Praise for #1 *New York Times* bestselling author Debbie Macomber

"Debbie Macomber tells women's stories in a way no one else does."
—*BookPage*

"Macomber is a skilled storyteller."
—*Publishers Weekly*

"No one writes stories of love and forgiveness like Macomber."
—*RT Book Reviews*

Praise for *Publishers Weekly* bestselling author Lee Tobin McClain

"*A Family for Easter* by Lee Tobin McClain is a beautiful story of deep friendship, and how it turns into lasting love and brings two families together into one."
—*Harlequin Junkie*

"Everything I look for in a book—it's emotional, tender, and an all-around wonderful story."
—RaeAnne Thayne, *New York Times* bestselling author, on *Low Country Hero*

Debbie Macomber is a #1 *New York Times* bestselling author and a leading voice in women's fiction worldwide. Her work has appeared on every major bestseller list, with more than 170 million copies in print, and she is a multiple award winner. Hallmark Channel based a television series on Debbie's popular Cedar Cove books. For more information, visit her website, www.debbiemacomber.com.

Publishers Weekly bestselling author **Lee Tobin McClain** read *Gone With The Wind* in the third grade and has been an incurable romantic ever since. When she's not writing angst-filled love stories with happy endings, she's probably cheering on her daughter at a gymnastics meet, mediating battles between her goofy golden-doodle puppy and her rescue cat or teaching aspiring writers in Seton Hill University's MFA program. She is probably not cleaning her house. For more about Lee, visit her website at www.leetobinmcclain.com.

#1 *New York Times* Bestselling Author

DEBBIE MACOMBER

LAUGHTER IN THE RAIN

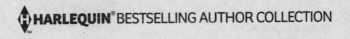

HARLEQUIN® BESTSELLING AUTHOR COLLECTION

ISBN-13: 978-1-335-08108-7

Laughter in the Rain

Copyright © 2019 by Harlequin Books S.A.

The publisher acknowledges the copyright holders of the individual works as follows:

Laughter in the Rain
Copyright © 1986 by Debbie Macomber

Engaged to the Single Mom
Copyright © 2015 by Lee Tobin McClain

Recycling programs for this product may not exist in your area.

Printed in U.S.A.

www.Harlequin.com

CONTENTS

Also available from Debbie Macomber

LAUGHTER IN THE RAIN

Debbie Macomber

One

"I'm so late. I'm so late."

The words were like a chant in Abby Carpenter's mind with every frantic push of the bike pedals. She was late. A worried glance at her watch when she paused at the traffic light confirmed that Mai-Ling would already be in Diamond Lake Park, wondering where Abby was. Abby should have known better than to try on that lovely silk blouse, but she'd seen it in the store's display window and couldn't resist. Now she was paying for the impulse.

The light turned green and Abby pedaled furiously, rounding the corner to the park entrance at breakneck speed.

Panting, she stopped in front of the bike stand and secured her lock around a concrete post. Then she ran across the lush green lawn to the picnic tables, where she normally met Mai-Ling. Abby felt a rush of relief when she spotted her.

Mai-Ling had recently immigrated to Minneapolis from Hong Kong. As a volunteer for the World Literacy Movement, Abby was helping the young woman learn to read English. Mai-Ling caught sight of her and waved eagerly. Abby, who'd been meeting her every Saturday afternoon for the past two months, was impressed by her determination to master English.

"I'm sorry I'm late," Abby apologized breathlessly.

Mai-Ling shrugged one shoulder. "No problem," she said with a smile.

That expression demonstrated how quickly her friend was adapting to the American way of speaking—and life.

Mai-Ling started to giggle.

"What's so funny?" Abby asked as she slid off her backpack and set it on the picnic table.

Mai-Ling pointed at Abby's legs.

Abby looked down and saw one red sock and one that was blue. "Oh, dear." She sighed disgustedly and sat on the bench. "I was in such a rush I didn't even notice." No wonder the salesclerk had given her a funny look. Khaki shorts, mismatched socks and a faded T-shirt from the University of Minnesota.

"I am laughing with you," Mai-Ling said in painstaking English.

Abby understood what she meant. Mai-Ling wanted to be sure Abby realized she wasn't laughing *at* her. "I know," she said as she zipped open the backpack and took out several workbooks.

Mai-Ling sat opposite Abby. "The man's here again," she murmured.

"Man?" Abby twisted around. "What man?"

Abby couldn't believe she'd been so unobservant. She felt a slight twinge of apprehension as she looked at the stranger. There was something vaguely familiar about him, and that bothered her. Then she remembered—he was the same man she'd seen yesterday afternoon at the grocery store. Had he been following her?

The man turned and leaned against a tree not more than twenty feet away, giving her a full view of his face. His tawny hair gleamed in the sunshine that filtered through the leaves of the huge elm. Beneath dark brows were deep-set brown eyes. Even from this distance Abby could see their intense expression. His rugged face seemed to be all angles and planes. He was attractive in an earthy way that would appeal to a lot of women and Abby was no exception.

"He was here last week," Mai-Ling said. "And the week before. He was watching you."

"Funny, I don't remember seeing him," she murmured, unable to disguise her discomfort.

"He is a nice man, I think. The animals like him. I am not worried about him."

"Then I won't worry, either," Abby said with a shrug as she handed Mai-Ling the first workbook.

In addition to being observant, Mai-Ling was a beautiful, sensitive and highly intelligent woman. Sometimes she became frustrated with her inability to communicate, but Abby was astonished at her rapid progress. Mai-Ling had mastered the English alphabet in only a few hours and was reading Level Two books.

A couple of times while Mai-Ling was reading a story about a woman applying for her first job, Abby's attention drifted to the stranger. She watched in astonishment as he coaxed a squirrel down the trunk of the tree. He pulled what appeared to be a few peanuts from his pocket and within seconds the squirrel was eating out of his hand. As if aware of Abby's scrutiny, he stood up and sauntered lazily to the nearby lakeshore. The instant he appeared, the ducks squawked as though recognizing an old friend. The tall man took bread crumbs from a sack he carried and fed them. Lowering himself to a crouch, he threw back his head and laughed.

Abby found herself smiling. Mai-Ling was right; this man had a way with animals—and women, too, if her pounding heart was anything to judge by.

A few times Mai-Ling faltered over a word, and Abby paused to help her.

The hour sped by, and soon it was time for the young woman to meet her bus. Abby walked Mai-Ling to the busy street and waited until she'd boarded, cheerfully waving to Abby from the back of the bus.

Pedaling her bicycle toward her apartment, Abby's thoughts again drifted to the tall, good-looking stranger. She had to admit she was enthralled. She wondered if he was attracted to her, too, since apparently he came to the park every week while she was there. But maybe she wasn't the one who attracted him; perhaps it was Mai-Ling. No, she decided. Mai-Ling had noticed the way the handsome stranger studied Abby. He was interested *in her*. Great, she mused contentedly; Logan Fletcher could do with some competition.

Abby pulled into the parking lot of her low-rise apartment building and climbed off her bike. Automatically she reached for her backpack, which she'd placed on the rack behind her, to get the apartment keys. Nothing. Surprised, Abby turned around to look for it. But it wasn't there. Obviously she'd left it at the park. Oh, no! She exhaled in frustration and turned, prepared to go and retrieve her pack.

"Looking for this?" A deep male voice startled Abby and her heart almost dropped to her knees. The bike slipped out from under her and she staggered a few steps before regaining her balance.

"Don't you know better than to sneak up on someone like that? I could have…" The words died on her lips as she whirled around to face the stranger. With her mouth hanging half open she stared into the deepest brown eyes she'd ever seen—the man from the park.

Her tongue-tied antics seemed to amuse him, but then it could have been her mismatched socks. "You forgot this." He handed her the backpack. Speechless, Abby took it and hugged it to her stomach. She felt grateful…and awkward. She started to thank him when another thought came to mind.

"How'd…how'd you know where I live?" The words sounded slightly scratchy, and she cleared her throat.

He frowned. "I've frightened you, haven't I?"

"How'd you know?" She repeated the question less aggressively. He hadn't scared her. If anything, she felt a startling attraction to him, to the sheer force of his masculinity. Logan would be shocked. For that matter, so was she. But up close, this man was even more appealing than he'd been at a distance.

"I followed you," he said simply.

"Oh." A thousand confused emotions dashed through her mind. He was so good-looking that Abby couldn't manage another word.

"I didn't mean to scare you," he said, regret in his voice.

"You didn't," she hurried to assure him. "I have an overactive imagination."

Shaking his head, he thrust his hands into his pants pockets. "I'll leave before I do any more damage."

"Please don't apologize. I should be thanking you. There's a Coke machine around the corner. Would you like to—"

"I've done enough for one day." Abruptly he turned to go.

"At least tell me your name." Abby didn't know where the request came from; it tumbled from her lips before she'd even formed the thought.

"Tate." He tossed it over his shoulder as he stalked away.

"Bye, Tate," she called as he opened his car door. When he glanced her way, she lifted her hand. "And thanks."

A smile curved his mouth. "I like your socks," he returned.

Pointedly she looked down at the mismatched pair. "I'm starting a new trend," she said with a laugh.

Standing beside her bike, Abby waited until Tate had driven away.

Later that night, Logan picked her up and they had hamburgers, then went to a movie. Logan's obligatory good-night kiss was...pleasant. That was the only way Abby could describe it. She had the impression that Logan kissed her because he always kissed her good-night. To her dismay, she had to admit that there'd never been any driving urgency behind his kisses. They'd been dating almost a year and the mysterious Tate was capable of stirring more emotion with a three-minute conversation than Logan had all evening. Abby wasn't even sure why they continued to date. He was an accountant whose office was in a building near hers. They had many of the same friends, and did plenty of things together, but their relationship was in a rut. The time had come to add a little spice to her life and Abby knew exactly where that spice would be coming from....

After Logan had left, Abby settled into the overstuffed chair that had once belonged to her grandfather, and picked up a new thriller she'd bought that week.

Dano, her silver-eyed cat, crawled into her lap as Abby opened the book. Absently she stroked the length of his spine. Her hand froze in midstroke as she discovered the hero's name: Logan. Slightly unnerved, she dropped the book and jumped up from her chair to look for the remote. Turning on the TV, she told herself she shouldn't feel guilty because she felt attracted to another man. The first thing she saw on the screen was a commercial for Logan Furniture's once-a-year sofa sale. Abby stared at the flashing name and hit the off button. This was crazy! Logan wouldn't care if she was interested in someone else. He might even be grateful. Their relationship was based on friendship and had progressed to romance, a romance that was more about routine than passion. If Abby was attracted to another man, Logan would be the first to step aside. He was like that—warm, unselfish, accommodating.

Her troubled thoughts on Saturday evening were only the beginning. Tate dominated every waking minute, which just went to prove how limited her social life really was. She liked Logan, but Abby longed for some excitement. He was so staid—yes, that was the word. *Staid.* Solid as a rock, and about as imaginative.

Logan came over to her apartment on Sunday afternoon, which was no surprise. He always came over on Sunday afternoons. They usually did something together, but never anything very exciting. More often than not Abby went over to his house and made dinner. Sometimes they watched a DVD. Or they played a game of backgammon, which he generally won. During the summer they'd ride their bikes, some of their

most pleasant dates had been spent in Diamond Lake
Park. Logan would lie on the grass and rest his head in
her lap while she read whatever thriller or mystery she
was currently devouring.

They'd been seeing each other so often that the last
time they had dinner at her parents', Abby's father had
suggested it was time they thought about getting married. Abby had been mortified. Logan had laughed and
changed the subject. Later, her mother had tactfully
reminded Abby that he might not be the world's most
exciting man, but he was her best prospect. However,
Abby couldn't see any reason to rush into marriage. At
twenty-six, she had plenty of time.

"I thought we'd bike around the park," Logan said.

The day was gloriously sunny and although Abby
wished Logan had proposed something more inventive, the idea *was* appealing. She enjoyed the feel of
the breeze in her hair and the sense of exhilaration that
came with rapid movement.

"Hi!" Abby and Logan were greeted by Patty Martin just inside the park's boundaries. "How's it going?"

"Fine," Logan answered for them as they braked to
a stop. "How about you?"

Patty had recently started to work in the same office
building as Logan, which was how Abby had met her.
Although Abby didn't know her well, she'd learned that
Patty was living with her sister. They'd talked briefly
at lunch one day, and Abby had invited her to join an
office-league softball team she and Logan had played
in last summer.

"I'm fine, too," Patty answered shyly and looked
away.

In some ways she reminded Abby of Mai-Ling, who

hadn't said more than a few words to her the first couple of weeks they'd worked together. Only as they came to know each other did Mai-Ling blossom. Abby herself had never been shy. The world was her friend, and she felt certain Patty would soon be comfortable with her, too.

"I can't talk now. I saw you and just wanted to say hello. Have fun, you two," Patty murmured and hurried away.

Confused, Abby watched her leave. The girl looked like a frightened mouse as she scurried across the grass. The description was more than apt. Patty's drab brown hair was pulled back from her face and styled unattractively. She didn't wear makeup and was so shy it was difficult to strike up a conversation.

After biking around the lake a couple of times, they stopped to get cold drinks. As they rested on a park bench, Logan slipped an affectionate arm around Abby's shoulders. "Have I told you that you look lovely today?"

The compliment astonished Abby; there were times she was convinced Logan didn't notice anything about her. "Thank you. I might add that you're looking very good yourself," she said with twinkling eyes, then added, "but I won't. No need for us both to get conceited."

Logan smiled absently as they walked their bikes out of the park. His expression was oddly distant; in some ways he hadn't been himself lately, but she couldn't put her finger on anything specific.

"Do you mind if we cut our afternoon short?" he asked unexpectedly.

He didn't offer an explanation, which surprised Abby. They'd spent most Sunday afternoons together for the past year. More surprising—or maybe not, considering her recent boredom with Logan—was the fact that Abby realized she didn't care. "No, that shouldn't be any problem. I've got a ton of laundry to do anyway."

Back at her apartment, Abby spent the rest of the afternoon doing her nails, feeling lazy and ignoring her laundry. She talked to her mother on the phone and promised to stop by sometime that week. Abby had been on her own ever since college. Her job as receptionist at an orthopedic clinic had developed with time and specialized training into a position as an X-ray technician. The advancement had included a healthy pay increase—enough to start saving for a place of her own. In the meanwhile, she relished her independence, enjoying her spacious ground-floor apartment, plus the satisfactions of her job and her volunteer work.

Several times over the next few days, Abby discovered herself thinking about Tate. Their encounter had been brief, but had left an impression on her. He was the most exciting thing that had happened to her in months.

"What's the matter with you?" Abby admonished herself. "A handsome man gives you a little attention and you don't know how to act."

Dano mewed loudly and weaved between her bare legs, his long tail tickling her calves. It was the middle of June and the hot summer weather had arrived.

"I wasn't talking to you." She leaned over to pet the cat. "And don't tell me you're hungry. I know better."

"Meow."

"You've already had your dinner."

"Meow. Meow."

"Don't you talk to me in that tone of voice. You hear?"

"Meow."

Abby tossed him the catnip mouse he loved to hurl

in the air and chase madly after. Logan had gotten it
for Dano. With his nose in the air, the cat ignored his
toy and sauntered into Abby's room, jumping up to sit
on the windowsill, his back to her. He ignored Abby,
obviously pining after whatever he could see outside.
In some obscure way, Abby felt that she was doing the
same thing to Logan and experienced a pang of guilt.

Since it was an older building, the apartments didn't
have air-conditioning, so Abby turned on her large fan.
Then, settling in the large overstuffed chair, she draped
one leg over the arm and munched on an apple as she
read. She was so engrossed in her thriller that when
she glanced at her watch, she gasped in surprise. Her
Tuesday evening painting class was in half an hour
and Logan would arrive in less than fifteen minutes.
He was always punctual, and although he seldom said
anything, she could tell by the set of his mouth that he
disliked it when she was behind schedule.

The "I'm late, I'm late" theme ran through her
mind as she vaulted out of the chair, changed pants
and rammed her right foot into her tennis shoe without
untying the lace. Whipping a brush through her long
brown hair, she searched frantically for the other shoe.

"It's got to be here," she told the empty room frantically. "Dano," she cried out in frustration. "Did you
take my shoe?"

She heard a faint indignant "meow" from the bedroom.

On her knees she crawled across the carpet, desperately tossing aside anything in her path—a week-old
newspaper, a scarf, a CD case, the mismatched pair of
socks she'd worn last Saturday and a variety of other
unimportant things.

She bolted to her feet when her apartment buzzer went off. Logan must be early.

She automatically let him into the building, threw open her door—and saw *Tate* standing in the hallway.

Abby felt the hot color seep up from her neck. He *would* come now, when she wasn't prepared and looking her worst.

He approached her apartment. "Hello," he said, staring down at her one bare foot. "Missing something?"

"Hello again." Her voice sounded unnaturally high. She bit her lip and tried to smile. "My shoe's gone."

"Walked away, did it?"

"You might say that. It was here a few minutes ago. I was reading and…" She dropped to her knees and lifted the skirting around the chair. There, in all its glory, was the shoe.

"Find it?" He was still in the doorway.

"Yes." She sat on the edge of the cushion and jerked her foot into the shoe.

"It might help if you untied the laces," he said, watching her with those marvelous eyes.

"I know, but I'm in a hurry." With her heel crushing the back of the shoe, Abby hobbled over to the door. "Come on in." She closed it behind him. "I'm—"

"Abby."

"Yes. How did you know?"

"I heard your friend say it at the park. And when I got to the lobby, I asked one of your neighbors." He frowned. "You should identify your guests before you let them in, you know."

"I know. I will. But I—was expecting someone else and…" Her words drifted off.

Smiling, he offered her his hand. "Tate Harding," he said.

A tingling sensation slipped up her arm at his touch. Tate's hand was calloused and rough from work. She successfully restrained her desire to turn it over and examine the palm. His handsome face was tanned from exposure to the elements. Tate was handsome, compellingly so.

"It looks as if I came at an inconvenient time."

"Oh, no," she hurried to assure him. She noticed that he'd released his grip, although she continued to hold her hand in midair. Self-consciously she lowered it to her side. "Sit down," she said, motioning toward her favorite chair. The hot color in her face threatened to suffocate her with its intensity.

Tate sat and lazily crossed his legs, apparently unaware of the effect he had on her.

Abby was shocked by her own reaction. She'd dated a number of men. She was neither naive nor stupid. "Would you like something to drink?" she asked as she hastily retreated to the kitchen, not waiting for his answer. Pausing, she frantically prayed that for once, just once, Logan would be late. No sooner had the thought formed than she heard the apartment buzzer again. This time she listened to her speaker.

"Abby?"

Logan. Abby hesitated, but let him in.

Tate had stood and opened the door by the time she turned around. Logan had arrived. When he stepped inside, the two men eyed each other skeptically. A slight scowl drew Logan's brows together.

"Logan, this is Tate Harding. Tate, Logan Fletcher."

Abby flushed uncomfortably and darted an apologetic look at them both.

"I thought we had a class tonight." Logan spoke somewhat defensively.

"This is my fault," Tate said, his gaze resting on Abby's face and for one heart-stopping moment on her softly parted lips. "I dropped by unexpectedly."

Logan's mouth thinned with displeasure and Abby pulled her eyes from Tate's. Logan had never been the jealous type, but then he'd never had reason or opportunity to reveal that side of his nature. Still, it surprised her. Abby hadn't considered this a serious relationship. It was more of a companionable one. Logan had understood and accepted that, or so she'd thought.

"I'll come back another time," Tate suggested. "You've obviously got plans with Logan."

"We're taking classes together," Abby rushed to explain. "I'm taking painting and Logan's studying chess. We drive there together, that's all."

Tate's smile was understanding. "I won't keep you, then."

"Nice to have met you," Logan stated, sounding as if he meant exactly the opposite.

Tate turned back and nodded. "Perhaps we'll meet again."

Logan nodded briskly. "Perhaps."

The minute Tate left Abby whirled around to face Logan. "That was so rude," she whispered fiercely. "For heaven's sake—you were acting like you owned me... like I was your property."

"Think about it, Abby," Logan said just as forcefully, also in a heated whisper. His dark eyes narrowed as he stalked to the other side of the room. "We've been dating exclusively for almost a year. I assumed that you would've developed some loyalty. I guess I was mistaken."

"Loyalty? Is that all our relationship means to you?" she demanded.

Logan didn't answer her. He walked to the door and held it open, indicating that if she was coming she needed to do it now. Silently Abby followed him through the lobby and into the parking lot.

The entire way to the community center they sat without speaking. The hard set of Logan's mouth indicated the tight rein he had on his temper. Abby forced her expression to remain haughtily cold.

They parted in the hallway, Logan taking the first left while Abby continued down the hall. A couple of the women she'd become friends with greeted her, but Abby had difficulty responding. She took twice as long as normal setting up her supplies.

The class, which was on perspective, didn't go well, since Abby's attention kept returning to the scene with Logan and Tate. Logan was obviously jealous. He'd revealed more emotion in those few minutes with Tate than in the past twelve months. Logan tended to be serious and reserved, while she was more emotional and adventurous. They were simply mismatched. Like her socks—one red, one blue. Logan had become too comfortable in their relationship these last months, taking too much for granted. The time had come for a change, and after tonight he had to recognize that.

After class they usually met in the coffee shop beside the center. Logan was already in a booth when she arrived there.

Wordlessly, Abby slipped into the seat across from him.

Folding her hands on the table, she pretended to study her nails, wondering if Logan was ever going to speak.

"Why are you so angry?" Abby finally asked. "I hardly know Tate. We only met a few days ago."

"How many times have you gone out with him?"

"None," Abby said righteously.

"But not because you turned him down." Logan shook his head grimly. "I saw the way you looked at him, Abby. It was all you could do to keep from drooling."

"That's not true," she denied vehemently—and realized he was probably right. She'd never been good at hiding her feelings. "I admit I find him attractive, but—"

"But what?" Logan taunted softly. "But you had this old boyfriend you had to get rid of first?" The hint of a smile touched his mouth. "And I'm not referring to my age." He was six years older than Abby. "I was pointing out that we've been seeing each other two or three times a week and suddenly you're not so sure how you feel about me."

Abby opened, then closed her mouth. She couldn't argue with what he'd said.

"That's it, isn't it?"

"Logan." She said his name on a sigh. "I like you. You know that. Over the past year I've grown very... fond of you."

"Fond?" He spat the word at her. "One is *fond* of cats or dogs—not men. And particularly not me."

"That was a bad choice of words," Abby agreed.

"You're not exactly sure what you feel," Logan said, almost under his breath.

Abby's fingers knotted until she could feel the pain

in her hands. Logan was right; she *didn't* know. She was attracted to Tate, but she knew nothing about him. The problem was that she liked what she saw. If her feelings for Logan were what they should be after a year, she wouldn't want Tate to ask her out so badly.

"You aren't sure, are you?" Logan said again.

She hung her head so that her face was framed by her dark hair. "I don't want to hurt you," she murmured.

"You haven't." Logan's hand reached across the table and squeezed her fingers reassuringly. "Beyond anything else, we're friends and I don't want to do anything to upset that friendship because it's important to me."

"That's important to me, too," she said and offered him a feeble smile. Their eyes met as the waitress came and turned over the beige cups and filled them with coffee.

"Do you want a menu?"

Abby couldn't have eaten anything and shook her head.

"Not tonight. Thanks, anyway," Logan answered for both of them.

"I don't deserve you," Abby said after the waitress had moved to the next booth.

For the first time all night Logan's lips curved into a genuine smile. "That's something I don't want you to forget."

For a few minutes they sipped their coffee in thoughtful silence. Holding the cup with both hands, she studied him. Logan's eyes were as brown as Tate's. Funny she hadn't remembered how brown they were. Tonight the color was intense, deeper than ever. They made quite a couple; she was so emotional—and he wasn't. Abby noticed that Logan's jaw was well-defined. Tate's jaw, although different, revealed that same quality—determination. With Logan, Abby recognized there was nothing he couldn't do if he wanted. Instinctively she knew the same was true of Tate.

She sensed that there were definite similarities between Logan and Tate, and yet she was reacting to them in different ways.

It seemed unfair that a man she'd seen only a couple of times could affect her like this. If she fell madly in love with someone, it should be Logan.

"What are you thinking about?" His words broke into her troubled thoughts.

Abby shrugged. "Oh, this and that," she said vaguely.

"You didn't even add sugar to your coffee."

Abby grimaced. "No wonder it tastes so awful."

Chuckling, he handed her the sugar canister.

Pouring some onto her spoon, Abby stirred it into her coffee. Logan had a nice mouth, she reflected. She couldn't remember thinking that in a long time. She had when they'd first met, but that was nearly two years ago. She watched him for a moment, trying to figure him out. Logan was so—Abby searched for the right word—sensible. Nothing ever seemed to rattle him. There wasn't an obstacle he couldn't overcome with cool reason. For once, Abby wanted him to do something crazy and nonsensical and fun.

"Logan." She spoke softly, coaxingly. "Let's drive to Des Moines tonight."

He looked at her as if she'd lost her mind. "Des Moines, Iowa?"

"Yes. Wouldn't it be fun just to take off and drive for hours—and then turn around and come home?"

"That's not fun, that's torture. Anyway, what's the point?"

Abby pressed her lips together and nodded. She shouldn't have asked. She'd known his answer even before he spoke.

The ride home was as silent as the drive to class. The tension wasn't nearly as great, but it was still evident.

"I have the feeling you're angry," Logan said as he parked in front of her building. "I'm sorry that spending the whole night on the road doesn't appeal to me. I've got this silly need for sleep. From what I understand, it affects older people."

"I'm not angry," Abby said firmly. She felt disappointed, but not angry.

Logan's hand caressed her cheek, curving around her neck and directing her mouth to his. Abby closed her eyes, expecting the usual feather-light kiss. Instead, Logan pulled her into his arms and kissed her soundly. Deeply. Passionately. Surprised but delighted, Abby groaned softly, liking it. Her hands slipped over his shoulders and joined at the base of his neck.

Logan had never kissed her with such intensity, such unrestrained need. His mouth moved over hers, and Abby sucked in a startled breath as pure sensation shot through her. When he released her, she sighed longingly and rested her head against his chest. Involuntarily, a picture of Tate entered her mind. This was what she'd imagined kissing *him* would be like....

"You were pretending I was Tate, weren't you?" Logan whispered against her hair.

Two

"Oh, Logan, of course I wasn't," Abby answered somewhat guiltily. She *had* thought of Tate, but she hadn't pretended Logan's kiss was Tate's.

He brushed his face along the side of her hair. Abby was certain he wanted to say something more, but he didn't, remaining silent as he climbed out of the car and walked around to her side. She smiled weakly as he offered her his hand. Logan could be such a gentleman. She was perfectly capable of getting out of a car by herself, but he always wanted to help. Abby supposed she should be grateful—but she wasn't. Those old-fashioned virtues weren't the ones that really mattered to her.

Lightly, he kissed her again outside her lobby door. Letting herself in, Abby was aware that Logan waited on the other side until he heard her turn the lock.

After changing into her long nightgown, Abby went into the kitchen and poured a glass of milk. She sat at the small round table and placed her feet on the edge of a chair, pulling her gown over her knees. Did she love Logan? The answer came almost immediately. Although he'd taken offense, "fond" had aptly described her feelings. She liked Logan, but Tate had aroused far more emotion during their short acquaintance. Downing the milk, Abby turned off the light and miserably decided to go to bed. Dano joined her, purring loudly as he arranged himself at her feet.

Friday evening, she begged off when Logan invited her to a movie, saying she was tired and didn't feel well. He seemed to accept that quite readily. And, in fact, she watched a DVD at home, by herself, and was in bed by ten, reading a new mystery novel, with Dano stretched out at her side.

Saturday afternoon, Abby arrived at the park a half-hour early, hoping Tate would be there and they'd have a chance to talk. She hadn't heard from him and wondered if he'd decided Logan had a prior claim to her affection. However, Tate didn't seem the type who'd be easily discouraged. She found him in the same spot as last week and waved happily.

"I was hoping you'd be here," she said eagerly and sat on the grass beside him, leaning her back against the massive tree trunk.

"My thoughts exactly," Tate replied, with a warm smile that elevated Abby's heart rate.

"I'm sorry about Logan," she told him, weaving her fingers through the grass.

"No need to apologize."

"But he was so rude," Abby returned, feeling guilty for being unkind. But she'd said no less to Logan himself.

Tate sent her a look of surprise. "He didn't behave any differently than I would have, had the circumstances been reversed."

"Logan doesn't own me," she said defiantly.

A smile bracketed the edges of his mouth. "That's one piece of news I'm glad to hear."

Their eyes met and he smiled. Abby could feel her bones melt. It was all she could do to smile back.

"Do you like in-line skating?"

"I love it." She hadn't skated since she was a teen at the local roller rink, but if Tate suggested they stand on their heads in the middle of the road, Abby probably would have agreed.

"Would you like to meet me here tomorrow afternoon?"

"Sure," she said without hesitating. "Here?" she repeated, sitting up.

"You *have* skated?" He gave her a worried glance.

"Oh, sure." Her voice squeaked, embarrassing her. "Tomorrow? What time?"

"Three," Tate suggested. "After that we'll go out for something to eat."

"This is sounding better all the time," Abby teased. "But be warned, I do have a healthy appetite. Logan says—" She nearly choked on the name, immediately wishing she could take it back.

"You were saying something about Logan," Tate prompted.

"Not really." She gave a light shrug, flushing involuntarily.

Mai-Ling stepped off the bus just then and walked toward them. Abby stood up. Brushing the grass from her legs, she smiled warmly at her friend.

"Why do you meet her every week?" Tate asked. The teasing light vanished from his eyes.

"I do volunteer work with the World Literacy Movement. Mai-Ling can read perfectly in Chinese, but she's an American now so I'm helping her learn to read and write English."

"Have you been a volunteer long?"

"A couple of years. Why? Would you like to help? We're always looking for volunteers."

"Me?" He looked stunned and a little shocked. "Not now. I've got more than I can handle helping at the zoo."

"The zoo?" Abby shot back excitedly. "Are you a volunteer?"

"Yes," Tate said as he stood and glanced at his watch. "I'll tell you more about it tomorrow. Right now I've got to get back to work before the boss discovers why I've taken extended lunch breaks the past four Saturdays."

"I'll look forward to tomorrow," Abby murmured, thinking she'd never known anyone as compelling as Tate.

"You met the man?" Mai-Ling asked as she came over to Abby's side and followed her gaze to the retreating male figure.

"Yes, I met him," Abby answered wistfully. "Oh, Mai-Ling, I think I'm in love!"

"Love?" Mai-Ling frowned. "The American word for love is bad."

"Bad?" Abby repeated, not comprehending.

"Yes. In English one word means many kinds of love."

Abby turned her attention from Tate to her friend and asked, "What do you mean?"

"In America, love for a husband is the same as... as love for chocolate. I heard a lady on the bus say she *loves* chocolate, then say she is in love with a new man." Mai-Ling shook her head in astonishment and disbelief. "In Chinese it is much different. Better."

"No doubt you're right," Abby said with a bemused grin. "I guess it's all about context."

Mai-Ling ignored that. "You will see the man again?"

"Tomorrow," Abby said dreamily. Suddenly her eyes widened. Tomorrow was Sunday, and Logan would expect her to do something with him. Oh, dear, this was becoming a problem. Not only hadn't she skated in years, but she was bound to have another uncomfortable confrontation with Logan. Her eager anticipation for tomorrow was quickly replaced by a sinking feeling in the pit of her stomach.

Abby spent another miserable night. She'd attempted to phone Logan and make up another excuse about not being able to get together, but he hadn't been home. She didn't feel it was right to leave a message, which struck her as cowardly. Consequently her sleep was fitful and intermittent. It wasn't as if Logan called and arranged a time each week; they had a simple understanding that Sundays were *their* day. Arrangements for most other days were more flexible. But Abby couldn't remember a week when they hadn't gotten together on a Sunday. Her sudden decision would be as readable as the morning headlines. Logan would know she was meeting Tate.

Abby's first inclination was not to be there when he arrived, but that was even more cowardly. In addition, Abby knew Logan well enough to realize that her attempts to dodge him wouldn't work. Either he'd go to the park and look for her or he'd drive to her parents' house and worry them sick.

By the time he did arrive, Abby's stomach felt as if a lead balloon had settled inside.

"Beautiful afternoon, isn't it?" Logan came over to her and slipped an arm around her waist, drawing her close to his side. "Are you feeling better?" he asked in a concerned voice. So often in the past year, Abby had longed for him to hold her like this. Now when he did, she wanted to scream with frustration.

"Yes, I'm…okay."

"What would you like to do?" he asked, nuzzling her neck and holding her close.

"Logan." Abby hesitated, and cleared her throat, feeling guilty. "I've got other plans this afternoon." Her voice didn't even sound like her own as she squeezed her eyes shut, afraid to meet his hard gaze.

A grimness stole into his eyes as his hand tightened. "You're seeing Tate, aren't you?"

Abby caught her breath at the ferocity of his tone. "Of course not!" She couldn't look at him. For the first time in their relationship, Abby was blatantly lying to Logan. No wonder she was experiencing this terrible guilt. For one crazy minute, Abby felt like bursting into tears and running out of the apartment.

"Tell me what you're doing, then," he demanded.

Abby swallowed at the painful lump in throat. "Last week you cut our time together short," she said. "I didn't ask where you were going. I don't feel it's too much to expect the same courtesy."

Logan's grip on her waist slackened, but he didn't release her. "What about later? Couldn't we meet for dinner? There's something I wanted to discuss."

"I can't," she said quickly. Too quickly. Telltale color warmed her face.

Logan studied her for a long moment, then dropped his arm. She should've been glad. Instead she felt chilled and suddenly bereft.

"Let me know when you're free." His words were cold as he moved toward the door.

"Logan," Abby called out to him desperately. "Don't be angry. Please."

When he paused and turned around, his eyes flickered over her. She couldn't quite read his expression but she knew it wasn't flattering. Wordlessly, he turned again and left.

Abby wanted to crawl into a hole, curl up and die. Logan deserved so much better than this. Any number of women would call her a fool—and they'd be right.

Dressed in white linen shorts and a red cotton shirt, Abby studied her reflection in the full-length mirror on the back of the bedroom door. Her hair hung in a long ponytail, practical for skating, she figured. Makeup did little to disguise the doubt and unhappiness in her eyes. With a jagged breath, Abby tied the sleeves of a sweater around her neck and headed out the door.

Tate was standing by the elm tree waiting for her. He was casually dressed in jeans and a V-neck sweater that hinted at curly chest hair. Even across the park, Abby recognized the quiet authority of the man. His virile look attracted the attention of other women in the vicinity, but Tate didn't seem to notice.

He started walking toward her, his smile approving as he surveyed her long legs.

"You look like you've lost your best friend," Tate said as he slid a casual arm around her shoulder.

Abby winced; his comment might be truer than he knew.

"Problem?" he asked.

"Not really." Her voice quavered, but she managed to

give him a broad smile. "I'm hoping we can rent skates. I don't have a pair."

"We can."

It didn't take long for Tate's infectious good mood to brighten Abby's spirits. Soon she was laughing at her bungling attempts to skate. A concrete pathway was very different from the smooth, polished surface of the rink. Either that, or it'd been longer than she realized since her last time on skates.

Tate tucked a hand around her hip as his movements guided hers.

"You're doing great." His eyes were smiling as he relaxed his grasp.

Laughing, Abby looked away from the pathway to answer him when her skate hit a rut and she tumbled forward, wildly thrashing her arms in an effort to remain upright. She would have fallen if Tate hadn't still been holding her. His hand tightened, bringing her closer. She faltered a bit from the effect of his nearness.

"I'm a natural," she said with a grin.

"A natural klutz," he finished for her.

They skated for two hours. When Tate suggested they stop, Abby glanced at her watch and was astonished by the time.

"Hungry?" Tate asked next.

"Famished."

The place Tate took her to was one of those relatively upscale restaurants that charged a great deal for its retro diner atmosphere, but where the reputation for excellent food was well-earned. Abby couldn't imagine Logan bringing her someplace like this. Knowing that made the outing all the more enticing.

When the waitress came, Abby ordered an avocado

burger with a large stuffed baked potato and strawberry shortcake for dessert.

Tate smiled. "I'll have the same," he told the waitress, who wrote down their order and stepped away from the table.

"So you do volunteer work at the zoo?" Abby was interested in learning the details he'd promised to share with her.

"I've always loved animals," he began.

"I could tell from the way you talked to the ducks and the squirrels," Abby inserted, recalling the first time she'd seen Tate.

He acknowledged her statement with a nod. "Even as a child I'd bring home injured animals—rabbits, raccoons, squirrels—and do what I could to make them well."

"Why didn't you become a veterinarian?"

Tate ignored the question. "The hardest part was setting them free once they were well. I might have been a veterinarian if things in my life had gone differently, but I'm good with cars, too."

"You're a mechanic?" Abby asked, already knowing the answer. The callused hands told her that her guess couldn't be far off.

"I work at Bessler's Auto Repair."

"Sure. I know it. That's across the street from the Albertsons' store."

"That's it."

So it *had* just been a coincidence that she'd seen Tate in the store; he worked in the immediate vicinity.

"I've been working there since I was seventeen," Tate added. "Jack Bessler is thinking about retirement these days."

"What'll happen to the shop?"

"I'm hoping to buy it," Tate said as he held his fork, nervously rotating it between two fingers.

Tate was uneasy about something. He ran his fingers up and down the fork, not lifting his gaze from his silverware.

Their meal was as delicious as Abby knew it would be. Whatever had bothered Tate was soon gone and the remainder of the evening was spent talking, getting to know each other with an eagerness that was as strong as their mutual attraction. They talked nonstop for hours, sauntering lazily along the water's edge and laughing, neither of them eager to bring their time together to a close.

When Abby finally got home it was nearly midnight. She floated into the apartment on a cloud of happiness. Even as she readied for bed, she couldn't forget how wonderful the night had been. Tate was a man she could talk to, really talk to. He listened to her and seemed to understand her feelings. Logan listened, too, but Abby had the impression that he sometimes felt impatient with her. But perhaps that wasn't it at all. Maybe she was looking for ways to soothe her conscience. His reaction today still shocked her; as far as she was concerned, they hadn't made any commitment to each other beyond that of friendship. Sometimes Abby wondered if she really knew Logan.

The phone rang fifteen minutes after she was in the door.

Assuming it was Tate, Abby all but flew across the room to answer it, not bothering to check call display. "Hello," she said in a low, sultry voice.

"Abby, is that you? You don't sound right. Are you sick?"

It was Logan.

Instantly, Abby stiffened and sank into the comfort of her chair. "Logan," she said in her normal voice. "Hi. Is something wrong?" He wouldn't be phoning this late otherwise.

"Not really."

"I just got in… I mean…" She faltered as her thoughts tripped over each other. "I thought you might be in bed, so I didn't call," she finished lamely. He was obviously phoning to find out what time she got home.

Deftly Logan changed the subject to a matter of no importance, confirming Abby's suspicions. "No," he said, "I was just calling to see what time you wanted me to pick you up for class on Tuesday."

Of all the feeble excuses! "Next time I go somewhere without you, do you want me to phone in so you'll know the precise minute I get home?" she asked crisply, fighting her temper as her hand tightened around the receiver.

His soft chuckle surprised her. "I guess I wasn't very original, was I?"

"No. This isn't like you, Logan. I've never thought of you as the jealous type."

"There's a lot you don't know about me," he answered on a wry note.

"I'm beginning to realize that."

"Do you want me to pick you up for class this week, or have you…made other arrangements?"

"Of course I want you to pick me up! I wouldn't want it any other way." Abby meant that. She liked Logan. The problem was she liked Tate, too.

Logan hesitated and the silence stretched between them. Abby was sure he could hear her racing heart over the phone. But she hoped he couldn't read the confusion in her mind.

After work on Monday afternoon, instead of heading back to her apartment and Dano, Abby stopped off at her parents' house.

"Hi, Mom." She sauntered into the kitchen and kissed her mother on the cheek. "What's there to eat?" Opening the refrigerator door, Abby surveyed the contents with interest.

"Abby," her mother admonished, "what's wrong?"

"Wrong?" Abby feigned ignorance.

"Abby, I'm your mother. I know you. The only time you show up in the middle of the week is if something's bothering you."

"Honestly, aren't I allowed an unexpected visit without parental analysis?"

"Did you and Logan have a fight?" her mother persisted.

Glenna Carpenter's chestnut hair was as dark as Abby's but streaked with gray, creating an unusual color a hairdresser couldn't reproduce. Glenna was a young sixty, vivacious, outgoing and—like Abby a doer.

"What makes you say that? Logan and I never fight." Abby chewed on a stalk of celery and closed the refrigerator. Taking the salt from the cupboard beside the stove she sprinkled some on it.

"Salt's bad for your blood pressure." Glenna took the shaker out of Abby's hand and replaced it in the cupboard. "Are you going to tell me what's wrong?"

She spoke in a warning tone that Abby knew better than to disregard.

"Honest, Mom, there's nothing."

"Abby." Sapphire-blue eyes snapped with displeasure.

Abby couldn't hold back a soft laugh. Her mother had a way of saying more with one glare than some women did with a tantrum.

Holding the celery between her teeth, Abby placed both hands on the counter and pulled herself up, sitting beside the sink.

"Abby," her mother said a second time.

"It's Logan." She gave a frustrated sigh. "He's become so possessive lately."

"Well, thank goodness. I'd have thought you'd be happy." Glenna's smiling eyes revealed her approval. "I was wondering how long it would take him."

"Mother!" Abby wanted to cry. Deep in her heart, she'd known her mother would react like this. "It's too late—I've met someone else."

Glenna froze and a shocked look came over her. "Who?"

"His name is Tate Harding."

"When?"

"A couple of weeks ago."

"How old is he?"

Abby wanted to laugh at her mother's questions. She sounded as if Abby was fifteen again and asking for permission to date. "He's twenty-seven and a hardworking, respectable citizen. I don't know how to explain it, Mom, but I was instantly attracted to him. I think I'm falling in love."

"Falling in love," Glenna echoed, reheating the day's

stale coffee and pouring herself a cup. Her hand shook as she lifted the mug to her mouth a couple of minutes later.

Abby knew her mother was taking her seriously when she drank coffee, which she usually reserved for mornings. A smile tugged at Abby's mouth, but she successfully restrained it.

"I know what you must be thinking," Abby said. "You don't even have to say it because I've already chided myself a thousand times. Logan's the greatest man in the world, but Tate is—"

"The ultimate one?"

The suppressed smile came to life. "You could say that."

"Does Logan know?"

"Of all the luck, they ran into each other at my apartment last week. It would've helped if they hadn't met like that."

"I think having Logan and Tate stumble into each other was more providential than you realize," Glenna murmured with infuriating calm. "I've always liked Logan. I think he's perfect for you."

"How can you *say* that?" Abby demanded indignantly. "We aren't anything alike. We don't even enjoy the same things. Logan can be such a stuffed shirt. And you haven't even met Tate."

"No." Her mother ran the tip of one finger along the rim of her mug. "To be honest, I could never understand why Logan puts up with you. I love you, Abby, but I know your faults as well as your strengths. Apparently Logan sees the same potential in you that I do."

"I can't believe my own mother would talk to me like this." Abby spoke to the ceiling, venting her irritation.

"I come to her to pour out my heart and seek her advice and end up being judged."

Glenna laughed. "I'm not judging you," she declared. "Just giving you some sound, motherly advice." An ardent light glowed from her eyes. "Logan loves you. He—"

"Mother," Abby interrupted. "How can you be so sure? If he does, which I sincerely doubt, then he's never told me."

"No, I don't imagine he has. Logan is waiting."

"Waiting?" Abby asked sarcastically. "For what? A blue moon?"

"No," Glenna said sharply and took a long, deliberate sip of her coffee, which must have tasted foul. "He's been waiting for you to grow up. You're impulsive and quick-tempered, especially when it comes to relationships. You expect him to take the lead and yet you resent him for it."

Abby gasped; she couldn't help it. Rarely had her mother spoken this candidly to her. Abby opened her mouth to deny the accusations, then closed it again. The words hurt, especially coming from her own mother, and she lowered her gaze to hide the onrush of emotional pain. Tears gathered in her eyes.

"I'm not saying these things to hurt you," Glenna continued softly.

"I know that." Abby grimaced. "You're right. I should be more honest, but I don't want to hurt Logan."

"Then tell him what you're feeling. Stringing him along would be unkind."

"But it's hard," Abby protested, wiping her eyes. "If I told him yesterday that I was going out with Tate he would've been angry. And miserable."

"And do you suppose he wasn't? I know Logan. If you said anything to him, he'd immediately step aside until you've settled things in your own mind."

"I know," Abby breathed in frustration. "But I'm not sure I want that, either."

"You mean you want to have your cake and eat it, too," Glenna said. "As the old cliché has it…"

"I never have understood that saying."

"Then maybe you'd better think about it, Abby."

"In other words you're telling me I should let Logan know how I feel about Tate."

"Yes. You can't have it both ways. You can't keep Logan hanging if you want to pursue a romance with this other man."

The seriousness of her mother's look, her words, transferred itself to Abby.

"Today," Glenna insisted. "Now, before you change your mind."

Slowly Abby nodded. She hopped down from the counter, prepared to talk to Logan. "Thanks, Mom."

Glenna Carpenter gave Abby a motherly squeeze. "I'll be thinking about you."

"You'll like Tate."

"I'm sure I will. You always did have excellent taste." Abby's smile was tentative.

She knew Logan was working late tonight, so she drove straight to his accounting firm, which was situated half a block from her own office. Karen, his assistant, had gone home, and Abby knocked at the outer office. Almost instantly the door opened and Logan gestured her inside.

"Abby." He beamed her a warm smile. "What a nice surprise. Come in, won't you."

Abby took the leather chair opposite his desk.

"Logan." Her fingers had knotted into a tight fist in her lap. "Can we talk?"

He looked down at his watch.

"It won't take long, I promise," she added hurriedly.

Leaning against the side of his desk, he crossed his arms. "What is it, Abby? You never look this serious about anything."

"I think you have a right to know that I was with Tate Harding yesterday." Her heart was hammering wildly as she said this.

"Abby, you're as readable as a child. I was aware from the beginning who you were with," he told her. "I only wish that you'd been honest with me."

"Oh, Logan, I do apologize for that."

"Fine. It's forgotten."

How could he be so generous? So forgiving? Just when she was about to explain that she wanted to continue seeing Tate, Logan reached for her, drawing her into his embrace. As his mouth settled over hers, he drew from her a response so complete that Abby was left speechless and all the more confused. He kissed her as if he couldn't get enough of her mouth, of *her*.

"I've got a client meeting in five minutes," Logan whispered as he massaged her shoulders. "But believe me, holding you is far more appealing. Promise me you'll drop by the office again."

Then he let her go, and she sank back into the chair.

Three

Abby punched the pillow and determinedly shut her eyes. She shouldn't be having so much trouble falling asleep, she thought, fighting back a loud yawn. Ten minutes later, she wearily raised one eyelid and glared at the clock radio. Two-thirty! She groaned audibly. Logan was responsible for this. He should've taken the time to listen to her. Now she didn't know when she'd work up the courage to talk to him about Tate.

And speaking of Tate… He'd phoned after dinner and suggested going to the zoo that weekend. Abby couldn't refuse him. Now she was paying the price—remorse and self-recrimination. Worse, it was all Logan's fault that she hadn't been able to explain the situation to him. She didn't mean to do anything behind his back. She liked both men, but the attraction she felt toward Tate was far more intense than the easy camaraderie she shared with Logan.

Bunching the pillow, Abby forced her eyes to close. She'd gone to Logan to tell him she wanted to date other men. She'd tried, really tried. What else could she do?

When the radio went off at six, Abby wanted to

scream. Sleep had eluded her the entire night. The few hours she'd managed to catch wouldn't be enough to see her through the day. Her eyes burned as she tossed aside the covers and sat on the edge of the bed.

More from habit than anything, Abby brushed her teeth and dressed. Coffee didn't help. And the tall glass of orange juice tasted like tomato, but she didn't open her eyes to investigate.

Half an hour later, she let herself into the clinic. The phone was already ringing.

"Morning." Cheryl Hansen, the receptionist, smiled at Abby before answering the call.

Abby returned the friendly gesture with a weak smile of her own.

"You look like the morning after a wild and crazy night," Cheryl said as Abby hung her jacket in the room off the reception area.

"It was wild and crazy, all right," Abby said after an exaggerated yawn. "But not the way you think."

"Another late night with Logan?"

Abby's eyes widened. "No!"

"Tate, then?"

"No. Unfortunately."

"I'm telling you, Ab, keeping track of your love life is getting more difficult all the time."

"I haven't got a love life," she murmured, unable to stop yawning. Covering her mouth, Abby moved to the end of the long hallway.

The day didn't get any better. By noon, she recognized that she couldn't possibly attend tonight's class with Logan. For one thing, she was too tired to concentrate on painting theory and technique. For another, as soon as he saw her troubled expression, he'd know immediately that she was deceiving him and seeing Tate again. And something she didn't need today was another confrontation with Logan. She didn't want to hurt him. But more than that—she didn't want to lie to him.

On her way back from lunch, Abby decided to call his office. Her guilt grew heavier at the pleasure in his voice.

"Abby! What's up?"

"Hi, Logan." She groaned inwardly. "I hope you don't mind me phoning you like this."

"Not at all."

"I'm not feeling well." She paused, her hand tightening around the receiver. "I was thinking that maybe it'd be best if I skipped class tonight."

"What's wrong?" His genuine concern was nearly her undoing. "You weren't well on Friday, either."

Did he really believe her excuse of Friday evening, which had been nothing but a way of avoiding him?

"You must be coming down with something," he said.

"I think so." *Like a terminal case of cowardice*, her mind shot back.

"Have you seen a doctor?"

"It isn't necessary. Not yet. But I thought I'd stay home again tonight and go to bed early," Abby mumbled, feeling more wretched every second.

"Do you need me to do anything for you?" His voice was laced with gentleness.

"No," she assured him quickly. "I'm fine. Really. I just thought I'd nip this thing in the bud and take it easy."

"Okay. But promise me that if you need anything, you'll call."

"Oh, sure."

Abby felt even worse after making that phone call. By the time she returned to her apartment late that afternoon her excuse for not attending her class had become real. Her head was throbbing unmercifully; her throat felt dry and scratchy and her stomach was queasy.

With her fingertips pressing her temple, Abby located the aspirin in the bathroom cabinet and downed two tablets. Afterward she lay on the sofa, the phone beside her, head propped up with a soft pillow, and closed her eyes. She didn't open them when the phone rang and she scrabbled around for it blindly.

"Hello." Her reluctant voice was barely above a whisper.

"Abby, is that you?"

She breathed easier. It was her mother.

"Hi, Mom."

"What's wrong?"

"I've got a miserable headache."

"What's bothering you?"

"What makes you think anything's bothering me?" Her mother displayed none of the sympathy Logan had.

"Abby, I know you. When you get a headache it's because something's troubling you."

Breathing deeply, Abby glanced at the ceiling with wide-open eyes, unable to respond.

"Did you talk to Logan yesterday?" Her mother resumed the interrogation.

"Only for a little while. He was on his way to a meeting."

"Did you tell him you want to continue seeing Tate?"

"I didn't get the chance," Abby said more aggressively than she'd intended. "Mom, I tried, but he didn't have time to listen. Then Tate phoned me and asked me out this weekend and...I said yes."

"Does Logan know?"

"Not yet," she mumbled.

"And you've got a whopper of a headache?"

"Yes." The word trembled on her lips.

"Abby." Her mother's voice took on the tone Abby knew all too well. "You've *got* to talk to Logan."

"I will."

"Your headache won't go away until you do."

"I know."

Dano strolled into the room and leaped onto the sofa, settling in Abby's lap. Grateful to have one friend left in the world, Abby stroked her cat.

It took her at least twenty minutes to work up enough fortitude to call Logan's home number. His phone rang six times, and Abby sighed, not leaving a message. She assumed he'd gone to class on his own, that he was on his way, so she didn't bother trying his cell. She'd talk to him tomorrow.

She closed her eyes again, wondering how—if— she could balance her intense attraction to Tate with her feelings of friendship for Logan. Friendship that sometimes hinted at more. His ardent kiss yesterday had taken her by surprise. But she *had* to tell him about Tate....

The apartment buzzer woke Abby an hour later. She sat up and rubbed the stiff muscles of her neck. Dano remained on her lap and meowed angrily when she stood, forcing the cat to leap to the floor.

"Yes?" she said into the speaker.

"It's Logan."

Abby buzzed him in. Her hand was shaking visibly as she unlocked the door. "Hi," she said in a high-pitched voice.

Logan stepped inside. "How are you feeling?"

"I don't know." She yawned, stretching her arms. "Better, I guess." Her attention was drawn to a white sack Logan was holding. "What's that?"

A crooked smile slanted his mouth. "Chicken soup. I picked some up at the deli." He handed her the bag. "I want to make sure you're well enough for the game tomorrow night."

Abby's head shot up. "Game? What game?"

"I wondered if you'd forgotten. We signed up a couple of weeks ago for the softball team. Remember?"

This was the second summer they were playing in the office league. With her recent worries, softball had completely slipped Abby's mind. "Oh, *that* game." Abby wanted to groan. She'd *never* be able to avoid Logan. Too many activities linked them together— work, classes and now softball.

She took the soup into the kitchen, removing the large plastic cup from the sack. The aroma of chicken and noodles wafted through the small room. Logan followed her in and slipped his arms around her waist from behind. His chin rested on her head as he spoke. "I woke you up, didn't I?"

She nodded, resisting the urge to turn and slip her arms around his waist and bury her face in his chest. "But it's probably a good thing you did. I've gotten a crick in my neck sleeping on the couch with Dano on my lap."

Logan's breath stirred the hair at the top of her head.

The secure feeling of his arms holding her close was enough to bring tears to her eyes.

"Logan." She breathed his name in a husky murmur. "Why are you so good to me?"

He turned her to face him. "I would've thought you'd have figured it out by now," he said as he slowly lowered his mouth to hers.

A sweetness flooded Abby at the tender possession of his mouth. She wanted to cry and beg him *not* to love her. Not yet. Not until she was sure of her feelings. But the gentle caress of his lips prevented the words from ever forming. Her hands moved up his shirt and over his shoulders, reveling in his strength.

His hands, at the small of her back, arched her closer as he inhaled deeply. "I've got to go or I'll be late for class. Will you be all right?"

Speaking was impossible and it was almost more than Abby could do to simply nod her head.

He straightened, relaxing his grip. "Take care of yourself," he said as his eyes smiled lovingly into hers.

Again it was all Abby could do to nod.

"I'll pick you up tomorrow at six-thirty, if you're up to it. We can grab a bite to eat after the game."

"Okay," she managed shakily and walked him to the door. "Thanks for the soup."

Logan smiled. "I've got to take care of the team's first-base player, don't I?" His mouth brushed hers and he was gone.

Leaning against the door, Abby looked around her grimly. If she felt guilty before, she felt wretched now.

Shoving the baseball cap down on her long brown hair, which she'd tied back in a loose ponytail, Abby couldn't stifle a sense of excitement. She did enjoy soft-ball. And Logan was right—she was the best first-base player the team was likely to find. Not to mention her hitting ability.

Logan wasn't as good a player but enjoyed himself as much as she did. He just didn't have the same com-petitive edge. More than once he'd been responsible for an error. But no one seemed to mind and Abby didn't let it bother her.

As usual he was punctual when he came to pick her up. "Hi. I can see you're feeling better."

"Much better."

The game was scheduled to be played in Diamond Lake Park, and Abby was half-afraid Tate would stum-ble across them. She wasn't sure how often he went into the park and— She reined in her worries. There was no reason to assume he'd show up or that he'd even recognize her.

Most of the team had arrived by the time Abby and Logan sauntered onto the field. The Jack and Jill Softball League was recreational. Of all their team members, Abby was the one who took the game most seriously. The team positions alternated between men and women. Since Abby played first base, a man was at second. Logan was in the outfield.

The team they were playing was from a local church that Abby remembered having beaten last summer.

Dick Snyder was their office team's coach and strat-egist. "Hope that arm's as good as last year," Dick said to Abby, who beamed at him. It was gratifying to be appreciated.

After a few warm-up exercises and practice pitches, their team left the field. Logan was up at bat first. Abby cringed at the stiff way he held himself. He wasn't a natural athlete, despite his biking prowess.

"Logan," she shouted encouragingly, "flex your knees."

He did as she suggested and swung at the next pitch. The ground ball skidded past the shortstop and Logan was safe on first.

Abby breathed easier and sent him a triumphant smile.

Patty Martin was up at bat next. Abby took one look at the shy, awkward young woman and knew she'd be an immediate out. Patty was new to the team this year, and Abby hoped she'd stick with it.

"Come on, Patty," she called out, hoping to instill some confidence, "you can do it!"

Patty held the bat clumsily and bit her lip as she glared straight ahead at the pitcher. She swung at the first three balls and missed each one.

Dick pulled Patty aside and gave her a pep talk before she took her place on the bench.

Abby hurried over to Patty and patted her knee. "I'm glad you decided to play with us." She meant that honestly. She suspected Patty could do with some friends.

"But I'm terrible." Patty stared at her clenched hands and Abby noticed how white her knuckles were.

"You'll improve," Abby said with more certainty than she felt. "Everyone has to learn, and believe me, every one of us strikes out. Don't worry about it."

By the time Abby was up to bat, there were two outs and Logan was still at first. Her standup double and a home run by the hitter following her made the score 3–0.

It remained the same until the bottom of the eighth.

Logan was playing the outfield when a high fly ball went over his head. He scrambled to retrieve it.

Frantically jumping up and down at first base, Abby screamed, "Throw the ball to second! Second." She watched in horror as Logan turned and faced third base. "Second!" she yelled angrily.

The woman on third base missed the catch, and the batter went on to make it home, giving his team their first run.

Abby threw her glove down and, with her hands placed defiantly on her hips, stormed into the outfield and up to Logan. "I told you to throw the ball to second."

He gave her a mildly sheepish look. "Sorry, Abby. All your hysterics confused me."

Groaning, Abby returned to her position.

They won the game 3–1 and afterward gathered at the local restaurant for pizza and pitchers of beer.

"You're really good," Patty said, sitting beside Abby.

"Thanks," she said, smiling into her beer. "I was on the high-school team for three years, so I had lots of practice."

"I don't know if I'll ever learn."

"Sure you will," Logan insisted. "Besides, we need you. Didn't you notice we'd be one woman short if it wasn't for you?"

Abby hadn't noticed that, but was pleased Logan had brought it up. This quality of making people feel important had drawn Abby to him on their first date.

"I'm awful, but I really like playing. And it gives me a chance to know all of you better," Patty added shyly.

"We like having you," Abby confirmed. "And you *will* improve." Patty seemed to want the reassurance that she was needed and appreciated, and Abby didn't mind echoing Logan's words.

They ate their pizzas and joked while making plans for the game the following Wednesday evening.

Dick Snyder and his wife gave Patty a ride home. Patty hesitated in the parking lot. "Bye, Abby. Bye, Logan," she said timidly. "I'll see you soon."

Abby smiled secretly to herself. Patty was attracted to Logan. She'd praised his skill several times that evening. Abby didn't blame her. Logan was wonderful. True, he wasn't going to be joining the Minnesota Twins any year soon—or ever. But he'd made it to base every time he was up at bat.

Logan dropped Abby off at her apartment, but didn't accept her invitation to come in for a glass of iced tea. To be honest, Abby was grateful. She didn't know how much longer she could hide from Logan that she was continuing to see Tate. And she refused to lie if he asked her. She planned to tell him soon…as soon as an appropriate opportunity presented itself.

The remainder of the week went smoothly. She didn't talk to Logan, which made things easier. Abby realized that Sunday afternoon with him would be difficult after spending Saturday with Tate, but she decided to worry about it then.

She woke Saturday morning with a sense of expectation. Tate was taking the afternoon off and meeting her in the park after she'd finished tutoring Mai-Ling. From there they were driving out to Apple Valley and the Minnesota Zoo, where he did volunteer work.

She wore a pale pink linen summer dress and had woven her long brown hair into a French braid. A glance in the mirror revealed that she looked her best.

Mai-Ling met her and smiled knowingly. "You and Tate are seeing each other today?"

"We're going to the zoo."

"The animal place, right?"

"Right."

Abby's attention drifted while Mai-Ling did her lesson. The woman's ability was increasing with every meeting. Judging by the homework Mai-Ling brought for Abby to examine, the young woman wouldn't be needing her much longer.

They'd finished their lesson and were laughing when Abby looked up and saw Tate strolling across the lawn toward her.

Again she was struck by the sight of this ruggedly appealing male. He was dressed in jeans, a tight-fitting T-shirt and cowboy boots.

His rich brown eyes seemed to burn into hers. "Hello, Abby." He greeted Mai-Ling, but his eyes left Abby's only for a second.

"I'll catch my bus," said Mai-Ling, excusing herself, but Abby barely noticed.

"You're looking gorgeous today," Tate commented, taking her hand in his.

A tingling sensation shot up her arm at his touch. Her nerves felt taut just from standing beside him. Abby couldn't help wondering what kissing Tate would be like. Probably the closest thing to heaven this side of earth.

"You seem deep in thought."

Abby smiled up at him. "Sorry. I guess I was."

They chatted easily as Tate drove toward Apple Valley. Abby learned that he'd been a volunteer for three years, working at the zoo as many as two days a week.

"What animals do you care for?"

Tate answered her without taking his eyes off the road. "Most recently I've been working with a llama for the Family Farm, but I also do a lot of work with birds. In fact, I've been asked to assist in the bird show."

"Will you?" Abby remembered seeing Tate that first day with the ducks....

"Yes."

"What other kinds of things do you do?"

Tate's returning smile was quick. "Nothing that glamorous. I help at feeding time and I clean the cages. Sometimes I groom and exercise the animals."

"What are you doing with the llama?"

"Mostly I've been working to familiarize him with people. We'd like Larry to join his brother in giving children rides."

Tate parked the car and came around to her side to open the passenger door. He kept her hand tucked in his as he led the way to the entrance.

"You love it here, don't you?" Abby asked as they cleared the gates.

"I do. The zoo gives us a rare opportunity to discover nature and our relationship to other living things. We have a responsibility to protect animals, as well as their habitats. Zoos, good zoos like this, are part of that." A glint of laughter flashed in his eyes as he turned toward her. "I didn't know I could be so profound."

Someone called out to Tate, and Abby watched him respond with a brief wave.

"Where would you like to start?"

The zoo was divided into five regions and Abby chose Tropics Trail, an indoor oasis of plants and animals from Asia.

As they walked, Tate explained what they were seeing, regaling her with fascinating bits of information. She'd been to the zoo before, but she'd never had such a knowledgeable guide.

Three hours later, it was closing time.

"Promise you'll bring me again," Abby begged, her eyes held by Tate's with mesmerizing ease.

"I promise," he whispered as he led her toward his car.

The way he said it made her feel weak in the knees, made her forget everything and everyone else. She lapsed into a dreamy silence on the drive home.

Tate drove back to Minneapolis and they stopped at a Mexican restaurant near Diamond Lake Park. Abby had passed it on several occasions but never eaten there.

A young Hispanic waitress smiled at them and led them to a table.

Tate spoke to the woman in Spanish. She nodded her head and turned around.

"What did you ask?" Abby whispered.

"I wanted to know if we could eat outside. You don't mind, do you? The evening is lovely."

"No, that sounds great." But she did mind. Because it immediately occurred to her that Logan might drive past and see her eating there with Tate. Abby managed to squelch her worries as she sat down at a table on the patio and opened her menu. She studied its contents, but her appetite had unexpectedly disappeared.

"You've got that thoughtful look again," Tate remarked. "Is everything okay, Abby?"

"Oh, sure," she said.

Abby decided what she'd order and took the opportunity to watch Tate as he reviewed the menu. His brow was creased, his eyes narrowed in concentration. When he happened to glance up and found her looking at him he set the menu aside.

An awkwardness followed. It continued until the waitress finally stopped at their table. Abby ordered cheese enchiladas and a margarita; Tate echoed her choice but asked for a Corona beer. "I had a good time today," Abby said in an attempt to breach the silence after the waitress left.

"I did, too." Tate sounded stiff, as if he suddenly felt uneasy.

"Is something wrong?" Abby asked after another silence.

It could have been Abby's imagination, but she sensed that Tate was struggling within himself.

"Tate?" she prompted.

He leaned forward and pinched the bridge of his nose before exhaling loudly. "No...nothing."

Long after he'd dropped her off at the apartment, Abby couldn't shake the sensation that something was troubling him. Twice he'd seemed about to speak, but both times he'd stopped himself.

Abby's thoughts were heavy as she drifted into sleep. Tomorrow she'd be spending the afternoon with Logan. She had to tell him she'd decided to see Tate; delaying it any longer was a grave disservice to them both—to Logan *and* to Tate.

Sunday afternoon, Logan sat on the sofa beside Abby and reached for her hand. She had to force herself not to snatch it away. So often in the past Abby had wanted Logan to be more demonstrative. And now that he was, it caused such turmoil inside her that she wanted to cry.

"You're looking pale, Abby. Are you sure you're feeling all right?" he asked her, his voice concerned.

"Logan, I've got to talk to you," she blurted out miserably. "I need to—"

"What you need is to get out of this stuffy apartment." He stood up, bringing her with him. Slipping an arm around her waist, Logan directed her out of the apartment and to his car.

Abby didn't have time to protest as he opened the door. She climbed inside and he leaned across to fasten her seat belt.

"Where are we going?" she asked, confused and unhappy as he backed out of the parking area.

"For a drive."

"I don't want to go for a drive."

Logan glanced away from the road long enough to narrow his eyes slightly at her. "Abby, what is it? You look like you're about to cry."

"I am." She swallowed convulsively and bit her bottom lip. "I want to go back to the apartment."

Logan pulled over and cut the engine. "Abby, what's wrong?" he asked solicitously.

Abby got out and leaned against the side of the car. The blood was pounding wildly in her ears. She hugged her waist with both arms.

"Abby?" he prompted softly as he joined her.

"I tried to tell you on Monday evening," she said. "I even went to your office, but you had some stupid meeting."

He didn't argue with her. "Is this about Tate?"

"Yes!" she shouted. "I went to the zoo with him yesterday. All week I've felt guilty because I know you don't want me to see anyone except you."

Abby chanced a look at him. He displayed no emotion, his eyes dark and unreadable. "Do you want to continue seeing him?" he asked carefully.

"I like Tate. I've liked him from the time we met," Abby admitted in a low whisper. "I don't know him all that well, but—"

"You want to get to know him better?" His eyes seemed to draw her toward him like a magnet.

"Yes," she whispered, gazing up at him.

"Then you should," he said evenly.

"Oh, Logan," she breathed. "I was hoping you'd understand."

"I do, Abby." He placed his hands deep inside his pants pockets and walked around the car, opening the passenger door.

"Where are we going?"

He looked mildly surprised. "I'm taking you home." The smile that touched the corners of his mouth didn't reach his eyes. "Abby, if you're seeing Tate, you won't be seeing me."

Four

Shocked, Abby stared at him, and her voice trembled slightly. "What do you mean?"

"Isn't it obvious?" Logan turned toward her. His eyes had darkened and grown more intense. There was an almost imperceptible movement along his jaw. "Remind me. How long have we been dating?" he asked, but his voice revealed nothing.

"You know how long we've been dating. About a year now. What's that got to do with anything?"

Logan frowned. "If you don't know how you feel about me in that length of time, then I can't see continuing a relationship."

Abby clenched her fist, feeling impotent anger well up within her. "You're trying to blackmail me, aren't you?"

"Blackmail you?" Logan snapped. He paused and breathed in deeply. "No, Abby, that isn't my intention."

"But you're saying that if I go out with Tate, then I can't see you," she returned with a short, bitter laugh. "You're not being fair. I like you both. You're wonderful, Logan, but...but so is Tate."

"Then decide. Which one of us do you want?"

Logan made it sound so simple. "I can't." She inhaled a shaky breath and raked a weary hand through her hair. "It's not that easy."

"Do you want Tate and me to slug it out? Is that it? Winner takes the spoils?"

"No!" she cried, shocked and angry.

"You've got the wrong man if you think I'll do that."

Tears spilled from Abby's eyes. "That's not what I want, and you know it."

"Then what *do* you want?" The low question was harsh.

"Time. I...I need to sort through my feelings. When did it become a crime to feel uncertain? I barely know Tate—"

"Time," Logan interrupted, but the anger in his tone didn't seem directed at her. "That's exactly what I'm giving you. Take as long as you need. When you've decided what you feel, let me know."

"But you won't see me?"

"Seeing you will be unavoidable. Our offices are half a block apart—and we have the softball team."

"Classes?"

"No. There's no need for us to go together or to meet each other there."

Tilting her chin downward, Abby swiped at her tears, trying to quell the rush of hurt. Logan could remove her from his life so effortlessly. His apparent indifference pierced her heart.

Without a word, he drove her back to the apartment building and parked, but didn't shut off the engine.

"Before you go," Abby said, her voice quavering, "would you hold me? Just once?"

Logan's hand tightened on the steering wheel until his knuckles were strained and white. "Do you want a comparison? Is that it?" he asked in a cold, stiff voice.

"No, that wasn't what I wanted." She reached for the door handle. "I'm sorry I asked."

Logan didn't move. They drew each breath in unison. Unflinching, their eyes held each other until Logan, his clenched jaw, hard and proud, became a watery blur and Abby lowered her gaze.

"Call me, Abby. But only when you're sure." The words were meant as a dismissal and the minute she was out of his car, he drove away.

Abby's knees felt so weak, she sat down as soon as she got inside her apartment. She was stunned. She'd expected Logan to be angry, but she'd never expected this—that he'd refuse to see her again. She'd only tried to be fair. Hurting Logan, or Tate for that matter, was the last thing she wanted. But how could she possibly know what she felt toward Tate? Everything was still so new. As she'd told Logan, they barely knew each other. They hadn't so much as kissed. But she and Logan were supposed to be friends....

She moped around the house for a couple of hours, then thought she'd pay her parents a visit. Her mother would be as shocked at Logan's reaction as she'd been. Abby needed reassurance that she'd done the right thing, especially since nothing had worked out as she'd hoped.

The short drive to her parents' house was accomplished in a matter of minutes. But there was no response to her knock; her parents appeared to be out. Belatedly, Abby recalled her mother saying that they were going camping that weekend.

Abby slumped on the front steps, feeling enervated

and depressed. Eventually she returned to her car, without any clear idea of where she should go or what she should do.

Never had a Sunday been so dull. Abby drove around for a time, picked up a hamburger at a drive-in and washed her car. Without Logan, the day seemed empty.

Lying in bed that night, Dano at her feet, Abby closed her eyes. If she'd missed Logan, he must have felt that same sense of loss. This could work both ways. Logan would soon discover how much of a gap she'd left in *his* life.

The phone rang Monday evening and Abby glanced at it anxiously. It had to be Logan, she thought hopefully. Who else would be calling? She didn't recognize the number, so maybe he had a new cell, she told herself.

"Hello," she said cheerfully. If it *was* Logan, she didn't want him to get the impression that she was pining away for him.

"Abby, it's Tate."

Tate. An unreasonable sense of disappointment filled her. What was the matter with her? This whole mess had come about because she wanted to be with Tate.

"How about a movie Friday evening?"

"I'd like that." She exhaled softly.

"You don't sound like yourself. Is something wrong?"

"No," she denied quickly. "What movie would you like to see?"

They spoke for a few more minutes and Abby managed to steer the conversation away from herself. For those few minutes, Tate helped her forget how miserable she was, but the feelings of loss and frustration returned the moment she hung up.

Tuesday evening, Abby waited outside the community center hoping to see Logan before class. She planned to give him a regal stare that would show how content she was without him. Naturally, if he gave any hint of his own unhappiness, she might succumb and speak to him. But either he'd arrived before her or after she'd gone into the building, because Abby didn't catch a glimpse of him anywhere. Maybe he'd even skipped class, but she doubted that. Logan loved chess.

The painting class remained a blur in her mind as she hurried out the door to the café across the street. She'd met Logan there after every class so far. He'd come; Abby was convinced of it. She pictured how their eyes would meet and intuitively they'd know that being apart like this was wrong for them. Logan would walk to her table, slip in beside her and take her hand. Everything would be there in his eyes for her to read.

The waitress gave Abby a surprised glance and asked if she was sitting alone tonight as she handed her the menu. Dejectedly Abby acknowledged that she was alone...at least for now.

When Logan entered the café, Abby straightened, her heart racing. He looked as good as he always did. What she didn't see was any outward sign of unhappiness...or relief at her presence. But, she reminded herself, Logan wasn't one to display his emotions openly. Their eyes met and he gave her an abrupt nod before sliding into a booth on the opposite side of the room.

So much for daydreams, Abby mused. Well, fine, he could sit there all night, but she refused to budge. Logan would have to come to her. Determinedly she studied the menu, pretending indifference. When she couldn't stand it any longer, she glanced at him from the corner of her eye. He now shared his booth with two other guys and was chatting easily with his friends. Abby's heart sank.

"I'm telling you, Mother," Abby said the next afternoon in her mother's kitchen. "He's blown this whole thing out of proportion."

"What makes you say that?" Glenna Carpenter closed the oven door and set the meat loaf on top of the stove.

"Logan isn't even talking to me."

"It doesn't seem like there's been much opportunity. But I wouldn't worry. He will tonight at the game."

"What makes you so sure of that?" Abby hopped down from her position on the countertop.

Glenna straightened and wiped her hands on her ever-present terry cloth apron. "Things have a way of working out for the best, Abby," she continued nonchalantly.

"Mom, you've been telling me that all my life and I've yet to see it happen."

Glenna chuckled, slowly shaking her head. "It happens every day of our lives. Just look around." Deftly she turned the meat loaf onto a platter. "By the way, didn't you say your game's at six o'clock?"

Abby nodded and glanced at her watch, surprised that the time had passed so quickly. "Gotta rush. Bye, Mom." She gave her mother a peck on the cheek. "Wish me well."

"With Logan or the game?" Teasing blue eyes so like her own twinkled merrily.

"Both!" Abby laughed and was out the door.

Glenna followed her to the porch, and Abby felt her mother's sober gaze as she hurried down the front steps and to her car.

* * *

Almost everyone was on the field warming up when Abby got there. Immediately her gaze sought out Logan. He was in the outfield pitching to another of the male players. Abby tried to suppress the emotion that charged through her. Who would've believed she'd feel so lost and unhappy without Logan? If he saw that Abby had arrived, he gave no indication.

"Hi, Abby," Patty called, waving from the bench.

Abby smiled absently. "Hi."

"Wait until you see me bat." Patty beamed happily, pretending to swing at an imaginary pitch. Then, placing her hand over her eyes as the fantasy ball flew into left field, she added, "I think I'll be up for an award by the end of the season."

"Good." Abby was preoccupied as she stared out at Logan. He looked so attractive. So vital. Couldn't he have the decency to develop some lines at his eyes or a few gray hairs? He *had* to be suffering. She was, although it wasn't what she'd wanted or expected.

"Logan took me to see the Twins play on Monday night and he gave me a few pointers afterward," Patty continued.

Abby couldn't believe what she was hearing. *A few pointers? I'll just bet he did!* Logan and Patty?

The shock must have shown in her eyes because Patty added hurriedly, "You don't mind, do you? When Logan phoned, I asked him about the two of you and he said you'd both decided to start seeing other people."

"No, I don't mind," Abby returned flippantly, remembering her impression last week—that Patty had a crush on him. "Why should I?"

"I…I just wanted to be sure."

If Patty thought she'd get an award for baseball, Abby was sure someone should nominate *her* for an Oscar. By the end of the game her face hurt from her permanent smile. She laughed, cheered, joked and tried to suggest that she hadn't a care in the world. At bat she was dynamite. Her pain was readily transferred to her swing and she didn't hit anything less than a double and got two home runs.

Once, Logan had patted her affectionately on the back to congratulate her, Abby had shot him an angry glare. It'd taken him only one day. *One day* to ask Patty out. That hurt.

"Abby?" Logan's dark brows rose questioningly. "What's wrong?"

"Wrong?" Although she gave him a blank look, she realized her face must have divulged her feelings. "What could possibly be wrong? By the way, Tate said hello. He wanted to be here tonight, but something came up." Abby knew her lie was childish, but she couldn't help her reaction.

She didn't speak to him again.

Gathering the equipment after the game, Abby tried not to remember the way Patty had positioned herself next to Logan on the bench during the game and how she made excuses to be near him at every opportunity.

"You're coming for pizza, aren't you?" Dick asked Abby for the second time.

Abby wanted to go. The get-togethers after the game were often more fun than the game itself. But she couldn't bear the curious stares that were sure to follow when Logan sat next to Patty and started flirting with her.

"Not tonight," Abby responded, opening her eyes

wide to give Dick a look of false candor. "I've got other plans." Abby noticed the way Logan's mouth curved in a mirthless smile. He'd heard that and come to his own conclusions. Good!

Abby regretted her hasty refusal later. The apartment was hot and muggy. Even Dano, her temperamental cat, didn't want to spend time with her.

After a cool shower, Abby fixed a meal of scrambled eggs, toast and a chocolate bar. She wasn't the least bit hungry, but eating was at least a distraction.

She couldn't concentrate on her newest suspense novel, so she sat on the sofa and turned on the TV. A rerun of an old situation comedy helped block out the image of Patty in Logan's arms. Abby didn't doubt that Logan had kissed Patty. The bright, happy look in her eyes had said as much.

Uncrossing her legs, Abby released a bitter sigh. She shouldn't care if Logan kissed a hundred women. But she did. It bothered her immensely—regardless of her own hopes and fantasies about Tate. She recognized how irrational she was being, and her confusion only increased.

With the television blaring to drown out the echo of Patty's telling her about the fun she'd had with Logan, Abby reached for the chocolate bar and peeled off the wrapper. The sweet flavor wouldn't ease the discomfort in her stomach, because Abby knew it wasn't chocolate she wanted, it was Logan. Feeling wretched again, she set the candy bar aside and leaned her head back, closing her eyes.

By Friday evening, Abby was convinced all the contradictory feelings she had about Logan could be summed up in one sentence: The grass is always greener on the other side of the fence. It was another of those clichés her mother seemed so fond of and spouted on a regular basis. She was surprised Glenna hadn't dragged this one into their conversations about Logan and Tate. The idea of getting involved with Tate had been appealing when she was seeing Logan steadily. It stood to reason that the reverse was also true—that Logan would miss her and lose interest in Patty. At least that was what Abby told herself repeatedly as she dressed for her date.

With her long brown hair a frame around her oval face, she put on more makeup than usual. With a secret little smile she applied an extra dab of perfume. Tate wouldn't know what hit him! The summer dress was one of her best—a pale blue sheath that could be dressed up or down, so she was as comfortable wearing it to a movie as she would be to a formal dinner.

When Tate arrived, he had on a pair of cords and a cotton shirt, open at the neck, sleeves rolled up. It was undeniably a sexy look.

"You're stunning," he said appreciatively, kissing her lightly on the cheek.

"Thank you." Abby couldn't restrain her disappointment. He'd looked at her the way one would a sister and his kiss wasn't that of a lover—or someone who intended to be a lover.

Still, they joked easily as they waited in line for the latest blockbuster action movie and Abby was struck by their camaraderie. It didn't take her long to realize that their relationship wasn't hot and fiery, sparked by mutual attraction. Instead, it was…friendly. Warm. Almost lacking in imagination. Ironically, that had been exactly her complaint about Logan….

Tate bought a huge bucket of popcorn, which they shared in the darkened theater. But Abby noted that he appeared restless, often shifting his position, crossing and uncrossing his legs. Once, when he assumed she wasn't watching, he laid his head against the back of the seat and closed his eyes. Was Tate in pain? she wondered.

Abby's attention drifted from the movie. "Tate," she whispered. "Are you okay?"

He immediately opened his eyes. "Of course. Why?"

Rather than refer to his restlessness, she simply shook her head and pretended an interest in the screen.

When they'd finished the popcorn, Tate reached for her hand. But Abby noted that it felt tense. If she didn't know better, she'd swear he was nervous. But Abby couldn't imagine what possible reason Tate would have to be nervous around her.

The evening was hot and close when they emerged from the theater.

"Are you hungry?" Tate asked, taking her hand, and again, Abby was struck by how unnaturally tense he seemed.

"For something cold and sinful," she answered with a teasing smile.

"Beer?"

"No," Abby said with a laugh. "Ice cream."

Tate laughed, too, and hand in hand they strolled toward the downtown area where Tate assured her he knew of an old fashioned ice-cream place. The Swanson Parlor was decorated in pink—pink walls, pink chairs, pink linen tablecloths and pink-dressed waitresses.

Abby decided quickly on a banana split and mentioned it to Tate.

"That does sound good. I'll have one, too."

Abby shut her menu and set it aside. This was the third time they'd gone for something to eat, and each time Tate had ordered the same thing she did. He didn't seem insecure. But maybe she was being oversensitive. Besides, it didn't make any difference.

Their rapport made conversation comfortable and lighthearted. They talked about the movie and other films they'd both seen. Abby discussed some of her favorite mystery novels and Tate described animal behavior he'd witnessed. But several times Abby noted that his laughter was forced. His gaze would become intent and his sudden seriousness would throw the conversation off stride.

"I love Minneapolis," Abby said as they left the ice-cream parlor. "It's such a livable city."

"I agree," Tate commented. "Do you want to go for a walk?"

"Yes, let's." Abby tucked her hand in the crook of his elbow.

Tate looked at her and smiled, but again Abby noted the sober look in his eyes. "I was born in California," he began.

"What's it like there?" Abby had been to New York but she'd never visited the West Coast.

"I don't remember much. My family moved to New Mexico when I was six."

"Hot, I'll bet," Abby said.

"It's funny, the kinds of things you remember. I don't recall what the weather was like. But I have a very clear memory of my first-grade teacher in Alburquerque, Ms. Grimes. She was pretty and really tall." Tate chuckled.

"But I suppose all teachers are tall to a six-year-old. We moved again in the middle of that year."

"You seem to have moved around quite a bit," Abby said, wondering why Tate had started talking about himself so freely. Although they had talked about a number of different subjects, she knew little about his personal life.

"We moved five times in as many years," Tate continued. "We had no choice, really. My dad couldn't hold down a job, and every time he lost one we'd pack up and move, seeking another start, another escape." Tate's face hardened. "We came to Minneapolis when I was in the eighth grade."

"Did your father finally find his niche in life?" Abby sensed that Tate was revealing something he rarely shared with anyone. She felt honored, but surprised. Their relationship was promising in some ways and disappointing in others, but the fact that he trusted her with his pain, his difficult past, meant a lot. She wondered why he'd chosen her as a confidante.

"No, Dad died before he ever found what he was looking for." There was no disguising the anguish in his voice. "My feelings for my father are as confused now as they were then." He turned toward Abby, his expression solemn. "I hated him and I loved him."

"Did your life change after he was gone?" Abby's question was practically a whisper, respecting the deep emotion in Tate's eyes.

"Yes and no. A couple of years later, I dropped out of school and got a job as a mechanic. My dad taught me a lot, enough to persuade Jack Bessler to hire me."

"And you've been there ever since?"

His mouth quirked at one corner. "Ever since."

"You didn't graduate from high school then, did you?"

"No."

That sadness was back in his voice. "And you resent that?" Abby asked softly.

"I may have for a time, but I never fit in a regular classroom. I guess in some ways I'm a lot like my dad. Restless and insecure. But I'm much more content working at the garage than I ever was in a classroom."

"You've worked there for years now," Abby said, contradicting his assessment of himself. "How can you say you're restless?"

He didn't acknowledge her question. "There's a chance I could buy the business. Jack's ready to retire and wants out from under the worry."

"That's what you really want, isn't it, Tate?"

"The business is more than I ever thought I'd have."

"But something's stopping you?" Abby could sense this more from his tension than from what he said.

"Yes." The stark emotion in his voice startled her.

"Are you worried about not having graduated from high school? Because, Tate, you can now. There's a program at the community center where I take painting classes. You can get what they call a G.E.D.—General Education Diploma, I think is what it means. Anyway, all you need to do is talk to a counselor and—"

"That's not it." Tate interrupted her harshly and ran a hand across his brow.

"Then what is it?" Abby asked, her smile determined.

Tate hesitated until the air between them was electric, like a storm ready to explode in the muggy heat.

"Where are you going with this discussion? What can I do to help? I don't understand." One minute Tate was exposing a painful part of his past, and the next he was growling at her. What was it with men? Something had been bothering him all evening. First he'd been restless and uneasy, then brooding and thoughtful, now angry. Nothing made sense.

And it wasn't going to. Abruptly he asked her if she was ready to leave.

He hardly said a word to her when he dropped her off at her apartment.

For a moment, Abby was convinced he'd never ask her out again.

"What about Sunday?" he finally said. "We can bring a picnic."

"Okay." But after this evening, Abby wasn't sure. He didn't sound as if he really wanted her company. "How about three o'clock?"

"Fine." His response was clipped.

Again he gave her a modest kiss, more a light brushing of their mouths than anything passionate or intense. Not a real kiss, in her opinion.

She leaned against the closed door of her apartment, not understanding why Tate was bothering to take her out. It seemed apparent that his interest in her wasn't romantic—although she didn't know what it actually was, didn't know what he wanted or needed from her. And for that matter, the bone-melting effect she'd experienced at their first meeting had long since gone. Tate was a handsome man, but he wasn't what she'd expected.

Maybe the grass wasn't so green after all.

After a restless Sunday morning, Abby decided that she'd go for a walk in the park. Logan often did before he came over to her place, and she hoped to run into him. She'd make a point of letting him know that their meeting was pure coincidence. They'd talk. Somehow she'd inform him, casually of course, that things weren't working out as she'd planned. In fact, yesterday, during her lesson with Mai-Ling, Tate hadn't come to the park, and she'd secretly been relieved. Despite today's picnic, she suspected that their romance was over before it could really start. And now she had doubts about its potential, anyway. Hmm. Maybe she'd hint to Logan that she missed his company. That should be enough to break the ice without either of them losing their pride. And that was what this came down to—pride.

The park was crowded by the time Abby arrived. Entering the grounds, she scanned the lawns for him and released a grateful sigh to find that he was sitting on a park bench reading. By himself. To her relief, Patty wasn't with him.

Deciding on her strategy, Abby stuck her hands in her pockets and strolled down the paved lane, hoping to look as if she'd merely come for a walk in the park. Their meeting would be by accident.

Abby stood about ten feet away, off to one side, watching Logan. She was surprised at the emotion she felt just studying him. He looked peaceful, but then he always did. He was composed, confident, in control. Equal to any situation. They'd been dating for almost a year and Abby hadn't realized that so much of her life was interwoven with Logan's. She'd taken him for granted until he was gone, and the emptiness he'd left behind had shocked her. She'd been stupid and insensitive. And heaven knew how difficult it was for her to admit she'd been wrong.

For several minutes Abby did nothing but watch him. A calm settled over her as she focused on Logan's shoulders. They weren't as broad or muscular as Tate's, but somehow it didn't matter. Not now, not when she was hurting, missing Logan and his friendship. Without giving it much thought, she'd been looking forward to Sunday all week and now she knew precisely why: Sundays had always been special because they were spent with Logan. It was Logan she wanted, Logan she needed, and Abby desperately hoped she wasn't too late.

Abby continued to gaze at him. After a while her determination to talk to him grew stronger. Never mind her pride—Logan had a right to know her feelings. He'd been patient with her far longer than she deserved. Her stomach felt queasy, her mouth dry. Just when she gathered enough courage to approach him, Logan closed his book and stood up. Turning around he looked in her direction, but didn't hesitate for a second. He glanced at his watch and walked idly down the concrete pathway toward her until he was within calling distance. Abby's breath froze as he looked her way, blinked and looked in the opposite direction. She couldn't believe he'd purposely avoid her and she doubted he would've been able to see her standing off to the side.

The moment she was ready to step forward, Logan stopped to chat with two older men playing checkers. From her position, Abby saw them motion for him to sit down, which he did. He was soon deep in conversation with them. The three were obviously good friends, although she'd never met the other men before.

Abby loitered as long as she could. Half an hour passed and still Logan stayed.

Defeated, Abby realized she'd have to hurry or be

late for her picnic with Tate. Silently she slipped from her viewing position and started across the grounds. When she glanced over her shoulder, she saw that Logan was alone on a bench again and watching a pair of young lovers kissing on the grass. Even from this distance, she saw a look of such intense pain cross his face, she had to force herself not to run to his side. He dropped his head in his hands and hunched forward as if a heavy burden was weighing on him.

Abby's throat clogged with tears until it was painful to breathe. They filled her eyes. Logan loved her and had loved her from the beginning, but she'd carelessly thrown his love aside. It had taken only a few days' separation to know with certainty that she loved him, too.

Tears rolled down her face, but Abby quickly brushed them aside. Logan wouldn't want to know she'd seen him. She'd stripped him of so much, it wouldn't be right to take his pride, as well. Today she'd tell Tate she wouldn't be seeing him again. If that was all Logan wanted, it would be a small price to pay. She'd run back to his arms and never leave him again.

By the time she got to her building, Tate was at the front door. They greeted each other and Tate told her about a special place he wanted to show her near Apple Valley.

She ran into her apartment to get a few things, then joined him in the car.

Both seemed preoccupied during the drive. Abby helped him unload the picnic basket, her thoughts racing at breakneck speed. She folded the tablecloth she'd brought over a picnic table while Tate spread out a blanket under a shady tree. They hardly spoke.

"Abby—"

"Tate—"

They both began together.

"You first," Abby murmured and sat down, drawing up her legs and circling them with both arms, then resting her chin on her bent knees.

Tate remained standing, hands in his pockets as he paced. Again, something was obviously troubling him.

"Tate, what is it?"

"I didn't know it would be so hard to tell you," he said wryly and shook his head. "I meant to explain weeks ago."

What was he talking about?

His gaze settled on her, then flickered to the ground. "I tried to tell you Friday night after the movie, but I couldn't get the words out." He ran a weary hand over his face and fell to his knees at her side.

Abby reached for his hand and held it.

"Abby." He released a ragged breath. "*I can't read.* I'll pay you any amount if you'll teach me."

Five

In one brilliant flash everything about Tate fell into place. He hadn't been captivated by her charm and natural beauty. He'd overheard her teaching Mai-Ling how to read and knew she could help him. That was the reason he'd sought her out and cultivated a friendship. She could help him.

Small things became clear in her mind. No wonder Tate ordered the same thing she did in a restaurant. Naturally their date on Friday night had been awkward. He'd been trying to tell her then. How could she have been so blind?

Even now he studied her intently, awaiting her response. His eyes glittered with pride, insecurity and fear. She recognized all those emotions and understood them now.

"Of course I'll teach you," she said reassuringly.

"I'll pay you anything you ask."

"Tate." Her grip on his hand tightened. "I wouldn't take anything. We're friends."

"But I can afford to pay you." He took a wad of bills from his pocket and breathed in slowly, glancing at the money in his hand.

Again Abby realized how difficult admitting his inability to read had been. "Put that away," Abby said calmly. "You won't be needing it."

Tate stuffed the bills back in his pocket. "You don't know how relieved I am to have finally told you," he muttered hoarsely.

"I don't think I could have been more obtuse," she said, still shocked at her own stupidity. "I'm amazed you've gotten along as well as you have. I was completely fooled."

"I've become adept at this. I've done it from the time I was in grade school."

"What happened?" Abby asked softly, although she could guess.

A sadness stole into his eyes. "I suppose it's because of all those times I was pulled out of school so we could move," he said unemotionally. "We left New Mexico in the middle of first grade and I never finished the year. Because I was tall for my age my mother put me in second grade the following September. The teacher wanted to hold me back but we moved again. And again and again." A bitterness infected his voice. "By the time I was in junior high and we'd moved to Minneapolis, I had devised all kinds of ways to disguise the fact that I couldn't read. I was the class clown, the troublemaker, the boy who'd do anything to get out of going to school."

"Oh, Tate." Her heart swelled with compassion.

Sitting beside her, Tate rubbed his hand across his face and smiled grimly. "But the hardest part was getting up the courage to tell you."

"You've never told anyone else, have you?"

"No. It was like admitting I have some horrible disease."

"You don't. We can fix this," she said. She was trying to reassure him and felt pathetically inadequate.

"Will you promise me that you'll keep this to yourself? For now?"

She nodded. "I promise." She understood how humiliated he felt, why he wanted his inability to read to remain a secret, and felt she had to agree.

"When can we start? There's so much I want to learn. So much I want to read. Books and magazines and computer programs…" He sounded eager, his gaze level and questioning.

"Is tomorrow too soon?" Abby asked.

"I'd say it's about twenty years too late."

Tate brought Abby back to her apartment two hours later. Tomorrow she'd call the World Literacy Movement and have them email the forms for her to complete regarding Tate. He looked jubilant, excited. Telling her about his inability to read had probably been one of the most difficult things he'd ever done in his life. She understood how formidable his confession had felt to him because now she had to humble herself and call Logan. And that, although major to her, was a small thing in comparison.

Abby wasn't unhappy at Tate's confession. True, her pride was stung for a moment. But overall she was relieved. Tate was the kind of man who'd always attract women's attention. For a brief time she'd been caught up in his masculine appeal. And if it hadn't been for Tate, it would have taken her a lot longer to recognize how fortunate she was to have Logan.

The thought of phoning him and admitting that she was wrong had been unthinkable a week ago. Had it only been a week? In some ways it felt like a year.

Abby glanced at the ceiling and prayed that Logan would answer her call. There was so much stored in her heart that she wanted to tell him. Her hand trembled as she lifted the receiver and tried to form positive thoughts. *Everything's going to work out. I know it will.* She repeated that mantra over and over as she dialed.

She was so nervous her fingers shook and her stomach churned until she was convinced she was going to be sick. Inhaling, Abby held her breath as his phone rang the first time. Her lungs refused to function. Abby closed her eyes tightly during the second ring.

"Hello."

Abby took a deep breath.

"Logan, this is Abby."

"Abby?" He sounded shocked.

"Can we talk? I mean, I can call back if this is inconvenient."

"I'm on my way out the door. Would you like me to come over?"

"Yes." She was surprised at how composed she sounded. "That would be great." She replaced the phone and tilted her head toward the ceiling. "Thank you," she murmured gratefully.

Looking down, Abby realized how casually she was dressed. When Logan saw her again, she wanted to bowl him over.

Racing into her room, she ripped the dress she'd worn Friday night off the hanger, then decided it wouldn't do. She tossed it across her bed. She tried on one outfit and then another. Never had she been more unsure about what she wanted to wear. Finally she chose a pair of tailored black pants and a white blouse with an eyelet collar. Simple, elegant, classic.

Abby was frantically brushing her hair when the buzzer went. *Logan.* She gripped the edge of the sink and took in a deep breath. Then she set down the brush, practiced her smile and walked into the living room.

"Hello, Abby," Logan said a moment later as he stepped into the apartment.

Her first impulse was to throw her arms around him and weep. A tightness gripped her throat. Whatever poise she'd managed to gather was shaken and gone with one look from him.

"Hello, Logan. Would you like to sit down?" She gestured toward the chair. Her gaze was fixed on his shoulders as he walked across the room and took a seat.

"And before you ask," he interjected sternly, "no, I don't want anything to drink. Sit down, Abby."

She complied, grateful because she didn't know how much longer her knees would support her.

"You wanted to talk?" The lines at the side of his mouth deepened, but he wasn't smiling.

"Yes." She laced her hands together tightly. "I was wrong," she murmured. Now that the words were out, Abby experienced none of the calm she'd expected. "I'm—I'm sorry."

"It wasn't a question of my being right or your being wrong," Logan said. "I'm not looking for an apology."

Abby's lips trembled and she bit into the bottom corner. "I know that. But I felt I owed you one."

"No." He stood and with one hand in his pocket paced the width of the carpet. "That's not what I wanted to hear. I told you to call me when you were sure it was me you wanted and not Tate." His eyes rested on her, his expression hooded.

Abby stood, unable to meet his gaze. "I *am* sure," she breathed. "I know it's you I want."

His mouth quirked in what could have been a smile, but he didn't acknowledge her confession.

"You have every right to be angry with me." She couldn't look at him, afraid of what she'd see. If he were to reject her now, Abby didn't think she could stand it. "I've missed you so much," she mumbled. Her cheeks flamed with color, and she couldn't believe how difficult this was. She felt tears in her eyes as she bowed her head.

"Abby." Logan's arms came around her shoulders, bringing her within the comforting circle of his arms. He lifted her chin and lovingly studied her face. "You're sure?"

The growing lump in her throat made speech impossible. She nodded, letting all the love in her eyes say the words.

"Oh, Abby..." He claimed her lips with a hungry kiss that revealed the depth of his feelings.

Slipping her arms around his neck, Abby felt him shudder with a longing he'd suppressed all these months. He buried his face in the dark waves of her hair and held her so tightly it was difficult to breathe.

"I've been so wrong about so many things," she confessed, rubbing her hands up and down his spine, reveling in the muscular feel of him.

Lowering himself to the sofa, Logan pulled Abby onto his lap. His warm breath was like a gentle caress as she wound her arms around his neck and kissed him, wanting to make up to him for all the pain she'd caused them both. The wild tempo of her pulse made clear thought impossible.

Finally, Logan dragged his mouth from hers. "You're sure?" he asked as if he couldn't quite believe it.

Abby pressed her forehead against his shoulder and nodded. "Very sure. I was such a fool."

His arm held her securely in place. "Tell me more. I'm enjoying this."

Unable to resist, Abby kissed the side of his mouth. "I thought you would."

"So you missed me?"

"I was miserable."

"Good!"

"Logan," she cried softly. "It wouldn't do you any harm to tell me how lonely *you* were."

"I wasn't," he said jokingly.

Involuntarily Abby stiffened and swallowed back the hurt. "I know. Patty mentioned that you'd taken her to the Twins game."

Logan smiled wryly. "We went with several other people."

"It bothers me that you could see someone else so soon."

"Honey." His hold tightened around her waist, bringing her closer. "It wasn't like you're thinking."

"But...you said you weren't lonely."

"How could I have been? I saw you Tuesday and then at the game on Wednesday."

"I know, but—"

"Are we going to argue?"

"A thousand kisses might convince me," she teased and rested her head on his shoulder.

"I haven't got the willpower to continue kissing you without thinking of other things," he murmured in her ear as his hand stroked her hair. "I love you, Abby. I've loved you from the first time I asked you out." His breathing seemed less controlled than it had been a moment before.

"Oh, Logan." Fresh tears sprang to her eyes. She started to tell him how much she cared for him, but he went on, cutting off her words.

"As soon as I saw Tate I knew there was no way I could compete with him. He's everything I'll never be. Tall. Movie-star looks." He shook his head. "I don't blame you for being attracted to him."

Abby straightened so she could look at this man she loved. Her hands framed his face. "You're a million things Tate could never be."

"I know this has been hard on you."

"But I was so stupid," Abby inserted.

He kissed her lightly, his lips lingering over hers. "I can't help feeling grateful that you won't be seeing him again."

Abby lowered her eyes. She *would* be seeing Tate, but not in the way Logan meant.

A stillness filled the room. "Abby?"

She gave him a feeble smile.

"You aren't seeing Tate, are you?"

She couldn't reveal Tate's problem to anyone. She'd promised. And not for the world would she embarrass him, especially when admitting he couldn't read had been so difficult. No matter how much she wanted to tell Logan, she couldn't.

"I'd like to explain," Abby replied, her voice trembling.

Logan stiffened and lightly pushed her from his lap. "I don't want explanations. All I want is the truth. Will you or will you not be seeing Tate?"

"Not romantically," she answered, as tactfully and truthfully as possible.

Logan's eyes hardened. "What other explanation could there be?"

"I can't tell you that," she said forcefully and stood up.

"Of course you can." A muscle worked in his jaw. "We're right back where we started, aren't we, Abby?"

"No." She felt like screaming at him for being so unreasonable. Surely he recognized how hard it had been for her to call him and admit she was wrong?

"Will you stop seeing Tate, then?" he challenged.

"I can't." Her voice cracked in a desperate appeal for him to understand. "We live in the same neighborhood…" she said, stalling for time as her mind raced for an excuse. "I'll probably run into him…. I mean, it'd be only natural, since he's so close and all."

"Abby," Logan groaned impatiently. "That's not what I mean and you know it. Will you or will you not be *seeing* Tate?"

She hesitated. Knowing what her promise was doing to her relationship with Logan, Tate would want him to know. But she couldn't say anything without clearing it with him first.

"Abby?"

"I'll be seeing him, but please understand that it's not the way you assume."

For an instant, Abby saw pain in Logan's eyes. The pain she witnessed was the same torment she was experiencing herself.

They stood with only a few feet separating them and yet Abby felt they'd never been further apart. Whole worlds seemed to loom between them. Logan's ego was at stake, his pride, and he didn't want her to continue seeing Tate, no matter what the reason.

"You won't stop seeing him," Logan challenged furiously.

"I can't," Abby cried, just as angry.

"Then there's nothing left to say."

"Yes," Abby said, "there is, but you're in no mood to hear it. Just remember that things aren't always as they appear."

"Goodbye, Abby," he responded. "And next time don't bother calling me unless—"

Abby stalked across the room and threw open the door. "Next time I won't," she said with a cutting edge.

Reaction set in the minute the door slammed behind him. Abby was so angry that pacing the floor did little to relieve it. How could Logan say he loved her in one breath and turn around and storm out the next? Yet, he'd done exactly that.

Once the anger dissipated, Abby began to tremble and felt the tears burning for release. Pride demanded that she forestall them. She wouldn't allow Logan to reduce her to that level. She shook her head and kept her chin raised. She wouldn't cry, she wouldn't cry, she repeated over and over as one tear after another slid down her cheeks.

"Who did you say was responsible for the literacy movement?" Tate asked, leafing respectfully through the first book.

"Dr. Frank Laubach. He was a missionary in the Philippines in the 1920s. At that time some of the island people didn't have a written language. He invented one and later developed a method of teaching adults to read."

"Sounds like he accomplished a lot."

Abby nodded. "By the time he died in 1970, his work had spread to 105 countries and 313 languages."

Tate continued leafing through the pages of the primary workbook. Abby wanted to start him at the most fundamental skill level, knowing his progress would be rapid. At this point, Tate would need all the encouragement he could get and the speed with which he completed the lower-level books was sure to help.

Abby hadn't underestimated Tate's enthusiasm. By the end of the first lesson he had relearned the alphabet and was reading simple phrases. Proudly he took the book home with him.

"Can we meet again tomorrow?" he asked, standing near her apartment door.

"I've got my class tomorrow evening," Abby explained, "but if you like, we could meet for a half hour before—or after if you prefer."

"Before, I think."

The following afternoon, Tate showed up an hour early, just after she got home from work, and seemed disappointed that Abby would be occupied with softball on Wednesday evening.

"We could get together afterward if you want," she told him.

Affectionately, Tate kissed her on the cheek. "I want."

Again she noted that his fondness for her was more like that of a brother—or a pupil for his teacher. She was grateful for that, at least. And he was wonderful to her. He brought over takeout meals and gave her small gifts as a way of showing his appreciation. The gifts weren't necessary, but they salvaged Tate's pride and that was something she was learning more about every day—male pride.

Abby was dressing for the game Wednesday evening when the phone rang. No longer did she expect or even hope it would be Logan. He'd made his position completely clear. Fortunately, call display told her it was her parents' number.

"Hello, Mom."

"Abby, I've been worried about you."

"I'm fine!" She forced some enthusiasm into her voice.

"Oh, dear, it's worse than I thought."

"What's worse?"

"Logan and you."

"There is no more Logan and me," she returned.

A strained silence followed. "But I thought—"

"Listen, Mom," Abby cut in, unwilling to listen to her mother's postmortem. "I've got a game tonight. Can I call you later?"

"Why don't you come over for dinner?"

"Not tonight." Abby hated to turn down her mother's invitation, but she'd already agreed to see Tate for his next lesson.

"It's your birthday Friday," Glenna reminded her.

"I'll come for dinner then," Abby said with a feeble smile. Her birthday was only two days away and she wasn't in any mood to celebrate. "But only if you promise to make my favorite dish."

"Barbecued chicken!" her mother announced. "You bet."

"And, Mom," Abby continued, "you were right about Logan."

"What was I right about?" Her mother's voice rose slightly.

"He does love me, and I love him."

Abby thought she heard a small, happy sound.

"What made you realize that?" her mother asked.

"A lot of things," Abby said noncommittally. "But I

also realized that loving someone doesn't make everything perfect. I wish it did."

"I have the feeling there's something important you're not telling me, Abby," Glenna said on a note of puzzled sadness. "But I know you will in your own good time."

Abby couldn't disagree with her mother's observation. "I'll be at your place around six on Friday," she murmured. "And thanks, Mom."

"What are mothers for?" Glenna teased.

The disconnected phone line droned in Abby's ear before she hung up, suddenly surprised to see that it was time to head over to the park. For the first time that she could remember, she didn't feel psyched up for the game. She wasn't ready to see Logan, which would be more painful than reassuring. And if he paid Patty special attention, Abby didn't know how she'd handle that. But Logan wouldn't do anything to hurt her. At least she knew him well enough to be sure of that.

The first thing Abby noticed as she walked onto the diamond was that Patty Martin had cut and styled her hair. The transformation from straight mousy-brown hair to short, bouncy curls was astonishing. The young woman positively glowed.

"What do you think?" Patty asked in a hurried voice. "Your hair is always so pretty and..." She let the rest of what she was going to say fade.

Abby held herself motionless. Patty had made herself attractive for Logan. She desperately wanted Logan's interest, and for all Abby knew, she was getting it. "I think you look great," Abby commented, unable to deny the truth or to be unkind.

"I was scared out of my wits," Patty admitted shyly. "It's been a long time since I was at the hairdresser's."

"Hey, Patty, they're waiting for you on the field," the team's coach hollered. "Abby, you, too."

"Okay, Dick," Patty called back happily, her eyes shining. "I've gotta go. We'll talk later, okay?"

"Fine." Softening her stiff mitt against her hand with unnecessary force, Abby ran to her position at first base.

Logan was practicing in the outfield.

"Abby," he called, and when she turned, she found his gaze level and unwavering. "Catch."

Nothing appeared to affect him. They'd suffered through the worst four days of their relationship and he looked at her as coolly and unemotionally as he would a...a dish of potato salad. She didn't respond other than to catch the softball and pitch it to second base.

The warm-up period lasted for about ten minutes. Abby couldn't recall a time she'd felt less like playing, and it showed.

"What's the matter, Ab?" Dick asked her at the bottom of the fifth after she'd struck out for the third time. "You're not yourself tonight."

"I'm sorry," she said with a frustrated sigh. Her eyes didn't meet his. "This isn't one of my better nights."

"She's got other things on her mind." Logan spoke from behind her, signaling that he was sitting in the bleachers one row above. "Her boyfriend just showed up, so she'll do better."

Abby whirled around to face Logan. "What do you mean by that?"

Logan nodded in the direction of the parking lot. Abby's gaze followed his movement and she wanted to groan aloud. Tate was walking toward the stands.

"Tate isn't my boyfriend." Abby's voice was taut with impatience.

"Oh, is that terminology passé?" Logan returned.

Stunned at the bitterness in him, Abby found no words to respond. They were both hurting, and in their pain they were lashing out at each other.

Logan slid from the bleachers for his turn at bat. Abby focused her attention on him, deciding she didn't want to make a fuss over Tate's unexpected arrival.

Logan swung wildly at the first pitch, hitting the ball with the tip of his bat. Abby could hear the wood crack as the ball went flying over the fence for a home run. Logan looked as shocked as Abby. He tossed the bat aside and ran around the bases to the shouts and cheers of his teammates. Abby couldn't remember Logan ever getting more than a single.

"Hi." Tate slid into the row of seats behind her. "You don't mind if I come and watch, do you?" he asked as he leaned forward with lazy grace.

"Not at all," Abby said blandly. It didn't make any difference now. She stared at her laced fingers, attempting to fight off the depression that seemed to have settled over her. She was so caught up in her own sorrows that she didn't see the accident. Only the startled cries of those around her alerted her to the fact that something had happened.

"What's wrong?" Abby asked frantically as the bench cleared. Everyone was running toward Patty, who was clutching her arm and doubled over in pain.

Logan's voice could be heard above the confusion. "Stand back. Give her room." Gently he aided Patty into a sitting position.

Even to Abby's untrained eye it was obvious that

Patty's arm was broken. Logan tore off his shirt and tied it around her upper body to create a sling and support the injured arm.

The words *hospital* and *doctor* were flying around, but everyone seemed stunned and no one moved. Again it was Logan who helped Patty to her feet and led her to his car. His calm, decisive actions imparted confidence to both teams. Only minutes before, Abby had been angry because he displayed so little emotion.

"What happened?" Abby asked Dick as they walked off the field.

"I'm not sure." Dick looked shaken himself. "Patty was trying to steal a base and collided with the second baseman. When she fell, she put out her arm to catch herself and it twisted under her."

"Will she be all right?"

"Logan seemed to think so. He's taking her to the emergency room. He said he'd let us know her condition as soon as possible."

The captain of the opposing team crossed the diamond to talk to Dick and it was decided that they'd play out the remainder of the game.

But without Logan the team was short one male player.

"Do you think your friend would mind filling in?" Dick asked somewhat sheepishly, glancing at Tate.

"I can ask."

"No problem," Tate said, smiling as he picked up Logan's discarded mitt and ran onto the field.

Although they'd decided to finish the game, almost everyone was preoccupied with the accident. Abby's team ended up winning, thanks to Tate, but only by a slight margin.

The group as a whole proceeded to the pizza parlor to wait for word about Patty.

Tate sat across the long wooden table from Abby, chatting easily with her fellow teammates. Only a few slices of the two large pizzas had been eaten. Their conversation was a low hum as they recounted their versions of the accident and what could have been done to prevent it.

Abby was grateful for Logan's clear thinking and quick actions. He wasn't the kind of skilled softball player who'd stand out, but he gave of himself in a way that was essential to every member of the team. Only a few days earlier she'd found Logan lacking. Compared to the muscular Tate, he'd seemed a poor second. Now she noted that his strengths were inner ones. Again she was reminded that if given the chance, she would love this man for the rest of her life.

Abby didn't see Logan enter the restaurant, but the immediate clamor caused her to turn. She stood with the others.

"Patty's fine," he assured everyone. "Her arm's broken, but I don't think that's news to anyone."

"When will she be back?"

"We want to send flowers or something."

"When do you think she'll feel up to company?"

Everyone spoke at once. Calmly Logan answered each question and when he'd finished, the mood around the table was considerably lighter.

A tingling awareness at the back of her neck told Abby that Logan was near. With a sweeping action he swung his foot over the long bench and joined her.

He focused on Tate, sitting across from Abby. "I wish I could say it's good to see you again," he said with stark unfriendliness.

"Logan, please!" Abby hissed.

The two men eyed each other like bears who'd violated each other's territory. Tate had no romantic interest in her, Abby was convinced of that, but Logan was openly challenging him and Tate wouldn't walk away from such blatant provocation.

Unaware of the dangerous undercurrents swirling around the table, Dick Snyder sauntered over and slapped Logan on the back.

"We owe a debt of thanks to Tate here," he informed Logan cheerfully. "He stepped in for you when you were gone. He batted in the winning run."

Logan and Tate didn't so much as blink. "Tate's been doing a lot of that for me lately, isn't that right, Abby?"

Wrenching her gaze from him, Abby stood and, with as much dignity and pride as she could muster, walked out of the restaurant and went home alone.

The phone was ringing when she walked into the apartment. Abby let it ring. She didn't want to talk to anyone. She didn't even want to know who'd called.

"Abby, would you take the bread out of the oven?" her mother asked, walking out to the patio.

"Okay." Abby turned off the broiler and pulled out the cookie sheet, on which slices of French bread oozed with melted butter and chopped garlic. Her enthusiasm for this birthday celebration was nil.

The doorbell caught her by surprise. "Are you expecting anyone?" she asked her mother, who'd returned to the kitchen.

"Not that I know of. I'll get it."

Abby was placing the bread slices in a warming basket when she heard her mother's surprised voice.

Turning, Abby looked straight at Logan.

Six

A shocked expression crossed Logan's face. "Abby." He took a step inside the room and paused.

"Hello, Logan." A tense silence ensued as Abby primly folded her hands.

"I'll check the chicken," Glenna Carpenter murmured discreetly as she hurried past them.

"What brings you to this neck of the woods?" Abby forced a lightness into her voice. He looked tired, as if he hadn't been sleeping well. For that matter, neither had Abby, but she doubted either would admit as much.

Logan handed her a wrapped package. "I wanted your mother to give you this. But since you're here— happy birthday."

A small smile parted her trembling lips as Abby accepted the brightly wrapped gift. He had come to her parents' home to deliver this, but he hadn't expected her to be there.

"Thank you." She continued to hold it.

"I, uh, didn't expect to see you." He stated the obvious, as though he couldn't think of anything else to say.

"Where else would I be on my birthday?"

Logan shrugged. "With Tate."

Abby released a sigh of indignation. "I thought I'd explained that I'm not involved with Tate. We're friends, nothing more."

She shook her head. They'd gone over this before. Another argument wouldn't help. Abby figured she'd endured enough emotional turmoil in the past few weeks. She still hadn't spoken to Tate about telling Logan the truth. But she couldn't, not with Tate feeling as sensitive as he did about the whole thing.

"Abby." Logan's voice was deadly quiet. "Don't you see what's happening? You may not think of Tate in a romantic light, but I saw the way he was looking at you in the pizza place."

"You openly challenged him." Abby threw out a few challenges of her own. "How did you expect him to react? You wouldn't have behaved any differently," she said. "And if you've come to ruin my birthday…then you can just leave. I've had about all I can take from you, Logan Fletcher." She whirled around, not wanting to face him.

"I didn't come for that." The defeat was back in his voice again.

Abby's pulse thundered in her ears as she waited for the sounds of him leaving—at the same time hoping he wouldn't.

"Aren't you going to open your present?" he said at last.

Abby turned and wiped away a tear that had escaped from the corner of her eye. "I already know what it is," she said, glancing down at the package. "Honestly, Logan, you're so predictable."

"How could you possibly know?"

"Because you got me the same perfume for my birthday last year." Deftly she removed the wrapping paper and held up the small bottle of expensive French fragrance.

"I like the way it smells on you," Logan murmured, walking across the room. He rested his hands on her shoulders. "And if I'm so predictable, you'll also recall that there's a certain thank-you I expect."

Any resistance drained from her as Logan pulled her into his embrace. Abby slid her arms around his neck and tasted the sweetness of his kiss. A wonderful languor stole through her limbs as his mouth brushed the sweeping curve of her lashes and burned a trail down her cheek to her ear.

"I love you, Logan," Abby whispered with all the intensity in her.

Logan went utterly still. Gradually he raised his head so he could study her. Unflinching, Abby met his gaze determined that he see for himself what her eyes and heart were saying.

"If you love me, then you'll stop seeing Tate," he said flatly.

"And if you love *me*, you'll trust me."

"Abby." Logan dropped his hands and stepped away. "I—"

"Oh, Logan." Glenna Carpenter moved out of the kitchen. "I'm glad to see you're still here. We insist you stay for dinner. Isn't that right, Abby?"

Logan held her gaze with mesmerizing simplicity.

"Of course we do. If you don't have another appointment," Abby said meaningfully.

"You know I don't."

Abby knew nothing of the kind, but didn't want to

argue. "Did you see the gift Logan brought me?" Abby asked her mother and held out the perfume.

"Logan is always so thoughtful."

"Yes, he is," Abby agreed and slipped an arm around his waist, enjoying the feel of him at her side. "Thoughtful, but not very original." Her eyes smiled into his, pleading with him that, for tonight, they could forget their differences.

Logan's arms slid just as easily around her. "But with that kind of thank-you, what incentive do I have for shopping around?"

Abby laughed and led the way to the back patio.

Frank Carpenter, Abby's father, was busy standing in front of the barbecue, basting chicken.

"Logan," he exclaimed and held out a welcoming hand. "This is a pleasant surprise. Good to see you."

Logan and her father had always gotten along and had several interests in common. For a time that had irked Abby. Defiantly she'd wanted to make it clear that she wouldn't marry a man solely because her parents thought highly of him. Her childish attitude had changed dramatically these past weeks.

Abby's mother brought another place setting from the kitchen to add to the three already on the picnic table. Abby made several more trips into the kitchen to carry out the salad, toasted bread and a glass of wine for Logan.

Absently, Logan accepted the glass from her and smiled, deep in conversation with her father. Happiness washed over Abby as she munched on a potato chip. Looking at the two of them now—Abby busy helping her mother and Logan chatting easily with her father—she figured there was little to distinguish them as unmarried.

Dinner and the time that followed were cheerful. Frank suggested a game of cards while they were eating birthday cake and ice cream. But Abby's mother immediately rejected the idea.

"I think Glenna's trying to tell me to keep my mouth shut because it's obvious you two want some time alone," Abby's father complained.

"I'm saying no such thing," Glenna denied instantly as an embarrassed flush brightened her cheeks. "We were young once, Frank."

"Once!" Frank scolded. "I don't know about you, but I'm not exactly ready for the grave."

"We'll play cards another time," Logan promised, ending a friendly argument between her parents.

"Double-deck pinochle," Frank prompted. "Best card game there is."

Glenna pretended to agree but rolled her eyes dramatically when Frank wasn't looking.

"Shall we?" Logan successfully contained a smile and held out his open palm to Abby. She placed her hand in his, more contented than she could ever remember being. After their farewells to her parents, Logan followed her back to her apartment, parking his car beside hers. He took a seat while Abby hurried into the next room.

"Give me a minute to freshen up," Abby called out as she ran a brush through her hair and studied her reflection in the bathroom mirror. She looked happy. The sparkle was back in her eyes.

She dabbed some of the perfume Logan had given her to the pulse points at her throat and wrists. Maybe this would garner even more of a reaction. He wasn't one to display a lot of emotion, but he seemed to be coming along nicely in that area. His kisses had produced an overwhelming physical response in Abby, and she was aware that his feeling for her ran deep and strong. It had been only a matter of weeks ago that she'd wondered why he bothered to kiss her at all.

"I suppose you're going to suggest we drive to Des Moines and back," Logan teased when she joined him a few minutes later.

"Logan!" she cried, feigning excitement. "That's a wonderful idea."

He rolled his eyes and and laid the paper on the sofa. "How about a movie instead?"

Abby gave a fake groan. "So predictable."

"I've been wanting to see this one." He pointed at an ad for the movie she'd seen with Tate.

"I've already been," Abby tossed back, not thinking.

"When?"

Abby could feel the hostility exuding from Logan. He knew. Without a word he'd guessed that Abby had been to the movie with Tate.

"Not long ago." She tried desperately to put the evening back on an even keel. "But I'd see it again. The film's great."

The air between them became heavy and oppressive.

"Forget the movies," Logan said and neatly folded the paper. He straightened and stalked to the far side of the room. "In fact, why don't we forget everything."

Hands clenched angrily at her sides, Abby squared her shoulders. "If you ruin my birthday, Logan Fletcher, I don't think I'll ever forgive you."

His expression was cold and unreadable. "Yes, but there's always Tate."

A hysterical sob rose in her throat, but Abby managed to choke it off. "I...I told you tonight that I loved you." Her voice wobbled treacherously as her eyes pleaded with his. "Doesn't that mean anything to you? Anything at all?"

Logan's gaze raked her from head to foot. "Only that you don't know the meaning of the word. You want both Tate *and* me, Abby. But you can't decide between us so you'd prefer to keep us both dangling until you make up your mind." His voice gained volume with each word. "But I won't play that game."

Abby breathed in sharply as a fiery anger burned in her cheeks. Once she would have ranted, cried and hurled her own accusations. Now she stood stunned and disbelieving. "If you honestly believe that, then there's nothing left to say." Her voice was calmer than she dared hope. Life seemed filled with ironies all of a sudden. Outwardly she presented a clearheaded composure while on the inside she felt a fiery pain. Perhaps for the first time in her life she was acting completely selflessly, and this was her reward—losing Logan.

Without another word, Logan walked across the room and out the front door.

Abby watched him leave with a sense of unreality. This couldn't be happening to her. Not on her birthday. Last year Logan had taken her to dinner at L'Hôtel Sofitel and given her—what else—perfume. A hysterical bubble of laughter slipped from her. He was predictable, but so loving and caring. She remembered how they'd danced until midnight and gone for a stroll in the moonlight. Only a year ago, Logan had made her birthday the most perfect day of her life. But this year he was ruining it.

Angry, hurt and agitated, Abby paced the living-room carpet until she thought she'd go mad. Dano had wandered into the living room when she and Logan came in, but had disappeared into her bedroom once he sensed tension. Figured. Not even her cat was interested in comforting her. Usually when she was upset she'd ride her bike or do something physical. But bike riding at night could be dangerous, so she'd go running instead. She changed into old jeans and a faded sweatshirt that had a picture of a Disneyland castle on the front. She had trouble locating her second tennis shoe, then threw it aside in disgust when the rainbow-colored lace snapped in two.

She sighed. Nothing had gone right today. Tate had been disappointed that she wasn't able to meet him. Because of that, she'd been fighting off a case of guilt when she went to her parents'. Then Logan had shown up, and everything had steadily and rapidly gone downhill.

Ripping a lace from one of her baseball shoes, Abby had to wrap it around the sole of the shoe several times. On her way out the door, she paused and returned to the bathroom. If she was going to go running, then she'd do it smelling better than any other runner in Minneapolis history. She'd dabbed perfume on every exposed part of her body when she stepped out the door.

A light drizzle had begun to fall. Terrific. A fitting end to a rotten day.

The first block was a killer. She couldn't be that badly out of shape, could she? She rode her bike a lot. And wasn't her running speed the best on the team?

The second block, Abby forced her mind off how out of breath she was becoming. Logan's buying her perfume made her chuckle. *Predictable. Reliable. Confident.* They were all words that adequately described Logan. But so were *unreasonable* and *stubborn*—traits she'd only seen recently.

The drizzle was followed by a cloudburst and Abby's hair and clothes were plastered against her in the swirling wind and rain. She shouldn't be laughing. But she did anyway as she raced back to her apartment. It was either laugh or cry, and laughing seemed to come naturally. Laughing made her feel better than succumbing to tears.

By the time Abby returned to her building, she was drenched and shivering. With her chin tucked under and her arms folded around her middle, she fought off the chill and hurried across the parking lot. She was almost at her building door when she realized she didn't have the keys. She'd locked herself out!

What more could go wrong? she wondered. Maybe the superintendent was home. She stepped out in the rain to see if the lights were on in his apartment, which was situated above hers. His place was dark. Of course. That was how everything else was going.

Cupping one hand over her mouth while the other held her stomach, Abby's laughter was mixed with sobs of anger and frustration.

"Abby?" Logan's urgent voice came from the street. Hurriedly he crossed it, took one look at her and hauled her into his arms.

"Logan, I'll get you wet," she cried, trying to push herself free.

"What happened? Are you all right?"

"No. Yes. I don't know," she murmured, sniffling miserably. "What are you doing here?"

Logan brought her out of the rain and stood with his back blocking the wind, trying to protect her from the storm. "Let's get you inside and dry and I'll explain."

"Why?" she asked and wrung the water from the hem of her sweatshirt. "So you can hurl insults at me?"

"No," he said vehemently. "I've been half-crazy wondering where you were."

"I'll just bet," Abby taunted unmercifully. "I'm surprised you didn't assume I was with Tate."

A grimace tightened his jaw, and Abby knew she'd hit her mark. "Are you going to be difficult or are we going inside to talk this out reasonably?"

"We can't go inside," she said.

"Why not?"

"Because I forgot my keys."

"Oh, Abby," Logan groaned.

"And the manager's gone. Do you have any more bright ideas?"

"Did you leave the bedroom window open?" he asked with marked patience.

"Yes, just a little, but—" A glimmer of an idea sparked and she smiled boldly at Logan. "Follow me."

"Why do I have the feeling I'm not going to like this?" he asked under his breath as Abby pulled him by the hand around to the back of the building.

"Here," she said, bending her knee and lacing her fingers together to give him a boost upward to the slightly open window.

"You don't expect to launch me through there, do you?" Logan glared at her. "I won't fit."

Rivulets of rain trickled down the back of Abby's

neck. "Well, I can't do it. You know I'm afraid of heights."

"Abby, the window's barely five feet off the ground."

"I'm standing here, drenched and miserable," she said, waving her hands wildly. "On my birthday, no less," she added sarcastically, "and you don't want to rescue me."

"I'm not in the hero business," Logan muttered as he hunched his shoulders to ward off the rain. "Try Tate."

"Fine, I'll do that." She stalked off to the side of the building.

"Abby?" He sounded unsure as she dragged over an aluminum garbage can.

"Go away!" she shouted. "I don't need you."

"What's the difference between going through the window using a garbage can or having me lift you through?"

"Plenty." She wasn't sure what, but she didn't want to take the time to figure it out. All she wanted was a hot bath and ten gallons of hot chocolate.

"You're being totally irrational."

"I've always been irrational. It's never bothered you before." Her voice trembled as she balanced her weight on the lid of the garbage can. She reached the window and pushed it open enough to crawl through when she felt the garbage can lid give way. "Logan!" she screamed, terror gripping her as she started to fall.

Instantly he was there. His arms gripped her waist as she tumbled off the aluminum container. Together they went crashing to the ground, Logan twisting so he took the worst of the fall.

"Are you okay?" he asked frantically, straightening and brushing the hair from her face.

Abby was too stunned and breathless to speak, so she just nodded.

"Now listen," he whispered angrily. "I'm going to lift you up to the windowsill and that's final. Do you understand?"

She nodded again.

"I've had enough of this arguing. I'm cold and wet and I want to get inside and talk some reason into you." He stood and wiped the mud from his hands, then helped her up. Taking the position she had earlier, he crouched and let her use his knee as a step as his laced fingers boosted her to the level of the window.

Abby fell into the bedroom with a loud thud, knocking the lamp off her nightstand. Dano howled in terror and dashed under the bed.

"Are you okay?" Logan yelled from outside.

Abby stuck her head out the window. "Fine. Come around to the front and I'll let you in."

"I'll meet you at your door."

"Logan." She leaned forward and smiled at him provocatively. "You *are* my hero."

He didn't look convinced. "Sure. Whatever you say."

Abby had buzzed open the front door and unlocked her own by the time he came around the building. His wet hair was dripping water down his face, and his shirt was plastered to his chest, revealing a lean, muscular strength. He looked as drenched and miserable as she felt.

"You take a shower while I drive home and change out of these." He looked down ruefully at his mud-spattered beige pants and rain-soaked shirt.

Abby agreed. Logan had turned and was halfway out

the door when Abby called him back. "Why are you here?" she asked, wanting to delay his leaving.

He shrugged and gave her that warm, lazy smile she loved. "I don't know. I thought there might be another movie you wanted to see."

Abby laughed and blew him a kiss. "I'm sure there is."

When Logan returned forty minutes later, Abby's hair was washed and blown dry and hung in a long French braid down the middle of her back. She'd changed into a multicolored bulky sweater and jeans.

Abby smiled. "We're not going to fight, are we?"

"I certainly hope not!" he exclaimed. "I don't think I can take much more of this. When I left here the first time I was thinking…" He paused and scratched his head. "I was actually entertaining the thought of driving to Des Moines and back."

"That's crazy." Abby tried unsuccessfully to hide her giggles.

"You're telling me?" He sat on the sofa and held out his arm to her, silently inviting her to join him.

Abby settled on the sofa, her head resting on his chest while his hand caressed her shoulder.

"Do you recall how uncomplicated our lives were just a few weeks ago?" Logan asked her.

"Dull. Ordinary."

"What changed all that?"

Abby was hesitant to bring Tate's name into the conversation. "Life, I guess," she answered vaguely. "I know you may misunderstand this," she added in a husky murmur, "but I don't want to go back to the way our relationship was then." He hadn't told her he loved her and she hadn't recognized the depth of her own feelings.

He didn't move. "No, I don't suppose you would."

Abby repositioned her head and placed the palm of her hand on his jaw, turning his face so she could study him. Their eyes met. The hard, uncompromising look in his dark eyes disturbed her. She desperately wanted to assure him of her love. But she'd realized after the first time that words were inadequate. She shifted and slid her hands over his chest to pause at his shoulders.

The brilliance of his eyes searched her face. "Abby." He groaned her name as he fiercely claimed her lips. His hand found its way to the nape of her neck, his fingers gently pulling dark strands free from the braid so he could twine them through his fingers.

His breathing deep, he buried his face in the slope of her neck. "Just let me hold you for a while. Let's not talk."

She agreed and settled into the warm comfort of his embrace. The staccato beat of his heart gradually returned to a normal pace and Abby felt content and loved. The key to a peaceful relationship was to bask in their love for each other, she thought, smiling. That, and not saying a word.

"What's so amusing?" Logan asked, his breath stirring the hair at the side of her face.

"How do you know I'm smiling?"

"I can feel it."

Abby tilted her head so she could look into his eyes. "This turned into a happy birthday, after all," she said.

Now he smiled, too. "Can I see you tomorrow?"

"If you weren't going to ask me, then I would've been forced to make some wild excuse to see *you*." Lovingly

Abby rubbed her hand along the side of his jaw, enjoying the slightly prickly feel of his beard.

"What would you like to do?"

"I don't care as long as I'm with you."

"My, my," he whispered, taking her hand. Tenderly he kissed her palm. "You're much easier to please than I remember."

"You don't know the half of it," she teased.

Logan stiffened and sat upright. "What's tomorrow?"

"The tenth. Why?"

"I can't, Abby. I've got something scheduled."

She felt a rush of disappointment but knew that if she was frustrated, so was Logan. "Don't worry, I'll survive," she assured him, then smiled. "At least I think I will."

"But don't plan anything for the day after tomorrow."

"Of course I'm planning something."

"Abby." He sounded tired and impatient.

"Well, it's Sunday, right? Our usual day. So I'm planning to spend it with you. I thought that was what you wanted."

"I do."

The grimness about his mouth relaxed.

Almost immediately afterward, Logan appeared restless and uneasy. Later, as she dressed for bed, she convinced herself that it was her imagination.

The lesson with Mai-Ling the following afternoon went well. It was the last reading session they'd have, since Mai-Ling was now ready to move on. She'd scheduled one with Tate right afterward, deciding that what Logan didn't know wouldn't hurt him. Tate was still painfully self-conscious and uncomfortable about telling anyone else, although his progress was remarkable and he advanced more quickly than any student she'd ever tutored, including the talented Mai-Ling. From experience, she could tell he was spending many hours each evening studying.

On her way back to her apartment late Saturday afternoon, Abby decided on the spur of the moment to stop at Patty's and see how she was recuperating. She'd sent her an email wishing her a rapid recovery and had promised to stop over some afternoon. Patty needed friends and Abby was feeling generous. Her topsy-turvy world had been righted.

She went to a drugstore first and bought half a dozen glossy magazines as a get-well gift, then drove to Patty's home.

Her sister answered the doorbell.

"Hi, you must be from the baseball team. Patty's gotten a lot of company. Everyone's been wonderful."

Abby wasn't surprised. Everyone on the team was warm and friendly.

"This must be her day for company. Come on in. Logan's with her now."

Seven

Abby was dismayed as the sound of Patty's laughter drifted into the entryway, but she followed Patty's sister into the living room.

Patty's broken arm was supported by a white linen sling and she sat opposite Logan on a long sofa. Her eyes were sparkling with undisguised happiness. Logan had his back to Abby, and it was all she could do not to turn around and leave. Instead she forced a bright smile and made an entrance any actress would envy. "Hello, everyone!"

"Hi, Abby!" Patty had never looked happier or, for that matter, prettier. Not only was her hair nicely styled, but she was wearing light makeup, which added color to her pale cheeks and accented her large brown eyes. She wore a lovely summer dress, a little fancy for hanging around the house, and shoes that were obviously new.

"How are you feeling?" Abby prayed the phoniness in her voice had gone undetected.

Logan stood up and came around the couch, but his eyes didn't meet Abby's probing gaze.

"Hello, Logan, good to see you again."

"Hello, Abby."

"Sit down, please." Patty pointed to an empty chair. "We've got a few minutes before dinner." Patty seemed oblivious to the tension between her guests.

"No, thanks," Abby murmured, faking another smile. "I can only stay a minute. I just wanted to drop by and see how you were doing. Oh, these are for you," she said, handing over the magazines. "Some reading material…"

"Thank you! And I'm doing really well," Patty said enthusiastically. "This is the first night I've been able to go out. Logan's taking me to dinner at the Sofitel."

Abby breathed in sharply and clenched her fist until her nails cut into her hand. Logan had taken her there only once, but Abby considered it their special restaurant. He could've taken Patty anyplace else in the world and it would've hurt, but not as much as this.

"Everyone's been great," Patty continued. "Dick and his wife were over yesterday, and a few others from the team dropped by. Those flowers—" she indicated several plants and bouquets "—are from them."

"We all feel terrible about the accident." Abby made her first honest statement of the visit.

"But it was my own fault," Patty said as Logan hovered stiffly on the other side of the room.

Abby lowered her eyes, unable to meet the happy glow in Patty's. A crumpled piece of wrapping paper rested on the small table at Patty's side. It was the same paper Logan had used to wrap Abby's birthday gift the day before. He *couldn't* have gotten Patty perfume. He wouldn't dare.

"You look so nice," Abby said. Her pulse quickened. What *had* Logan brought Patty? She thought she recognized that scent.... "Is that a new perfume you're wearing?"

"Yes, as a matter of fact, Logan—"

"Hadn't we better be going?" Logan said as he made a show of glancing at his watch.

Patty looked flustered. "Is it time already?"

Following her cue, Abby glared at Logan and took a step in retreat. "I should go, too." A contrived smile curved her mouth. "Have a good time."

"I'll walk you to your car," Logan volunteered.

Walking backward Abby gestured with her hands, swinging them at her sides to give a carefree impression. "No, that isn't necessary. Really. I'm capable of finding my own way out."

"Abby," Logan said under his breath.

"Have a wonderful time, you two," Abby continued, her voice slightly high-pitched. "I've only been to the Sofitel once. The food was fantastic, but I can't say much for my date. But I no longer see him. A really ordinary guy, if you know what I mean. And so predictable."

"I'll be right back." Logan directed his comment to Patty and gripped Abby by the elbow.

"Let me go," she seethed.

Logan's grip relaxed once they were outside the house. "Would you let me explain?"

"Explain?" She threw the word in his face. "What could you possibly say? No." She waved her hand in front of his chest. "Don't say a word. I don't want to hear it. Do you understand? Not a word."

"You're being irrational again," Logan accused, apparently having difficulty keeping his rising temper in check.

"You're right," she agreed. "I've completely lost my sense. Please forgive me for being so closed-minded." Her voice was surprisingly even but it didn't disguise the hurt or the feeling of betrayal she was experiencing.

"Abby."

"Don't," she whispered achingly. "Not now. I can't talk now."

"I'll call you later."

She consented with an abrupt nod, but at that point, Abby realized, she would have agreed to anything for the opportunity to escape.

Her hand was shaking so badly that she had trouble sliding the key into the ignition. This was crazy. She felt secure in his love one night and betrayed the next.

Abby didn't go home. The last thing she wanted to do was sit alone on a Saturday night. To kill time, she visited the Mall of America and did some shopping, buying herself a designer outfit that she knew Logan would hate.

The night was dark and overcast as she let herself into the apartment. Hanging the new dress in her closet, Abby acknowledged that spending this much money on one outfit was ridiculous. Her reasons were just as childish. But it didn't matter; she felt a hundred times better.

The phone rang the first time at ten. Abby ignored it. Logan. Of course. When it started ringing at five-minute intervals, she simply unplugged it. There was nothing she had to say to him. When they spoke again, she wanted to feel composed. Tonight was too soon. She wasn't ready yet.

Calm now, she changed into her pajamas and sat on the sofa, brushing her long hair in smooth, even strokes.

Reaction would probably set in tomorrow, but for now she was too angry to think.

Half an hour later, someone pressed her buzzer repeatedly. Annoying though it was, she ignored that, too.

When there was a banging at her door, Abby hesitated, then continued with her brushing.

"Come on, Abby, I know you're in there," Logan shouted.

"Go away. I'm not dressed," she called out sweetly.

"Then get dressed."

"No!" she yelled back.

Logan's laugh was breathless and bitter. "Either open up or I'll tear the stupid door off its hinges."

Just the way he said it convinced Abby this wasn't an idle threat. And to think that only a few weeks ago she'd seen Logan as unemotional. Laying her brush aside, she walked to the door and unlatched the safety chain.

"What do you want? How did you get into the building? And for heaven's sake, keep the noise down. You're disturbing the neighbors."

"Some guy from the second floor recognized me and opened the lobby door. And if you don't let me in to talk to you, I'll do a lot more than wake the neighbors."

Abby had never seen Logan display so much passion. Perhaps she should've been thrilled, but she wasn't.

"Did you and Patty have a nice evening?" she asked with heavy sarcasm.

Logan glanced briefly at his hands. "Reasonably nice."

"I apologize if I put a damper on your *date*," she returned with smooth derision. "Believe me, had I known about it, I would never have visited Patty at such an inopportune time. My timing couldn't have been better— or worse, depending on how you look at it."

"Abby," he sighed. "Let me in. Please."

"Not tonight, Logan."

Frustration furrowed his brow. "Tomorrow, then?"

"Tomorrow," she agreed and started to close the door.
"Logan," she called and he immediately turned back.
"Without meaning to sound like I care a whole lot, let
me ask you something. Why did you give Patty the
same perfume as me?" Some perverse part of herself
had to know.

His look was filled with defeat. "It seemed the thing
to do. I knew she'd enjoy it, and to be honest, I felt sorry
for her. Patty needs someone."

Abby's chin quivered as the hurt coursed through
her. Pride dictated that she maintain a level gaze.
"Thank you for not lying," she said and closed the door.

Tate was waiting for her when Abby entered the park
at eleven-thirty Sunday morning. Since her Saturday
sessions with Mai-Ling had come to an end, Abby was
now devoting extra time on weekends to Tate.

"You look like you just stepped out of the dentist's
chair," Tate said, studying her closely. "What's the matter? Didn't you sleep well last night?"

She hadn't.

"You work too hard," he told her. "You're always
helping others. Me and Mai-Ling…"

Abby sat on the blanket Tate had spread out on the
grass and lowered her gaze so that her hair fell forward,
hiding her face. "I don't do nearly enough," she dis-
agreed. "Tate," she said, raising her eyes to his. "I've
never told anyone the reason we meet. Would you mind
if I did? Just one person?"

Unable to sleep, Abby had considered the various

reasons Logan might have asked Patty out for dinner. She was sure he hadn't purposely meant to hurt her. The only logical explanation was that he wanted her to experience the same feelings he had, since she was continuing to see Tate. And yet he'd gone to pains to keep her from knowing about their date. Nothing made sense anymore. But if she could tell Logan the reason she was meeting Tate, things would be easier....

Tate rubbed a weary hand over his eyes. "This is causing problems with you and—what's-his-name— isn't it?"

Abby didn't want to put any unnecessary pressure on Tate so she shrugged her shoulders, hoping to give the impression of indifference. "A little. But I don't think Logan really understands."

"Is it absolutely necessary that he know?"

"No, I guess not." Abby had realized it would be extremely difficult for Tate to let anyone else learn about his inability to read—especially Logan.

"Then would it be too selfish of me to ask that you don't say anything?" Tate asked. "At least not yet?" A look of pain flashed over his face, and Abby understood anew how hard it was for him to talk about his problem. "I suppose it's a matter of pride."

Abby's smile relaxed her tense mouth. The relationship among the three of them was a mixed-up matter of pride, and she didn't know whose was the most unyielding.

"No, I don't mind," she replied, and opened her backpack to take out some books. "By the way, I want to give you something." She handed him three of her favorite Dick Francis books. "These are classics in the mystery genre. They may be a bit difficult for you in the beginning, but I think you'll enjoy them."

Tate turned the paperback copy of *The Danger* over and read the back cover blurb. "His business is kidnapping?" He sounded unsure as he raised his eyes to hers.

"Trust me. It's good."

"I'll give it a try. But it looks like it'll take me a while."

"Practice makes perfect."

Tate laughed in the low, lazy manner she enjoyed so much. "I've never known anyone who has an automatic comeback the way you do." He took a cold can of soda and tossed it to her. "Let's drink to your wit."

"And have a celebration of words." She settled her back against the trunk of a massive elm and closed her eyes as Tate haltingly read the first lines of the book she'd given him. It seemed impossible that only a few weeks before he'd been unable to identify the letters of the alphabet. But his difficulty wasn't attributed to any learning disability, such as she'd encountered in the past with others. He was already at a junior level and advancing so quickly she had trouble keeping him in material, which was why she'd started him on a novel. Unfortunately, his writing and spelling skills were advancing at a slower pace. Abby calculated that it wouldn't take more than a month or two before she could set him on his own with the promise to help when he needed it. Already he'd voiced his concerns about an application he'd be filling out for the bank to obtain a business loan. She'd assured him they'd go over it together.

Abby hadn't been home fifteen minutes when Logan showed up at her building. She buzzed him in and opened the door, but for all the emotion he revealed, his face might have been carved in stone.

"Are you going to let me inside today?" he asked, peering into her apartment.

"I suppose I'll have to."

"Not necessarily. You could make a fool of me the way you did last night."

"Me?" she gasped. "You don't need *me* to make you look like a fool. You do a bang-up job of it yourself."

His mouth tightened as he stepped into her apartment and sank down on the sofa.

Abby sat as far away from him as possible. "Well?" She was determined not to make this easy.

"Patty was in a lot of pain when I drove her to the hospital the night of the accident," he began.

"Uh-huh." She sympathized with Patty but didn't know why he was bringing this up.

Logan's voice was indifferent. "I was talking to her, trying to take her mind off how much she was hurting. It seems that in all the garble I rashly said I'd take her to dinner."

"I suppose you also—rashly—suggested the Sofitel?" She felt chilled by his aloofness and she wasn't going to let him off lightly.

An awkward silence followed. "I don't remember that part, but apparently I did."

"Apparently so," she returned with forced calm. "Maybe I could forget the dinner date, but not the perfume. Honestly, Logan, that was a rotten thing to do."

Impatience shadowed his tired features. "It's not what you think. I got her cologne. Not perfume."

"For heaven's sake," she said, exasperated. "Can't you be more original than that?"

"But it's the truth."

"I know that. But you can't go through life giving women perfume and cologne every time the occasion calls for a gift. And, even worse, you chose the same scent!"

"It's the only one I know." He shook his head. "All right, the next time I buy a woman a gift, I'll take you along."

"The next time you buy a woman a gift," she interrupted in a stern voice, "it had better be me."

He ignored her statement. "Abby, how could you believe I'm attracted to Patty?"

She opened her mouth and closed it again. "Maybe I can believe that you really do care about me. But I've seen the way Patty looks at you. It wouldn't take more than a word to have her fall in love with you. I don't want to see her hurt." Or any of them for that matter, Abby mused. "I don't believe you're using Patty to make me jealous," she said honestly. "I mean, I wondered about it but then decided you weren't."

"I'm glad you realize that much." He breathed out in obvious relief.

"But I recognize the looks she's giving you, Logan. She wants you."

"And Tate wants you!"

Abby's shoulders sagged. "Don't go bringing him into this discussion. It's not right. We were talking about you, not me."

"Why not? Isn't turnabout fair play?" The contempt in his expression made her want to cry.

"That's tiddlywinks, not love," she said saucily.

"But if Patty looks at me with adoring eyes, it only mirrors the way Tate looks at you."

"Now you're being ridiculous," she said, annoyed by his false logic.

Slowly Logan rubbed his chin. "It's always amazed me that you can twist a conversation any way you want."

"That's not true," she said, hating the fact that he'd turned the situation around to suit himself.

"All right, let's put it like this—if you mention Patty Martin, then I mention Tate Harding. That sounds fair to me."

"Fine." She flipped a strand of hair over her shoulder. "I won't mention Patty again."

"Are you still seeing him?"

"Who?" Abby widened her eyes innocently.

Logan's jaw tightened grimly. "I want you to promise me that you won't date Harding again."

Abby stared at him.

"A simple yes or no. That's all I want."

The answer wasn't even difficult. She *wasn't* dating him. "And what do I get in return?"

He bent his head to study his hands. "Something that's been yours for over a year. My heart."

At his words, all of Abby's defensive anger melted. "Oh, Logan," she whispered, emotion bringing a misty happiness to her eyes.

"I've loved you so long, Abby, I can't bear to lose you." There could be no doubt of his sincerity.

"I love you, too."

"Then why are you on the other side of the room when all I want to do is hold you and kiss you?"

The well of tenderness inside her overflowed. She rose from her sitting position. "In the interests of fairness, I think we should meet halfway. Okay?"

He chuckled as he stood, coming to her, but his eyes

revealed a longing that was deep and intense. A low groan rumbled from his throat as he swept her into his arms and held her as if he never wanted to let her go. He kissed her eyes, her cheeks, the corner of her mouth until she moaned and begged for more.

"Abby." His voice was muffled against her hair. "You're not going to sidestep my question?"

"What question?" She smiled against his throat as she gave him nibbling, biting kisses.

His hands gripped her shoulders as he pulled her slightly away from him so he could look into her face. "You won't be seeing Tate again?"

She decided not to make an issue of semantics. He *meant* date, not see. What she said in response was the truth. "I promise never to date anyone else again. Does that satisfy you?"

He linked his hands at the small of her back and smiled deeply into her eyes. "I suppose it'll have to," he said, echoing her remark when she'd let him in.

"Now it's your turn."

"What would you like?"

"No more dating Patty, okay?"

"I agree," he replied without hesitation.

"Inventive gift ideas."

He hesitated. "I'll try."

"You're going to have to do better than that."

"All right, all right, I agree."

"And—"

"There's more?" he interrupted with mock impatience.

"And at some point in our lives I want to drive to Des Moines."

"Fine. Shall we seal this agreement with a kiss?"

"I think it would be only proper," Abby said eagerly as she slid her arms around his waist and fit her body to his.

His large hands framed her face, lifting her lips to meet his. It lacked the urgency of their first kiss, but was filled with promise. His breathing was ragged when he released her, but Abby noted that her own wasn't any calmer.

Not surprisingly, their truce held. Maybe it was because they both wanted it so badly. The next Sunday they met at her place for breakfast, which Abby cooked. Later, they drove over to her parents' house and during their visit Frank Carpenter speculated that the two of them would be married by the end of the year. A few not-so-subtle questions about the "date" popped up here and there in the conversation. But neither of them seemed to mind. Logan was included in Abby's every thought. This was the way love was supposed to be, Abby mused as they returned to her apartment.

After changing clothes, they rode their bikes to the park and ate a picnic lunch. After that, with Logan's head resting in her lap, Abby leaned against an elm tree and closed her eyes. This was the same tree that had supported her back during more than one reading session with Tate. A guilty sensation attacked the pit of her stomach, but she successfully fended it off.

"Did you hear that Dick Snyder wants to climb Mount Rainier this summer?" Logan asked unexpectedly, as he chewed lazily on a long blade of grass.

In addition to softball, Dick's passion was mountains. She'd heard rumors about his latest venture, but hadn't been all that interested.

"Yeah, I heard that," she murmured. "So?"

"So, what do you think?"

"What do I think about what?" Abby asked.

"They need an extra man. It sounds like the expedition will be cancelled otherwise." Logan frowned as he looked up at her.

"Climbing the highest mountain in Washington State should be a thrill—for some people. They won't have any trouble finding someone. Personally, I have trouble making it over speed bumps," she teased, leaning forward to kiss his forehead. "What's wrong?"

He smiled up at her and raised his hands to direct her mouth to his. "What could possibly be wrong?" he whispered as he moved his mouth onto her lips for a kiss that left her breathless.

The next week was the happiest of Abby's life. Logan saw her daily. Monday they went to dinner at the same Mexican restaurant Tate had taken her to weeks before. The food was good, but Abby's appetite wasn't up to par. Again, Abby dismissed the twinge of guilt. Tuesday he picked her up for class, but they decided to skip school. Instead they sat in the parking lot and talked until late. From there they drove until they found a café where they could enjoy their drinks outside. The communication between them had never been stronger.

Tate phoned Abby at work on Wednesday and asked her to meet him at the park before the softball game. He wanted to be sure his application for the business loan had been filled out correctly. Uneasy about being in public with him, for fear Logan would see or hear about it, Abby promised to stop off at his garage.

Later, when Logan picked her up for the game she was short-tempered and restless.

"What's the matter with you tonight?" he complained

as they reached the park. "You're as jumpy as a bank robber."

"Me?" She feigned innocence. "Nervous about the game, I guess."

"You?" He looked at her with disbelief. "Ms. Confidence? You'd better tell me what's really bothering you. Fess up, kid."

She felt her face heat with a guilty blush. "Nothing's wrong."

"Abby, I thought we'd come a long way recently. Won't you tell me what's bothering you?"

Logan was so sincere that Abby wanted to kick herself. "Nothing. Honest," she lied and tried to swallow the lump in her throat. She hated this deception, no matter how minor it really was.

"Obviously you're not telling the truth," he insisted, and a muscle twitched in his jaw.

"What makes you say that?" She gave him a look of pure innocence.

"Well, for one thing, your face is bright red."

"It's just hot, that's all."

He released a low breath. "Okay, if that's the way you want it."

Patty was in the bleachers when they arrived, and waved eagerly when she saw Logan. Abby doubted she'd noticed that Abby was with him.

"Your girlfriend's here," Abby murmured sarcastically.

"My girlfriend is walking beside me," Logan said. "What's gotten into you lately?"

Abby sighed. "Don't tell me we're going over all of that again?" She didn't wait for him to answer. Instead she ran onto the field, shouting for Dick to pitch her the ball.

The game went smoothly. Patty basked in the attention everyone was giving her and had the team sign her cast. Abby readily agreed to add her own comment, eager to see what Logan had written on the plaster. But she couldn't locate it without being obvious. Maybe he'd done that on purpose. Maybe he'd written Patty a sweet message on the underside of her arm, where no one else could read it. The thought was so ridiculous that Abby almost laughed out loud.

They lost the game by a slim margin, and Abby realized she hadn't been much help. During the get-together at the pizza place afterward she listened to the others joke and laugh. She wanted to join in, but tonight she simply didn't feel like partying.

"Are you feeling all right?" Logan sat beside her, holding her hand. He studied her with worried eyes.

"I'm fine," she answered and managed a halfhearted smile. "But I'm a little tired. Would you mind taking me home?"

"Not at all."

They got up and, with Logan's hand at the small of her back, they made their excuses and left.

The silence in the car was deafening, but Abby did her best to ignore the unspoken questions Logan was sending her way.

"How about if I cook dinner tomorrow?" Abby said brightly. "I've been terrible tonight and I want to make it up to you."

"If you're not feeling well, maybe you should wait."

"I'm fine. Just don't expect anything more complicated than hot dogs on a bun." She was teasing and Logan knew it.

He parked outside her building and kissed her gently. Abby held on to him compulsively as if she couldn't bear to let him go. She felt caught in a game of cat and mouse between Tate and Logan—a game in which she was quickly becoming the loser.

The following evening, Abby was putting the finishing touches on a salad when Logan came over.

"Surprise," he said as he held out a small bouquet of flowers. "Is this more original than perfume?" he asked with laughing eyes.

"Hardly." She gave him a soft brushing kiss across his freshly shaven cheek as she took the carnations from his hand. "Mmm, you smell good."

Logan picked a tomato slice out of the salad and popped it into his mouth. "So do you."

"Well, if you don't like the fragrance, you have only yourself to blame."

"Me? You smell like pork chops." He slipped his arms around her waist from behind and nuzzled her neck. "You know I could get used to having dinner with you every single night." The teasing quality left his eyes.

Abby dropped her gaze as her heart went skyrocketing into space. She knew what he was saying. The question had entered her mind several times during the past few days. These feelings they were experiencing were the kind to last a lifetime. Abby wanted to share Logan's life. The desire to wake up with him at her side every morning, to marry him and have his children, was stronger than any instinct. She loved this man and wanted to be with him always.

"I think I could get used to that, too," she admitted softly.

Someone knocked at the door, breaking into their conversation. Impatiently Logan glanced at it. "Are you expecting anyone? One of your neighbors?"

"You," she said. "Here, turn these. I'll see who it is and get rid of them." She handed him the spatula.

Abby's hand was shaking as she grasped the knob, praying it wouldn't be Tate. If she was lucky, she could ask him to leave before Logan knew what was happening.

Her worst fears were realized when she pulled the door open halfway.

"Hi. Someone let me into the lobby."

"Hello, how are you?" she asked in a hushed whisper.

"I'm returning the books you lent me. I really enjoyed them." Tate gave her a funny look. "Is this a bad time or something?"

"You might say that," she breathed. "Could you come back tomorrow?"

"Sure, no problem. Is it Logan?"

Abby nodded, and as she did, the door was opened all the way.

"Hello, Tate," Logan greeted him stiffly. "I've been half-expecting you. Why don't you come inside where we can all visit?"

Eight

The two men regarded each other with open hostility.

Glancing from one to the other, Abby paused to swallow a lump of apprehension. Her worst fears had become reality. She wanted to blurt out the truth, explain to Logan exactly why she was seeing Tate. But one look at the two of them standing on either side of the door and Abby recognized the impossibility of making any kind of explanation. Like rival warlords, the two blatantly dared each other to make the first move.

Logan loomed at her side exuding bitterness, surprise, hurt and anger. He held himself still and rigid.

"I'll see you tomorrow, Abby?" Tate spoke at last, making the statement a question.

"Fine." Abby managed to find her voice, which was low and urgent. She wanted to scream at him to leave. If pride wasn't dominating his actions, he'd recognize what a horrible position he was putting her in. Apparently maintaining his pride was more important than the problem he was causing her. Abby's eyes pleaded with Tate, but either he chose to ignore the silent entreaty or he didn't understand what she was asking.

The enigmatic look on Tate's face moved from Logan to Abby. "Will you be all right? Do you want me to stay?"

"Yes. No!" She nearly shouted with frustration. He'd read the look in her eyes as a plea for help. This was crazy. This whole situation was unreal.

"Tomorrow, then," Tate said as he took a step in retreat.

"Tomorrow," Abby confirmed and gestured with her hand, begging him to leave.

He turned and stalked away.

Immobile, Abby stood where she was, waiting for Logan's backlash.

"How long have you been seeing each other?" he asked with infuriating calm.

If he'd shouted and decried her actions, Abby would have felt better; she could have responded the same way. But his composed manner relayed far more adequately the extent of his anger.

"How long, Abby?" he repeated.

Her chin trembled and she shrugged.

His short laugh was derisive. "Your answer says quite a bit."

"It's not what you think," she said hoarsely, desperately wanting to set everything straight.

His jaw tightened forbiddingly. "I suppose you're going to tell me you and Tate are just good friends. If that's the case, you can save your breath."

"Logan." Fighting back tears of frustration, Abby moved away from the door and turned to face him. "I need you to trust me in this."

"Trust you!" His laugh was mocking. "I asked you to decide which one of us you wanted. You claimed you'd made your decision. You even went so far as to assure me you wouldn't be seeing Tate again." The intense anger darkened the shadows across his face, making the curve of his jaw look sharp and abrupt.

"I said I wouldn't *date* him again," she corrected.

"Don't play word games with me," he threw back at her. "You knew what I meant."

She merely shook her head, incapable of arguing. Why *couldn't* he trust her? Why hadn't Tate just *told* him? Why, why, why.

"I suspected something yesterday at the game," Logan continued wryly. "That guilty look was in your eyes again. But I didn't want to believe what I was seeing."

Abby lowered her gaze at the onrush of pain. This deception hadn't been easy for her. But she was bound by her promise to Tate. She couldn't explain the circumstances of their meetings to Logan; only Tate's permission would allow her to do that. But Tate couldn't risk his pride to that extent and she wouldn't ask him to.

Logan's short laugh was bitter with irony. "Yet, when the doorbell rang, I knew immediately it was Tate. To be honest, I was almost glad, because it clears away the doubts in my mind."

Determinedly he started for the door, but Abby's hand delayed him. "Don't go," she whispered. "Please." Her fingers tightened around his arm, wanting to bind him to her forever, beginning with this moment. "I love you and…and if you love me, then you'll trust me."

"Love?" he repeated in a contemptuous voice. "You don't know the meaning of the word."

Stunned, Abby dropped her hand and with a supreme effort met his gaze without emotion. "If that's what you think, maybe it would be better if you did leave."

Logan paused, his troubled expression revealing the inner storm raging within him.

"I may be wrong, but I was brought up to believe that love between two people required mutual trust," Abby added.

One corner of his mouth quirked upward. "And I assumed, erroneously it seems, that love required honesty."

"I…I bent the truth a little."

"Why?" he demanded. "No." He stopped her from explaining. "I don't want to know. Because it's over. I told you before that I wouldn't be kept dangling like a schoolboy while you made up your mind."

"But I *can't* explain now! I may never be able to tell you why."

"It doesn't matter, Abby, it's over," Logan said starkly, his expression impassive.

Abby's stomach lurched with shock and disbelief. Logan didn't mean that. He wouldn't do that to them.

Without another word he walked from the room. The door slammed as he left the apartment. He didn't hesitate or look back.

Abby held out her hand in a weak gesture that pleaded with him to turn around, to trust her. But he couldn't see her, and she doubted it would've had any effect on him if he had. Unshed tears were dammed in her throat, but Abby held her head up in a defiant gesture of pride. The pretense was important for the moment, as she calmly moved into the kitchen and turned off the stove.

Only fifteen minutes before, she had stared lovingly into Logan's eyes, letting her own eyes tell him how much she wanted to share his life. Now, swiftly and without apparent concern, Logan had rejected her as carelessly and thoughtlessly as he would an old pair of shoes. Yet Abby knew that wasn't true. He *did* love her. He couldn't hold her and kiss her the way he did without loving her. Abby knew him as well as he knew her. But then, Abby mused, she had reason to doubt that Logan knew her at all.

Even worse was the fact that Abby recognized she was wrong. Logan deserved an explanation. But her hands were bound by her promise to Tate. And Tate had no idea what that pledge was doing to her and to her relationship with Logan. She couldn't believe he'd purposely do this, but Tate was caught in his own trap. He viewed her as his friend and trusted teacher. He felt fiercely protective of her, wanting in his own way to repay her for the second chance she was giving him by teaching him to read.

Logan and Tate had disliked each other on sight. The friction between them wasn't completely her fault, Abby realized. The ironic part was that for all their outward differences they were actually quite a bit alike.

When Abby had first met Tate that day in the park she'd found him compelling. She'd been magnetically drawn to the same strength that had unconsciously bound her to Logan. This insight had taken Abby weeks to discover, but it had come too late.

The weekend arrived in a haze of emotional pain. Tate phoned Friday afternoon to tell her he wouldn't be able to meet her on Saturday because he was going to the bank to sign the final papers for his loan. He invited her to dinner in celebration, but she declined. Not meeting him gave Abby a reprieve. She wasn't up to facing anyone right now. But each minute, each hour, the hurt grew less intense and life became more bearable. At least, that was what she tried to tell herself.

She didn't see Logan on Sunday, and forced herself

not to search for him in the crowded park as she took a late-afternoon stroll. This was supposed to be their day. Now it looked as if there wouldn't be any more lazy Sunday afternoons for them.

Involved in her melancholy thoughts, Abby wandered the paths and trails of the park, hardly noticing the people around her.

Early that evening, as the sun was lowering in a purple sky, Abby felt the urge to sit on the damp earth and take in the beauty of the world around her. She needed the tranquillity of the moment and the assurance that another day had come and gone and she'd made it through the sadness and uncertainty. She reflected on her feelings and actions, admitting she'd often been headstrong and at times insensitive. But she was learning, and although the pain of that growth dominated her mind now, it, too, would fade. Abby stared at the darkening sky and, for the first time in several long days, a sense of peace settled over her.

Sitting on the lush grass, enjoying the richness of the park grounds, Abby gazed up at the sky. These rare, peaceful minutes soothed her soul and quieted her troubled heart. If she were never to see Logan again, she'd always be glad for the good year they'd shared. Too late she'd come to realize all that Logan meant to her. She'd carelessly tossed his love aside—with agonizing consequences.

The following afternoon Abby called Dick Snyder about Wednesday's softball game. Although she was dying for the sight of Logan, it would be an uncomfortable situation for both of them.

"Dick, it's Abby," she said when he answered. She suddenly felt awkward and uneasy.

"Abby," Dick greeted her cheerfully. "It's good to hear from you. What's up?"

An involuntary smile touched the corners of her mouth. No-nonsense Dick. He climbed mountains, coached softball teams, ran a business with the effectiveness of a tycoon and raised a family; it was all in a day's work, as he often said. "Nothing much, but I wanted you to know I won't be able to make the game on Wednesday."

"You, too?"

"Pardon?" Abby didn't know what he meant.

"Logan phoned earlier and said he wouldn't be at the game, either. Are you two up to something we should know about?" he teased. "Like running off and getting married?"

Abby felt the color flow out of her face, and her heart raced. "No," she breathed, hardly able to find her voice. "That's not it at all."

Her hand was trembling when she replaced the receiver a couple of minutes later. So Logan had decided not to play on Wednesday. If he was quitting softball, she could assume he'd also stop attending classes on Tuesday nights. The possibility of their running into each other at work was still present, since their offices were only half a block apart, but he must be going out of his way to avoid any possible meeting. For that matter, she was doing the same thing.

Soon Abby's apartment began to feel like her prison. She did everything she could to take her mind off Logan, but as the weeks progressed, it became more and more difficult. Much as she didn't want to talk to anyone or provide long explanations about Logan's absence, Abby couldn't tolerate another night alone. She had to get out. So after work the following Wednesday, she got in her car and started to drive.

Before she realized where she was headed, Abby pulled into her parents' driveway.

"Hi, Mom," Abby said as she let herself in the front door.

Her father was reading the paper, and Abby paused at his side. She placed her hand on his shoulder, kissing him lightly on the forehead. "What's that for?" Frank Carpenter grumbled as his arm curved around her waist. "Do you need a loan?"

"Nope," Abby said with forced cheer. "I was just thinking that I don't say *I love you* nearly enough." She glanced up at her mother. "I'm fortunate to have such good parents."

"How sweet," Glenna murmured softly, but her eyes were clouded with obvious worry. "Is everything all right?"

Abby restrained the compulsion to cry out that *nothing* was right anymore. Not without Logan. She left almost as quickly as she'd come, making an excuse about hurrying home to feed Dano. That weak explanation hadn't fooled her perceptive mother. Abby was grateful Glenna didn't pry.

Another week passed and Abby didn't see Logan. Not that she'd expected to. He was avoiding her as determinedly as she did him. Seeing him would only mean pain. She lost weight, and the dark circles under her eyes testified to her inability to sleep.

Sunday morning, Abby headed straight for the park, intent on finding Logan. Even a glimpse would ease the pain she'd suffered without him. She wondered if his face would reveal any of the same torment she had endured. Surely he regretted his lack of trust. He must miss her—perhaps even enough to set aside their differences and talk to her. And if he did, Abby knew she'd readily respond. She imagined the possible scenes that might play out—from complete acceptance on his part to total rejection.

There was a certain irony in her predicament. Tate had been exceptionally busy and she hadn't tutored him at all that week. He was doing so well now that it wouldn't be more than a month before he'd be reading and writing at an adult level. Once he'd completed the lessons, Abby doubted she'd see him very often, despite the friendship that had developed between them. They had little in common and Tate had placed her on such a high pedestal that Abby didn't think he'd ever truly see her as a woman. He saw her as his rescuer, his salvation—not a position Abby felt she deserved.

She sat near the front entrance of the park so she wouldn't miss Logan if he showed up. She made a pretense of reading, but her eyes followed each person entering the park. By noon, she'd been waiting for three hours and Logan had yet to arrive. Abby felt sick with disappointment. Logan came to the park every Sunday morning. Certainly he wouldn't change that, too—would he?

Defeated, Abby closed her book and meandered down the path. She'd been sitting there since nine, so she was sure she hadn't missed him. As she strolled through the park, Abby saw several people she knew and paused to wave but walked on, not wanting to be drawn into conversation.

Dick Snyder's wife was there with her two school-aged children. She called out Abby's name.

"Hi! Come on over and join me. It'll be nice to have an adult to talk to for a while." Betty Snyder chatted easily, patting an empty space on the park bench. "I keep telling Dick that one of these days *I'm* going mountain climbing and leaving him with the kids." Her smile was bright.

Abby sat on the bench beside Betty, deciding she could do with a little conversation herself. "Is he at it again?" she asked, already knowing the answer. Dick thrived on challenge. Abby couldn't understand how anyone could climb anything. Heights bothered her too much. She remembered once—

"Dick and Logan."

"Logan?" His name cut into her thoughts and a tightness twisted her stomach. "He's not climbing, is he?" She didn't even try to hide the alarm in her voice. Logan was no mountaineer! Oh, he enjoyed a hike in the woods, but he'd never shown any interest in conquering anything higher than a sand dune.

Betty looked at her in surprise. She'd obviously assumed Abby would know who Logan was with and what he was up to.

"Well, yes," Betty hedged. "I thought you knew. The Rainier climb is in two weeks."

"No, I didn't." Abby swallowed. "Logan hasn't said anything."

"He was probably waiting until he'd finished learning the basics from Dick."

"Probably," Abby replied weakly, her voice fading as terror overwhelmed her. Logan climbing mountains? With a dignity she didn't realize she possessed, Abby met Betty's gaze head-on. It would sound ridiculous to tell Betty that this latest adventure had slipped Logan's mind. The fact was, Abby knew it hadn't. She recalled Logan's telling her that Dick was looking for an extra climber. But he hadn't said it as though he was considering it *himself.*

Betty continued, apparently trying to fill the stunned silence. "You don't need to worry. Dick's a good climber. I'd go crazy if he weren't. I have complete and utter confidence in him. You shouldn't worry about Logan. He and Dick have been spending a lot of time together preparing for this. Rainier is an excellent climb for a first ascent."

Abby heard almost nothing of Betty's pep talk and her heart sank. This had to be some cruel hoax. Logan was an accountant. He didn't have the physical endurance needed to ascend fourteen thousand feet. He wasn't qualified to do any kind of climbing, let alone a whole mountain. Someone else should go. Not Logan.

Not the man she loved.

Betty's two rambunctious boys returned and closed around the women, chatting excitedly about a squirrel they'd seen. The minute she could do so politely, Abby slipped away from the family and hurried out of the park. She had to get to Logan—talk some sense into him.

Abby returned to her apartment and got in her car. She drove around, dredging up the nerve to confront Logan. If he was out practicing with Dick, he wouldn't be back until dark. Twice she drove by his place, but his parking space was empty.

After a frustrating hour in a shopping mall, Abby sat through a boring movie and immediately drove back to Logan's. For the third time she saw that he hadn't returned. She drove around again—for how long she was unsure.

Abby couldn't comprehend what had made him decide to do this. A hasty decision wasn't like him. She wondered if this crazy mountain-climbing expedition was his way of punishing her; if so, he'd succeeded beyond his expectations. The only thing left to do was confront him.

Abby drove back to Logan's building, telling herself that the sooner they got this settled, the better. Relief washed over her at the familiar sight of his car.

She pressed his apartment buzzer, but Logan didn't respond. She tried again, keeping her finger on it for at least a minute. And still Logan didn't answer.

Abby decided she could sit this out if he could. Logan wasn't fooling her. He was there.

When he finally answered and let her into the building lobby, Abby ran in, rushing up to his third-floor apartment. He'd opened the door and she stumbled ungracefully across the threshold. Regaining her balance—and her breath—she turned to glare angrily at him.

"Abby." Logan was holding a pair of headphones. "Were you waiting long?" He closed the door, placing the headset on a shelf. "I'm sorry I didn't hear you, but I was listening to a CD."

Regaining her composure, Abby straightened. "Now listen here, Logan Fletcher." She punctuated her speech with a finger pointed at him. "I know why you're doing this, and I won't let you."

"Abby, listen." He murmured her name in the soft way she loved.

"No," she cried. "I *won't* listen!"

He held her away from him, one hand on each shoulder. Abby didn't know if this was meant to comfort her or to keep her out of his arms. Desperately she wanted his arms around her, craved the comfort she knew was waiting for her there.

"You don't need to prove anything to me," she continued, her voice gaining in volume and intensity. "I love you just the way you are. Logan, you're more of a hero than any man I know, and I can't—no," she corrected emotionally, "I *won't* let you do this."

"Do what?"

She looked at him in stunned disbelief. "Climb that stupid mountain."

"So you did hear." He sighed. "I was hoping none of this would get back to you."

"Logan," she gasped. "You weren't planning to let me know? You're doing this to prove some egotistical point to me and you weren't even going to let me know until it was too late? I can't believe you'd do that. I simply can't believe it. You've always been so logical and all of a sudden you're falling off the deep end."

Now it was his turn to look flabbergasted. "Abby, sit down. You're becoming irrational."

"I am not," she denied hotly, but she did as he suggested. "Logan, please listen to me. You can't go traipsing off to Washington on this wild scheme. The whole idea is ludicrous. Crazy!"

He knelt beside her and she framed his face with both hands, her eyes pleading with his.

"Don't you understand?" she said. "You've never climbed before. You need experience, endurance and sheer nerve to take on a mountain. You don't have to prove anything to me. I love you just the way you are. Please don't do this."

"Abby," Logan said sternly and pulled her hand free, holding her fingers against his chest. "This decision is mine. You have nothing to do with it. I'm sorry this upsets you, but I'm doing something I've wanted to do for years."

"Haven't you listened to a word I've said?" She yanked her hands away and took in several deep breaths. "You could be killed!"

"You seem to be confusing the issues. My desire to make this climb with Dick and his friends has nothing to do with you."

"Nothing to do with me?" she repeated frantically. Had Logan gone mad? "If you think for one instant that I'm going to let you do this, then you don't know me, Logan Fletcher."

He stood up, and smoothed the side of his hair with one hand as he regarded her quizzically. "You seem to be under the mistaken impression that I'm doing this to prove something to you."

"You may not have admitted it to yourself, but that's exactly the reason you are." She shook her head frantically. "You're climbing this crazy mountain because you want to impress me."

Logan's short laugh was filled with amusement. "I'm doing this, Abby, because I want to. My reasons are as simple as that. You're making it sound like I'm going in front of a firing squad. Dick's an experienced climber. I expect to be perfectly safe," he said matter-of-factly.

"I don't believe you could be so naive," she told him flatly, "about the danger of mountain-climbing *or* about your own motivations."

"Then that's your problem."

"But...you could end up dead!"

"I could walk across the street and be hit by a car to-morrow," Logan replied with infuriating calm.

Abby couldn't stand his quiet confidence another second. She leaped to her feet and stalked across the floor, gesturing wildly with her hands, unable to clarify her thoughts enough to reason with him. Pausing, she took a moment to compose herself. "If this is something you always wanted to do, how come I've never heard about it before?"

"Because I knew what your reaction would be—and I was right. I—"

"You're so caught up in the excitement of this adventure, you can't see how crazy it is," Abby interrupted, not wanting him to argue with her. He *had* to listen.

Logan took her gently by the shoulders and turned her around. "I think you should realize that nothing you say is going to change my mind."

"I drove you to this—" Her voice throbbed painfully.

"No," he cut in abruptly and brushed a hand across his face. "As I keep telling you, this is something I've always wanted to do, whether you like it or not."

"I don't like it and I don't believe it."

"That's too bad." Logan breathed in harshly. "But unlike certain people I know, I don't bend the truth. It's true, Abby."

Abby's mouth twisted in a smile. "And you weren't even going to tell me."

His look was grudging. "I think you can understand why."

Abby shut her eyes and groaned inwardly.

"Now if you'll excuse me, I really do need to get back to the audio book I'm listening to. It's on climb-ing. Dick recommended it."

"I thought you were smarter than this. I've never heard of anything so stupid in my life," she said waspishly, lashing out at him in her pain.

His smile was mirthless as if he'd expected that kind of statement from her.

"I'm sorry," she mumbled as she studied the scuffed-up toe of her shoe. The entire day had been crazy. "I didn't mean that."

A finger under her chin lifted her eyes to his. "I know you didn't." For that instant all time came to a halt. His eyes burned into hers with an intensity that stole her breath.

Seemingly of their own volition, her hands slid over his chest. She wound her arms around his neck and stood on the tips of her toes as she fitted her mouth over his. The slow-burning fire of his kiss melted her heart. Every part of her seemed to be vibrantly alive. Her nerves tingled and flared to life.

Angrily Logan broke the kiss. "What's this?" he said harshly. "My last kiss before I face the firing squad?"

"Hardly. I expect you to come back alive." She paused, frowning at him. "If you don't, I swear I'll never forgive you."

He rammed his hands into his pants pockets. Then, as if he couldn't bear to look at her, he stalked to the other side of the room. "If I don't come back, why would it matter? We're not on speaking terms as it is."

From somewhere deep inside her, Abby found the strength to swallow her pride and smile. "That's something I'd like to change."

"No," he said without meeting her gaze.

"You're not leaving for two weeks. During that time you won't be able to avoid seeing me," she went on. "I don't mind telling you that I plan to use every one of those days to change your mind."

"It won't work, Abby," he murmured.

"I can try. I—"

"What I mean is that I have two weeks before the climb, but we're flying in early to explore several other mountains in the Cascade Range."

"The Cascades?" From school, Abby remembered that parts of the Cascade mountain range in Washington State had never been explored. This made the whole foolish expedition even more frightening.

"My flight leaves tomorrow night."

"No," she mumbled miserably, the taste of defeat filling her.

"There's a whole troop who'll be seeing us off. If you're free, you might want to come, too."

Abby noted that he didn't ask her to come, but merely informed her of what was happening. Sadly she shook her head. "I don't think so, Logan. I refuse to be a part of it. Besides, I'm not keen on tearful farewells and good wishes."

"I won't ask anything from you anymore, Abby."

"That's fine," she returned more flippantly than she intended. Involuntary tears gathered in her eyes. "But you'd better come back to me, Logan Fletcher. That's all I can say."

"I'll be back," he told her confidently.

Not until Abby was halfway home did she realize that Logan hadn't said he was coming back *to her*.

Later that night Abby lay in bed while a kaleidoscope of memories went through her mind. She recalled the most memorable scenes of her year-long relationship with Logan. One thing was clear: she'd been blind and stupid not to have appreciated him, or recognized how much she loved him.

Staring at the blank ceiling, she felt a tear roll from the corner of her eye and fall onto the pillow. Abby was intensely afraid for Logan.

The following afternoon, when Abby let herself into her apartment, the phone was ringing.

Abby's heart hammered in her throat. Maybe Logan was calling to say goodbye. Maybe he'd changed his mind and would ask her to come to the airport after all.

But it was her mother.

"Abby." Glenna's raised voice came over the line. "I just heard that Logan's joining Dick Snyder on his latest climb."

"Yes," Abby confirmed in a shaky voice, wondering how her mother had found out about it. "His plane's leaving in—" she paused to check her watch "—three hours and fifteen minutes. Not that I care."

"Oh, dear, I was afraid of that. You're taking this hard."

"Me? Why would I?" Abby attempted to sound cool and confident. She didn't want her mother to worry about her. But her voice cracked and she inhaled a quivering breath before she was able to continue. "He's in Dick's capable hands, Mother. All you or I or anyone can do is wait."

The hesitation was only slight. "Sometimes you amaze me, Ab."

"Is that good or bad?" Some of her sense of humor was returning.

"Good," her mother whispered. "It's very good."

The more Abby told herself she wouldn't break down and go to the airport, the more she realized there was nothing that could stop her.

A cold feeling of apprehension crept up her back and extended all the way to the tips of her fingers as Abby drove. Her hands felt clammy, but that was nothing compared to her stomach. The churning pain was almost more than she could endure. Because she hadn't been able to eat all day, she felt light-headed now.

Abby arrived at the airport and the appropriate concourse in plenty of time to see the small crowd of well-wishers surrounding Dick, Logan and company. They obviously hadn't checked in for their flight. Standing off to one side, Abby chose not to involve herself. She didn't want Logan to know she'd come. Almost everyone from the softball team was there, including Patty. She seemed more quiet and subdued than normal, Abby noted, and was undoubtedly just as worried about Logan's sudden penchant for danger as she herself was.

Once Abby thought Logan was looking into the crowd as if seeking someone. Desperately she wanted to run to him, hold him and kiss him before he left. But she was afraid she'd burst into tears and embarrass them both. Logan wouldn't want that. And her pride wouldn't allow her to show her feelings.

When it came time for Logan and the others to check in and go through security, there was a flurry of embraces, farewells and best wishes. Then almost everyone departed en masse.

Abby waited, studying the departures board until she knew his plane had left.

Nine

Abby rolled out of bed, stumbled into the kitchen and turned on the radio, anxious to hear the weather report. They were in the midst of a July heatwave.

Cradling a cup of coffee in her hands, Abby eyed the calendar. In a few days Logan would be home. Each miserable, apprehensive day brought him closer to her.

Betty Snyder continued to hear regularly from Dick about the group's progress as they trekked over some of the most difficult of the Cascade mountains. Trying not to be obvious, Abby phoned Betty every other day or so, to hear whatever information she could impart. Abby still didn't know the true reasons Logan had joined this venture, but believed they were the wrong ones.

The first week after his departure, Abby received a postcard. She'd laughed and cried and hugged it to her breast. An email would've been nice. Or a phone call. But she'd settle—happily—for a postcard. Crazy, wonderful Logan. Anyone else would have sent her a scene of picturesque Seattle or at least the famous mountain he was about to climb. Not Logan. Instead he sent her a picture of a salmon.

His message was simple:

How are you? Wish you were here. I saw you at
the airport. Thank you for coming. See you soon.
Love, Logan

Abby treasured the card more than the bottles of expensive French perfume he'd given her. Even when several other people on the team received similar messages, it didn't negate her pleasure. The postcard was tucked in her purse as a constant reminder of Logan. Not that Abby needed anything to jog her memory; Logan was continually in her thoughts. And although the message on the postcard was impersonal, Abby noted that he'd signed it with his love. It was a minor thing, but she held on to it with all her might. Logan did love her, and somehow, some way, they were going to overcome their differences because what they shared was too precious to relinquish.

"Disturbing news out of Washington State for climbers on Mount Rainier…" the radio announced.

Abby felt her knees go weak as she pulled out a kitchen chair and sat down. She immediately turned up the volume.

"An avalanche has buried eleven climbers. The risk of another avalanche is hampering the chances of rescue. Six men from the Minneapolis area were making a southern ascent at the time of the avalanche. Details at the hour."

A slow, sinking sensation attacked Abby as she placed a trembling hand over her mouth.

During the news, the announcer related the sketchy details available about the avalanche and fatalities and concluded the report with the promise of updates as they became available. Abby ran for the TV and turned it to an all-news channel. She heard the same report over and over. Each word struck Abby like a body blow, robbing her lungs of oxygen. Pain constricted her chest. Fear, anger and a hundred emotions she couldn't identify were all swelling violently within her. When the telephone rang, she nearly tumbled off the chair in her rush to answer it.

Please, oh, please don't let this be a call telling me Logan's dead, her mind screamed. *He promised he'd come back.*

It was Betty Snyder.

"Abby, do you have your radio or TV on?" she asked urgently. Her usual calm manner had evaporated.

"Yes… I know," Abby managed shakily. "Have you heard from Dick?"

"No." Her soft voice trembled. "Abby, the team was making a southern ascent. If they survived the avalanche, there's a possibility they'll be trapped on the mountain for days before a rescue team can reach them." Betty sounded as shocked as Abby.

"We'll know soon if it's them."

"It's not them," Betty continued on a desperate note, striving for humor. "And if it isn't, I'll personally kill Dick for putting me through this. We should hear something soon."

"I hope so."

"Abby," Betty asked with concern, "are you going to be all right?"

"I'll be fine." But hearing the worry in her friend's voice did little to reassure her. "Do you want me to come over? I can take the day off…"

"Dick's mother is coming and she's a handful. You go on to work and I'll call you if I hear from Dick—or anyone."

"Okay." Her friends at the clinic and on the team would need reassurance themselves and Abby could quickly relay whatever messages came through. She'd check her computer regularly for any breaking news.

"Everything's going to work out fine." Betty's tone was low and wavering and Abby realized her friend expected the worst.

The day was a living nightmare; every nerve was stretched taut. With each ring of the office phone her pulse thundered before she could bring it under control and react normally.

Keeping busy was essential for her sanity those first few hours. But by quarter to five she'd managed to settle her emotions. The worst that could've happened was that Logan was dead. The worst. But according to the news, no one from the Minneapolis area was listed among those missing and presumed dead. Abby decided to believe they were fine; there was no need to face any other possibility until necessary.

After work Abby drove directly to Betty's. She hadn't realized how emotionally and physically drained she was until she got there. But she forced herself to relax before entering her friend's home, more for Betty's sake than her own.

"Have you heard anything?" she asked calmly as Betty let her in the front door. She could hear the TV in the background.

"Not a word." Betty studied Abby closely. "Just what's on the news. The hardest part is not knowing."

Abby nodded and bit her bottom lip. "And the waiting. I won't give up my belief that Logan's alive and well. He must be, because I'm alive and breathing. If anything happened to Logan, I'd know. My heart would know if he was dead." Abby recognized that her logic was questionable, but she expected her friend to understand better than anyone else exactly what she was saying.

"I feel the same thing," Betty confirmed.

Dick's mother had gone home and Abby stayed for a while to keep Betty and the kids company. Then she went to her apartment to change clothes and watch the latest update on TV. The television reporter wasn't able to relate much more than what had been available that morning.

Tate was waiting for her at the little Mexican restaurant where they met occasionally and raised his hand when she entered. They'd arranged this on the weekend, and Abby had decided not to change their plans. She needed the distraction.

Her relationship with Tate had changed in the past weeks. He'd changed. Confident and secure now, he often came to her with minor problems related to the business material he was reading. She was his friend as well as his teacher.

"I didn't know if you'd cancel," Tate said as he pulled out a chair for her. "I heard about the accident on Mount Rainier."

"To be honest, I wasn't sure I should come. But I would've gone crazy sitting at home brooding about it," Abby admitted.

"Any news about Logan?"

Abby released a slow, agonizing breath. "Nothing."

"He'll be fine," Tate said. "If anyone could take care of himself, I'd say it was Logan. He wouldn't have gone if he didn't know what to expect and couldn't protect himself."

Abby was surprised by Tate's insights. She wouldn't have thought that Tate would be so generous in his comments.

"I thought you didn't like Logan." She broached the subject boldly. "It seemed that every time you two were around each other, fireworks went off."

Tate lifted one shoulder in a dismissive shrug. "That's because I didn't like his attitude toward you."

"How's that?"

"You know. He acted like he owned you."

The problem was that he held claim to her heart and it had taken Tate to show Abby how much she loved Logan. Her fingers circled the rim of the glass and she smiled into her water. "In a way he does," she whispered. "Because I love him, and I know he loves me."

Tate picked up the menu and studied it. "I'm beginning to realize that...." he murmured. "Look, I'll try to talk to him, if that'll help."

Abby reached across the table and squeezed his hand "Thanks, Tate."

The waitress approached them. "Are you ready to order?"

Abby glanced at the menu and nodded. "I'll have the cheese enchiladas."

"Make that two," Tate said absently. "No." He paused. "I've changed my mind. I'll have the pork burrito."

Abby tried unsuccessfully to disguise her amusement.

"What's so funny?" Tate asked.

"You. Do you remember the first few times we went out to eat? You always ordered the same thing I did. I'm pleased to see you're not still doing it."

"It became a habit." He paused. "I owe you a great deal, Abby, more than I'll ever be able to repay."

"Nonsense." They were friends, and their friendship had evolved from what it had been in those early days, but his gratitude sometimes made her uncomfortable.

"Maybe this will help show a little of my appreciation." Tate pulled a small package from inside his pocket and handed it to her.

Abby was stunned, her fingers numb as she accepted the beautifully wrapped box. She raised her eyes to his. "Tate, please. This isn't necessary."

"Hush and open your gift," he instructed, obviously enjoying her surprise.

When she pulled the paper away, Abby was even more astonished to see the name of a well-known and expensive jeweler embossed across the top of the case. Her heart was in her throat as she shook her head disbelievingly. "Tate," she began. "I—"

"Open it." An impish light glinted in his eyes.

Slowly she raised the lid to discover a lovely intricately woven gold chain on a bed of blue velvet. Even with her untrained eye, Abby recognized that the chain was of the highest quality. A small cry of undisguised pleasure escaped before she could hold it back.

"Tate!" She could hardly take in its beauty. For the first time in months she found herself utterly speechless.

"Abby?"

"I…I can't believe it. It's beautiful."

"I knew you'd like it."

"Like it! It's the most beautiful necklace I've ever seen. Thank you." Abby smiled at him. "But you shouldn't have. You know that, don't you?"

"If you say so."

"*Now* he's agreeable." Abby smiled as she spoke to the empty chair beside her. "Here, help me put it on."

Tate stood and came around to her side of the table. He took the chain from its plush bed and laid it against the hollow of her throat. Abby bowed her head and lifted the hair from the back of her neck to make it easier for Tate to fasten the necklace.

When he returned to his chair, Abby felt a warm glow. "I still think you shouldn't have done this, but to be honest, I'm glad you did."

"I knew the minute I saw it in the jeweler's window that it was exactly what I was looking for. If you want the truth, I'd been searching for weeks for something special to give you. I want to thank you for everything you've done for me."

Abby didn't think Tate realized what a small part she'd played in his tutoring. He'd done all the real work himself. He was the one who'd sought her out with a need and admitted that need—something he'd never been able to do before, having always hidden his inability. Abby doubted Tate recognized how far he'd come from the day he'd followed her home from the park.

Later, when Abby undressed for bed, she fingered the elegant chain, remembering Tate's promise. Maybe now he'd be willing to explain to Logan why Abby had met with him. The chain represented his willingness to help repair her relationship with Logan. That would be the most significant gift he could possibly give her.

Before leaving for work the next morning, Abby checked the news. Nothing. Then she phoned Betty in case there'd been any calls during the night. There hadn't been, and discouragement sounded in Betty's voice as she promised to phone Abby's office if she heard anything.

At about ten that morning, Abby had just finished updating the chart on a young teen who'd visited the clinic, when she glanced up and saw Betty in the doorway.

Abby straightened and stood immobile, her heart pumping at a furious rate. Suddenly, she went cold with fear. She couldn't move or think. Even breathing became impossible. Betty would've come to the office for only one reason, she thought. Logan was dead.

"Betty," she pleaded in a tortured whisper, "tell me. What is it?"

"He's fine! Everyone is. They were stuck on the slopes an extra night, but made it safely to camp early this morning. I just heard—Dick called me."

Abby closed her eyes and exhaled a breath of pure release. Her heart skipped a beat as she moved across the room. The two women hugged each other fiercely as tears of happiness streaked their faces.

"They're on their way home. The flight will land sometime tomorrow evening. Everyone's planning to meet them at the airport. You'll come, won't you?"

In her anger and pain Abby had refused to see him off with the others…until the last minute. She wouldn't be so stubborn about welcoming him home. Abby doubted she'd be able to resist hurling herself into his arms the instant she saw him. And once she was in his arms, Abby defied anyone to tear her away.

"Abby? You'll come, won't you?" Betty's soft voice broke into her musings.

"I'll be there," Abby replied, as the image of their reunion played in her mind.

"I thought you'd want to be." Her friend gave her a knowing look.

Logan was safe and coming home. Abby's heart leaped with excitement and she waited until it resumed its normal pace before returning to her desk.

"Tonight," Abby explained to Tate at lunch on Thursday. She swallowed a bite of her pastrami sandwich. "Their flight's arriving around nine-thirty. The team's planning a get-together with him and Dick on Friday night. You're invited to attend if you'd like."

"I just might come."

Tate surprised her with his easy acceptance. Abby had issued the invitation thoughtlessly, not expecting Tate to take her up on it. For that matter, it might even have been the wrong thing to do, since Logan would almost certainly be offended.

"I was beginning to wonder if you were ever going to invite me to any of those social functions your team's always having."

"Tate." Abby glanced up in surprise. "I had no idea you wanted to come. I wish you'd said something earlier." Now she felt guilty for having excluded him in the past.

"Sure," Tate chimed in defensively. "They'll take one look at a mechanic and decide they've got something better to do."

"Tate, that's simply not true." And it wasn't. He'd be accepted as would anyone who wished to join them. Plenty of friends and coworkers attended the team's social events.

"It might turn a few heads." Tate expelled his breath as if he found the thought amusing.

"Oh, hardly."

"You don't think so?" he asked hopefully.

Tate's lack of self-confidence was a by-product of his inability to read. Now that reading was no longer a problem, he would gain that new maturity. She was already seeing it evolve in him.

Moonlight flooded the ground. The evening was glorious. Not a cloud could be seen in the crystal-blue sky as it darkened into night. Slowly, Abby released a long, drawn-out sigh. Logan would land in a couple of hours and the world had never been more beautiful. She paused to hum a love ballad playing on the radio, thrilled by the romantic words.

She must have changed her clothes three times, but everything had to be perfect. When Logan saw her at the airport, she wanted to look as close to an angel as anything he would find this side of heaven.

She spent half an hour on her hair and makeup. Nothing satisfied her. Tight-lipped, Abby realized she couldn't suddenly make herself into an extraordinarily beautiful woman. Sad but true. She could only be herself. She dressed in a soft, plum-colored linen suit and a pink silk blouse. Dissatisfied with her hair, Abby pulled it free of the confining pins and brushed it until it shimmered and fell in deep natural waves down the middle of her back. Logan had always loved her hair loose....

A quick glance at her watch showed her that she was ten minutes behind schedule. Grabbing her purse, Abby hurried out to her car—and she noticed that it was running on empty. Everything seemed to be going wrong....

Abby pulled into a service station, splurging on full

service for once instead of pumping her own. *Hurry*, she muttered to herself as the teenager took his time.

"Do you want me to check your oil?"

"No, thanks." Abby handed him the correct change, plus a tip. "And don't bother washing the window."

Inhaling deep breaths helped take the edge off her impatience as she merged onto the freeway. A mile later an accident caused a minor slowdown.

By the time she arrived at the airport, her heart was pounding. Checking the arrivals board revealed that Logan's flight was on schedule.

Abby ran down the concourse. Within minutes the team, as well as Karen, Logan's assistant, came into sight.

Warmth stole over Abby as she saw Logan, a large backpack slung over one shoulder. His face was badly sunburned, the skin around his eyes white from his protective eye gear. He looked tanned and more muscular than she could remember. His eyes searched the crowd and paused on her, his look thoughtful and intense.

Abby beamed, wearing her brightest smile. He was so close. Close enough to reach out and touch if it weren't for the people crowding around. Abby's heart swelled with the depth of her love. His own eyes mirrored the longing she was sure he could see in hers. These past weeks were all either of them would need to recognize that they should never be apart again.

Abby edged her way toward him and Dick. The others who'd come to greet Logan were chatting excitedly, but Abby heard none of their conversation. Logan was back! Here. Now. And she loved him. After today he'd never doubt the strength of her feelings again.

In her desire to get to Logan quickly, Abby nearly stumbled over an elderly man. She stopped and apol-

ogized profusely, making sure the white-haired gentleman wasn't hurt. As she straightened, she heard
someone call out Logan's name.

In shocked disbelief, Abby watched as Patty Martin ran across the room and threw herself dramatically
into Logan's arms. He dropped his pack. Sobbing, she
clung to him as if he'd returned from the dead. Soon
the others gathered around, and Dick and Logan were
completely blocked from Abby's view.

The bitter taste of disappointment filled her mouth.
Logan should have pushed the others aside and come
to her. *Her* arms should be the ones around him. *Her*
lips should be the ones kissing his.

Proudly Abby decided she wouldn't fight her way
through the throng of well-wishers. If Logan wanted
her, then she was here. And he knew it.

But apparently he didn't care. Five minutes later, the
small party moved out of the airport and progressed to
the parking lot. As far as Abby could tell, Logan hadn't
so much as looked around to see where she was.

After all the lonely days of waiting for Logan, Abby
had a difficult time deciding if she should attend the
party being held at a local buffet restaurant in his and
Dick's honor the following evening. If he hadn't come
to her at the airport, then what guarantee did she have
that he wouldn't shun her a second time? The pain lingered from his first rejection. Abby didn't know if she
could bear another one.

To protect her ego on Friday night Abby dressed casually in jeans and a cotton top. She timed her arrival
so she wouldn't cause a stir when she entered the restaurant. As she'd expected, and as was fitting, Logan

and Dick were the focus of attention while they relived their tales of danger on the high slopes.

Abby filled her plate and took a seat where she could see Logan. She knew she wouldn't be able to force down any dinner; occasionally she rearranged the food in front of her in a pretence of eating.

Sitting where she was, Abby could observe Logan covertly. Every once in a while he'd glance up and search the room. He seemed to be waiting for someone. Abby would've liked to believe he was looking for her, but she could only speculate. The tension flowed out of her as she witnessed again the strength and vitality he exuded. That experience on the mountain had changed him, just as it had changed her.

Unable to endure being separated any longer, Abby pushed her plate aside and crossed the room to his table. Logan's eyes locked with hers as she approached. Someone was speaking to him, but Abby doubted that Logan heard a word of what was being said.

"Hello, Logan," she said softly. Her arms hung nervously at her sides. "Welcome home."

"It's good to see you, Abby." His gaze roamed her face lovingly. He didn't need to pull her into his arms for Abby to know what he was feeling. It was all there for her to read. Her doubts, confusion and anxiety were all wiped out in that one moment.

"I'm sorry about what happened at the airport." His hand clasped hers. "There wasn't anything I could do."

Their eyes held as she studied his face. Every line, every groove, was so familiar. "Don't apologize. I understand." Who would've believed a simple touch could cause such a wild array of sensations? Abby felt shaky and weak just being this close to him. A tingling warmth ran up the length of her arm as he gently enclosed her in his embrace.

"Can I see you later?"

"You must be exhausted." She wanted desperately to be with him, but she could wait another day. After all this time, a few more hours wouldn't matter.

"Seeing you again is all the rest I need."

"I'll be here," she promised.

Dick Snyder tapped Logan on the shoulder and led him to the front row of tables. After a few words from Dick about their adventure, Logan stood and thanked everyone for their support. He relayed part of what he'd seen and the group's close brush with death.

The tables of friends and relatives listened enthralled as Logan and Dick spoke. Hearing him talk so casually about their adventures was enough to make Abby's blood run cold. She'd come so close to losing him.

Abby stood apart from Dick and Logan while they shook everyone's hand as they filed out the door and thanked them for coming. When the restaurant began to empty Logan hurried across the room and brought Abby to his side. She wasn't proud of feeling this way, but she was glad Patty hadn't come. Abby was also grateful that Tate had called to say he couldn't make it. In an effort to assure him he'd be welcome another time, Abby invited him to the team picnic scheduled that Sunday in Diamond Lake Park. Tate promised to be there if possible.

Logan led her into the semidarkened parking lot and turned Abby into his arms. There was a tormented look in his eyes as he gazed down on her upturned face.

"Crazy as it sounds, the whole time we were trapped on that mountain, I was thinking that if I didn't come back alive you'd never forgive me." With infinite tenderness he kissed her.

"I wouldn't have forgiven you," she murmured and smiled up at him in the dim light.

"Abby, I love you," he said. "It took a brush with death to prove how much I wanted to come home to you."

His mouth sought hers and with a joyful cry, Abby wrapped her arms around him and clung. Tears of happiness clouded her eyes as Logan slipped his hands into the length of her hair. He couldn't seem to take enough or give enough as he kissed her again and again. Finally he buried his face in the slope of her neck.

He held her face as he inhaled a steadying breath. "When I saw you across the restaurant tonight, it was all I could do to be polite and stay with the others."

Abby lowered her eyes. "I wasn't sure you wanted to see me."

"You weren't sure?" Logan said disbelievingly. He slid his hands down to rest on the curve of her shoulders. His finger caught on the delicate gold chain and he pulled it up from beneath her blouse.

Abby went completely still. Logan seemed to sense that something wasn't right as his eyes searched hers.

"What's wrong?"

"Nothing."

His eyes fell on the chain. "This is lovely and it's far more expensive than you could afford. Who gave it to you, Abby? Tate?"

Ten

Abby pressed her lips so tightly together that they hurt. "Yes, Tate gave me the necklace."

"You're still seeing him, aren't you?" Logan dropped his hands to his sides and didn't wait for her to respond. "After everything I've said, you still haven't been able to break off this relationship with Tate, have you?"

"Tate has nothing to do with you and me," she insisted, inhaling deeply to hide her frustration. After the long, trying days apart, they *couldn't* argue! Abby wanted to cry out that she loved him and nothing else should matter. She should be able to be friends with a hundred men if she loved only him. Her voice shaking, she attempted to salvage their reunion. "I know this is difficult for you to understand. To be honest, I don't know how I'd feel if you were to continue seeing Patty Martin."

His mouth hardened. "Then maybe I should."

Abby realized Logan was tired and impatient, but an angry retort sprang readily to her lips. "You certainly seem to have a lot in common with Patty—far more than you do with me."

"The last thing I want to do is argue."

"I don't, either. My intention in coming tonight wasn't to defend my actions while you were away. And yes—" she paused to compose herself, knowing her face was flushed "—I did see Tate."

The area became charged with an electricity that seemed to spark and crackle. The atmosphere was heavy and still, pressing down on her like the stagnant air before a thunderstorm.

"I think that says everything I need to know," he said with quiet harshness.

Abby nodded sharply, forcing herself to meet his piercing gaze. "Yes, I suppose it does." She took a step backward.

"It was kind of you to come and welcome me back this evening." A muscle twitched in his jaw. "But as you can imagine, the trip was exhausting. I'd like to go home and sleep for a week."

Abby nodded, trying to appear nonchalant. "Perhaps we can discuss this another time."

Logan shook his head. "There won't be another time, Abby."

"That decision is yours," she said calmly, although her voice trembled with reaction. "Good night, Logan."

"Goodbye, Abby."

Goodbye! She knew what he was saying as plainly as if he'd screamed it at her. Whatever had been between them was now completely over.

"I expect you'll be seeing a lot more of Logan now that he's back," Tate commented from her living room the following afternoon.

Abby brought out a sandwich from the kitchen and

handed it to him before taking a seat. "We've decided to let things cool between us," she said with as much aplomb as she could manage. "Cool" was an inadequate word. Their relationship was in Antarctica. They'd accidentally run into each other that morning while Abby was doing some grocery shopping and had exchanged a few stilted sentences. After a minute Abby could think of nothing more to say.

"You know what I think, Tate?" Abby paid an inordinate amount of attention to her sandwich. "I've come to the belief that love is a highly overrated emotion."

"Why?"

Abby didn't need to glance up to see the amusement in Tate's face. Instead she took the first bite of her lunch. How could she explain that from the moment she realized how much she loved Logan, all she'd endured was deep emotional pain. "Never mind," she said at last, regretting that she'd brought it up.

"Abby?" Tate's look was thoughtful.

She leaped to her feet. "I forgot the iced tea." She hurried into the kitchen, hoping Tate would let the subject drop.

"Did I tell you the bank approved my loan?"

Returning with their drinks, Abby grinned. "That's great!"

"They phoned yesterday afternoon. Bessler's pleased, but not half as much as I am. I have a lot to thank you for, Abby."

"I'm so happy for you," Abby said with a quick nod. "You've worked hard and deserve this." Abby knew how relieved Tate was that the loan had gone through. He'd called Abby twice out of pure nerves, just to talk through his doubts.

Tomorrow afternoon they were going to attend the picnic together and although Abby was grateful for Tate's friendship, she didn't want to give her friends the wrong impression. Logan had already jumped to conclusions. There was nothing to say the others wouldn't, too. Tate was a friend—a special friend—but their relationship didn't go beyond that. It couldn't, not when she was in love with Logan.

"Abby," Tate said quietly. "I'm going to talk to him."

Sunday afternoon Abby was preoccupied as she dressed in shorts and a Twins T-shirt for the picnic. She was glad Tate was going with her, glad he'd promised to explain, but she hoped Logan didn't do or say anything to make him uncomfortable.

Logan. The unhappiness weighed down on her heart. Her thoughts were filled with him every waking minute. Even her dreams involved him. This misunderstanding, this lack of trust, had to stop once and for all. From the moment Logan had left for Washington, Abby had longed for Tate to explain the situation and heal her relationship with Logan. She'd assumed that as time went on they'd naturally get back together. Now, just the opposite was proving to be true. With every passing hour, Logan was drifting further and further out of her life. Yet her love was just as strong. Perhaps stronger. Whether Tate went through with his confession and whether it changed things remained to be seen.

Since Tate was meeting her at the park, Abby got there early and found a picnic table for them. When Logan came, he claimed the table directly across from hers and Abby felt the first bit of encouragement since they'd last spoken. As quickly as the feeling came, it vanished. Logan set out a tablecloth and unpacked his cooler without so much as glancing her way. Only a few feet separated her from him, but it felt as if their distance had never been greater. He gave no indication that he'd seen her. Even her weak smile had gone unacknowledged.

Soon they were joined by the others, chatting and laughing. A few men played horseshoes while the women sat and visited. The day was glorious, birds trilled their songs from the tree branches and soft music came from someone's CD player. Busy putting the finishing touches on a salad, Abby sang along with the music. The last thing in the world she felt like doing was singing, but if she didn't, she'd start crying.

Tate arrived and Abby could see by the way he walked that he was nervous. He'd met some of the people at the softball game. Still, he looked surprised when one of the guys called out a greeting. The two men talked for a minute and Tate joined her soon afterward.

"Hi."

"There's no need to be nervous," she said, smiling at him.

"What? Me nervous?" he joked. "They're nice people, aren't they?"

"The best."

"Even Logan?"

"Especially Logan."

Tate was silent for a moment. "Like I said, I'll see what I can do to patch things up between you two."

Unhurriedly, she raised her gaze to his. "I'd appreciate that."

His returning smile told her how difficult revealing

his past would be. Abby hated to ask him to do it, but there didn't seem to be any other way.

As he wandered off, Abby laced her fingers tightly and sat there, searching for Logan. He was standing alone with his back to her, staring out over the still, quiet lake.

Abby spread out a blanket between the two picnic tables and lay down on it, pretending to sunbathe. She must have drifted off, because the low-pitched voices of Tate and Logan were what stirred her into wakefulness.

"Seems to me you've got the wrong table," Logan was saying. "Your girlfriend's over there."

"I was hoping we could talk."

"I can't see that there's much to talk about. Abby's made her decision."

The noises that followed suggested that Logan was arranging drinks on the table and ignoring Tate as much as possible. Abby resisted the urge to roll over and see exactly what was happening.

"Abby's a friend," Tate said next. "No more and no less."

"You two keep saying that." Logan sounded bored.

"It's the truth."

"Sure."

There was a rustling sound and faintly Abby could hear Tate stumbling over the awkward words in the list of ingredients on the side of a soda can.

"What are you doing?" Logan asked.

"Reading," Tate explained. "And for me that's some kind of miracle. You see, until I met Abby here in the park helping Mai-Ling, I couldn't read."

A shocked silence followed his announcement.

"For a lot of reasons, I never properly learned," Tate

continued. "Then I found Abby. Until I met her, I didn't know there were good people like her who'd be willing to teach me."

"Abby taught you to read?" Logan was obviously stunned.

"I asked her not to tell anyone. I suppose that was selfish of me in light of what's happened between you two. I don't have any excuse except pride."

Someone called Logan's name and the conversation was abruptly cut off. Minutes later someone else announced that it was time to eat. Abby joined the others, helping where she could. She and Tate were sitting with Dick and Betty when she felt Logan's eyes on her. The conversation around her faded away. The space between them seemed to evaporate as she turned and boldly met his look. In his eyes she read anger, regret and a great deal of inner pain.

When it came time to pack up her things and head home, Abby found Tate surrounded by a group of single women. He glanced up and waved. "I'll call you later," he told her cheerfully, clearly enjoying the attention he was receiving.

"Fine," she assured him. She hadn't gotten as far as the parking lot when Logan caught up with her.

He grabbed her shoulder as he turned her around. The anger she'd thought had been directed inward was now focused on her.

"Why didn't you tell me?" he demanded.

"I couldn't," she said simply. "Tate asked me not to."

"That's no excuse," he began, then paused to inhale a shuddering breath. "All the times I questioned you about meeting Tate, you were tutoring him. The least you could've done was tell me!"

"I already told you Tate was uncomfortable with that. Even now, I don't think you appreciate what it took for him to admit it to you," she explained slowly, enunciating each word so there'd be no misunderstanding. "I was the first person he'd ever told about this problem. It was traumatic for him and I couldn't go around telling others. Surely you can understand that."

"What about me? What about *us*?"

"My hands were tied. I asked you to trust me. A hundred times I pleaded with you to look beyond the obvious."

Logan closed his eyes and emitted a low groan. "How could I have been so stupid?"

"We've both been stupid and we've both learned valuable lessons. Isn't it time to put all that behind us?" She wanted to tell him again how much she loved him, but something stopped her.

Hands buried deep in his pockets, Logan turned away from her, but not before Abby saw that his eyes were narrowed. The pride in his expression seemed to block her out.

Abby watched in disbelief. The way he was behaving implied that *she'd* been the unreasonable, untrusting one. The more Abby thought about their short conversation as she drove home, the angrier she got.

Pacing her living room, she folded her arms around her waist to ward off a sudden chill. "Of all the nerve," she snapped at Dano, who paraded in front of her. The cat shot into her bedroom, smart enough to know when to avoid his mistress.

Yanking her car keys out of her purse, Abby hurried outside. She'd be darned if she'd let Logan end things like this.

His car was in its usual space, and he'd just opened the driver's door. She marched over, standing directly in front of him.

Logan frowned. "What's going on?"

She pointed her index finger at his chest until he backed up against the car.

"Now listen here, Logan Fletcher. I've had about all I can take from you." Every word was punctuated with a jab of her finger.

"Abby? What's the problem?"

"You and that stubborn pride of yours."

"Me?" he shouted in return.

"When we're married, you can bet I won't put up with this kind of behavior."

"Married?" he repeated incredulously. "Who said anything about marriage?"

"I did."

"Doesn't the man usually do the asking?" he said in a sarcastic voice.

"Not necessarily." Some of her anger was dissipating and she began to realize what a fool she was making of herself. "And…and while we're on the subject, you owe me an apology."

"You weren't entirely innocent in any of this."

"All right. I apologize. Does that make it easier on your fragile ego?"

"I also prefer to make my own marriage proposals."

Abby paled and crossed her arms. She wouldn't back down now. "Fine. I'm waiting."

Logan squared his shoulders and cleared his throat. "Abby Carpenter." His voice softened measurably. "I want to express my sincere apology for my behavior these past weeks."

"Months," she inserted with a low breath.

"All right, months," Logan amended. "Although you seem to be rushing the moment, I don't suppose it would do any harm to give you this." He pulled a diamond ring from his pocket.

Abby nearly fell over. Her mouth dropped open and she was speechless as he lifted her hand and slipped the solitaire diamond on her ring finger. "I was on my way to your place," he explained as he pulled her into his embrace. "I've loved you for a long time. You know that. I hadn't worked out a plan to steal your heart away from Tate. But you can be assured I wasn't going to let you go without a struggle."

"But I love—"

His lips interrupted her declaration of love. Abby released a small cry of wonder and wound her arms around his neck, giving herself to the kiss as his mouth closed over hers.

Gradually Logan raised his head, and his eyes were filled with the same wonder she was experiencing. "I talked to Tate again after you left the park," Logan said in a husky murmur. "I was a complete fool."

"No more than usual." Her small laugh was breathless.

"I'll need at least thirty years to make it up to you."

"Change that to forty and you've got yourself a deal."

His eyes smiled deeply into hers. "Where would you like to honeymoon?"

Abby's eyes sparkled. "Des Moines—where else?"

* * * * *

Books by Lee Tobin McClain

HQN Books

Safe Haven

Low Country Hero
Low Country Dreams

Love Inspired

Redemption Ranch

A Soldier's Return
The Soldier's Redemption
The Twins' Family Christmas
The Nanny's Secret Baby

Rescue River

Engaged to the Single Mom
His Secret Child
Small-Town Nanny
The Soldier and the Single Mom
The Soldier's Secret Child
A Family for Easter

Christmas Twins

Secret Christmas Twins

Lone Star Cowboy League: Boys Ranch

The Nanny's Texas Christmas

Don't miss *Low Country Christmas*, the next book
in the Safe Haven series from HQN!

ENGAGED TO THE SINGLE MOM

Lee Tobin McClain

I owe much appreciation
to my Wednesday-morning critique group—
Sally Alexander, Jonathan Auxier, Kathy Ayres,
Colleen McKenna and Jackie Robb—
for being patient through genre shifts
while gently insisting on excellence. Thanks also
to my colleagues at Seton Hill University,
especially Michael Arnzen, Nicole Peeler
and Albert Wendland, whose support and
encouragement keep me happily writing.
Ben Wernsman helped me brainstorm story ideas,
and Carrie Turansky read an early draft
of the proposal and critiqued it most helpfully.
I'm grateful to be working with my agent,
Karen Solem, and my editor, Shana Asaro—dog
lovers both—who saw the potential of the story
and helped me make it better. Most of all, thanks
belong to my daughter, Grace, for being patient
with her creative mom's absentmindedness
and for offering inspiration, recreation and
eye-rolling, teenage-style love every step of the way.

One

"You can let me off here." Angelica Camden practically shouted the words over the roar of her grandfather's mufflerless truck. The hot July air, blowing in through the pickup's open windows, did nothing to dispel the sweat that dampened her neck and face.

She rubbed her hands down the legs of the full-length jeans she preferred to wear despite the heat, took a deep breath and blew it out yoga-style between pursed lips. She could do this. Had to do it.

Gramps raised bushy white eyebrows as he braked at the top of a long driveway. "I'm taking you right up to that arrogant something-or-other's door. You're a lady and should be treated as one."

No chance of that. Angelica's stomach churned at the thought of the man she was about to face. She'd fight lions for her kid, had done the equivalent plenty of times, but this particular lion terrified her, brought back feelings of longing and shame and sadness that made her feel about two inches tall.

This particular lion had every right to eat her alive. Her heart fluttered hard against her ribs, and when she took a deep breath, trying to calm herself, the truck's exhaust fumes made her feel light-headed.

I can't do this, Lord.

Immediately the verse from this morning's devotional, read hastily while she'd stirred oatmeal on Gramps's old gas stove, swam before her eyes: *I can do all things through Him who gives me strength.*

She believed it. She'd recited it to herself many times in the past couple of difficult years. She could do all things through Christ.

But this, Lord? Are you sure?

She knew Gramps would gladly go on the warpath for her, but using an eighty-year-old man to fight her battles wasn't an option. The problem was hers. She'd brought it on herself, mostly, and she was the one who had to solve it. "I'd rather do it my own way, Gramps. Please."

Ignoring her—of course—he started to turn into the driveway.

She yanked the handle, shoved the truck door open and put a booted foot on the running board, ready to jump.

"Hey, careful!" Gramps screeched to a stop just in front of a wooden sign: A Dog's Last Chance: No-Cage Canine Rescue. Troy Hinton, DVM, Proprietor. "DVM, eh? Well, he's still a—"

"Shhh." She swung back around to face him, hands braced on the door guards, and nodded sideways toward the focus of her entire life.

Gramps grunted and, thankfully, lapsed into silence.

"Mama, can I go in with you?" Xavier shot her a pleading look—one he'd perfected and used at will, the rascal—from the truck's backseat. "I want to see the dogs."

If she played this right, he'd be able to do more than just see the dogs during a short visit. He'd fulfill a dream, and right now Angelica's life pretty much revolved around helping Xavier fulfill his dreams.

"It's a job interview, honey. You go for a little drive with Gramps." At his disappointed expression, she reached back to pat his too-skinny leg. "Maybe you can see the dogs later, if I get the job."

"You'll get it, Mama."

His brilliant smile and total confidence warmed her heart at the same time that tension attacked her stomach. She shot a glance at Gramps and clung harder to the truck, which suddenly felt like security in a storm.

He must have read her expression, because his gnarled hands gripped the steering wheel hard. "You don't have to do this. We can try to get by for another couple of weeks at the Towers."

Seeing the concern in his eyes took Angelica out of herself and her fears. Gramps wasn't as healthy as he used to be, and he didn't need any extra stress on account of her. Two weeks at the Senior Towers was the maximum visit from relatives with kids, and even though she'd tried to keep Xavier quiet and neat, he'd bumped into a resident who used a walker, spilled red punch in the hallway and generally made too much noise. In other words, he was a kid. And the Senior Towers was no place to raise a kid.

They'd already outstayed their welcome, and she knew Gramps was concerned about it. She leaned back in to rub his shoulder. "I know what I'm doing. I'll be fine."

"You're sure?"

She nodded. "Don't worry about me."

But once the truck pulled away, bearing with it the only two males in North America she trusted, Angelica's strength failed her. She put a hand on one of the wooden fence posts and closed her eyes, shooting up a desperate prayer for courage.

As the truck sounds faded, the Ohio farmland came to life around her. A tiny creek rippled its way along the driveway. Two fence posts down, a red-winged blackbird landed, trilling the *oka-oka-LEE* she hadn't heard in years. She inhaled the pungent scent of new-mown hay.

This was where she'd come from. Surely the Lord had a reason for bringing her home.

Taking another deep breath, she straightened her spine. She was of farm stock. She could do this. She reached into her pocket, clutched the key chain holding a cross and a photo of her son in better days, and headed toward the faint sound of barking dogs. Toward the home of the man who had every reason to hate her.

As the sound of the pickup faded, Troy Hinton used his arms to lift himself halfway out of the porch rocker. In front of him, his cast-clad leg rested on a wicker table, stiff and useless.

"A real man plays ball, even if he's hurt. Get back up and into the game, son." His dad's words echoed in his head, even though his logical side knew he couldn't risk worsening his compound fracture just so he could stride down the porch steps and impress the raven-haired beauty slowly approaching his home.

Not that he had any chance of impressing Angelica

Camden. Nor any interest in doing so. She was one mistake he wouldn't make again.

His dog, Bull, scrabbled against the floorboards beside him, trying to stand despite his arthritic hips. Troy sank back down and put a hand on the dog's back. "It's okay, boy. Relax."

He watched Angelica's slow, reluctant walk toward his house. Why she'd applied to be his assistant, he didn't know. And why he'd agreed to talk to her was an even bigger puzzle.

She'd avoided him for the past seven years, ever since she'd jilted him with a handwritten letter and disappeared not only from his life, but from the state. A surge of the old bitterness rose in him, and he clenched his fists. Humiliation. Embarrassment. And worse, a broken heart and shattered faith that had never fully recovered.

She'd arrived in her grandfather's truck, but the old man had no use for him or any of his family, so why had he brought her out here for her interview? And why wasn't he standing guard with a shotgun? In fact, given the old man's reputation for thrift, he'd probably use the very same shotgun with which he'd ordered Troy off his hardscrabble farm seven years ago.

Troy had come looking for explanations about why Angelica had left town. Where she was. What her letter had meant. How she was surviving; whether she was okay.

The old man had raved at him, gone back into the past feud between their families over the miserable acre of land he called a farm. That acre had rapidly gone to seed, as had Angelica's grandfather, and a short while later he'd moved into the Senior Towers.

In a way, the old man had been abandoned, too, by the

granddaughter he'd helped to raise. Fair warning. No matter how sweet she seemed, no matter what promises she made, she was a runner. Disloyal. Not to be counted on.

As Angelica approached, Troy studied her. She was way thinner than the curvy little thing she'd been at twenty-one. Her black hair, once shiny and flowing down her back in waves, was now captured in a careless bun. She wore baggy jeans and a loose, dusty-red T-shirt.

But with her full lips and almond-shaped eyes and coppery bronze skin, she still glowed like an exotic flower in the middle of a plain midwestern cornfield. And doggone it if his heart didn't leap out of his chest to see her.

"Down, boy," Troy ordered Bull—or maybe himself—as he pushed up into a standing position and hopped over to get his crutches.

His movements must have caught the attention of Lou Ann Miller, and now she hobbled out the front screen door.

She pointed a spatula at him. "You get back in that chair."

"You get back in that kitchen." He narrowed his eyes at the woman who'd practically raised him. "This is something I have to do alone. And standing up."

"If you fall down those steps, you'll have to hire yet another helper, and you've barely got the charm to keep me." She put her hands on bony hips. "I expect you to treat that girl decent. What I hear, she's been through a lot."

Curiosity tugged at him. People in town were too kind to tell him the latest gossip about Angelica. They danced around the subject, sparing his ego and his feelings.

What had Angelica been through? How had it affected her?

The idea that she'd suffered or been hurt plucked at the chords of his heart, remnants of a time he'd have moved mountains to protect her and care for her. She'd had such a hard time growing up, and it had made him feel ten feet tall that she'd chosen him to help her escape her rough past.

Women weren't the only ones who liked stories of knights in shining armor. Lots of men wanted to be heroes as well, and Angelica was the kind of woman who could bring out the heroic side of a guy.

At least for a while. He swallowed down his questions and the bad taste in his mouth and forced a lightness he didn't feel into his tone. "Who says I won't treat her well? She's the only person who's applied for the job. I'd better." Looking at his cast, he could only shake his head. What an idiot he'd been to try to fix the barn roof by himself, all because he didn't want to ask anyone for help.

"I'll leave you alone, but I'll know if you raise your voice," Lou Ann warned, pointing the spatula at him again.

He hopped to the door and held it for her. Partly to urge her inside, and partly to catch her if she stumbled. She was seventy-five if she was a day, and despite her high energy and general bossiness, he felt protective.

Not that he'd be much help if she fell, with this broken leg.

She rolled her eyes and walked inside, shaking her head.

When he turned back, Angelica was about ten feet away from the front porch. She'd stopped and was watching him. Eyes huge, wide, wary. From here, he could see the dark circles under them.

Unwanted concern nudged at him. She looked as though she hadn't slept, hadn't been eating right. Her clothes were worn, suggesting poverty. And the flirty sparkle in her eyes, the one that had kept all the farm boys buying gallons of lemonade from her concession stand at the county fair...that was completely gone.

She looked defeated. At the end of her rope.

What had happened to her?

Their mutual sizing-up stare-fest lasted way too long, and then he beckoned her forward. "Come on up. I'm afraid I can't greet you properly with this bum leg."

She trotted up the stairs, belying his impression that she was beaten down. "Was that Lou Ann Miller?"

"It was." He felt an illogical urge to step closer to her, which he ascribed to the fact that he didn't get out much and didn't meet many women. "She runs my life."

"Miss Lou Ann!" Angelica called through the screen door, seemingly determined to ignore Troy. "Haven't seen you in ages!"

Lou Ann, who must have been directly inside, hurried back out.

Angelica's face broke into a smile as she pulled the older woman into a gentle hug. "It's so nice to see you! How's Caleb?"

Troy drummed his fingers on the handle of his crutch. Caleb was Lou Ann's grandson, who'd been in Angelica's grade in school, and whom Angelica had dated before the two of them had gotten together. He was just one of the many members of Angelica's fan club back then, and Troy, with his young-guy pride and testosterone, had been crazy jealous of all of them.

Maybe with good reason.

"He's fine, fine. Got two young boys." Lou Ann held Angelica's shoulders and studied her. "You're way too thin. I'll bring out some cookies." She glared at Troy. "They're not for you, so don't you go eating all of them."

And then she was gone and it was just the two of them.

Angelica studied the man she'd been so madly in love with seven years ago.

He was as handsome as ever, despite the cast on his leg and the two-day ragged beard on his chin. His shoulders were still impossibly broad, but now there were tiny wrinkles beside his eyes, and his short haircut didn't conceal the fact that his hairline was a little higher than it used to be. The hand he held out to her was huge.

Angelica's stomach knotted, but she forced herself to reach out and put her hand into his.

The hard-calloused palm engulfed hers and she yanked her hand back, feeling trapped. She squatted down to pet the grizzled bulldog at Troy's side. "Who's this?"

"That's Bull."

She blinked. Was he calling her on her skittishness?

That impression increased as he cocked his head to one side. "You're not afraid of me, are you?"

"No!" She gulped air. "I'm not afraid of you. Like I said when we texted, I'm here to apply for the job you advertised in the *Tribune*."

He gestured toward one of the rockers. "Have a seat. Let's talk about that. I'm curious about why you're interested."

Of course he was. And she'd spent much of last night sleepless, wondering how much she'd have to tell him to get the job she desperately needed, the job that would make things as good as they could be, at least for a while.

Once she sat down, he made his way back to his own rocker and sat, grimacing as he propped his leg on the low table in front of him.

She didn't like the rush of sympathy she felt. "What happened?"

"Fell off a roof. My own stupid fault."

That was new in him, the willingness to admit his own culpability. She wondered how far it went.

"That's why I need an assistant with the dogs," he explained. "Lou Ann helps me around the house, but she's not strong enough to take care of the kennels. I can't get everything done, and we've got a lot of dogs right now, so this is kind of urgent."

His words were perfectly cordial, but questions and undercurrents rustled beneath them.

Angelica forced herself to stay in the present, in sales mode. "You saw my résumé online, right? I worked as a vet assistant back in Boston. And I've done hospital, um, volunteer work, and you know I grew up in the country. I'm strong, a lot stronger than I look."

He nodded. "I've no doubt you could do the work if you wanted to," he said, "but why would you want to?"

"Let's just say I need a job."

He studied her, his blue eyes troubled. "You haven't shown your face in town for seven years. Even when you visit your grandfather, you hide out at the Senior Towers. If I'm giving you access to my dogs and my computer files and my whole business, especially if you're able to live here on the grounds, I need to know a little more about what you've been up to."

He hadn't mentioned his main reason for mistrusting her, and she appreciated that. She pulled her mind out of the past and focused on the living arrangement, one of the main reasons this job was perfect for her. "I'm very interested in living in. Your ad said that's part of the job?"

"That's right, in the old bunkhouse." He gestured toward a trim white building off to the east. "I figured the offer of housing might sweeten the deal, given that this is just a temporary job."

"Is it big enough for two?"

"Ye-es." He leaned back in the rocker and studied her, his eyes hooded. "Why? Are you married? I thought your name was still Camden."

"I'm not married." She swallowed. "But I do have a son."

His eyebrows lifted. "How old is your son?"

"Is that important?" She really, really didn't want to tell him.

"Yes, it's important," he said with a slight sigh. "I can't have a baby or toddler here. It wouldn't be safe, not with some of the dogs I care for."

She drew in a breath. Now or never. "My son's six, almost seven." She reached a hand out to the bulldog, who'd settled between them, rubbed it along his wrinkled head, let him sloppily lick her fingers.

"Six! Then…"

She forced herself to look at Troy steadily while he did the math. Saw his eyes harden as he realized her son must have been conceived right around the time she'd left town.

Heat rose in her cheeks as the familiar feeling of shame twisted her insides. But she couldn't let herself go there. "Xavier is a well-behaved kid." At least most of the time. "He loves animals and he's gentle with them."

Troy was still frowning.

He was going to refuse her, angry about the way she'd left him, and then what would she do? How would she achieve the goal she'd set for herself, to fulfill as many of Xavier's wishes as she could? This was such a perfect arrangement.

"I really need this job, Troy." She hated to beg, but for Xavier, she'd do it.

He looked away, out at the fields, and she did, too. Sun on late-summer corn tassels, puffy clouds in a blue sky. Xavier would love it so.

"If you ever felt anything for me…" Her throat tightened and she had to force out the words. "If any of your memories about me are good, please give me the job."

He turned back toward her, eyes narrowing. "Why do you need it so badly?"

She clenched her hands in her lap. "Because my son wants to be close to Gramps. And because he loves animals."

"Most people don't organize their careers around their kids' hankerings."

She drew in a breath. "Well, I do."

His expression softened a little. "This job…it might not be what you want. It's just until my leg heals. The doc says it could be three, four months before I'm fully back on my feet. Once that happens, I won't need an assistant anymore."

She swallowed and squeezed her hands together.

Lord, I know I'm supposed to let You lead, but this seems so right. Not for me, but for Xavier, and that's what matters. It is of You, isn't it?

No answer from above, but the roar of a truck engine pierced the country quiet.

Oh no. Gramps was back too soon. He'd never gotten along with Troy, never trusted him on account of his conflicts with Troy's dad. But she didn't want the two men's animosity to get in the way of what both she and her son wanted and needed.

The truck stopped again at the end of the driveway. Gramps got out, walked around to the passenger door.

She surged from her chair. "No, don't!" she called, but the old man didn't hear her. She started down the porch steps.

Troy called her back. "It's okay, they can come up. Regardless of what we decide about the job, maybe your son would like to see the dogs, look around the place."

"There's nothing he'd like better," she said, "but I don't want to get his hopes up if this isn't going to work out."

Troy's forehead wrinkled as he stared out toward the truck, watching as Gramps helped Xavier climb out.

Angelica rarely saw her son from this distance, and now, watching Gramps steady him, her hand rose to her throat. He looked as thin as a scarecrow. His baseball cap couldn't conceal the fact that he had almost no hair.

Her eyes stung and her breathing quickened as if she were hyperventilating. She pinched the skin on the back of her hand, hard, and pressed her lips together.

Gramps held Xavier's arm as they made slow progress down the driveway. The older supporting the younger, opposite of how it should be.

Troy cleared his throat. "Like I said, the job won't be long-term. I… It looks like you and your son have some…issues. You might want to find something more permanent."

His kind tone made her want to curl up and cry for a couple of weeks, but she couldn't go there. She clenched her fists. "I know the job is short-term." Swallowing the lump that rose in her throat, she added, "That's okay with us. We take things a day at a time."

"Why's that?" His gaze remained on the pair making their slow way up the driveway.

He was going to make her say it. She took a shuddering breath and forced out the words. "Because the doctors aren't sure how long his remission will last."

Troy stared at Xavier, forgetting to breathe. Remission? "Remission from what?"

Angelica cleared her throat. "Leukemia. He has…a kind that's hard to beat."

Every parent's nightmare. Instinctively he reached out to pat her shoulder, the way he'd done so many times with pet owners worried about seriously ill pets.

She flinched and sidled away.

Fine! Anger flared up at the rejection and he gripped the porch railing and tamped it down. Her response was crystal clear. She didn't want any physical contact between them.

But no matter his own feelings, no matter what Angelica had done to him, the past was the past. This pain, the pain of a mother who might lose her child, was in the present, and Angelica's worn-down appearance suddenly made sense.

And no matter whose kid Xavier was…no matter

who she'd cheated on him with...the boy was an innocent, and the thought of a child seriously, maybe terminally, ill made Troy's heart hurt.

Again he suppressed his emotions as his medical
instincts went into overdrive. "What kind of doctors
has he seen? Have you gotten good treatments, second
opinions?"

She took a step back and crossed her arms over her
chest. "I can't begin to tell you how many doctors and
opinions."

"But are they the best ones? Have you tried the
Cleveland—"

"Troy!" She blew out a jagged breath. "Look, I don't
need medical interference right now. I need a job."

"But—"

"Don't you think I've done everything in my power
to help him?" She turned away and walked down the
steps toward her son. Her back was stiff, her shoulders rigid.

He lifted a hand to stop her and then let it fall. *Way
to go, Hinton. Great social skills.*

He'd find out more, would try to do something to
help. Obviously Angelica hadn't done well financially
since she left him and left town. Xavier's father must
have bolted. And without financial resources, getting
good medical care wasn't easy.

"Mom! Did you get the job?"

Angelica shot Troy a quick glance. "It's still being
decided."

The boy's face fell. Then he nodded and bit his lip.
"It's okay, Mama. But can we at least see the dogs?"

"Absolutely," Troy answered before Angelica could
deny the boy. Then he hobbled down the porch stairs

and sank onto the bottom one, putting him on a level with the six-year-old. "I'm Troy," he said, and reached out to shake the boy's hand.

The boy smiled—wow, what a smile—and reached out to grasp Troy's hand, looking up at his mother for reassurance.

She nodded at him. "You know what to say."

Frowning with thought, the boy shook his head.

"Pleased to…" Angelica prompted.

The smile broke out again like sunshine. "Oh yeah. Pleased to meet you, sir. I'm Xavier." He dropped Troy's hand and waved an arm upward, grinning. "And this is my grandpa. My *great*-grandpa."

"I've already had the pleasure." Troy looked up and met the old man's hostile eyes.

Camden glared down at him, not speaking.

Oh man. Out of the gazillion reasons not to hire Angelica, here was a major one. Obviously her grandfather was an important part of her life, one of her only living relatives. If she and Xavier came to live here, Troy would see a lot of Homer Camden, something they'd managed to avoid for the years Angelica was out of town.

Of course, he'd been working like crazy himself. Setting up his private practice, opening the rescue, paying off debt from vet school, which was astronomical even though his family had helped.

Troy pushed himself to his feet and got his crutches underneath him. "Dogs are out this way, if you'd like to see them." He nodded toward the barn.

"Yes!" Xavier pumped his arm. "I asked God to get me a bunch of dogs."

"Zavey Davey…" Angelica's voice was uneasy. "Remember, I don't have the job yet. And God doesn't always—"

"I know." Xavier sighed, his smile fading a little. "He doesn't always answer prayers the way we want Him to."

Ouch. Kids were supposed to be all about Jesus Loves Me and complete confidence in God's—and their parents'—ability to fix anything. But from the looks of things, young Xavier had already run up against some of life's hard truths.

"Come on, Gramps." When the old man didn't move, Xavier tugged at his arm. "You promised you'd be nice. Please?"

The old man's face reddened. After a slight pause that gave Troy and Angelica the chance to glance at each other, he turned in the direction Troy had indicated and started walking, slowly, with Xavier.

Angelica touched Troy's arm, more like hit him, actually. "Don't let him go back there if you don't want to give me the job," she growled.

Even angry, her voice brushed at his nerve endings like rich, soft velvet. Her rough touch plucked at some wildness in him he'd never given way to.

Troy looked off over the cornfields, thinking, trying to get control of himself. He didn't trust Angelica, but that sweet-eyed kid…how could he disappoint a sick kid?

Homer Camden and the boy were making tracks toward the barn, and Troy started after them. He didn't want them to reach the dogs before he'd had a chance to lay some ground rules about safety. He turned to make sure Angelica was following.

She wasn't. "Well?" Her arms were crossed, eyes narrowed, head cocked to one side.

"You expect me to make an instant decision?"

"Since my kid's feelings are on the line…yeah. Yeah, I do."

Their eyes locked. Some kind of stormy electrical current ran between them.

This was bad. Working with her would be difficult enough, since feelings he thought he'd resolved years ago were resurfacing. He'd thought he was over her dumping him, but the knowledge that she'd conceived a child with someone else after seeming so sincere about their decision to wait until marriage… His neck felt as tight as granite. Yeah. It was going to take a while to process that.

Having her live here on the grounds with that very child, someone else's child, the product of her unfaithfulness…he clenched his jaw against all the things he wanted to say to her.

Fools vent their anger, but the wise hold it back. It was a proverb he'd recently taught the boys in his Kennel Kids group, little dreaming how soon and how badly he'd need it himself.

"Mom! Come on! I wanna see the dogs!" Xavier was tugging at his grandfather's arm, jumping around like a kid who wasn't at all sick, but Troy knew that was deceptive. Even terminally ill animals went through energetic periods.

Could he deprive Xavier of being with dogs and of having a decent home to live in? Even if having Angelica here on the farm was going to be difficult?

When he met her eyes again, he saw that hers shone with unshed tears.

"FAST FIVE" READER SURVEY

Your participation entitles you to:
* ✳ Up to 4 FREE BOOKS and Thank-You Gifts Worth Over $20!

Complete the survey in minutes.

Suspense

Romance

Get Up to 4 **FREE** Books

Your Thank-You Gifts include up to **4 FREE BOOKS** and **2 MYSTERY GIFTS**. There's no obligation to purchase anything!

See inside for details.

Dear Reader,

Since you are a lover of our books, your opinions are important to us... and so is your time.

That's why we made sure your **"FAST FIVE" READER SURVEY** can be completed in just a few minutes. Your answers to the five questions will help us remain at the forefront of women's fiction.

And, as a thank-you for participating, we'd like to send you up to **4 FREE BOOKS** and **FREE THANK-YOU GIFTS!**

Try **Essential Suspense** featuring spine-tingling suspense and psychological thrillers with many written by today's best-selling authors.

Try **Essential Romance** featuring compelling romance stories with many written by today's best-selling authors.

Or TRY BOTH!

Enjoy your gifts with our appreciation,

Pam Powers

To get up to
4 FREE BOOKS & THANK-YOU GIFTS:

✱ Quickly complete the "Fast Five" Reader Survey
and return the insert.

"FAST FIVE" READER SURVEY

1	Do you sometimes read a book a second or third time?	○ Yes ○ No
2	Do you often choose reading over other forms of entertainment such as television?	○ Yes ○ No
3	When you were a child, did someone regularly read aloud to you?	○ Yes ○ No
4	Do you sometimes take a book with you when you travel outside the home?	○ Yes ○ No
5	In addition to books, do you regularly read newspapers and magazines?	○ Yes ○ No

YES! Please send me my Free Rewards, consisting of **2 Free Books from each series I select** and **Free Mystery Gifts**. I understand that I am under no obligation to buy anything, as explained on the back of this card.

❏ **Essential Suspense** (191/391 MDL GNRN)
❏ **Essential Romance** (194/394 MDL GNRN)
❏ **Try Both** ((191/391 & 194/394) MDL GNRY)

FIRST NAME	LAST NAME

ADDRESS

APT.#	CITY

STATE/PROV.	ZIP/POSTAL CODE

READER SERVICE—Here's how it works:

"Okay," he said around a sigh. "You're hired."

Her face broke into a sunshiny smile that reminded him of the girl she'd been. "Thank you, Troy," she said softly. She walked toward him, and for a minute he thought she was going to hug him, as she'd been so quick to do in the past.

But she walked right by him to catch up with her son and grandfather. She bent over, embraced Xavier from behind and spoke into his ear.

The boy let out a cheer. "Way to go, Mama! Come on!"

They hurried ahead, leaving Troy to hop along on his crutches, matching Angelica's grandfather's slower pace.

"Guess you hired her," the old man said.

"I did."

"Now you listen here." Camden stopped walking, narrowed his eyes, and pointed a finger at Troy. "If you do anything to hurt that girl, you'll have me to contend with."

Troy took a deep breath and let it out slowly. He was doing this family a favor, but he couldn't expect gratitude, not with the history that stood between them. "I have no plans to hurt her. Hoping she'll be a help to me until I'm back on my feet." He glanced down. "Foot."

"Humph." Camden turned and started making his way toward the barn again. "Heard you fell off a roof. Fool thing to do."

Troy gritted his teeth and swung into step beside Camden. "According to my brother and dad, you've done a few fool things in your day." This was a man who'd repeatedly refused a massive financial package that would have turned his family's lives around, all in favor of keeping his single-acre farm that stood in the middle of the Hinton holdings.

Not that Troy blamed the old man, particularly. Troy's father was an arrogant, unstable man with plenty of enemies. Including Troy himself, most of the time.

Even after Homer Camden's health had declined, forcing him to move into the Senior Towers, he clung stubbornly to the land. Rumor had it that his house had fallen into disrepair and the surrounding fields were nothing but weeds.

Not wanting to say something he'd regret, Troy motored ahead on his crutches until he reached Xavier and Angelica, who'd stopped at the gate.

"If you wait there," he said to them, "I'll let the dogs out into the runs." The breeze kicked up just as he passed Angelica, and the strawberry scent of her hair took him back seven years, to a time when that smell and her gentle, affectionate kisses had made him light-headed on a regular basis.

"Wait. Mr. Hinton." Xavier was breathing hard. "Thank you...for giving Mama...the job." He smiled up at Troy.

Troy's throat constricted. "Thank you for talking her into doing it," he managed to say, and then swung toward the barn.

He was going to do everything in his power to make that boy well.

Inside, joyful barks and slobbery kisses grounded him. His dogs ranged in age and size but tended toward the large, dark-coated bully breeds. The dogs no one else wanted to take a risk with: pit bulls, aggressive Dobermans and Rotties, large mutts. They were mixed in with older, sicker dogs whose owners couldn't or wouldn't pay the vet bills to treat them.

He moved among them, grateful that he'd found his calling in life.

Yes, he was lonely. Yes, he regretted not having a family around him, people to love. But he had his work, and it would always be there. Unlike people, dogs were loyal and trustworthy. They wouldn't let you down.

He opened the kennel doors to let them run free.

When he got back outside, he heard the end of Homer Camden's speech. "There's a job might open up at the café," he was saying, "And Jeannette Haroldson needs a caregiver."

For some reason that went beyond his own need for a temporary assistant, Troy didn't want the old man to talk her out of working for him. "Look, I know you've got a beef with the Hintons. But it's my dad and my brother who manage the land holdings. My sister's not involved, and I just run my rescue."

"That's as may be, but blood runs true. Angie's got other choices, and I don't see why—"

"That's why, Grandpa." Angelica pointed to Xavier. He'd knelt down beside the fence, letting the dogs lick him through it. On his face was an expression of the purest ecstasy Troy had ever seen.

All three adults looked at each other. They were three people at odds. But in that moment, in complete silence, a pact arose between them: whatever it takes, we'll put this child first and help him be happy.

Two

Angelica watched her son reach thin, bluish fingers in to touch the dogs. Listened to Troy lecture them all about the rules for safety: don't enter the pens without a trained person there, don't let the dogs out, don't feed one dog in the presence of others. Her half-broken heart sang with gratitude.

Thanks to God, and Troy, Xavier would have his heartfelt wish. He'd have dogs—multiple dogs—to spend his days with. He'd have a place to call home. He'd have everything she could provide for him to make his time on this earth happy.

And if Xavier was happy, she could handle anything: Troy's intensity, the questions in his eyes, the leap in her own heart that came from being near this too-handsome man who had never been far from her thoughts in all these years.

"Do you want to see the inside of the barn?" Troy asked Xavier.

"Sure!" He sounded livelier than he had in weeks.

Troy led the way, his shoulders working the crutches.

He was such a big man; he'd probably had to get the extra-tall size.

Gramps patted her back, stopping her. "I don't like it," he said, "but I understand what you're doing."

She draped an arm around his shoulders. "Thanks. That means a lot."

"Think I'll wait in the truck, though," he said. "Being around a Hinton sticks in my craw."

"Okay, sure." Truthfully, she was glad to see Gramps go. She doubted that he and Troy could be civil much longer.

She held Xavier's hand as they walked into the barn and over to the dog pens. The place was pretty clean, considering. Troy must have been wearing himself out to keep it that way.

As Xavier and Troy played with the dogs, she looked around, trying to get a clue into the man. She wandered over to a desk in the corner, obviously a place where he did the kennel business, or some of it.

And there, among a jumble of nails and paper clips, was a leather-studded bracelet she hadn't seen in seven years. She sucked in a breath as her heart dove down, down, down.

She closed her eyes hard, trying to shut out the memories, but a slide show of them raced through her mind. First date, whirlwind courtship and the most romantic marriage proposal a girl from her background could have imagined. For a few months, she'd felt like a princess in a fairy tale.

Back then, as an engaged couple, they'd helped with the youth group and had gotten the kids True Love Waits bracelets—leather and studs for the guys, more delicate chains for the girls. There had been a couple of extra ones, and one night when the waiting had been difficult, she and Troy had decided to each wear one as a reminder.

Carefully, she picked up the leather band. Her eyes filled with tears as she remembered stroking it on his arm, sometimes jokingly tugging at it when their kisses had gotten too passionate. Back in those innocent, happy days.

She'd ripped hers off and thrown it away on the most awful night of her life. The night she'd turned twenty-one and stupidly gone out with a bunch of friends to celebrate. The night she'd had too much to drink, realized it and accepted the offer of an older acquaintance to walk her home.

The night her purity and innocence and dreams of waiting for marriage had been torn forcibly away.

The next day, when Troy had noticed her bracelet was missing, she'd lied to him, telling him it must have fallen off.

But he'd continued to wear his, joking that he probably needed the reminder more than she did.

"Hey." He came up behind her now. When he noticed what she was holding, his eyebrows shot up and he took a step back.

She dropped it as if it were made of hot metal. "I'm sorry. That's not my business. I just happened to see it and…got carried away with the memories."

He nodded, pressed his lips together. Turned away.

That set face had to be judging her, didn't it? Feeling disgust at her lack of purity.

She'd been right to leave him. He could never have accepted her after what happened, although knowing him, he'd have tried to pretend. He'd have felt obligated to marry her anyway.

"Mom! Come see!" Xavier cried.

"Xavier!" He'd gone into a section of the barn Troy had warned them was off-limits. "I'm sorry," she said to Troy, and hurried over to her son. "You have to follow the rules! You could get hurt!"

"But look, Mama!" He knelt in front of a small heap of puppies, mostly gray and white, all squirming around a mother who lay on her side. Her head was lifted, her teeth bared.

"Careful of a mama dog," Troy said behind her. "Pull him back a foot or two, will you, Angelica? These little guys are only two weeks old, and the mom's still pretty protective."

She did, hating the crestfallen expression on Xavier's face. This ideal situation might have its own risks.

And then Troy reached down, patted the mother dog and carefully lifted a tiny, squirming puppy into Xavier's lap.

Xavier froze, then put his face down to nuzzle the puppy's pink-and-white snout. It nudged and licked him back, and then two more puppies crawled into his lap, tumbling over each other. Yips and squeals came from the mass of warm puppy bodies.

"Mom," Xavier said reverently. "This is *so* cool."

Angelica's heart did a funny little twist. She reached out and squeezed Troy's arm before she could stop herself.

"Do we really get to live here? Can we sleep in the barn with the puppies?"

Troy laughed. "No, son. You'll stay in a bunkhouse. Kind of like an Old West cowboy. Want to see?"

"Sure!" His eyes were on Troy with something like hero worship, and worry pricked at Angelica's chest. Was Xavier going to get too attached to Troy?

Then again, if it would make him happy... Angelica swallowed hard and shut out thoughts of the future. "Let's go!" she said with a voice that was only slightly shaky.

When they reached the bunkhouse and walked inside, Angelica felt her face break out into a smile. "It's wonderful, Troy! When did you do all this work on it?" She remembered the place as an old, run-down outbuilding, but now modern paneling and new windows made it bright with sunshine on wood. It needed curtains, maybe blue-and-white gingham. The rough-hewn pine furniture was sparse, but with a few throw pillows and afghans, the place would be downright homey.

A home. She'd wanted one forever, and even more after she'd become a mom.

Troy's watchful eyes snapped her out of her happy fantasies. "You like it?"

"It's fantastic." She realized he'd never answered her question about when he'd done the work.

"You're easy to please." His voice was gruff.

She smiled and squatted down beside Xavier. "We both are. Pretty near perfect, isn't it, Zavey Davey?"

"Yes. Sure, Mama."

Her ear was so attuned to his needs that she heard the slight hesitation in his voice. "What's wrong?" she asked, keeping her voice low to make the conversation private, just between her and her son. "Isn't this everything you've always wanted?"

"Yes. Except..." He wrinkled his freckled nose as though he was trying to decide something.

"What? What is it, honey?"

He pressed his lips together and then lost the battle with himself, shrugged and grinned winningly at her. "It's the last thing on my list, Mama."

The last thing. Her heart twisted tight. "What? What do you need?"

He leaned over and whispered into her ear, "A dad."

When Angelica emerged from the bunkhouse the next Saturday, every nerve in Troy's body snapped to attention. Was this the same woman who'd been working like a ranch hand this week, wearing jeans and T-shirts and boots, learning the ropes in the kennel?

It was the first time he'd seen her in a top that wasn't as loose as a sack. And was that makeup on her eyes, making them look even bigger?

"What?" she asked as she walked up beside him. She seemed taller. He looked down and saw that she was wearing sandals with a little heel, too.

Angelica had always been cute and appealing. But now she was model-thin, and with her hair braided back, her cheekbones stood out in a heart-shaped face set off by long silver earrings. A pale pink shirt edged with lace made her copper-colored skin glow. With depth and wisdom in her brown eyes, and a wry smile turning up the edges of her mouth, she was a knockout.

And one he needed to steer clear of. Beauty didn't equate to morality or good values, and one whirl with this little enchantress had just about done him in.

Though to be fair, he didn't know the rest of her story. And he shouldn't judge. "Nothing. You look nice."

"Do you have the keys?"

"What?"

"Keys." She held out her hand.

He had to stop staring. The keys. He pulled them out of his pocket and handed them over.

She wasn't here for him. She was here because she needed something, and when she got it, she'd leave. He knew that from experience.

"Bye, Mama!" Xavier's voice was thin, reedy, but for all that, cheerful.

When he turned, he saw Xavier and Lou Ann standing on the porch, waving.

"You be good for Miss Lou Ann." Angelica shook her finger at Xavier, giving him a mock-stern look.

"I will, Mama."

Lou Ann put an arm around the boy. "We'll have fun. He's going to help me do some baking."

"Thank you!" Angelica shot a beaming smile toward the porch, and Troy's heart melted a little more.

With him, though, she was all business. "Let's get going. If we're to get there by nine, we don't have time to stand around."

She walked toward the truck, and he couldn't help noticing how well her jeans fit her slender frame.

Then she opened the passenger door and held it for him.

He gritted his teeth. Out of all the indignities of being injured, this had to be the worst. He liked to drive, liked to be in control, liked to open the door for a lady. Not have the door held for him. That was a man's proper role, pounded into him from childhood. No weakness; no vulnerability. Men should be in charge.

While his years in college and vet school, surrounded by capable and brilliant professional women, had knocked some feminist sense into his head, his alpha-male instincts were as strong as ever.

"You need help getting in?" she asked.

Grrrr. "I have a broken leg. I'm not paralyzed." He swung himself into the truck, grunting with the awkward effort.

"Sor-ry." She shrugged and walked back around to the driver's side.

When they headed down the driveway, he said, "Take a right up there at the stop sign."

She did, rolling down her window at the same time. Hot, dusty July air blew tendrils of her hair loose, but she put her head back and breathed it in deeply, a tiny smile curving her full lips.

He liked that she'd stayed a farm girl, not all prissy and citified. Maybe liked it a little too much. "Slow down, this is a blind curve. Then go left after that barn."

"Troy." She shifted gears with complete competence. "I grew up here, remember? I know how to get to town."

Of course she did. She was a capable assistant...and no more. He needed to focus on his weekly vet clinic and how he was going to manage it on crutches. Forget about Angelica.

Easier said than done.

Angelica turned down the lane that led into town, trying to pay attention to the country air blowing through the truck's open windows rather than on the man beside her. He'd been staring at her nonstop since she came outside today. She already felt self-conscious, all dolled up, and Troy's attitude made it worse. She wasn't sure if he was judging her or...something else, but his gaze made her feel overheated, uncomfortable.

Or maybe the problem was that she'd dressed up on purpose, with the notion of finding a dad—or a temporary stand-in for one—to fulfill Xavier's wish. The thought of putting herself out there for men to approach made her feel slightly ill; dating was the last thing she wanted to do. And it wasn't likely that anyone would want damaged goods like her, not likely she'd attract interest, but she had to try. She'd promised herself to make her son's days happy, since she couldn't be sure how many he had left, and she was going to do her best.

Once they reached the residential area that surrounded Rescue River's downtown, Angelica's stomach knotted. Everyone in town knew about what she'd done to Troy, their beloved high school quarterback and brilliant veterinarian and all-around good guy. No doubt her own reputation was in the gutter.

There was the town's famous sign, dating back to Civil War years when the tiny farm community had been home to several safe houses on the Underground Railroad:

Rescue River, Ohio.

All Are Welcome, All Are Safe.

Funny, she didn't feel so safe now. She cruised past the bank and the feed store, and then thoughts of herself vanished when she saw the line of people snaking around the building that housed Troy's veterinary practice. "Wow. Looks like your clinic is a success."

"Lots of people struggling these days."

"It's free?"

He nodded, pointed. "Park right in front. They always save me a place."

She noticed a few familiar faces turning toward their truck. Someone ran to take a lawn chair out of the single remaining parking spot and she pulled in, stopped and went around to see if Troy needed help getting out. But he'd already hopped down, so she grabbed his crutches out of the back and took them to him.

"Here." She handed him the crutches, and his large, calloused hand brushed hers.

Something fluttered inside her chest. She yanked her hand back, dropping a crutch in the process.

"Hey, that you, Angie? Little Angie?"

She turned to see a tall, skinny man, his thin hair pulled back in a ponytail, his face stubbly. She cocked her head to one side. "Derek? Derek Moseley?"

"It *is* you!" He flung an easy arm around her and she shrugged away, and then suddenly Troy was there, stepping between them. "Whoa, my friend," he said. "Easy on my assistant."

"I'm fine!" She took another sidestep away.

Derek lifted his hands like stop signs. "Just saying hi to my old buddy's little sister, Doc." He turned to Angelica. "Girl, I ain't seen you in ages. How's your brother?"

She shook her head. "I don't see him much myself. He's overseas, doing mission work."

"Carlo? A missionary?"

"Well, something like that." In reality, her brother, Carlo, was halfway between a missionary and a mercenary, taking the word of God to people in remote areas where he was as likely to be met with a machete as a welcome.

"Carlo's a great guy. Tell him I said hello."

"I will." That evaluation was spot-on—her brother was a great guy. Carlo was the one who'd gone to Gramps and told him he had to take her in when their parents' behavior had gone way out of control. He'd been sixteen; she'd been nine. He'd gone out on his own then, had his dark and dangerous times, but now he'd found Jesus and reformed. He wrote often, sent money even though she told him not to, probably more than he could afford. But she didn't see him enough and she wished he'd come home. Especially now, with Xavier's health so bad.

A shuffling sound broke into her consciousness. She looked around for Troy and saw him working his way toward the clinic on his crutches, large medical bag clutched awkwardly at his side.

She hurried to him. "Here, let me carry that."

"I can get it."

Stepping in front of him, she took hold of the bag. "Probably, but not very well. This is what you're paying me for."

He held on to the bag a second longer and then let it go. "Fine."

As they walked toward the clinic, people greeted Troy, thanked him for being there, asked about his leg. The line seemed endless. Most people held dogs on leads, but a few had cat carriers. One man sat on a bench beside an open-topped cardboard box holding a chicken.

How would Troy ever take care of all these people? "The clinic's only until noon, right? Do you have help?"

"A vet tech, whenever he gets here. And I stay until I've seen everyone. We work hard. You up for this?"

She was and they did work hard; he wasn't lying. The morning flew by with pet after pet. She held leashes for Pomeranians and pit bulls, got scratched by a frightened tomcat with a ripped ear and comforted a twenty-something girl who cried when her two fluffy fur-ball puppies, one black and one white, had to get shots. She wrote down the particulars of rescue situations people told Troy about. Dogs needed rabies shots and ear medicine, X-rays and spaying. If it was something he couldn't do right at the moment, he made a plan to do it later in the week.

She asked once, "Can you even do surgery, with your leg?"

"My leg doesn't hurt as much as that guy's hurting," he said, scratching the droopy ears of a basset-beagle mix with a swollen stomach. The owner was pretty sure he'd swallowed a baby's Binky. "Feed him canned pumpkin to help things along," he told the owner. "If he doesn't pass it within three days, or if he's in more pain, call me."

A fiftysomething lady came in with a small, scruffy white dog wrapped in a towel. "Afraid he's got to be put to sleep, Doc." Her voice broke as she lifted the skinny animal to the metal exam table.

Angelica moved closer and patted the woman's back, feeling completely ineffectual. She wanted to help, but sometimes there wasn't anything you could do.

"Let's not jump to that conclusion." Troy picked up the whimpering little creature, ignoring its feeble effort to bite at him. He felt carefully around the dog's abdomen and examined its eyes and ears. "I'm guessing pancreatitis," he said finally, "but we'll need to do some blood work to be sure."

"What's that mean, Doc?" the woman asked. "I don't have much extra money…and I don't want him to suffer." She buried her face in her hands.

Angelica's throat ached. She could identify. She found a box of tissues and brought it over.

"Hey." Troy put a hand on the woman's shoulder.

"Let's give treatment a try. If you can't afford the medicine, we'll work something out."

"Is he even likely to live?"

"Fifty-fifty," Troy admitted. "But I'm not a quitter. We can bring the dog to the farm if you don't have time to do the treatments. Aren't you a night waitress out at the truck stop?"

She nodded. "That's the other thing. I can't stick around home to care for him. I gotta work to pay my rent."

"Let me take him to the farm, then," Troy said. "It's worth it. He may have years of running around left. Don't you want me to try?"

"You'd really do that for him?" Hope lit the woman's face as she carefully picked up the little dog and cradled him to her chest. When she looked up, her eyes shone. "You don't know how much this means to me, Doc. He's been with me through two divorces and losing my day job and a bout with cancer. I want to be able to give back to him. I'll donate all my tips when I get them."

"Give what you can. That's all I ask." He told Angelica what to do next and took the dog away.

A man in jeans and a scrub top strode into the clinic then, and Angelica studied him as he greeted Troy. He must be the vet tech they'd been waiting for.

"Buck," Troy said. "How goes it?"

Buck. So that was why he looked so familiar—he was an old classmate, one of the nicer boys. "Hey," she greeted him. "Remember me?"

"Is that you, Angie?" A smile lit his eyes. "Haven't seen you in forever. How's your grandpa?"

They chatted for a few minutes while Troy entered data into a computer, preparing for the next appointment. Buck kept smiling and stepped a little closer, and Angelica recognized what was happening: he *like* liked her, as her girlfriends back in Boston would say. She took a step away.

And then it dawned on her: Buck would be a perfect guy to help fulfill Xavier's dream. Oh, not to marry, she couldn't go that far, but if she could find a nice, harmless man to hang out with some in the evenings, watch some family shows with, play board games with…that didn't sound half-bad. Xavier would be thrilled.

Come on, flirt with the man. You used to be good at it.

But she barely remembered how to talk to a man that way. And anyway, it felt like lying. How could she pretend to have an interest in a nice guy like Buck just to make her son happy? Maybe this wasn't such a good plan after all.

When Troy came back, ready for the next patient, Buck cocked his head to one side. "Are you two together? I remember you used to—"

"No!" they both said at the same time.

"Whoa, okay! I just thought you were engaged, back in the day."

Angelica felt her face heat. "I'm just his assistant while he gets back on his feet," she explained as the next patient came in.

"Glad to hear you've come to your senses about him," Buck joked.

Troy's lips tightened and he turned away, limping over to greet a couple with a cat carrier who'd just walked in.

"You back in town for a while?" Buck looked at Angelica with sharpened interest.

"Yes. For a…a little while."

"Long enough to have dinner with an old friend?"

He was asking her out. To dinner, and really, what would be the harm? This was what she wanted.

"Sure," she said. "I'll have dinner with you."

"Saturday night? Where are you staying?" He touched her shoulder to usher her over to the side of the exam area, and she forced herself not to pull away.

They agreed on a time and exchanged phones to punch in numbers.

When she looked up, Troy was watching them, eyes narrowed, jaw set.

She shook her hair back. There was no reason for him to feel possessive. What had been between them was long gone.

So why did she feel so guilty?

Three

By the time they'd gotten back to the farm, it was suppertime and Troy's blood was boiling as hot as the pot of pasta on the stove.

Did Angelica have to make her date plans right in front of him? And with Buck Armstrong?

But it wasn't his business, and he had no reason to care. He just needed some time to himself.

Which apparently he wasn't going to get, because the minute they set down their things, Xavier was pulling at his hand. "Mr. Troy, Mr. Troy, we're all going to have dinner together!"

Great. He smiled down at the boy. How was he going to get out of this?

"Xavier, honey." Angelica knelt down beside her son. "We'll have dinner at the bunkhouse. We can't impose."

She tugged the ponytail holder out of her hair, and the shiny locks flowed down her back. Her hand kneaded Xavier's shoulder. She was all loving mother.

And all woman.

"But, Mama! Wait till you see what Miss Lou Ann and me cooked!"

Lou Ann rubbed Xavier's bald head. "I'm sorry, Angelica. I told him we could probably all eat together. We picked zucchini and tomatoes from the garden and cooked up some of that ratatouille."

"And we made a meat loaf, and I got to mix it up with my hands!"

The boy sounded so happy. Troy's throat tightened as he thought about how Angelica must feel, cherishing every moment with him and wondering at the same time whether he'd ever make meat loaf again, whether this was the last chance for this particular activity.

Angelica glanced up at him, eyebrows raised. "Maybe we'll get together another time. Mr. Troy's been working all day and he's tired. Let's let him rest."

What was he supposed to do now, squash down all of this joy? And he had to admit that the thought of having company for dinner in the farmhouse kitchen didn't sound half-bad, except that the pretty woman opposite him was hankering after another man.

At the thought of Angelica dating Buck Armstrong, something dark twisted his insides. With everything he knew about Buck, he should warn her off, and yet it would serve her right to go out with him and find out what he was really like.

"Can we stay, Mr. Troy?"

He looked at the boy's hopeful eyes. "Of course." His words sounded so grudging that he added, "Sounds like a good meal you fixed."

"It is good, and wait till you see dessert!"

By the time Xavier helped Lou Ann serve dessert—sliced pound cake, topped with berries and whipped cream—he looked beat. But his smile was joyous. "I had so much fun this afternoon, Mama!"

Troy praised the food, which was really good, thanks he was sure to Lou Ann's guidance. But his stomach was turning, wouldn't let him really enjoy it.

Angelica looked beautiful at the other end of the table, her black hair tumbling down past her shoulders and her cheeks pink as apples. And now, with Xavier so happy, she didn't seem as worried as usual; the little line that tended to live between her eyebrows was gone, and her smile flashed frequently as Xavier described all that he and Lou Ann had done that day.

Troy had always wanted this. He wanted a warm, beautiful woman and cute, enthusiastic children at his table, wanted to be the man of the family. And this sweet, feisty pair seemed to fit right into his home and his heart. But he had to keep reminding himself that this wasn't his and it wouldn't last.

Looking at Xavier, he couldn't believe the child had been so sick and might relapse at any moment. Yeah, he was drooping, getting tired, but he was so full of life that it made no sense that God might take him away.

Any more than it made sense that God would put him and his siblings in a loveless family, let alone give Angelica all the heartaches she'd endured growing up, but that was God for you—making sense wasn't what He was about. That was why Troy had stopped trusting Him, starting taking most things into his own hands. He believed, sure; he just didn't trust. And he sure didn't want to join the men's Bible study his friend Dion was always bugging him about.

"This little one needs to get to bed," Lou Ann said. "Troy, I know you can't carry much with those crutches, but why don't you at least help her with the doors and such?"

"Oh, you don't have to—" Angelica stood, looking suddenly uncomfortable. "We've already taken too much of your time. We can make it."

But Troy moved to intercept her protest. "Come on, pal. Let's get you out to bed."

Angelica started gathering Xavier's pills and toys and snacks together, stuffing them into a Spider-Man backpack. Before she could bend to pick Xavier up, Troy leaned on one crutch, steadied himself with a hip against the table and picked up the boy himself. He was amazingly light. He nestled right against Troy's chest and Troy felt his heart break a little. He glanced over at Angelica and saw that she had tears in her eyes. "Ready?" he asked. Then, gently, he put her son in her arms, taking the boy's backpack to carry himself.

She bit her lip, turned and headed off, and he grabbed his crutches and followed her. They walked out to the bunkhouse together and Troy helped Angelica lay Xavier in his bed, noticing the homey touches Angelica had put around—a teddy bear, a poster of a baseball player, a hand-knitted afghan in shades of blue and brown. It was a boy's room, and it should be filling up with trophies from Little League games. They said every kid got a trophy these days, and wasn't that awful? But not Xavier. This kid hadn't had the opportunity to play baseball.

Not yet.

Angelica knelt beside the bed. "Let's thank God for today."

"Thank You, God, for letting me cook dinner. And for Lou Ann. And the dogs."

Angelica was holding Xavier's hand. "Thank You for giving us food and love and each other."

"Bless all the people who don't have so much," they said together.

"And, God, please get me a daddy before..." Xavier trailed off, turned over.

Whoa. Troy's throat tightened.

"Night, sweetie, sleep tight." Angelica's voice sounded choked.

"Don't let the bedbugs... Love you, Mama." The words were fading off and the boy was asleep.

They both stood looking down at him, Troy on one side of the bed and Angelica on the other.

"Did he say he wants a...dad?" Troy ventured finally.

Angelica nodded.

"Does his dad ever spend time with him?"

She looked up at him. "No. Never."

"Does he even know him?"

Her lips tightened. "I... Look, Troy, I don't want to talk about that."

"Sure." But he'd like to strangle the guy who'd loved and left her, and not just because he remembered how difficult it had been to keep his hands off Angelica back when they were engaged. He took a deep breath and loosened his tightly clasped fists. She'd gotten pregnant with Xavier right around the time she left town, so was Xavier's dad—the jerk—from here or from elsewhere? She hadn't married him, apparently, but... "If the guy knew Xavier, knew what he was like and what he's facing, surely he'd be willing—"

"No."

"No?"

"Just...no, okay?" She stood and stalked out to the living room, and Troy wondered whether he'd ever stop putting his plaster-covered foot in his mouth around her.

* * *

The next Saturday, Angelica touched up her hair with a curling wand and applied blush and mascara. And tried not to throw up.

She didn't want to go out on a date. But there was no other way to get Xavier off her case.

In fact, he was beside her now, hugging her leg. "You never had a date before, Mama."

She laughed. "Yes, I did. Back in the day. Before you."

"Did you go on dates with my dad?"

All Xavier knew was that his father had died. He hadn't ever asked whether Angelica and his father had been married, and Angelica hoped he didn't go there any time soon. For now, she would stick as close to the truth as possible. "No, not with him, but with a few other guys." She tried to deflect his attention. "Just like I'm doing now. Do I look all right?"

"You're beautiful, Mama."

She hugged him. "Thanks, Zavey Davey. You're kinda cute yourself."

"Do I get to meet him? Because I want to see, you know, if he's the right kind of guy for us."

"My little protector. You can meet him sometime, but not now. Miss Lou Ann is going to come over and play with you. And I think I hear her now."

Sure enough, there was a knock on the bunkhouse door. Xavier ran over to get it while Angelica fussed with herself a little more. She'd much rather just stay home with Xavier tonight. What if Buck tried something? She knew him to be a nice guy, but still…

"Well, how's my little friend for the evening?" Lou Ann asked, pinching Xavier's cheek. "You set up for a

Candy Land marathon, or are we building a fort out of sheets and chairs?"

"You'll build a fort with me?" Xavier's eyes turned worshipful. "Mom always says it's too messy."

"It's only too messy if we don't clean up later. And we will, right?"

"Right. I'll get the extra sheets."

As soon as he was out of the room, Lou Ann turned to Angelica. "You look pretty," she said. "Somebody's already cranky, and when he sees you looking like that..." She smacked her lips. "Sparks are gonna fly."

That was the last thing she needed. Her face heated and she changed the subject. "Xavier can stay up until eight-thirty. He gets his meds and a snack half an hour before bed." She showed Lou Ann the pills and the basket of approved snacks.

"That's easy. Don't worry about us." Lou Ann leaned back and looked out the window. "I think your friend just pulled in."

"I wanna see him!" Xavier rushed toward the window, dropping the stack of sheets he'd been carrying.

"Well," Lou Ann said, "that's just fine, because I want to claim the best spot in the fort."

Xavier spun back to Lou Ann. "I'm king of the fort!"

"You'd better get over here and help me, then."

Thank you, Angelica mouthed to Lou Ann, and slipped out the door.

Buck emerged from his black pickup, looking good from his long jean-clad legs to his slightly shaggy brown curls. Any girl would feel fortunate to be dating such a cute guy, Angelica told herself, trying to lighten the lead weight in her stomach.

He's a nice guy. And it's for Xavier. "Hi there!"

"Well, don't you look pretty!" He walked toward her, loose limbed.

To her right, the front door of the main house opened. Troy. He came out on the porch and stood, arms crossed. For all the world as if he were her father.

She narrowed her eyes at him, trying to ignore his rougher style of handsome, the way his broad shoulders, leaning on his crutches, strained the seams of his shirt. She was through with Troy Hinton, and he was most certainly through with her, wouldn't want anything to do with her if he knew the truth.

She deliberately returned her attention to Buck. He reached her and opened his arms.

Really? Was a big hug normal on a first date? It had been so long…and she'd been so young… She took a deep breath and allowed him to hug her, at the same time wrinkling her nose. Something was wrong…

"Baby, it's great to see you. Man, feels good to hug a woman." Buck's words were slurred. And yes, that smell was alcohol, covered with a whole lot of peppermint.

She tried to pull back, but he didn't let go.

Panic rose in her. She stepped hard onto his foot. "Let go," she said, loud, right in his ear.

From the corner of her eye, the sight of Troy made her feel secure.

"Sorry!" Buck stepped back. "I didn't mean… I was just glad…oh man, you look so good." He moved as though he was going to hug her again.

She sidestepped. "Buck. How much have you had to drink?"

"What?" He put an arm around her and started guiding her toward his truck. "I had a drink before I came over. One drink. Don't get uptight."

Could that be true? Without a doubt, she was uptight around men. But this felt wrong in a different way. "Wait a minute. I...I think we should talk a little bit before we go."

"Sure!" He shifted direction, guiding her toward a bench and plopping down too hard, knocking into her so that she sat down hard, too.

She drew in a breath and let it out in a sigh. He was drunk, all right. It wasn't just her being paranoid. But now, how did she get rid of him?

"I really like you, Angelica," he said, putting an arm around her. He pulled her closer.

She scooted away. "Look, Buck, I can't... I don't think I can go out with you. You've had too much to drink."

"One drink!" He sounded irritated.

Angelica stood and backed away. Couldn't something, just once, be easy? "Sorry, friend, but I can't get in the truck with you. And you shouldn't be driving, either."

There was a sound of booted feet, and then Troy was beside her. "She's right, Buck."

"What you doing here, Hinton?"

"I live here, as you very well know."

"Well, I'm taking this little lady out for a meal, once—"

"You're not going anywhere except home. As soon as your sister gets here to pick you up."

"Oh man, you didn't call Lacey!" Buck staggered to his feet, his hand going to his pocket. He pulled out truck keys. "This has been a bust."

Angelica glanced at Troy, willing him to let her handle it. She had plenty of experience with drunk people, starting with her own parents. "Can I see the car keys a minute?"

He held them out, hope lighting up his face. "You gonna come after all? I'll let you drive."

She took the keys. "I'm not going, and sorry, but you're not fit to drive yourself, either."

He lunged to get them back and Troy stuck out a crutch to trip him. "You're not welcome on this property until you're sober."

Angelica kept backing off while, in the distance, a Jeep made clouds on the dusty road. That must be Buck's sister.

So she could go home now. Back inside. Face Xavier and tell him the date was off.

Except she couldn't, because tears were filling her eyes and blurring her vision. She blinked hard and backed up as far as the porch steps while Troy greeted the woman who'd squealed up in the Jeep.

The woman pushed past Troy, poked a finger in Buck's chest and proceeded to chew him out. Then she and Troy helped him into the passenger seat. They stood beside the Jeep for a minute, talking.

When Angelica turned away, she realized that Xavier could see her here if he looked out the window. Hopefully he was too deep into fort-building to notice, but she wasn't ready to see him and she couldn't take the risk. She headed out to the kennels at a jog. Grabbed one of the pit bulls she'd been working with, a black-and-white beauty named Sheena, attached a leash to her and started walking down the field road as unwanted, annoying tears came faster and faster.

She sank to her knees beside a wooden fence post,

willing the tears to stop, hugging the dog that licked her cheek with canine concern.

"Get yourself together, girlie. Nobody said life's a tea party."

Gramps's words, harsh but kindly meant, had guided her through the storms of adolescence and often echoed in her mind.

Today, for some reason, they didn't help. She squeezed her eyes shut and tried to pray, but the tears kept coming.

After long moments, one of the verses she'd memorized during Xavier's treatment came into her mind.

Fear not, for I am with you; be not dismayed, for I am your God; I will strengthen you, I will help you, I will uphold you with My righteous right hand.

Slowly, peace, or at least resignation, started to return. But every time she thought about Xavier and how disappointed he'd be, the tears overflowed again.

A hand gripped her shoulder, making her start violently. "You that upset about Buck?" Troy asked.

She shook her head, fighting for control. It wasn't about Buck, not really. He was a small disappointment in the midst of a lot of big ones, but it was enough to push her over the edge. She couldn't handle the possibility of losing Xavier, the only good thing in her life, and yet she had to handle it. And she had to stay strong and positive for him.

It was pretty much her mantra. She breathed in, breathed out. *Stay strong*, she told herself. *Stay strong.*

A couple of minutes later she was able to accept Troy's outstretched hand and climb to her feet. He took the dog leash from her and handed her an ancient-looking, soft bandanna. "It's not pretty, but it's clean."

She nodded and wiped her eyes and nose and came back into herself enough to be embarrassed at how she must look. She wasn't one of those pretty, leak-a-few-tears criers; she knew her eyes must be red and puffy, and she honked when she blew her nose. "Sorry," she said to him.

"For what?"

She shook her head, and by unspoken agreement they started walking. "Sorry to break down."

"You're entitled."

The sun was setting now, sending pink streaks across the sky, and a slight breeze cooled the air. Crickets harmonized with bullfrogs in a gentle rise and fall. Angelica breathed in air so pungent with hay and summer flowers that she could almost taste it, and slowly the familiar landscape brought her calm.

"You know," Troy ventured after a few minutes, "Buck Armstrong's not really worth all that emotion. Not these days. If I'd known you were this into dating him, I might have warned you he has a drinking problem."

She laughed, and that made her cry a little more, and she wiped her eyes. "It's not really about Buck."

He didn't say anything for a minute. Then he gave her shoulder a gentle squeeze. "You've got a lot on your plate."

"I've got a plan, is what I've got," she said, "and I was hoping Buck could be a part of it." Briefly, she explained her intention of finding a stand-in dad for Xavier.

Troy shook his head. "That's not going to work."

"What do you mean?"

"He's a smart kid. He'll know. You can't just pretend you're dating someone so that he'll think he's getting a dad."

"I can if I want to." They came to a crossroads and she glanced around. "I'm not ready to go back home and admit defeat yet, and I don't want him looking out the window and seeing me cry."

"Come the back way, by the kennel."

Sheena, the dog she'd brought with her, jumped at a squirrel, and Troy let her off the lead to chase it. She romped happily, ears flopping.

"So you think getting a dad will make Xavier happy? Even if it's a fake dad?"

"It's not fake! Or, well, it is, but for a good reason." She reached into her pocket and pulled out the picture she always carried, Xavier in happier times. "Look at that face! For all I know, he'll never be really healthy again." She cleared her throat. "If I can make his life happy, I'm going to do it."

He studied the picture. "He played Little League?"

She swallowed hard around the lump in her throat. "T-ball. He'd just started when he was diagnosed. He had one season."

"He started young."

She nodded. "They let him start a few weeks before his birthday, even though officially they aren't supposed to start until they turn four."

"Because he was sick?"

She shook her head. "Because he was so good. He loved it." Tears rushed to her eyes again and she put her hands to her face.

"Hey." He took the sloppy bandanna from her hand, wiped her eyes and nose as if she were a child, and pulled her to his chest. And for just a minute, after a reflexive flinch, Angelica let herself enjoy the feeling. His chest was broad and strong, and she heard the slow beating of his heart. She aligned her breath with his and it steadied her, calmed her.

In just a minute, she'd back away. Because this was dangerous and it wasn't going anywhere. Troy wouldn't want a woman like Angelica, not really, so letting an attraction build between them was a huge mistake.

Troy patted Angelica's back and breathed in the strawberry scent of her hair, trying to remind himself why he needed to be careful.

He wanted to help Angelica and Xavier in the worst way. His heart was all in with this little family. But that heart was broken, wounded, not whole.

He felt her stiffen in his arms, as though she was just realizing how close he was. For the thousandth time since he'd reencountered her, he wondered about her skittishness around men. Or was it just around him? No, he'd seen her tense up when Armstrong had hugged her, too.

Carefully, he held her upper arms and stepped away. Her face was blotched and wet, but she still looked beautiful. Her Western-style shirt was unbuttoned down to a modest V, sleeves rolled up to reveal tanned forearms. Her jeans clung to her slim figure. Intricate silver earrings hung from her ears, sparkling against her wavy black hair.

"Come on," he said gruffly, "let's go in the house. We'll get you something to drink."

"Okay." She looked up at him, her eyes vulnerable, and he wanted nothing more than to protect her.

Don't go there, fool.

They walked back along the country road as the last bit of sun set in a golden haze. A few dogs barked out their farewell to the day. At the kennel, they put Sheena back inside, and then he led Angelica up to the house.

He loved his farm, his dogs, his life. He had so much. But what right did he have to be happy when Angelica's problems were so big?

How could he help her?

An idea slammed into him, almost an audible voice. *You could marry her.*

Immediately he squelched the notion. Ridiculous. No way. He wouldn't go down that path. Not again, not after what she'd done to him.

And even outside of the way she'd dumped him, he'd never seen a good marriage. He didn't know how to be married; didn't know how to relate to people that way; didn't know how to keep a woman happy or make it last. He didn't want to be like his dad, the person who failed his wife. He didn't want to let Xavier down.

But the point was, he thought as he held the door for her, Xavier might not have the time to be let down. Xavier needed and wanted a dad now, and Troy already knew the boy liked him.

As they walked into the kitchen, he remembered proposing to Angelica the last time. Then he'd been all about wanting to impress her, to sweep her away. He'd hired Samantha Weston, who usually used her small plane for crop dusting, to sky-write his proposal at sunset during an all-town Memorial Day picnic. Angelica had laughed, and cried, and joyously accepted. Her friends had clustered around them, and he'd presented her with a diamond way too big for a new vet with school loans to pay off.

He still had that ring, come to think of it. He'd stuffed it in his sock drawer when she mailed it back to him, and he'd never looked at it again.

It was upstairs right now. He could go and get it. Help her handle this massive challenge life had given her. And Xavier... Boy, did he want to help that kid!

Angelica perched on a kitchen stool and rested her chin in her hands. "I guess the idea of Buck as a pretend husband does seem kinda crazy, when I think about it," she admitted. "Anyway, enough about me. How long has Buck had a drinking problem?"

"Since he lost his wife and child," Troy said. "Not only that, but he served a couple of tours in Afghanistan. Which is why I cut the guy a break and let him work at my weekend clinic. I've offered him a full-time job, too, but only if he'll stay sober for six months first. So far, he hasn't been able to do that."

"That's so sad." She bit her lip. "I hope he's going to be okay tonight. I felt bad, but there was no way I was getting into a truck with him."

"And no way he could be Xavier's pseudodad."

"No."

He cracked open a Pepsi and handed it to her. "Here. Sugar and caffeine. It'll make you feel better."

"Always. Thanks." She swung her feet. "Remember buying me a Coke at the drugstore, that very first time we went out?"

He nodded. "And I remember how you sat there drinking it and explaining to me your dating rules. No kissing until the third date. No parking. No staying out past eleven."

"I know, and it wasn't even Gramps making those rules, it was me. I was so scared of getting myself into the same bad situations that landed my folks in trouble. Plus, my brother told me I should be careful about you. Since you were an older man and all." She smiled up at him through her lashes.

His heart rate shot through the ceiling. "Your brother was protective," he said, trying to keep his voice—and his thoughts—on something other than how pretty she was. One question still nagged at him: if she'd had all those rules, then how had she ended up unmarried and pregnant?

"Xavier really misses my brother. Carlo lived near us in Boston for a while, and he's the one who got Xavier involved in T-ball. He did the whole male influence thing, until he got the call to go overseas." She flashed Troy a smile. "If I keep thinking about Carlo I'll get sad again. Save me, Bull!" She slid off the stool and sat cross-legged on the floor. The old bulldog climbed into her lap, and she leaned down and let him lick her face.

"Whoa, Bull, be a gentleman! She'll pass out from your breath!" But he couldn't help enjoying Angelica's affectionate attitude toward his dog. A lot of women didn't want a smelly old dog anywhere around their stockings and fancy dresses, but Angelica was a blue-jeans girl from way back.

He sank down beside her, petting Bull. "So, what are you going to do now? About your plan, I mean?"

She shook her head. "I don't know. I guess I'll have to disappoint him. I mean, I'm not the most outgoing person when it comes to dating, and I don't want to mislead any guys about where it's all headed." She forced a smile. "Know any eligible bachelors I could snare?"

"Me," he heard himself saying. "You could marry me."

Four

As he watched the color drain from Angelica's face, Troy's chest tightened and he wished he could take back his words. What had he just said? What had he been thinking?

Cynical doubts kicked at the crazy adrenaline rush coursing through his body. Why would he want to propose to Angelica again when she'd dumped him without explanation before? He'd already done what he could to help her and her son. He'd given her a job and provided a place to live, but this was way beyond the call of duty.

He opened his mouth to say so, but she held up a hand.

"Look, it's amazingly kind of you to offer that, especially after…after everything. You've already done so much for us. But I could never expect anything like that. And I couldn't marry someone without…"

He crossed his arms over his chest. "Without loving him?"

"I was going to say…" She lowered her head and let out a sigh. "Never mind."

Suddenly warm, he stood, grabbed a crutch

and limped across the room. He flicked on the air-conditioning and fiddled with the thermostat on the wall.

She'd brought up all the very same objections he'd had himself. She'd given him a way to back out.

So why did he feel so let down?

She scrambled to her feet, watching him as if he were a wild animal she had to protect herself from. All comfort, all closeness between them was gone. "Um, I should go." Her hand on the screen door handle, she stilled. "Uh-oh."

"What's wrong?" He came up behind her and looked over her shoulder out the door as the scent of her hair tickled his nose.

In the outdoor floodlight he saw Xavier was running toward the house, his face furrowed. Teary hiccups became more audible as he got closer. Behind him, Lou Ann followed at a dangerously fast pace, huffing and puffing and calling the boy.

Angelica opened the screen door just as Xavier got to the top of the porch steps. She knelt, and Xavier ran into her arms, causing her to reel backward.

Troy balanced on his crutch and reached out to steady the pair. "Whoa there, partner, slow down!"

"Is it true?" Xavier demanded. "What Miss Lou Ann said?"

At that moment the lady in question arrived at the top of the front porch steps. "Xavier!" She paused for breath. "You come...when I call you. I'm sorry," she added, turning to Angelica. "I said something I shouldn't have. It upset him."

"She said it wasn't going to work out for that man to be my daddy, and I might not get a daddy!"

"Come on in, baby." Angelica scooped her son into her arms and struggled to her feet, shrugging off Troy's attempt to help her. She carried Xavier inside. "Is it okay if we talk a minute in here?"

"Sure."

And then he watched her focus entirely on her son. She sat down on the couch and pulled the boy, all angular arms and long legs, in her lap. "So tell me more about those tears, mister."

"I want a daddy!" he sulked. "I thought you were gonna get me one."

She rubbed his hairless head. "I know how much you want a dad. You want to be like other kids."

"I want somebody to play T-ball with me and take me fishing." Behind the words, Troy heard a poignant yearning for all Xavier wanted and might not get, all he'd missed during the long months of treatment.

"I know," Angelica said, rocking a little. "I know, honey."

"So why did you send that man away?"

She shot a glance at Troy. "He wasn't feeling well."

"So he might come back when he's better?"

Slowly, Angelica shook her head. "No, honey. Turns out he's not right for us."

Tears welled in the boy's eyes again, but she pulled his head against her chest. "Shh. I know it's hard, but we have to let God do His work. He takes care of us, remember?"

"Sometimes He does a bad job!"

Angelica chuckled, a low vibration that brushed along Troy's nerve endings. "He never does a bad job, sweetie. Sometimes you and I can't understand His ways, but He's always taking care of us. We can relax because of that."

Her voice sounded totally confident, totally sure, and Troy wished for some of that certainty for himself.

She was such a good mother. She knew exactly how to reach her son, even when he was upset. She could listen, handle his bratty moments and get him to laugh. She was meant to mother this boy, and most of the resentment Troy felt about her pregnancy fell away. Whatever had happened, whatever mistakes she'd made, she'd paid for them. And as she said, God was always taking care of things. He'd given one sick young boy the perfect mother.

Who, when she met his eyes over the child's head and gave him a little smile, looked like the perfect wife, as well.

A week later, Angelica was chopping vegetables for stew and marveling at how quickly they'd settled into a routine. Lou Ann took an online class every Tuesday and Thursday, so those days, Angelica started dinner for all of them while Xavier rested.

As she chopped the last carrot, though, Xavier burst into the kitchen. "Can I go outside and see Mr. Troy and the dogs?"

Thrilled to see this sign of improved energy, she nonetheless narrowed her eyes at him. "What are you doing off the couch? You're supposed to rest from two to four every afternoon. Doctor's orders."

"I don't want to rest anymore. Besides, it's almost four."

"Is it really?" She looked at the clock. "Three-thirty isn't four, buster." But it was close. Where had the time gone? Troy had been wonderful about letting her set up a flexible schedule around Xavier, but she needed to get back out to the kennels at four. She bit the inside of her cheek.

"I want to go outside." Xavier's lower lip pushed out.

"That's not going to work, honey. After you rest, you need to stay in here with Miss Lou Ann so I can work."

"But I wanna go outside!" Xavier yelled.

Angelica dried her hands on a dishcloth and shot up a prayer for patience. Then she knelt in front of Xavier. "Inside voice and respect, please."

"Sorry." He didn't sound it, but she stood up anyway. With a sick kid, you had to choose your battles.

"I see someone's feeling better." Troy limped into the kitchen, wearing jeans and a collared shirt. His shoulder muscles flexed as he hopped nimbly over on his crutches.

He looks good! was her first thought, and it made her cheeks heat up. "I didn't know you were here today. Thought you had vet patients in town."

"I come home early on Thursdays. Snagged a ride with our receptionist." He was looking at her steadily, eyebrows raised a little, as if he could read her mind. How embarrassing!

Xavier tugged at his leg. "Can I come outside with you, Mr. Troy? Please?"

"It's okay with me, buddy." Troy reached down to pat Xavier's shoulder. "But what does your mom say? She's the boss."

"I can't let him follow you around and bother you."

"I think you and Xavier were at the doctor's last week, so you wouldn't know that Thursdays are special. I do some other stuff."

"Stuff I can do with you?" Xavier was staring up at Troy, eyes wide and pleading.

Angelica bit back a smile. Her son, the master manipulator. "Honey, we have to respect—"

"Actually," Troy interrupted, "this might be a really good activity for Xavier. If you're willing."

"What is it?" She covered the stew pot and lowered the gas heat.

"Dog training. Takes a lot of patience." He winked at her. "Some kid training, too. Let him come with me, and then you come out, too, in a little while. I may need some help."

"Please, Mom?"

She threw up her hands. "I give up. Go ahead."

She watched out the window as Xavier and Troy walked off together. Troy was getting more and more agile with his crutches, and she suspected he'd be off them soon. His head was inclined to hear what Xavier was saying, and as for her son, he was chattering away so joyously that she was glad she'd let him go with Troy.

She wanted him to be happy, and right now, somehow, that happiness was all tied up in Troy. Troy and the dogs. Pray God it would last.

"They look more like father and son than most father and sons," Lou Ann said, walking into the room with an armload of books and paperwork. "That's good for Troy. He didn't have a great relationship with his own dad. Still doesn't, for that matter."

"I remember, but I never knew why." Angelica reached down to scratch Bull's head. "Go back to your bed, buddy. I'm done cooking, and Daddy says no table scraps for you."

"That doesn't keep him from begging, though." Lou

Ann put her laptop and books on the built-in desk in the corner of the kitchen. "Clyde Hinton is a hard man, especially with his boys. His older son fought back, and that's why the two of them can work together now. Troy, though, wasn't having any of it. He shut the door on his dad a long time ago. They hardly ever see each other."

"Interesting." During their engagement, she and Troy hadn't visited much with his father, and the little time they'd spent at Troy's family home was stiff and uncomfortable.

Settling into a chair at the kitchen table, Lou Ann put her feet up on one of the other chairs and stretched. "Where's Xavier going, anyway? I'm ready to play some *Extreme Flight Simulator* with him. Clear my brain from all that psychology."

"Troy's taking him out to the kennels." Angelica turned to the woman who was rapidly becoming a good friend. "I'm so impressed you're working on your degree online."

"Never had the chance before," Lou Ann said, "and it's a kick. I always did like school, just never had time to really pursue it. And Troy insists on paying for it. Says it's the least he can do since I agreed to come back to work for him."

"Wow, I didn't know that."

"There's a lot of things you don't know about that man," Lou Ann said. "He's not one to toot his own horn."

Angelica tucked that away for consideration. "He's sure being good to Xavier. Though he doesn't know what he's getting into, taking him out to the kennels. He'll have to watch him like a hawk, and he won't get any of his own work done."

"It's Thursday, isn't it?" Lou Ann glanced up at the calendar on the wall. "Thursdays, he has the rascals over. Maybe he's going to get Xavier involved with them."

"The rascals, huh?" Just what Xavier needed. "Who are they?"

One side of Lou Ann's mouth quirked up. "They're some kids I wouldn't work with to save my life, but somehow Troy has them helping at the kennel, training dogs and cleaning cages. He's a rescuer, always has been."

"Dangerous kids?" Angelica paused in the act of handing Lou Ann a cup of coffee.

"No, not dangerous. Just full of beans. Relax!" Lou Ann reached for the coffee, took a sip and put it down on the table. "Thanks, hon. There are some real poor folks in this county. Kids who live on hardscrabble farms, hill people just up from down South, migrants who've set up their trailers at the edge of some field."

"Sounds like the way I grew up," Angelica said wryly.

"That's right." Lou Ann looked thoughtful for a minute. "Anyway, when Troy was…well, when he went through a rough spot a while back, Pastor Ricky approached him about setting up a program for those kids. Troy went along, because a lot of them hadn't a notion of the right way to take care of a dog. It's grown, and now he's got ten or twelve coming every week to help out."

"That's amazing, with everything else he does."

"He'd help anyone in the world. What doesn't come so easy to him is taking help himself."

"I'm going to go out." Angelica rinsed the cutting

board and stood it in the drainer. "Just as soon as I get those bathrooms clean."

"You go ahead now," Lou Ann said. "I can tell you're a little worried about your boy. I think you'll like what you see."

"Thanks." Impulsively, she gave the older woman a hug.

Five minutes later, Angelica was leaning on the fence outside the kennel, watching Xavier run and play with dogs and boys of all sizes, shapes and colors. He looked so happy that it took Angelica's breath away. She didn't know she was crying until Troy came up beside her and ran a light finger under each eye.

She jerked back, not comfortable with the soft, tender touch.

"You okay?"

She drew in a breath and let it out in a happy sigh. "I'm fine. And I'm so grateful to you for letting Xavier have some normal kid moments."

Troy frowned. "He doesn't get to do stuff like this often?"

She shook her head. "He's been in treatment so much that he hasn't had the chance to play with other boys. Let alone a bunch of dogs."

"It's good for the kids. They need to get their energy out in an accepting environment. And I need someone to play with the dogs. Easy there, Enrique!" he called to a boy who was roughhousing with a small white mutt a little too vigorously.

"Sorry, Señor Troy." The boy in question backed off immediately, then knelt and petted the dog.

"Hey, that's the little dog from the clinic! The owner thought he was going to die!"

Troy nodded, looking satisfied. "He's responding to the medication. He should be able to go back home within a week. I know Darlene will be glad. She calls every couple of days."

She studied Troy's profile. He helped dogs who needed it, owners who couldn't pay, kids who'd grown up without advantages. And of course, he was helping her and Xavier.

"Anyway, thanks for giving my son this opportunity."

When he looked down at her, arms propped on the fence beside hers, she realized how close together they were.

The thought she'd been squelching for the past week, the topic she'd been dodging the couple of times Troy had brought it up, burst into the front of her mind: he'd asked her to marry him just a week ago. He was a man of his word. She could have this. She could have a home, a farm, a man who liked to help others. Most of all, a father for Xavier.

But she'd struggled so long alone that being here, in this perfect life, felt scary, almost wrong. She didn't deserve it.

The other thing she'd been trying not to think about made its way to the surface. She was tainted, dirty. In his heart, Troy would want someone pure. He'd said it enough times when they were engaged—how important it was to him that she'd never been with anyone, that she'd saved herself for marriage. *"I'm a jealous guy,"* he'd said. *"I want you all for my own."*

She tore her eyes away from him, cleared her throat and focused on Xavier, who was rolling on the grass while a couple of the pit bull puppies, already bigger and steadier than they'd been a week ago, licked his face.

She had to live in the moment and focus on all the benefits this lifestyle was bringing her son. And stay as far as possible away from this man who'd proposed marriage.

Troy was a good person, even a great one, but she wasn't a rescue dog. She needed to be with a man who loved her and could accept her mistakes and her past.

"Mom!" Xavier came over, panting, two high red spots on his cheeks. "This is so much fun. Did you see how I was throwing the Frisbee with the guys?"

When he said "the guys," his tone rang with amazed, self-conscious pride. He'd never been one of the guys, but it was high time he started. And Troy was helping make that happen. "I missed your Frisbee throwing, buddy," she said, "but I'll watch it the next time, okay?"

When she glanced up at Troy to thank him again, she found him staring down at her with a look in his dark eyes that was impossible to read. Impossible to look away from, too. She caught her breath, licked her lips.

As if from a great distance, she heard Xavier calling her name, felt him tugging at her hand. "Hey, Mom, I had a great idea," he was saying.

She shook her head a little, blinked and turned to look at her son. "What's the idea, honey?"

"Do you think Mr. Troy could be my dad?"

Five

Xavier's words were still echoing in Troy's mind the next day. He was riding shotgun—man, he hated that, but the doctor hadn't yet cleared him to drive—while his friend Dion Grant drove his van. They were taking a group from their church, including Angelica and Xavier, to weed the garden at the Senior Towers.

"Do you think Mr. Troy could be my dad?"

He listened to the group's chatter as they climbed out of the van and pulled garden tools from the back. *Could* he become Xavier's dad? Angelica's husband?

It seemed as if those questions hovered in the air every time he was around Angelica. She'd never responded to his proposal, and yesterday she'd brushed aside Xavier's words and scolded the child.

But was the thought so repugnant to her? Once, she'd wanted to marry him.

Sure, she'd left him, apparently for someone else, since she immediately became pregnant. Knowing her now, he didn't think she'd cheated on him while they were together; she wouldn't have had that in her.

But if she'd fallen in love with someone else and been

too embarrassed to admit it…maybe when she'd gone to visit her aunt that summer…

The moment he emerged from the driver's seat, a small hand tugged at his. "Dad! Dad!"

"Xavier!" Angelica hurried up behind Xavier and put her hands on his shoulders. "Honey, you can't call Mr. Troy 'Dad.'" Her face was bright red, and she wouldn't meet Troy's eyes.

"It's okay." Troy patted her shoulder.

"No, it's really not." Angelica kept her voice low and nodded sideways toward the row of ladies sitting on the porch of the Senior Towers. "Let's just hope nobody heard. Come on, Zavey Davey," she said, "you have a playdate with your new friend Becka from church."

"A girl?" Xavier groaned.

"Yes, and she's a lot of fun. Her mom said you two were going to hunt for bugs in the park. She has a magnifying glass."

Xavier screwed up his face and looked thoughtful.

"And she's into soccer, so maybe you two can kick around a soccer ball."

"Okay. That's cool."

Troy watched as Angelica led her son toward a one-story house set between the Senior Towers and the town park. Her long hair was caught up in a high ponytail, and she wore old jeans and a T-shirt emblazoned with a Run for Shelter/Stop Domestic Violence logo. When had she gotten time to do a charity run, with all she had on her plate? And how did she manage to put zero time into her appearance and still look absolutely gorgeous?

"Breathe, buddy." His friend Dion gave him a light punch in the arm. "Didn't know she was your baby mama, but half the town will pretty soon."

"What? She's not my baby mama," Troy said automatically, and then met his friend's eyes. "Uh-oh. Who all heard what Xavier just said?"

"Miss Minnie Falcon, for one." Dion nodded toward the front porch of the Senior Towers.

Troy shrugged and lifted his hands, palms up. "Xavier's not my kid, but he wants me to be his dad. Guess he's decided to pretend it's so."

"You could do a lot worse than those two."

"Yeah. Except she dumped me once before, and she doesn't want anything but a professional relationship with me."

"You sure about that, my friend?"

He wasn't sure of anything and he felt too confused to discuss the subject. "Come on, we'd better start weeding or the ladies are going to outshine us."

He'd brought a low lawn chair so he could weed without bending his injured leg. Working the earth, just slightly damp from a recent rain, felt soothing to Troy, and he realized he'd been spending too much time indoors, doing paperwork and staying late at his office in town. The dirt was warm and pungent with an oniony scent. Nearby, he could hear the shouts of kids at the park and the occasional car or truck driving by.

Even after Angelica returned and started weeding across the gardens from him, he didn't sweat it. The jokes and chatter of the group, most of whom knew each other well from years of adult Sunday school class together, made for an easy feeling. He was glad they'd come.

"Hey, beautiful, when did you get back to town?"

The voice, from a passerby, sounded pleasant enough, but he turned to see who was calling a member of the group "beautiful" with the tiniest bit of snarkiness in his tone. It took a minute, but he recognized the guy from a few classes behind him in high school, dressed in a scrub shirt and jeans. Logan Filmore. Brother of a friend of his. Guy must be in some kind of medical field now.

And of course, he was speaking to Angelica.

Troy's eyes flashed to her and read her concern, even distaste.

He pushed to his feet, grabbed a crutch and limped across the garden to stand beside her. "How's it going?"

"Okay." She looked uneasily at Logan, who'd stopped in front of them.

The guy looked at Troy and seemed to read something in his eyes, because he took a step back. He gave Angelica a head-to-toes once-over, then waved and walked on, calling, "Nice to see you" over his shoulder.

Angelica squatted back down and Troy eased himself down beside her.

"Someone you know?"

She yanked a thistle out of the ground. "Sort of."

"Is there anything I can do?"

Another weed hit the heap in the center of the garden. "Stop talking about it?"

He lifted his hands, palms up. "Okay. Just trying to help."

For several minutes they pulled weeds in silence. Troy was totally aware of her, though: the glow of her skin, the fine sheen of sweat on her face, the vigorous, almost angry way she tugged weeds.

Finally she turned her face partway toward him. "I'm sorry. I…I used to know him and I really dislike him. Thanks for coming over."

"Sure." A few more weeds hit the pile. "I like helping you, you know."

"Thanks."

"I like it a lot." He wanted to protect her from people like the guy who'd just passed by. He wanted to protect her full-time. Of course, he mainly wanted to marry her for Xavier's sake. That was all.

He reached across her to tug on a vine. Their hands brushed.

He was expecting her to jerk away, but she didn't; she just went a little still.

That gave him the hope he needed. "You still haven't answered my question," he said quietly.

"What question was that?"

"About whether you'd marry me."

She laughed a little. "Oh, that."

"Yes, that. Have you thought about it?"

She shut her eyes for a moment. "I've hardly thought of anything else."

"And?"

"And…I don't know."

"Fair enough," he said. "But is there anything I could do to help you decide?"

She gave him a narrow-eyed look and for a moment, he thought she was going to scold him. "Yes," she said finally. "You could tell me why you want to do it."

"That's easy. I want to do it because Xavier wants a dad. And because I like helping you."

Her mouth got a pinched look. If he hadn't known better, he'd have thought she felt hurt. "Those aren't… those aren't the reasons people get married."

"Are they bad reasons, though?"

She shook her head, staring at the ground. "They're not bad, no. They're fine. Kind. Good."

"Then what's standing in the way?"

She shrugged, looked away. There was a fine film of tears over her eyes. "Nothing. I don't know."

"Look," he said, touching her under the chin with one finger, lifting her face toward his. "Let's do it. Let's surprise Xavier." He didn't know what was making him force the issue.

Maybe something he saw in her eyes. Some part of her wanted to. And maybe it was for Xavier, or mostly so; but he had a funny feeling that she saw him as a man and was drawn to him.

"We'd be doing it for Xavier." She stared at him, her eyes huge.

"Yes, for Xavier. So, are you saying yes?"

"I think I am."

He nodded. "Then…let's seal it with a kiss." He leaned over and ever so gently brushed her lips with his.

It was meant to be just a friendly peck on the lips, but he lingered a couple of seconds, feeling the tingle of awareness he'd felt before but something else, too, something deeper.

She gasped and jerked away. "We'll…have to figure out…what kind of boundaries…" She trailed off, still staring at him. "You know."

She looked so appealing that he wanted to kiss her again, a real kiss. But the defenseless look on her face got to him and he pulled her into his arms, as slow and light and careful as if she were a wounded animal. "We'll figure it out," he whispered into her soft, dark hair.

"Mom! Can I? Can I?"

Angelica turned away from the church group and from Troy, standing just a little too close for comfort, to greet her son. It was late afternoon, and they were all saying their goodbyes in front of the weeded, re-mulched Senior Towers gardens.

Running ahead of Becka and her mom, Xavier looked so...normal. His striped shirt was mud-stained, his legs pumping sturdily beneath thrift-store gym shorts. Joy flooded her to see how healthy he looked. And what a relief to get out of the sticky, messy, impossibly emotional situation with Troy and back to what grounded her.

"Can you what, honey?" She knelt to catch Xavier as he ran into her arms, relishing the sweaty, little-boy smell of him.

"Can I play soccer with Becka? Her mom is the coach of the team!"

She hugged him close. "We'll see."

"You say that when you mean no!" Xavier pulled away. "Please, Mom?"

Becka and her mom arrived and Angelica stood up. "Thanks so much for watching him," she said.

"Well, I may have done something wrong." Becka's mom wore shorts and a T-shirt, her hair back in a no-nonsense ponytail under a baseball cap. "Becka and I were talking about soccer practice tonight, and when Xavier was interested, I told him he could join the team."

Angelica felt her eyebrows draw together. "Hmm. I'm not sure."

"Mom!"

"We'll have to see." Angelica bit her lip. She wanted him to be able to do it, to do everything a normal, healthy boy could do, but... "Soccer's pretty strenuous, isn't it?"

"At this age? No more so than normal play." Linda Mason gave her trademark grin. "The kids run around a lot, yeah. And I try to teach them some skills. But it's not competitive. It's just for fun."

"Practice is tonight, Mom!"

"Tonight?" Xavier hadn't had his usual afternoon rest. "I don't think so, sweetie. That's just too much."

A light touch warmed her shoulder. Troy. Her heart skittered as she looked back at him.

He raised an eyebrow, squeezed her shoulder once and then reached out to shake Linda's hand. "Hey, Linda. He'd need a sports physical anyway, wouldn't he?"

"Exactly." Linda nodded. "What we could do, if you don't think it's too much, is to have him come over to the park for a half-hour practice session I do with some of the kids, before the official practice. But you're right, Troy, he couldn't actually be on the team until getting a physical."

Angelica flashed Troy a grateful smile. She hadn't known that kids needed physicals for team sports, and it made the perfect delay tactic.

Xavier's face fell, and tears came to his eyes. "I just wanna play!"

"Then you have to get a physical, buddy!" Angelica gave him a one-armed hug. "All the kids have to get physicals. I'm sure Becka did, right?"

"Yeah, and I had to get a shot."

Xavier grimaced. "Yuck."

As the kids started comparing horror stories about doctors and needles, the three adults sat down on the bench outside the Senior Towers. "I'm really sorry," Linda said. "I didn't mean to get him all excited. But he seems like a great kid, and he had so much fun kicking around a ball with Becka. I'm sure he'd be good at soccer."

"We'll see what the doctor says," Troy said.

Angelica stared at him. "Excuse me?"

"Um, I'm going to go check on the kids." Linda looked from one to the other, frank curiosity in her eyes. "If that half-hour practice is okay, I'll walk them over to the park. Come on over and watch."

"Okay," Angelica said distractedly as Linda herded the kids toward the park. What did Troy mean, acting as if he had some say in Xavier's life? "Look, I'm sure you didn't mean it this way, but it sounded like you thought we'd all go to the doctor together."

"That's what I was thinking." Troy raised his eyebrows and met her eyes. "Is that a problem?"

"I don't want you to think you're the authority on Xavier after knowing him for, what, three weeks?"

"I can tell," Troy said mildly. "But after all, I'm going to be his father."

Angelica stared at him, momentarily speechless. Adrenaline flooded her body, and her breathing quickened.

She'd have to set some boundaries. She was so used to having full say about Xavier and what he did, how he lived—whether he could play soccer, for instance—and now Troy was wanting to get all high-handed.

In most matters, she'd be fine collaborating with Troy. But where Xavier was concerned, not so much.

"Some people say a two-parent family is good for this very reason." Troy sounded maddeningly calm. "A lot of moms are a little more protective. Dads help kids get out there and see the world."

"Look, you have no experience being a parent, and you don't know what Xavier's been through."

"Come on, let's walk. You want to see him play, don't you?"

"Um…yes! Of course!" Angelica stood, feeling a stiffness in her neck that bespoke a headache to come. "But we're not done talking about this."

How had Troy so smoothly taken control? She had to admit, looking up at him as he strode by her side, ushering her around a broken spot in the sidewalk, nodding to people he knew, that something about his confidence felt good. That it attracted her. She had to admit it, but… "Listen, this is making me a little uncomfortable," she said. "I'm used to having control of Xavier, and I'm not sure I'm willing to give that up."

He nodded. "I understand. I feel like I should have some say, but of course, you're his mom."

"And I make the decisions."

He slanted his eyes down at her. "Right. Okay. You make…the final decisions. Right."

She had to laugh. "Boy, that was pretty hard for you to say. Control much, do you?"

"You know me."

She did. She'd known him for a long time. But this new, older version, a little less driven, a little more humble… Wow. Despite all the craziness in her life, a core of excitement and hope was building inside her.

They approached the park together. Large oaks and maples provided shade against the late-afternoon sun, shining bright in a sky spotted with a few puffy white clouds. Kids shouted and ran around the old-fashioned swings and slide. Ragweed and earth scents mingled with the savory smell of someone's grilled burgers.

On the other side of town, a train on its late-afternoon run made a forlorn whistle.

A family sprawled on a blanket together: Mom, Dad, a boy about Xavier's age and a toddler girl with curly red hair and an old-fashioned pink romper. The little girl put her arms around the boy and hugged him, and the father and mother exchanged a smile. Angelica's heart caught. That was what she'd always longed for: a loving man who could share in the raising of the children. A little sister for Xavier.

But that wasn't in the cards for her. What Troy was proposing was purely a marriage of convenience. She had to remember the limits, the reason he'd proposed at all: he wanted to help her, and especially to help Xavier. It wasn't romantic, it wasn't love. Nothing of the kind. Troy was a rescuer, and she and Xavier just so happened to be in need of some rescuing.

They walked over to the area where Linda was leading Xavier, Becka and three other kids through some soccer drills. "He seems to be doing okay," Troy said. "What do you think?"

Tugging her thoughts away from what couldn't be changed, she studied her son, noticing the high spots of color in his cheeks. "He's getting tired. But I'll let him stay for the half hour. I'll make sure he gets some extra rest tomorrow."

They sat down on the bleachers by the soccer field. Troy took her hand and squeezed it, and warmth and impossible hope flooded through her.

"We should talk about those other boundaries," Troy said.

"What… Oh." When she saw the meaningful look in his eyes she knew exactly what he was talking about. The physical stuff.

"I'm attracted to you. You can probably tell."

Angelica looked down. She was attracted to him, too, or she thought she was. What else would her breathless, excited feeling be about? But she was too afraid to say so. Too afraid to tell him about all her issues. She pulled her hand away and pressed her lips together to keep herself from blurting out this shameful part of her past.

After a minute, he let out a sigh. "We don't have to hold hands or kiss or anything like that. I know you're doing this for Xavier, not for love. I want the same thing. I want to take care of you and Xavier, but I won't put pressure on you."

"Right." Her heart felt as if it were shrinking in her chest.

"Now, what about our…personal lives?" He looked at her sideways, raising an eyebrow.

Did he have any idea how handsome he was? "What?"

"I mean your…social life."

What was he talking about?

"Other men, Angelica."

"Other…ooooh." She shook her head. "It's not an issue. I don't date." In fact, she'd never really been in love with anyone but Troy.

"You sure?" He looked skeptical.

"I'm sure!" She looked away. This was the best someone like her could hope for.

Other families were arriving for the soccer game. Mothers in pretty clothes with designer handbags, kids with proper soccer garb. In her garden-stained jeans and T-shirt, carrying her discount-store purse, Angelica wondered if she could ever fit in. If the other families would look askance at Xavier for his murky background, his lack of a father, his mismatched, thrift-shop clothes.

Being with Troy was a chance to be a real part of the community. She wouldn't impose on him to buy her fancy things, but she'd happily accept decent clothing and soccer duds for Xavier. Would happily accept Troy's good name in the town, too, paving the way for her son to be accepted and have friends.

Troy was giving her a lot, and he was even saying he wouldn't expect the physical side of marriage in return.

She should be grateful instead of wanting more.

Six

Two days later, on a rainy Monday, Angelica was cleaning out kennels when the door burst open and two women stalked in, slamming it behind them.

"Where is he?" one of them asked loudly over the dogs' barking.

She started to put down her shovel and then paused, wondering if she should keep it for self-defense. "Where's who?"

"The boy. Xavier."

Angelica's fingers tightened on the handle of the shovel. "Why do you want to see Xavier?"

As the dogs' barking subsided, one of the women stepped forward into the light, and Angelica recognized her. "Daisy! I haven't seen you in—"

Troy's sister, Daisy, held out one hand like a stop sign. "Don't try to be nice."

Angelica studied the woman she'd once called a friend. Just a couple of years older than Angelica, she wore purple harem pants and a gold shirt. Her hair flowed down her shoulders in red curls, and rings glittered on every finger. Short, adorably chubby and always full of life, she'd been Angelica's main ally in Troy's family back when she and Troy were engaged. Angelica had hoped they'd be friends again one day.

But Daisy pointed a finger at Angelica. "I want to see my nephew, and I want to see him now."

"Your nephew? Wait a minute. What's going on? What's got you mad?"

"What's got me mad is that I have a nephew who's six years old and I've never even met him. I may not ever be going to have children of my own, but I've always wanted to be an aunt. And now I hear I've been one for years and the boy's been kept from me!"

"Oh, Daisy." Things were starting to fall into place. "Xavier isn't your nephew."

The other woman, whom Angelica didn't recognize, stepped forward—tall and thin, with streaked hair and Asian features. "We heard it on good faith from Miss Minnie Falcon."

Of course. The day of weeding at the Senior Towers. News traveled fast. Angelica shook her head. "Come on, you guys. Sit down. Miss Minnie's got it wrong, but I can explain."

"You've got some explaining to do, all right." Daisy made her way over to Troy's office area and pulled out the desk chair, clearly at home here. "I was already mad at you for what you did to Troy, but this beats all. And I'm sorry, but you were engaged to Troy, and then you left, and now you have a kid. How can he not be my nephew?"

Angelica perched on a crate and gestured to the other woman to do the same.

The woman held out a hand to Angelica. "I'm Susan, Daisy's best friend," she said, "and I'm here to keep her from becoming violent."

"It's nothing to joke about!" Daisy glared at her friend.

Angelica leaned forward. "Daisy, I can tell you for sure that Troy isn't Xavier's father." She explained Xavier's desire for a father and how he'd wishfully called Troy Dad.

"But word was you and Troy were all over each other," Daisy said skeptically.

"All over each other." Angelica rubbed her chin. She was tempted to tell the ladies what was really going on, except she hated to do that without Troy. They hadn't had the chance to discuss what they'd tell the world about their so-called engagement; Xavier didn't even know, because once Xavier knew, everyone in town would know.

She needed time to prepare, but there wasn't any. "Listen," she said, "I'm gonna go get Troy."

"Don't you try to hide behind him. He's a sucker where you're concerned."

"Daisy," the other woman said in a low voice. "We shouldn't judge. Especially considering we came straight from Bible group."

"Even Jesus got righteously angry." Daisy sulked, but then she nodded at her friend. "You're right. I'm not giving you much of a chance, Angelica, am I? But the truth is, I always really liked you, and when you dumped Troy, you dumped me, too. And now to hear that you've actually had a baby... That pretty much beats all."

"Let me get Troy."

"No, I'll text him."

Before Angelica could stop her, Daisy was on her phone, and a couple of minutes of awkward small talk later, Troy walked in. "What's going on?"

Angelica's mind raced through the possible outcomes

of this confrontation. They weren't great. If they didn't reveal their marriage of convenience now, it would make Daisy mad, and as Daisy went, so went the family. On the other hand, if they did explain that it wasn't a real marriage, that would get out, too. And that was exactly what she didn't want Xavier to find out.

Without thinking it through, she walked over to Troy and put an arm around him. "Honey," she said. "Can we spill the beans a tiny bit early and tell Daisy and Susan our news?"

When Angelica put her arm around him, Troy almost fell off his crutches. She was so resistant to getting physically close that her act of affection stunned him. It took another moment for him to realize what she'd said.

Really? She wanted to tell his sister, who knew everyone in town and loved to talk, about their pseudo-engagement?

Troy blinked in the dark kennel. Automatically, he hobbled over—his leg was bad today—toward one of the barking dogs in the front, a fellow named Crater for the ugly scar in the middle of his back, and opened the gate of his kennel. Crater leaped with joy and Troy knelt awkwardly to rub and pet him.

Then he looked back at Angelica.

She cocked her head to one side and raised her eyebrows. She must have had a reason for what she'd done; she wasn't one to playact for no reason. And if he was going to marry her, maybe even to make it a good marriage, he needed to show her his trust. "Are you sure about this?"

"I think we should tell them." She was communicating with her eyes, willing him to say something, and he only hoped he'd get it right.

"Okay," he said, pushing himself to his feet and limping over to drape an arm around Angelica's shoulders. "Guys… Angelica and I have decided to get married."

There were no happy hugs, no shouts of joy. Daisy's lips pressed together. "Are you sure that's a good idea?"

"Of course," he said. "We've…settled our differences." He tightened his arm around Angelica for emphasis and noticed that she was shaking. "Hey, it's okay. It's Daisy. She'll be happy for us!" He glared at his sister. "Won't you?"

"Are you kidding?" Daisy was nothing if not blunt. "I can't be happy to watch you setting yourself up for another fall."

He felt Angelica cringe.

"Daisy!" Susan put a hand on her hip. "Be nice."

Troy rubbed Angelica's shoulder a little, still feeling her tension. "Look, the past is water under the bridge. We've started over, and we'd appreciate it if you would be supportive." He frowned at Daisy. "For all of us, especially Xavier."

He watched as his opinionated sister struggled with herself. Finally she nodded. "All right," she said. "I'll do my best."

Angelica chimed in. "You said you'd always wanted to be an aunt. Well, now you'll be one. Xavier will be thrilled to have a bigger family. We've been pretty much…" She cleared her throat. "Pretty much on our own, since my aunt passed away."

For the millionth time, he wondered what had happened to make her leave him and leave town. And what had happened to Xavier's father.

Apparently he wasn't the only one. "One thing I've

got to know," Daisy said. "Who's Xavier's father if it's not Troy?"

The question hung in the air. It was what Troy had wanted to ask but hadn't had the guts to. Trust Daisy to get the difficult topics out into the open.

Angelica didn't speak. She was staring at the ground as if the concrete floor held the answer to Daisy's question.

"Well?" Daisy prompted. "If we're all starting fresh, what better basis than honesty?"

Angelica looked up, shot a glance at Troy and then lifted her chin and met Daisy's eyes. "I'm not at liberty to share that information," she said. "It's Xavier's story, and when he's old enough, he'll decide who he wants to share it with. Until then, it's private."

"Does he even know?" Daisy blurted.

"No!" Angelica stood, crossed her arms and paced back and forth. "And I'd appreciate all of you avoiding the topic with him. He's not old enough to understand, and I don't want him to start questioning. Not yet."

Something ugly twisted in Troy's chest. He wanted to know, if only so he could watch out for the guy, keep him away from her in the future, know his enemy. To have that unknown rival out there made the hairs on the back of his neck stand up.

"I guess that makes sense," Daisy said doubtfully.

"Thank you for respecting my son's right to privacy."

As he accepted the forced hugs of his sister and pretended to be an excited, normal fiancé to Angelica, Troy had to wonder whether they were doing the right thing.

"I don't know, man." Troy's friend Dion, the police chief of Rescue River, sat across from him at the table of the Chatterbox Café later that afternoon. They were drinking coffee and Troy had confided the truth about the marriage of convenience, knowing Dion could keep a secret. "I just don't know. You say you're doing it for Xavier, but Father God has His plans for that boy. What if He takes him young, him being so sick with leukemia? You going to divorce Angelica then?"

"No!" Troy's coffee cup clattered into the saucer, liquid sloshing over the sides. "I wouldn't leave her, not in her time of need, not ever."

"Think she'll stay with you?"

Troy drew in a breath and let it out in a sigh. "I hope so, but I can't know for sure. She left me before."

"And she won't tell you who the daddy is?"

Troy shook his head. "Says it's between her and Xavier, and she doesn't want the whole town to know before he does. Says it's his story to tell."

Dion shook his head. "That's a nice theory. But a man and his wife shouldn't have secrets." He rubbed a hand over his nearly shaved head. "Secrets destroy a marriage. I'm living proof of that."

Troy nodded. Dion didn't talk much about his marriage, but Troy knew there had been rough patches. Then they'd straightened things out, and then Dion's wife had passed away. Dion had turned to God and he had a deeper faith than anyone else Troy knew, which was why he'd come to his friend with his own issue. "Do I try to force it out of her, though?" he asked. "Is it even my right to know?"

"All kinds of reasons to know about paternity," Dion pointed out. He paused while the waitress, a little too interested in their conversation, poured them some more coffee. "Thanks, Felicity," he said to her. "We won't be needing anything else."

After she left, Troy chuckled. "She's curious what we're talking about, and she's even more curious what you're doing Friday night."

Dion shook his head. "Got a date with the baseball game on TV, just like usual. Anyway, what if something happened to Angelica? You'd need to know Xavier's story. For his health, if nothing else, it's important to know who his daddy is."

"I guess."

"Something else. Everybody in town gonna think you're the daddy. Some already do. You okay with that?"

"What people say doesn't matter."

Dion looked out the window, a little smile on his face. "Maybe not," he said finally. "But you won't look like the good guy anymore. People might think you've been neglecting your duties."

"What the gossips say doesn't matter. Period."

"Okay." Dion studied him. "I believe you. Still, you gotta know."

"You've convinced me of that."

"Talk to her, man. But pray first. Because it's not easy to be calm about the guy who got your girl pregnant, but in this situation, calm is what you'll have to be."

Troy nodded thoughtfully. How was he going to bring this up? One thing Dion was sure right about—he needed every bit of help the good Lord could offer him. Only thing was, he hated asking for help of any kind. Even from God.

Seven

Angelica was in the kitchen washing breakfast dishes when she heard the screeching of brakes out on the road.

"Zavey?"

No answer.

She grabbed a dish towel on her way out the door, drying her hands as she climbed the slight rise to where she could see the road.

Her heart seemed to stop. Xavier was on his knees beside the road, screaming.

She practically flew over the ground until she reached him and saw the situation.

In front of Xavier, a couple of feet from the edge of the road, Bull lay in the gravel, his sturdy body twisted at an odd angle. A car was pulled halfway into the ditch across the road, and in front of it, a middle-aged woman pressed her hand to her mouth.

Heart pounding, Angelica knelt by her son, patting his arms and legs, examining him. "Are you okay?"

Xavier gulped and nodded and pointed toward Bull. "I'm... It's my fault... I let him off his lead. I wanted him to play fetch." His voice rose to a wail. "I think he's dead."

"I'm sorry, I'm so sorry!" The driver came over and sank to her knees beside them, her voice shaking, tears streaking her face. "I didn't see the dog, he came running out so fast..."

And suddenly Troy was there, kneeling awkwardly beside Bull.

"Oh, honey." Angelica scooped Xavier up into her arms, reached out a hand to pat the stranger's shoulder and leaned toward Troy and Bull, her heart aching at the sight of the still, twisted dog. "Is...is he alive?"

Busy examining Bull, Troy didn't answer, so she set Xavier down and instructed him to stay out of Troy's way. She took information from the distraught driver and walked her back to her vehicle, promising to call and let her know how the dog was, making sure the woman was calm enough to drive and able to back her car out of the ditch.

And then she knelt beside Troy and Xavier, putting her arm around her son.

"I'm sorry I let him off his lead! It's my fault!" Xavier buried his face in her shoulder, weeping.

"Shh. It was an accident. You didn't know." She bit her lip and touched Troy's arm. "Is he breathing?"

Troy took one quick glance toward them and then went back to examining the dog. "Yes, but he's pretty badly injured. I'd like to do surgery right away. Here. No time to get to town." He scanned the area. "Can you grab me a big board out of the shed? There's a stack beside the door."

"Of course. Xavier, stay here." She ran to the shed and came back with a piece of plywood.

"Give me your hoodie," Troy was saying to Xavier. "I'm going to wrap Bull up in it. T-shirt, too, buddy."

Xavier shucked his hoodie and started pulling off his T-shirt, shivering in the chilly morning air.

Her son was so vulnerable to colds. "But, Troy, he shouldn't—"

"I can do it, Mom!" Xavier's trembly voice firmed up and he sniffed loudly and wiped his face on the T-shirt before handing it over to Troy.

"We need to keep Bull warm," Troy explained in a calm voice, slipping out of his own much larger T-shirt and kneeling to cover the old bulldog. "And," he said, lowering his voice so only Angelica could hear, "Xavier needs to help."

Gratitude spread through Angelica's chest. "Thank you." She knelt and helped him ease the dog onto the wide wooden plank she'd found.

Bull yelped once and his old eyes opened, then closed again. His breathing came in hard bursts.

Together, Angelica and Troy lifted the makeshift stretcher. Once, Troy lurched hard to one side, and it took both Xavier and Angelica to steady Bull. Angelica's heart twisted when she saw that a smear of blood had gotten on Xavier's hand. With his medical history, he was oversensitive to blood.

But he just wiped his hand on his jeans. "Where are your crutches, Mr. Troy?"

"Dumped 'em. Come on."

Worry pinged Angelica's heart. Troy had been to the doctor just yesterday and had gotten another full cast and a warning that he was putting too much weight on his leg.

"Can you fix him?" Xavier asked as they walked toward the kennel building.

Troy glanced down at Xavier. "They say I'm good," he tried to joke, but his voice cracked. He was limping badly now.

Angelica gulped in a breath. "Who can I call to help?"

"Buck's my only trained surgical assistant, but I'm not having him on the property. I'll manage."

"I'll help as best I can." But how would she do that? she wondered; Lou Ann wasn't here and Xavier needed her. He couldn't watch the surgery.

They got Bull to the kennel and onto the small examining table Troy had for emergencies.

"You've gotta fix him, Mr. Troy! I love him!"

"I know, son." Troy turned to Xavier. "Watch him, and if he starts to move, hold him while I wash up and prep. Angelica, you help him."

"Okay. But I don't think Xavier should stick around."

By the time Troy had assembled his instruments and gotten back to the dog, he had to lean hard on the operating table, and Angelica saw his face twist with pain.

How would he stand, possibly for several hours, and do delicate surgery without help?

Angelica hurried Xavier outside and pulled out her phone. Buck had given her his number when they were going to go out, and hopefully... Good, she'd never deleted it. She hit the call button.

"Hey, Angie," he said, sounding sleepy.

"I've got an emergency," she said, not bothering to greet him. "Listen, are you sober?"

"Yeah. Just woke up."

"Can you come out to the farm and help Troy with a surgery? Bull is hurt."

"Be right there."

She went back in and helped Troy hold Bull still and administer something with a needle. As he ran careful hands over the dog's leg, his face was set, jaw clenched.

"Is he gonna be okay, Mr. Troy?" Xavier asked from the doorway.

Angelica and Troy met each other's eyes over the table.

"I don't know," Troy said, his voice husky. "I'm going to do my very best. You've been a big help."

The dog's laceration looked bad, but as Troy continued to examine it, his face relaxed a little. "I don't think any internal organs are affected, though we can't be sure about that. It's the leg I'm worried about. I'll try to pin it, but I'm not sure it'll work."

"You can fix him. Right?" Xavier's voice was hopeful.

Troy turned to her son. "It's hard to tell," he said. "He's an older guy, and I had to give him strong medicine to make him sleep. That's hard on him. And his leg might be the more serious injury. We just don't know, buddy."

The anesthetic had set in and Troy was just starting to clean the wound when a car sounded. "Can you see who that is?" Troy said without looking up.

She went out, opened the door and let Buck in. "He's just getting started," she said. "Let me walk back with you. He doesn't know you're here."

Buck, already dressed in scrubs, followed her in.

"Troy, I have Buck here to help you."

Troy's shoulders stiffened. "How'd you manage that?"

"I have his number from before."

No answer.

"Stone-cold sober, man, and ready to help." Buck pulled on some gloves. He glanced up at Troy's face. "Whoa, chill. I'm here by invitation. And truth is, you look like you could use the help. Sure you didn't get hit, too?"

Troy's glance at Angelica was as cold as ice.

She swallowed hard. "I'm going to tend to Xavier. He needs to get inside, get cleaned up and rest."

"Fine." He turned away.

Letting her know things were anything but fine.

The surgery took longer than Troy expected, and operating on his own pet threw professional objectivity right out the window. Armstrong's help was crucial, but even with it, the outcome was touch and go.

Discouraged, his leg on fire with the pain of standing without support for several hours, Troy cleaned up while Buck finished bandaging Bull. Troy watched the younger man easily manage the heavy dog in one arm while he opened the crate door with the other, and the anger he'd shoved aside during the delicate surgery rushed back in.

Since when was Angelica in touch with Buck? How often did they talk, get together? Why hadn't she mentioned the friendship if, in fact, it was innocent?

He could barely manage to thank Buck, and the other man's cheerful "Anytime, my man" rang as guilty in Troy's ears. When they walked out together, Buck held the door for him and then checked his phone and jogged off toward his Jeep and swung in. Leaving Troy to hobble toward the house on both crutches, wanting nothing more than some pain medication and a place to put his leg up.

Angelica greeted him at the door. "How is he?"

Just looking at her made his stomach roil. "The dog or your boyfriend?"

She paled. "What?"

He clenched his jaw. "Bull is resting peacefully, but it'll be a few days before we know how well he does. He did come out of the anesthesia, so he's at least survived that."

"Oh, that's wonderful." She backed away from the door to let him by. "But, Troy, what did you mean by that other crack?"

He spun, faced her down. "Why did you keep Armstrong's phone number? How long have you had something going on with him?"

Her forehead wrinkled. "I don't have anything going on with anybody."

To Troy's ears, her denial sounded forced. He squeezed his eyes shut and turned away from her. "I'm beat. I'm going to get some rest."

"I'll take care of the dogs," she said, her voice hesitant. "But I don't want to have this stand between us. I had Buck's phone number because I never deleted it from before. Not because I'm seeing him."

"Yeah, right." Troy had heard so many denials all his life. He remembered his mother's lies to his father, remembered the first time he'd seen her driving by with another man and realized that she wasn't telling the truth about her whereabouts.

Angelica herself had left him to sleep with another man.

It crushed him that Angelica was seeing Buck. He'd half expected something like this to happen, but not so soon. He'd never thought she would cheat on him even before the wedding.

In fact, he'd even thought she had feelings for him. He felt his shoulders slump, as if the bones that held up his body had turned to jelly. Women were treacherous and his own meter of awareness was obviously broken.

Fool that he was.

"Listen," she said now, stepping in front of him as he tried to leave the room. A high flush had risen to her cheeks, and her eyes sparked fire. "I don't appreciate what you're accusing me of. I have no feelings for Buck. I barely know the man."

He leaned against the wall as exhaustion set in. "You were all set to date him. The only obstacle was his drinking. Well, he's sober today, so go for him."

"I. Don't. Want. Him. I never did. And anyway, I'm getting married to you."

"Yeah, well, we both know how real that marriage is," he said bitterly. "It's a sham, for your convenience and Xavier's. You said you never dated, but obviously that wasn't true."

"You're not listening."

"I don't listen to lies."

She shook her head, staring at him, her brown eyes gone almost black. "You're insulting my integrity and I don't appreciate that. I'm committed to you until we decide different. Which it looks like you're doing right now."

"It's not me who made the decision to seek comfort elsewhere." He rubbed the back of his neck. "Tell me, when you act all scared about being touched, is that fake? Or are you just repulsed by me?"

"Is it... Oh man." Her hands went to her hips. "You are making me so mad, Troy Hinton. Just because your parents had their problems—and yeah, I know about that, I heard it from your sister—it doesn't mean you get free rein to accuse me of whatever other women have done to you."

"I'm not..." He paused. Maybe he was. He didn't know. "Look, I'm too tired to think. Can we just put this whole conversation on hold for now?"

"What, so you can build up even more of a case against me? No way." She was small but she was determined and she obviously wasn't budging. "I'm not letting you do this, Troy. I'm not letting you fall in hate with me."

"Why not? Wouldn't it be easier for you?"

She heaved out a sigh and looked up at the ceiling. "No, it wouldn't be easier and it wouldn't be right. Stop judging me!"

"I wasn't—"

"Yes, you were," she pressed on, stepping in closer. "To think I'm dating Buck in all my spare time—which if you haven't noticed, is nonexistent—is totally insulting. As well as ridiculous. So can it and apologize before I whack you one."

That unexpected image made him smile. "You're scaring me, Angelica."

"Mom will do it, too. What do you mean, Mom's dating Buck ? And how's Bull?"

They both froze. In the doorway stood Xavier, in sweats and a T-shirt, his hair sticking up in all directions. He swayed a little and grabbed on to the door frame.

Angelica knelt before him, steadying him with a hand on his shoulder. "Honey! I didn't know you were up from your rest."

"I heard you guys fighting. Is Bull okay?" He looked plaintively up at Troy.

Hard as it was to kneel on one leg with his casted leg stuck awkwardly out beside him, he got himself down to Xavier's level. "Bull is sleeping. The drugs we gave him during the surgery made him tired. But he's looking pretty good for an old guy."

Xavier wasn't to be placated with that. "Is he gonna die?"

Troy's heart clenched in his chest. This was a kid too familiar with death. "I can't promise you that he won't, because he's an old dog. The accident was hard on him, and surgery is, too. But I did my best, and we're going to take good care of him. Okay?"

"Can I see him?"

Troy glanced at Angelica. "How about we bring him inside in a couple of hours, once he's gotten some rest? Okay?"

Angelica and Xavier nodded, both looking serious, and Troy's chest clenched painfully. He cared for both of them way too much. He wanted to protect them, wanted to answer Xavier's questions, wanted to help him heal.

Wanted to trust Angelica.

Now that he'd come down from his angry high, now that he was looking at the sunshine on her black hair as she leaned forward to hug her son, he thought he must have been crazy to accuse her.

But at the same time, there was that nagging doubt.

"You better get some rest, Troy." Angelica's tone was guarded. "And we'll do the same, right, Zavey? We'll have a quiet day. Because tomorrow, we get to go meet your teacher and see your classroom. Just a couple of weeks until school starts."

Troy nudged Xavier with his crutch. "That's a big deal, buddy. You're going to have a blast."

Concern darkened Angelica's eyes and she was biting her lip. He knew she wanted Xavier to go to school, wanted him to have as normal a life as possible for as long as possible.

He headed toward the stairs but turned back to look at Angelica. She was ushering Xavier toward the door, but he was dawdling over a handheld video game. Angelica stopped, looking half patient and half exasperated, and then she squeezed her eyes shut. He saw her lips moving.

He felt like an utter cad. She was dealing with the worst thing a mother could face, the possible death of her child, and doing it beautifully, focusing on Xavier and his needs. Given his health issues, educating him at home would have been easier, but Xavier was a social kid and needed friends, so she'd called umpteen social workers and school administrators and the school nurse to figure out a way he could attend as much as possible and make up his work when he had to be out. She was super stressed out, and how had he supported her?

By calling her out for cheating, when she'd just been trying to help him. At least he thought so.

He scrubbed a hand over his face and headed up the stairs. Reopening their discussion would likely just result in more misunderstanding. He had to get a little rest.

And then he'd get up and be a better man. With God's help.

Eight

As soon as the school secretary buzzed them in, Angelica marched into Xavier's new elementary school—her own alma mater—holding Xavier by one hand.

Immediately memories assailed her, brought on by the smell of strong cleaning chemicals and the sight of cheerful, bright alphabet letters hanging from the ceiling. She could almost feel the long patchwork skirt brushing her first-grade legs and taste the peanut-butter-and-sprouts sandwiches that had marked her as just a little different from the other kids.

Behind her, Gramps was breathing hard, and she paused to hold the office door open for him. Gramps had driven them there because he knew how important this was. They all wanted to see Xavier have a real childhood, and a big part of that was a regular school.

The other reason Gramps had driven her was that Troy had taken the truck to drive himself and Bull into town today for a consultation with another vet. He wasn't supposed to drive with his cast, but he'd insisted that they keep this appointment for Xavier, that he could manage driving with his left foot.

She knew the real reason he didn't want her to drive him: he was still a little mad at her. Well, fine. She was mad at him, too. Things hadn't been the same since he had accused her of dating Buck on the sly, an idea that would be laughable except he so obviously took it seriously.

It made her feel hopeless about their relationship. If he was that quick to suspect her morals when she'd called Buck in to help him, how would he react to finding out about her assault?

And underneath her anger, a dark thread of shame twisted through her gut. She *had* gone out drinking. She'd even flirted. If she hadn't, if she'd stayed safely at home by herself, she wouldn't have been assaulted.

But she couldn't think about that now; she had to gear up to fight yet another battle for Xavier. Had to get the right teacher and the best classroom situation for him. "Hello, I'm here to see Dr. Kapp," she said to the plump, middle-aged secretary who was working the desk in the front office.

"Okay, and this must be Xavier," the woman said, smiling down at him. "Welcome to your new school! Dr. Kapp will be right out."

Xavier's grin was so wide it made his eyes crinkle and his cheeks go round as red apples.

Meanwhile, Angelica took deep breaths, trying not to be nervous. Dr. Kapp had always been strict, and she must be ancient now, probably even more set in her ways. How would she respond to Angelica, who'd been notorious in the town for having parents who bummed around in their ancient Volkswagen minivan, spent too much time in bars and sold weed?

While Gramps and Xavier looked at a low showcase

of children's art, Angelica tried to forget about Troy and prepare for the battle ahead.

Please, Lord, help me remember. I'm not that mixed-up little hippie girl anymore. I'm Your child and You're here with me.

"Well, Angelica Camden! It's been a long time." Dr. Kapp's tone was dry. "So you have a son now."

Was that accusation in her voice? Angelica couldn't be sure, but she felt it. "Hello," she said, extending her hand to the woman whose close-cropped hair and dark slacks and jacket still made her look like an army general. *God's child. God's child.* "It *has* been a long time."

"I know you're here to talk about your son, but I think we have all the necessary information." Dr. Kapp's eyebrows went up, suggesting Angelica was wasting her time. "Was there something else before you meet Xavier's teacher and see the classroom?"

Angelica glanced back at Gramps for support, but he'd sat down heavily in one of the chairs in the waiting section of the office. Xavier had come over to press against her leg in an uncharacteristic display of neediness. So he was scared, too.

Angelica swallowed. "I'd like to talk to you about Xavier's placement in first grade." She'd rehearsed these words, but her voice still wobbled like the little girl she'd been. She drew in a deep breath. "I understand one of the first-grade teachers is a man, and I'd like for him to be in that class."

Dr. Kapp nodded. "A lot of parents want to choose their child's teacher, but we don't do things that way. I've placed Xavier in Ms. Hayashi's classroom. I think you'll like her."

"Go see if Gramps wants to play tic-tac-toe," Angelica said to Xavier, who was staring up at Dr. Kapp with a sort of awe.

Once he'd gotten out of earshot, she spoke quickly. "I'm a single mother, and that's why I'd like for him to have a male influence."

Dr. Kapp nodded. "That's understandable, but from what you said on the phone, Xavier may have some special needs. That's why we've placed him in Ms. Hayashi's class. She's dual-certified in special education, and I think she's the best choice for Xavier."

So Dr. Kapp wasn't just being autocratic. Angelica bit her lip. "Yes, the doctors said his chemo might have caused some cognitive delays, so a teacher who gets that makes a difference, for sure. I just…don't have many men in his life, and I think that's important for him."

Dr. Kapp nodded toward Gramps and Xavier, heads bent over Gramps's cell phone. "Looks like he has one good male influence, at least."

"Yes, and I'm so thankful. But—"

"Tell you what," Dr. Kapp interrupted. "Why don't I take you down to see Ms. Hayashi? She's here now, setting up her classroom. I'm sure she'll be glad to talk to you about Xavier, and then if you're still feeling dissatisfied, we can talk. I know it's a special situation, but I just have a hunch that Ms. Hayashi is going to be the right placement for Xavier."

Troy parked the truck in the elementary school parking lot. Man, it felt good to be in the driver's seat again, but the doctor had been right about how he shouldn't drive. He could tell he was overdoing it. He used his crutches to make his way to the school's front door.

As he waited to be buzzed in, feelings from his past

flooded him. The fun of going to school, the escape from the tension in his family, the relief of making new friends who didn't know anything about his big fancy home. He started to walk into the office when he saw Angelica, her grandfather and Xavier following—could that be Kapp the cop, still running this place?—around a corner in the brightly painted hallway ahead, and he followed them. "Hey, sorry to be late."

"He's gonna be my dad!" Xavier said proudly to the school principal.

Troy's heart constricted at the boy's trusting comment. What had he, Troy, done to deserve that affection and trust? Nothing, but there it was, and it got to him. Made him want to earn it by being a really good dad to Xavier.

"Some say he always was the boy's dad," Gramps muttered, frowning at Troy.

Troy's fist clenched. Homer Camden was even older than Dr. Kapp, but someday he was going to get Troy put in jail for assault on a senior citizen.

"Gramps!" Angelica hissed, nodding sideways at Xavier, who fortunately had darted over to the wall to examine a fire alarm.

As the principal walked over to explain the fire alarm and caution Xavier never to pull it unless there was a fire, Camden glared at Troy. "Just saying what I've heard around town," he said in a lower voice.

Troy glared back. What an idiot. "If you want to talk to me about something, we'll talk later where the boy won't hear."

"Let's do that." He muttered, "Sorry" to Angelica as he walked over to study the fire alarm with Xavier and the principal.

"How's Bull?" Angelica asked. "Is he going to be okay?"

"Yeah, did you bring him with you?" Back at Angelica's side, Xavier wrapped his arms around his mom's legs and looked worriedly up at Troy.

Troy hesitated. "He's…he's not doing that well. He might need another operation. He's staying at the office in town for now."

"Oh no!" Xavier's eyes filled with tears. "He's gonna have to get his leg cut off and it's my fault!"

Immediately Troy squatted down, barely stabilizing himself on one crutch, his bad leg awkwardly out in front. "If Bull's leg has to be amputated, we'll do everything we can to help him do okay with it. Most dogs are just fine with three legs. There's even a special name for three-legged dogs."

"What is it?"

"Tripod," he said, tapping his palm with three fingers of his other hand. "See? One, two, three."

"I have to talk to Ms. Hayashi," Angelica said. "Do you think—"

Troy got it. "Hey, buddy," he said to Xavier as he shoved himself painfully to his feet. "What do you think about seeing the gym and the lunchroom first? Let Mom talk to your new teacher, and then we'll come back and look around the classroom. Okay?"

"Sure!" Xavier reached up and gripped Troy's hand where it rested on the handle of his crutch.

Troy looked at Homer Camden, red-faced and frowning, and for a split second, he got the image of a man who didn't know what to do with his feelings, who was jealous of a new man in Xavier's and Angelica's life, and who wanted only the best for them. He sighed. "Want to come along?"

Thank you, Angelica mouthed to him before disappearing into the classroom.

"Guess I can," Homer Camden groused. "If you can't handle the boy alone."

It was going to be a long half hour. But he'd do it for Angelica. He'd do almost anything for her, if she'd let him, even though he wasn't at all sure that was wise.

"Where's the lunchroom?" Xavier asked as the three of them headed down the hall.

"Straight down thataway," Camden said, pointing, before Troy could answer.

"Wait a minute," Troy said, "did you go to this school, too?"

Camden nodded. "I was a member of the first graduating class. Back then, it was the new K-eight building, and I was here for seventh and eighth grade."

"That's cool, Gramps!" Xavier grabbed the older man's hand and swung his arms between the two of them, practically pulling Troy off his crutches.

"Back in those days," Camden said, "a lot of farm kids only finished eighth grade, so it truly was a graduation."

"What about you?" Troy had never thought about the old man's schooling, or lack thereof.

"Oh, I finished high school," Gramps said, a note of pride in his voice. "I was always good at math and science. English, not so much."

"Me, too," Troy said as they entered the school lunchroom, where a summer of cleaning couldn't quite erase the smell of sour milk and peanut butter. "That's why vet school had more appeal than, say, lawyering."

"But don't get too friendly," Gramps said as Xavier ran around looking at the colorful posters and sitting in various chairs. "I want to know why you're taking such an interest in Angelica and her son. Is there something you want to tell me?"

"Well, you know about our engagement." He felt duplicitous still, talking about something that might not happen. But it might. He was willing to marry Angelica and be a father to Xavier; he'd meant it when he'd offered, and he would stick with it.

"Is that because you're Xavier's dad?" Camden asked bluntly.

Troy stopped, turned and faced the other man. "No. I don't know who Xavier's father is. I'd like to, but so far, Angelica hasn't been willing to tell me."

Camden studied him. "I'm supposed to believe that? When you were engaged and spending practically every evening together?"

"It's not up to me what you believe," Troy said, "but it's the truth. Angelica and I had decided to wait until marriage." He couldn't keep the bitterness out of his voice. "Why she decided to change that plan, and with whom, I have no idea. But it wasn't me."

Camden crossed his arms over his chest and shook his head. "Guessin' that don't sit right," he said finally. "I always thought it was you. Thought you'd gotten her pregnant and then sent her away. But when you said you were marrying her now, you really threw me off."

Troy drew in a breath. "So you don't know what happened, who the father is?" He knew he shouldn't probe, should only discuss this with Angelica, but it felt like important information, and she wouldn't tell him. Maybe if he knew…

Camden shook his head. "Can't help you there."

"Come see this, Gramps!" Xavier was calling, and the two of them headed over just in time to stop him from squirting an entire container of ketchup into the sink. Plenty had gotten onto his shirt and shorts as well, and the two of them looked at each other with guilty expressions, obviously thinking the same thing: *we're going to be in trouble with Angelica*. A few paper towels later, they headed toward the gym.

"Do you know how to play basketball, Mr. Troy?"

"I sure do. I used to play at this school."

"Were you that tall then?"

Troy laughed. "No, son. I wasn't very tall at all."

"He was a pip-squeak. A lot smaller than you. I remember him in those days."

That hadn't occurred to Troy before, that Homer Camden had known him as a kid. On a whim, Troy put down his crutches. Camden grabbed a basketball, and they took turns lifting Xavier up to shoot baskets.

When they headed back toward the classroom, Xavier rested his hand on Troy's crutch again.

Which made Troy feel that all was right with the world. When had this boy put such a hold on his heart, enough to make him even see the good in Homer Camden?

When Xavier walked into the classroom between Troy and Gramps, tears sprang to Angelica's eyes. It felt as if all of her dreams were coming true.

She'd always wished her son could have a real father. And she'd hoped he could go to a regular school. It hadn't happened for kindergarten, because of all of his treatments, so this was his first opportunity.

"Hey, cool!" Xavier ran into the room and sat down at one of the desks. "I'm ready!"

"And is your name Sammy?" asked Ms. Hayashi.

Angelica was pretty sure she liked this teacher, who turned out to be the friend who'd come to the kennel with Daisy. She seemed very knowledgeable about children with medical issues, and her educational background was impeccable.

Her tight jeans, Harley-Davidson T-shirt and biker boots weren't everyone's idea of a first-grade teacher, even one who was at the school early to move books and set up her classroom. From Gramps's raised eyebrows, she could tell he thought the same. Angelica hoped the woman wouldn't intimidate Xavier.

But her son put his hands on his hips and spoke right up. "I'm not Sammy, I'm Xavier!"

"Aha. And do you know what letter your name starts with?" The woman squatted effortlessly in front of Xavier.

Xavier nodded eagerly. "An *X*, and I can write it, too!"

His enthusiasm made Angelica smile. They'd been practicing letters for months, and she'd taught him to write his name, but it had taken quite a while. His treatment had caused some cognitive issues that might or might not go away, according to the various nurses and social workers they'd dealt with.

"That's good. Can you find your desk?"

"How can I…"

The woman put a hand to her lips, took Xavier's hand and pointed to the sign on the front of the desk where he'd been sitting. "See? It's Ssssammy," she said, emphasizing the *S*. "What we need to do is to find your desk, the one that says 'Xavier.'"

He frowned and nodded. "With an *X*."

"Yes, like this." She held her fingers crossed.

Xavier did the same with his hands. "I remember. Your nails are cool. I like purple."

"Me, too. Let's find that *X*."

So far, the woman hadn't even said hello to Troy or Gramps, but Angelica didn't care. She was impressed by Ms. Hayashi's educational focus and by how much learning was already taking place.

If only her son would remain healthy enough to benefit from it.

He'd woken up with a fever several mornings this week, which filled her with the starkest terror. Fear of relapse stalked every parent of a cancer kid. But, according to Dr. Lewis, all they could do was wait and see.

"Come see my new desk, Mr. Troy!"

Troy limped over, and Angelica followed, her arm around Gramps. Who didn't look as disgruntled as he had looked before. As Xavier showed with pride how the desk opened and closed, and Troy pretended amazement over the schoolbooks inside, Angelica snapped pictures and pondered.

She'd wanted Xavier to have a male role model. And maybe he already did.

Nine

Angelica was paying bills the next Saturday morning—thanking God for the job that allowed her to—
when she heard a tapping on the door. Her heart did a
double thump. Since she hadn't heard a car drive up, it
had to be Troy.

They hadn't talked since their visit to Xavier's classroom and the closeness that had come out of that. She
didn't know what to think of their up-and-down relationship. One minute he was mad at her about Buck, and
then the next day he was acting like the sweetest father
Xavier could possibly have, making her fall hard for him.

"Hey." Outlined in the early-morning sunlight, his
well-worn jeans and faded T-shirt made him look as
young as when they'd been engaged. But now his shoulders bulged with the muscles of someone who ran a
farm and lifted heavy animals and equipment. Running
her hands up those arms, over his shoulders, as she'd
done back then…it would feel totally different now.

"Hey yourself." When her words came out low,
husky, she looked away and cleared her throat. "What's
up? Everything okay at the kennels?"

He blinked. "The kennels are fine, but I wondered if you could help me with Bull." He nodded downward, and for the first time she realized that the bulldog was sitting patiently beside him, his wrinkly face framed by his recovery collar.

"Hey, big guy!" Feeling strangely warm, she knelt down to pet Bull, and he obligingly pushed up into a crooked standing position and wagged his stub of a tail.

"Is he okay?" She looked up at Troy. Man, was he handsome!

"He's doing pretty well. I can't tell for sure until the stitches are out, and it's time to do that. Then we'll see how he gets around."

He was saying it all without taking his eyes off her, and the intensity in his gaze seemed to be about more than the dog.

She looked down, focusing on Bull, feeling confused. Between her own feelings and the way Troy was looking at her, she was starting to feel as though they had an actual relationship.

Except they didn't. It was all about business and Xavier. Because if Troy knew the truth about her and her past and why she'd left, he'd never have anything to do with her. And what kind of relationship could you build on secrets and shame?

Back to business. "I need to get Xavier up and give him some breakfast," she said. "When were you thinking?"

He shrugged. "Whenever."

Something about the way he said it made her think of him rattling around his big house. Weekends could be so lonely when you were single. She knew it well, but at least she'd always had Xavier. "Would you...would you want to have breakfast with us first? I can make us something."

His face lit up. "Sure would. I'm strictly a cold cereal guy when I'm trusting my own cooking, but I do like breakfast food."

"Pancakes are my specialty." She didn't add that there'd been many nights when pancakes were all they could afford for dinner. "You go wake up Xavier. He'll love the surprise of it."

"Even better, how about if Bull and I wake him up together? We could probably even take the stitches out right here, if you don't mind my using your front porch as an exam room."

"Perfect." They smiled at each other as the sunlight came in the windows, their gazes connecting just a little too long. And then Angelica spun away and walked toward the kitchen, weak-kneed, her smile widening to where it almost hurt.

Half an hour later, she looked around the kitchen table and joy rose in her. Xavier was just starting to sprout a few patches of hair and his grin stretched wide. Troy sniffed appreciatively at the steaming platter of pancakes. Beneath the table, Bull sighed and flopped onto his side.

"Let's pray," she suggested, and they all took hands while Xavier recited a short blessing. Then she dished up pancakes and warm syrup to all of them.

"Delicious," Troy said around a mouthful.

"Mom's a good cook."

He swallowed. "Obviously." Then, a few bites later: "I'm impressed that you sit down at the table for meals and start them with prayer."

Angelica chuckled. "I could let you go on thinking we do that at every meal, but the truth is, there are plenty of nights when we eat off the coffee table and watch *Fresh Prince* reruns."

"Yeah, that's fun!" Xavier shoved another bite into his mouth.

"And we don't always remember to pray, either. I'm not a perfect mom *or* a perfect Christian."

Troy put a hand over hers. "Perfectly imperfect."

Yeah, if only you knew.

Later, Troy went and got his exam bag and then called Bull out to the porch, putting his crutches aside and lifting the dog down the hard-to-maneuver step. In every painstaking move, she saw his care for the old bulldog.

She got Xavier involved in a new video game, then went outside and petted Bull while Troy gathered his materials for removing stitches. "Hey, buddy, you gonna get your fancy collar off, huh?"

As if answering her, Bull pawed at the recovery collar that formed a huge bell around his neck.

"I'm going to try him without it," Troy said. "It's been driving him crazy, and he can't get around that well with it on. Depends on whether he'll leave the leg alone."

He put his hand on the dog and turned to her. "Angelica, I have to apologize."

She tipped her head to the side. "For what?"

"For going off on you that day. You were right. This guy wouldn't have survived without my having Buck to help me. I owe you."

She lifted an eyebrow. "You *were* quick to judge."

"I know. And I'm sorry. I'm kind of a Neanderthal

where you're concerned." He looked at her with a possessive intensity that flooded her with warmth.

Troy had grown, for sure. He could see when he was wrong and apologize. And he definitely had a softer heart these days. It looked as if he was blinking back tears when he gazed down at his old dog.

She didn't dare focus on what else his words evoked in her.

Troy removed Bull's stitches with skilled hands while she held the dog's head still and murmured soothing words. But as Troy examined the dog's leg more carefully, moving it back and forth, he frowned. "The range of movement isn't good," he said. "This is what my buddy the specialist warned me about. Once he starts to walk on it, I'm worried what will happen."

"Is there anything we can do?"

"Not right now," he said, still moving Bull's leg, intensely focused. "We'll have to watch him for a few more days, see how he does when he's free to move around."

After the stitches were removed, Angelica insisted on carrying Bull back to Troy's house. She'd noticed how badly Troy was limping, and it wouldn't do for him to ditch his crutches and carry Bull himself.

As she knelt beside Bull's crate, helping the dog settle in and petting him, Troy came up behind her and put a hand on her shoulder. After an initial flinch, she relaxed into his touch. Which felt amazing.

"So you were right about getting Buck's help and I was wrong," he said. "But I'm right about something else. Will you listen to me?"

She kept petting Bull, superaware of Troy's hand on her shoulder. "Okay."

"I want to take Xavier to a new doctor for his physical tomorrow."

She let go of Bull and scooted around to look at Troy. "What?"

"I found a new doctor for Xavier," he repeated. "We scored big-time. Great cancer doctor, hard to get, but he's an old friend of mine from college so I called in a favor. He's at the Cleveland Clinic, just about an hour and fifteen minutes away."

Before she could analyze her own response, it was out of her mouth. "No."

"What?" He looked startled.

"He likes the doctor we've started seeing here. I'd rather go to him. Anyway, it's just a simple physical for school and sports." She stood. "And I have to get back to Xavier."

He grabbed his crutches and held the door for her. "I'll walk with you if you'll listen."

"I listened. And then I said no." She started walking back toward the bunkhouse.

He followed. "Angelica, this is a really good doctor. Someone who specializes in leukemia."

"No."

"Wait." He turned toward her, leaning on his crutches, and looked hard into her eyes. "Why not? Why really?"

She looked away from his intensity. Why didn't she want a great new cancer doctor for Xavier? She took in a deep breath and started walking again. "Because I'm scared."

He fell into step beside her. "Of what? It can only be good for Xavier."

She stared at the hard dirt beneath their feet. "What if this doesn't work out?"

"What are you talking about?"

She glanced over at him. The morning they'd spent together, the delight of Xavier's happiness, of Troy's appreciation for her cooking, all of it made this so hard to say. "Look, I know the chances of us—you and me, this so-called engagement—making it are fifty-fifty at best. So what if we don't? What if you decide you don't want to go through with the marriage, or even if we do go through with it, that you don't want to stay? What are Xavier and I supposed to do then?"

He stared at her and then, slowly, shook his head. "You don't trust me, do you?"

"It's not you necessarily." She shrugged. "But why would you stick with us? What's in it for you? People don't just do things out of the goodness of their hearts."

They'd reached the bunkhouse porch, and he waited while she climbed the steps, then hopped up behind her. "What world have you been living in? Around here, people do things to help others all the time."

"Sure, give them a ride or watch their dog when they go on vacation. But marry someone? Stand by a kid with serious health issues? That's way, way beyond the call of duty, Troy. I appreciate your willingness, and for Xavier's sake, I have to give it a try. But—"

He tugged her down onto the porch swing and then sat next to her, held out a hand to touch her chin, ran his thumb ever so lightly over her lips. "Really? It's just for Xavier's sake?"

She stared at him, willing herself to stay still and explore the mix of feelings that his touch evoked. But she couldn't handle it. She scooted away and stood, and at a safe distance, pacing, she switched back to a safer topic. "Xavier hates changing doctors. If our relationship doesn't work, I certainly can't afford a fancy specialist. So that's why I'd rather just stick with the doctor we've been going to since we moved here."

"So you'd rather go with safe and mediocre."

"Dr. Lewis comes highly recommended," she protested.

"By whom?"

"Gramps and his friends." At his expression, she flared up. "I know you don't like Gramps, but he's been in the area forever, and all of his friends have medical issues, as does he. They know doctors."

"Geriatric doctors, not pediatricians. Look, this is a great opportunity. He'll get the athletic physical times ten. We're really blessed to see this guy, Ange."

Ange. It was what he'd called her when they were engaged, and hearing it thrust her back to that time. His excitement did, too.

Back then, she would have joined in readily, would have shared his optimism; she'd have been eager to try something new and take a risk.

But now, given her life experiences since that time, her stomach clenched. "I think Dr. Lewis will be just fine."

"Not really." He was getting serious now, leaning in, crossing his arms. "I asked around about Dr. Lewis. He's been in practice forty years. He isn't likely to be up on the latest research."

Angelica's spine stiffened and she felt her face getting hot. "I researched all the CHIP-eligible doctors within fifty miles. He's by far the best of those."

"Of those." His tone had gone gentle. "I'm not questioning that you did the best you could—"

"He seems really experienced. And Xavier liked him when we went when we first arrived in town."

He sighed. "Look, I just don't understand why you're not excited about this. It's a chance for your son to have the very best care around. Don't you want that?"

"Of course I do," she said, forcing herself not to strangle the guy. "But listen, would you? It's hard for Xavier to handle a new doctor. He's suffered through a lot of them. I don't want to make a change when it might not be permanent."

He leaned over and clamped a hand on her forearm. "I'm not going to fall through. I'm here for you!"

She stared at him, meeting his eyes, trying to read them. But something about his expression took her breath away and she pulled free and turned to look out over the fields, biting her lip.

God, what do I do?

She wanted to trust Troy. She wanted to trust God, and hadn't she been praying for better medical treatment? Hadn't she had her own issues with Dr. Lewis's wait-and-see attitude?

Xavier banged out the front door, sporting a T-shirt Angelica hadn't seen before, and she pulled him toward her, hands on shoulders, to read it.

Rescue River Midget Soccer.

"Where'd you get this, buddy?"

He smiled winningly. "Becka gave it to me. It's her old one. But she said I can get a new one as soon as I'm 'ficial on the team."

Angelica's heart gave a little thump as she put her

arms around him, noticing he was warm and sweaty. He must have been running around inside.

He wanted this so badly, and she did, too. But she worried about whether it was the right thing to do.

Here Troy was offering her an opportunity to get the best medical opinion, even on something so minor as whether a six-year-old could play soccer. Shouldn't she be grateful, and thanking God, rather than trying to escape their good fortune?

Even if it poked at her pride?

She took a deep breath. "Guess what! Mr. Troy found us a new doctor for you, a really good one. We're going to get you a super soccer checkup, to make sure you're ready to do your best."

The next day at the clinic, watching his friend and expert cancer doctor, Ravi Verma, examine Xavier's records and latest test results, Troy heaved a sigh of relief.

He had to admire the way Angelica was handling this. He knew he'd gone beyond the boundaries when he pulled strings to make the appointment, but he just couldn't stand to think that they were making do with a small-town doctor when the best medical care in the world was just another hour's drive away.

Obviously Angelica hadn't loved his approach, but she wasn't taking it out on Xavier. She'd pep-talked him through today's blood tests and played what seemed like a million games of tic-tac-toe as a distraction. Now she had an arm around her son as he leaned against her side.

She was a great mom. She was also gorgeous, her hair curlier than she usually wore it and tumbling over her shoulders, her sleeveless dress revealing shapely bronzed arms and legs.

Troy swallowed and shifted in his plastic chair. Man, this consultation room was small. And warm.

The doctor cleared his throat and turned to them. "There's so much that looks good on his chart and in the testing," he said, "but I'm afraid his blasts are up just a little."

"No!" Angelica's hand flew to her mouth, her eyes suddenly wide and desperate.

Troy pounded his fist on his knee. Just when things had been going so well. "What does that mean, Ravi?"

His friend held up a hand. "Maybe nothing, and I can see why my colleague Dr. Lewis wanted to wait—"

"He didn't even tell us about it!" Angelica sounded anguished.

"And that's common. The impulse not to alarm the patient about what might be a normal fluctuation."

"Might be…or might be something else?" Angelica's throat was working, and he saw her taking breath after breath, obviously trying to calm herself down. She stroked Xavier's back with one hand; her other hand gripped the chair arm with white knuckles. "What can we do about it?"

Ravi nodded. "Let's talk about possibilities. The first, of course, is to wait and see."

"Let's do that." Xavier buried his head in Angelica's skirt. He sounded miserable.

"Other options?" Troy heard the brusqueness in his own voice, but he couldn't seem to control his tone. Hadn't had the practice Angelica had.

"There is an experimental treatment for this kind of…probable relapse."

Angelica's shoulders slumped. "Probable relapse?"

Ravi's dark eyes flashed sympathy. "I'm afraid so.

You see, his numbers have crept up again since his last test. Not much at all, so not necessarily significant, but from what I have seen in these cases…" He reached out and put a hand on Angelica's. "I think it might be best to treat it aggressively."

"Treat it how?" Angelica's voice was hoarse, and Troy could hear the tears right at the edge of it.

Xavier looked up at his mother. "Mom?"

"We'll figure it out, buddy." She smiled down reassuringly and stroked his hair with one hand. The other dug into the chair's upholstery so hard it looked as if she was about to rip it.

"The traditional protocol is radiation and chemo, quite intensive and quite…challenging on the patient."

Angelica pressed her lips together.

Troy leaned forward. "Is there another option?"

"Yes, the experimental treatment I mentioned. Cell therapy. Using the body's own immunological cells. Now, most of the participants in the trial are adults, but there is one other child, a girl of about twelve. It's possible I could talk my colleagues into allowing Xavier in, if he passes the tests."

"Isn't that going to be really expensive? We don't have good insurance."

"In an experimental trial, the patient's medications are fully funded. However…" He looked up at Angelica. "There may be some expenses not covered by our grant or your insurance."

"That's not a problem," Troy said. "Is this new treatment what you'd recommend?" he pressed.

Ravi looked at Xavier's bent head with eyes full of compassion. "If he were one of my own, this is the approach I would take."

Angelica opened her mouth and then closed it again. Shut her eyes briefly, and then turned back to Ravi. "How difficult is the treatment?"

"That is the wonder of it. It is noninvasive and not harmful as far as cancer treatments go because it uses the body's own cells. Of course, there are the usual tests and injections…" He reached down and patted Xavier's shoulder. "Nothing about cancer is easy for a child."

"I don't want a treatment." Xavier's head lifted to look at his mother. "I want to play soccer."

She lifted him into her lap and clasped him close. "I know, buddy. I want that, too."

Troy leaned toward the pair, not sure whether to touch Xavier or not. In the mysteries of sick children, he was a rank beginner. He had to bow to the expertise of Ravi, and especially of Angelica. At most, he was a mentor and a friend to the boy. "Buddy, this could make you well."

"It never did before." Xavier's expression held more discouragement than looked right on that sweet face. "Mom, I don't want a treatment."

"We'll talk about it and think about it. And pray about it." She straightened her back and squared her shoulders and Troy watched, impressed, as she took control of the situation. "Listen, I think Mr. Troy is feeling worried. And I also think I have a bag of chocolate candy in my purse. Could you get him some?"

Xavier sniffed and nodded and reached for her purse. She let him dig in it, watching him with the most intense expression of love and fierce care that he'd ever seen on a woman's face.

"Here it is!"

"Give Mr. Troy the first choice." She took back the

purse and reached in herself, pulling out a creased sheet of paper. While Xavier fumbled through the bag of candy, patently ignoring her instruction to let Troy go first, Angelica skimmed down a list and started pelting Ravi with questions.

Troy imagined he could see the sweat and tears of their history with cancer on that well-worn paper. He didn't pray often enough, but now he thanked God for allowing him the honor of helping Angelica cope.

He focused on Xavier for a few minutes while the other two talked, bandying about terms and phrases he'd not heard even with his vet school history. Finally Angelica folded the paper back up, glanced over at Xavier and frowned. "Is there time for me to think about this?"

"Of course," Ravi said, "but it's best to get started early, before his numbers go up too high. If there is any chance you'll be interested in participating, we should start the paperwork now."

She closed her eyes for a moment, drew in a slow breath and then opened her eyes and nodded. "Let's do it."

During the little flurry of activity that followed— forms to fill out, a visit from the office manager to pin down times and details, some protests from Xavier— Troy kept noticing Angelica's strength, her fierceness and her decision-making power. She'd grown so much since he knew her last, and while he'd been aware of it before, he was even more so now. She had his total respect.

And she deserved a break. When Xavier's protests turned into crying and the office manager started talking about initial tests that would be costly but not covered by the trial's grant, he nudged the boy toward her.

"Why don't you two go out and get some fresh air, maybe hit the park across the street? I need to talk to my friend here for a minute. And I'll settle up some of the financial details with the office manager and then come on out."

"Can we go, Mom?"

She pressed her lips together and then nodded. "I'll be in touch," she said to Ravi. She mouthed a thank-you to Troy, and then the two of them left.

Troy stood, too, knowing his friend's time was valuable, but Ravi gestured him back into the chair. "You cannot escape without telling me about her."

"She's…pretty special. And so is the boy."

"I see that." Ravi nodded. "They've not had an easy road, I can tell from the charts. Lots of free clinics, lots of delays."

"Has it affected the outcome?"

"No, I think not. It has just been hard on both of them."

"What are his chances of getting into the trial?"

"Honestly? Fifty-fifty. We have to look more deeply into all his previous treatments and his other options. But I will do my best."

"Thank you." And Troy made a promise to himself: he *would* make sure they got in. And, God willing, the treatment would make Xavier well.

That night, Angelica was helping Lou Ann clean up the kitchen—they'd all eaten together again—while Troy and Xavier sat in the den building something complicated out of LEGO blocks. The sound of the two of them laughing was a pleasant, quiet backdrop to the clattering of pots and dishes, and Angelica didn't know she was sighing until Lou Ann called her on it. "What's going on in your mind, kiddo?"

Angelica smiled at the older woman. "I'm just... wishing this could go on forever."

"Which part? With Xavier, or with Troy?"

"Both."

"Xavier we pray about. Is there a problem with your engagement we should take to the Lord, too?"

Lou Ann didn't know that the engagement was for show, and normally Angelica felt that was right and would have continued the deception. But something in the older woman's sharp eyes told her that she'd guessed the truth. "Yes," she said slowly, "we could use some prayer. I just don't know that it will work, not really."

"Why's that?" Lou Ann carried the roaster over to the sink and started scrubbing it.

Angelica wiped at the counter aimlessly. "Well, because I... I don't know, I just don't believe it can happen."

Lou Ann shook her head. "Why the two of you can't see what's under your noses, that you love each other, I don't know."

"We don't love each other!" And then Angelica's hand flew to her mouth. If the fact that their engagement was a sham hadn't been out before, it was now.

"I think you have more feelings than you realize," the older woman said. "So what's holding you back, really?"

Angelica leaned against the counter, abandoning all pretense of working. "I...I just don't believe he'll love me. Don't believe I'm able to keep him."

"The man's crazy about you!"

Lou Ann's automatic, obviously sincere response made Angelica's breath catch. "You really think so?"

"Yep."

Lou Ann's certainty felt amazing, but Angelica couldn't let herself trust it. "That's because he doesn't know much about me. If he did, he'd feel differently."

Lou Ann pointed at her with the scrubber stick. "What did you do that's so all-fired awful?"

Angelica shook her head. "Nothing. I…I can't talk about it."

"If it's about Xavier's daddy," Lou Ann said with her usual shrewdness, "I think you should let it go. The past is the past."

"Not when you have a child by it," Angelica murmured, starting to scrub again.

"Look," Lou Ann said, "all of us have sinned. Every single one. If you'd look at the inside of my soul, it would be as stained and dirty as this greasy old pan."

"You? No way!"

"You'd be surprised," Lou Ann said. "For one thing, I wasn't always as old and wrinkled as I am now. I had my days of running around. Ask your grandfather sometime."

Angelica laughed. "Gramps already told me you were the belle of the high school ball. In fact, I think he has a crush on you still."

Lou Ann's cheeks turned a pretty shade of pink. "I doubt that. But the point is, we've all done things we're not proud of. I ran around with too many boys in my younger days, and I've also done my share of gossiping and coveting. Not to mention that I don't love my neighbor as well as I should."

When Angelica tried to protest, Lou Ann held out

a hand. "Point is, we're all like that. We've all sinned and fallen short, that one—" she pointed the scrubber toward the den where Troy was "—included. So don't go thinking your sins, whatever they are, make you worse than anyone else. Without Jesus, we'd all be on the same sinking ship."

"I guess," Angelica said doubtfully. She knew that was doctrine, and in her head she pretty much believed it. In her heart, though, where it mattered, she felt worse than other people.

"I think you need to sit down and talk to the man," Lou Ann said. "The two of you spend all your time with Xavier, and you don't ever get any couple time to grow your relationship and get to know each other."

"But our connection…well, you've pretty much guessed that it's mainly about Xavier."

"But it shouldn't be," Lou Ann said firmly. "You two should build your own bond first, like putting on your oxygen mask in a plane before you help your kid. If Mom and Dad aren't happy, the kids won't be happy. Xavier needs to see that you two have a stable, committed relationship. That's what will help him."

Angelica sighed. "You're probably right." She'd been thinking about it a lot: the fact that their pretend engagement had grown out of their control and was now of a size to need some tending. Half the town knew they were engaged, and more important, her own feelings had grown beyond pretend to real. She didn't want to think about ending the engagement, partly because of what it would do to Xavier, but also because of what it would do to her.

"You need to get to know him as he is now, not just the way he was seven years ago. Things have changed.

He writes articles in veterinary journals now, and other vets come to consult with him. He's way too busy. And on the home front, his dad's not getting any younger, and Troy needs to make his peace with him. You're the one with the big, immediate issues in the form of that special boy in there, but Troy has his own problems to solve. You need to figure out if you can help him do that."

"Sit down. Take a break." Angelica nudged Lou Ann aside and reached for the scrubber, attacking the worst of the pots and pans. "I've been selfish, haven't I?"

"Not at all. You're preoccupied, and that makes sense. But promise you'll talk to him soon. Maybe even tell him some of that history that's got you feeling so down on yourself."

Angelica sighed. The thought of bringing up their engagement, of having that difficult talk, seemed overwhelming, but she could tell Lou Ann wasn't going to let it go. "All right," she said. "I'll try."

Ten

Angelica strolled toward the field beside the barn, more relaxed than she had felt in a week.

She'd tried to work up the courage to talk to Troy about their relationship, even to tell him the truth about why she'd left him, but it hadn't happened. Finally this morning, she'd turned the whole thing over to God. If He wanted her to talk to Troy, He had to open up the opportunity, because she couldn't do it on her own strength.

Red-winged blackbirds trilled and wild roses added a sweet note to the usual farm fragrances of hay and the neighboring cattle. Beyond the barn, she could hear boys shouting and dogs barking as Troy's Kennel Kids tossed balls for the dogs.

Today—praise the Lord—she'd gotten word that Xavier was accepted into the clinical trial. He'd go for his treatment in a couple of days, and Dr. Ravi was reassuring about everything. The treatment wouldn't be difficult, and he was optimistic that the trial would work, told stories of patients' numbers improving and "positive preliminary findings."

Impulsively she lifted her hands to the sky, feeling the breeze kiss her arms. *Lord, thank You, thank You.*

She rounded the corner of the barn and froze.

One of the Kennel Kids, older and at least twice Xavier's size, loomed over him, fist raised threateningly.

"Hey!" Poised to run to her son, she felt a restraining hand on her shoulder.

"Let him try to handle it himself," Troy said.

She yanked away. "He can't fight that kid! Look at the size difference!"

"Just watch." Troy's voice was still mild, but there was a note of command that halted her. "Wendell always pulls his punches, so don't worry."

Clenching her fist, still primed to run to her son, she paused.

Xavier smiled up guilelessly at the other boy. "Hey, I'm sorry my ball hit you. My pitching stinks."

"Leave him alone, Wendell. He's just a kid." One of the other boys put an arm around Xavier.

The bigger boy drew in a breath, and then his fisted hand dropped. "Yeah, well, don't hit me again. Or else."

One of the puppies jumped into the mix, and as if no threat had ever existed, the group broke into a kaleidoscope of colorful balls and yipping puppies and running boys.

As her adrenaline slowly dissipated, Angelica leaned against the wall of the barn and sank down to a sitting position.

"I want to go give Wendell some positive feedback. He's getting better about controlling his anger."

"I'm still working on that myself," she snapped at him, but halfheartedly. She knew it was good for Xavier to socialize with other kids, but these rough-around-the-edges boys scared her.

She watched Troy walk over and speak briefly with Wendell and then clap him on the back. Xavier, completely unmoved by his near brush with getting the tar kicked out of him, was rolling with one of the puppies.

Taking deep breaths, she willed herself to calm down. She hated the way Troy was high-handed with her, but after all, he was right, wasn't he? Xavier had handled the situation himself just fine and was fitting in nicely with the other boys. If she'd run in to save him, that might not be the case.

A few minutes later, Troy came back and sat down beside her. "You mad at me?"

"Yes and no." She watched as one of the other boys threw a ball back and forth with Xavier. The other boy was older; in fact, most of the boys were, but Xavier was holding his own. It reminded her of what a good athlete he could be.

If he got the chance.

And that was where Troy had been incredibly, incredibly helpful. "Listen," she said. "I don't necessarily like being told how to mother my kid, but there are times when you're right." She smiled up at him. "Dr. Ravi called today."

Troy's head jerked toward her, his face lighting up. "And?"

"And Xavier gets into the trial."

"That's fantastic!" He threw his arms around her.

No, no, no. She couldn't breathe, couldn't survive, couldn't stand it. She pushed hard at his brawny chest.

"Hey, fine, sorry!" He dropped his arms immediately and scooted backward, his eyebrows shooting up.

She gulped air. "It's fine. I'm sorry. I just…" Blinking rapidly, she came back from remembered darkness—something she'd had years of practice at doing—and offered Troy a shaky smile. "I'm so grateful that you made us see Dr. Ravi. He's wonderful. And I like that he's going forward aggressively with the treatment. I really, really want Xavier to have it. This could make all the difference."

"I'm glad." Troy continued to look a little puzzled. "But you're still mad at me?"

Mad wasn't the word. She knew she should launch into the talk she'd promised Lou Ann she'd have with Troy. She looked out across the fields and breathed deeply of the farm-scented air.

And changed the subject. "Look, I know I'm overprotective. It kind of comes with the territory of parenting a seriously ill child."

"Of course."

"And I was worried about that bigger kid hitting him. Xavier tends to bruise and bleed easily, or he did when he was in active disease. I try to make sure he doesn't fall a lot and all that."

"Should I have stopped them? I struggle with how much to intervene and how much to let them work it out themselves so they can build better social skills." He studied his hands, clasped between his upraised knees. "Thing is, a lot of these boys are out on their own much of the time. I spend such a small fraction of their lives with them. So I feel like they need to practice solving some of their conflicts themselves. We usually talk it over in group, after they've gotten some of their energy out." He shrugged. "I'm just a vet with a heart to help kids. I don't know sometimes if I'm doing it right."

"You do a great job," she said warmly.

"Thanks." And then he was looking at her again, and she spoke nervously to make the moment pass. "Parenting is like that for me. I never know if there's something I should do differently. Xavier's going to go to school, and he'll have to learn to handle the playground himself. I won't be there to intervene for him, so I guess that's something I'd better get used to."

"We can help each other out. We're a good partnership." He reached out and squeezed her shoulder.

She cringed away instinctively. And when she saw the hurt look on his face, she felt awful.

She opened her mouth to apologize and then closed it again. What was she going to say? How could she explain?

Nervously she pulled a bandanna out of her pocket and wiped off her suddenly sweaty neck and face. The thing was, she didn't know if she was going to get over this, ever. Being touched was hard for her. Oh, she could hug Xavier, did that all the time, and his childish affection was a balm to her spirit. When she stayed with Aunt Dot right after being assaulted, and indeed for years afterward until that wonderful woman had died a year ago, they'd shared hugs galore. And her girlfriends were always hugging on her and plenty of nurses had let her weep in their arms.

Female nurses.

It was only when a man hugged her that she freaked out.

Troy was regarding her seriously. His blue eyes showed hurt and some anger, too. "Look, I'm sorry," he said. "I guess I didn't realize how much you... Well, how much you don't want me near you. That's a problem. How are we…" He broke off, got awkwardly to his feet, favoring his hurt leg. "I better go check on the boys."

He limped off and she wanted to call him back, to apologize, to say she'd work on it, really she would. But the thing was, it had been seven years and she still wasn't over the assault.

She hadn't been motivated to get over it before because she hadn't dated anyone and she hadn't wanted a man around.

But Troy was doing so much for them. Moreover, when he touched her, she felt something uncurl within her, and that as much as anything made her shy away.

There'd been plenty of chemistry between them when they were engaged. Now, though, everything felt different.

She stared absently out at cornfields with tassels almost head high. Above her, the sky shone deep blue with puffy clouds.

She'd seen a counselor right along with her obstetrician, at her aunt's insistence, and the woman had been wonderful and had helped her a lot. But Angelica hadn't wanted to date. Hadn't wanted to open herself up to love—and the accompanying dangers and risks—again.

Still didn't, if the truth be told. She'd rather stay in her safe, comfortable little shell. But Troy was so good with Xavier, and Xavier needed a dad. Holding back like this was selfish of her. She had to fix this.

If she wanted to love again, a part of loving was hugging and kissing and all the intimate physicality created by the same God who'd made the corn and the sky and the sweaty little boys and jumping, bounding dogs in front of her.

She let her head drop into her hands. *Lord, I can't do this myself. Please help me heal. Help me learn to love.*

Slowly, as she listened for God's voice, as she breathed in the wonders of His creation, she felt herself relaxing. She didn't know if it would work for her. She certainly didn't want to tell Troy the reasons for her pain, because she knew he would judge her.

But maybe God would give her a pass on that. Maybe He'd let her have this relationship and let Xavier have a dad—a dad who could do amazing things with his connections, who could actually help Xavier heal—and she wouldn't have to tell Troy the sordid side of her past. Wouldn't have to tell him about her own culpability in what had happened to her.

Because no matter what her therapist had said, Angelica knew the truth. She'd gotten drunk and silly and flirty, and she'd been mad at Troy for not coming out to celebrate her birthday, and she'd been flattered when a handsome older man wanted to walk her home.

It wasn't pretty and it wasn't nice, and she'd regret it for the rest of her life.

God in His amazing excellence had turned it to good. God had brought her Xavier and he was the purpose of her life now, the thing that gave it meaning. And she, flawed as she was, loved him as fiercely as any mother could love any child, despite his bad beginning. God had done that much for them, overlooking her sins.

She could only hope and pray that He'd heal her enough to let her go forward with the marriage to Troy.

Troy strode away from Angelica and out toward the driveway. He just needed a minute to himself.

Apparently, though, he wasn't going to get it, because heading toward him was a police cruiser. Like any red-blooded American male who'd occasionally driven faster than he should, he tensed…until he realized that Dion was at the wheel.

Even seeing his friend didn't make him smile as he walked up to the driver's-side window.

"What's wrong with you, old man?"

Troy shrugged. He'd talk to Dion about almost anything, they were those kinds of friends, but there was a time and a place. "What brings you out my way? You're working nights. You should be home catching Zs."

"Yeah, had an issue." Dion jerked his head toward the backseat and lowered the rear window.

There, on a towel, was the saddest-looking white pit bull Troy had ever seen. Ears down, cringing against the backseat, quivering, skin and bones.

Troy's heart twisted.

"Found her chained to an abandoned house. You got your work cut out for you with this one."

Troy opened the rear car door and wasn't really surprised when the dog shrank against the back of the seat and bared her teeth. "Problem is, I've got the Kennel Kids here today."

"I know you do. I'm gonna help out for a bit while you take care of this little mama. Those boys could use an hour with a cop who's not out to arrest them."

Troy focused in on the word *mama*. "She's pregnant?"

"Oh yeah. It rains, it pours."

Troy drew in a breath and let it out in a sigh. "Okay. Lemme run get a crate and—"

Shaking his head, Dion turned off the engine and got out. "Can't crate her, man. She freaks."

"How'd you get her into the cruiser?" As always, when there was a hurting animal nearby, Troy went into superfocus, forgetting everything else, trying to figure out how to help it. He braced his hands on the car roof and leaned in, studying the dog.

Dion gave his trademark low chuckle. "One of the guys had a sandwich left over from lunch."

"Gotcha. Be right back."

Minutes later, with the help of a piece of chicken, the dog was out of the cruiser and in one of the runs right beside where the boys were playing.

"See what you can do, my man," Dion said, then strode over to the group of boys in the field, who went silent at the sight of the tall, broad-shouldered man in full uniform.

Troy watched for a minute. Angelica was with them, and he saw her greet Dion. The two of them spoke, and then Dion squatted down to pet one of the dogs.

A couple of the boys came closer. Dion greeted them and apparently made some kind of a joke, because the boys laughed.

So that would be okay. Dion was great with kids; in fact, some of these boys probably knew him pretty well already, though not for as innocent a reason as his visit here today.

Using treats, Troy tried to get the dog to relax and come to him, but she cowered as far away as possible. From this distance, he could see her distended belly and swollen teats. She'd probably give birth in a week or two.

Xavier, for one, would be excited. He loved the puppies best, and though he was having a blast with the ones already here, watching them grow and playing with them, new babies would thrill him beyond belief. For that reason, Troy was glad they had a mama dog, though he had to wonder about this one's story.

Right on schedule, his sister pulled into the driveway. She helped with the Kennel Kids whenever she could.

"C'mere, Lily." On an impulse he named the dog for her white coat, even if she was more gray than white at the moment. He threw a treat to within a few inches of her nose, and she made several moves toward it, then jerked back. Finally she dove far enough forward to grab the dog biscuit and retreat, and he praised her lavishly. Still when he moved toward her, she backed away, growling.

He settled in, back against the fence, watching the boys, Dion, Angelica and his sister.

Dion said something to Angelica and she laughed, and Troy felt a burning in his chest. Would Angelica go for his best friend?

A year older than Troy, Dion had been a little more suave with the ladies when they played football together in high school. But Troy had never felt jealous of the man…until this moment.

He tried to stifle the feeling, but that just made his heart rate go up, made him madder. Yeah, he was possessive, especially where Angelica was concerned. Nothing to be proud of, but the truth.

He watched Angelica and noticed that, while she was friendly to Dion, she kept a good few feet between them. Not like his sister, who often put an affectionate hand on Dion's arm or fist-bumped him after a joke.

Relief trickled in. Looked as though Angelica wasn't attracted.

He tossed another treat to the dog, and this time she

dove for it and ate it immediately. He scooted a couple of feet closer, still staying low so he didn't look big and threatening to her. She let out a low growl but didn't attack.

He tossed another treat halfway between them, and the dog considered a moment, then crept forward to grab it.

He reached out toward the dog with a piece of food in his hand. This was a risk, as he might get bitten, but he figured it wasn't likely. He had a sense about this one. She wanted help.

A moment later, his instinct was rewarded when she accepted food out of his hand.

He fed her several more pieces and then reached toward her. She backed away, a low growl vibrating in her chest.

Righteous anger rose in him. He'd like to strangle the person who'd mistreated this sweet dog. Maybe ruined her for a home with a family. Fear did awful things to an animal.

Or a person.

It hit him like a two-by-four to the brain.

The dog was reacting the way Angelica reacted.

It was pretty obvious why, in the dog's case: people had treated her badly, and she'd learned to be afraid.

So who'd been mean to Angelica? What had they done? And when?

He jumped up, moved toward the dog and she lunged at him, teeth bared. He backed away immediately. He should know better than to approach a scared dog when he was feeling this agitated; she could sense it.

Had Angelica been abused or attacked?

No, not possible. He spun around and marched over to the kennels, grabbed a water bowl for the dog, filled it.

He had no idea what had gone on in Angelica's life in the years they'd been apart. She could very well have gotten into a bad relationship. And given that she'd apparently been poor, she could have lived in bad areas where risks were high and safety wasn't guaranteed.

He needed to talk to his social-worker sister. He took the water bowl back to the new dog's run and set it down, keeping a good distance from her. Then he beckoned to Daisy.

She came right over. "Hey, bro, what's happening with Xavier and Angelica? Did you find out about the cancer trial?"

"Xavier got in. We're pretty happy."

Hands on hips, she studied him. "Then what's eating you?"

"You know me too well. And you understand women, and I don't."

She raised her eyebrows. "What's up?"

He looked out at the cornfields. "If a woman was… abused, say, or attacked…how would she react? Wouldn't she tell people what happened?"

Daisy cocked her head to one side. "Probably, but maybe not. Why?"

"Why wouldn't she tell?"

"Well…"

He could see her social work training kick in as she thought about it.

"Sometimes women are ashamed. Sometimes their attacker threatens them. Sometimes they're in denial, or they just want to bury it."

He nodded. "Okay, it makes sense that they might

not want to report it, to have it be common knowledge. But if they have close family or friends who would help them…"

"Are you talking about a rape?"

The word slammed into him. And the doors of his mind slammed shut. That couldn't have happened. Not to Angelica. *Please, God, no.*

Daisy crossed her arms over her chest and narrowed her eyes at him. "Whatever you're thinking, you need to talk to that person about it. Not to me."

He nodded, because he couldn't speak.

"So go do it."

He drew in a breath, sighed it out. "Cone of silence?"

"Of course."

Slowly he walked over to where Dion leaned against a fence, talking to a rapt group of boys. Angelica knelt a short distance away beside the pen they'd made to keep Bull safe from too much activity but still included in the fun. She was rubbing the old dog's belly, praising him for how his leg was healing, telling him he'd feel better soon. She looked pensive and beautiful and she didn't hear him coming.

Deliberately he touched her shoulder, and just as he now expected, she jumped and frowned toward him.

He hated being right. "We have to talk," he said to her. "Soon."

Eleven

The next Saturday night, Angelica listened to the closing notes of the praise band and wished she felt the love the musicians had been singing about.

Sometime during the past month, coming to Saturday night services with Lou Ann, Troy and Xavier had become the highlight of her week. The focus on God's love, the sense of being part of a community of believers and the growing hope of a future here—all of it made church wonderful. But tonight, she'd been too jittery to enjoy it.

She felt Troy's gaze on her—again—and scooted toward the edge of the padded pew. "I've got to go get Xavier."

"No, that's okay." Lou Ann sidled past her and out of the pew. "I'll do it."

Oh. Rats.

Troy turned to greet the family next to them, and, hoping he hadn't heard her exchange with Lou Ann, she started edging out of the pew. Grabbing her purse, she stood and took a sideways step, then another.

Suddenly some kind of hook caught her wrist, and

she looked down to see the crook of a wooden cane tugging at her.

She spun back toward him. "Troy! What are you doing?"

"I knew this thing was good for something," he said, holding up the cane he'd borrowed from Lou Ann and offering her a repentant grin. Then he scanned the room. "The place is emptying out. We can have some privacy. Do you mind staying a minute?"

Yes, I mind! She bit her lip, shook her head and sank back down onto the pew. It was probably better to stay here in the sanctuary than to go off somewhere by themselves. Somewhere she might feel that strange sense in her stomach again, that sense of...

Being attracted.

Yeah, that.

She hadn't felt it for years—in fact, she hadn't felt it since she was engaged to Troy—and it was making her crazy.

"We've got to talk about why you jump every time I touch you."

"Don't open that can of worms, Troy," she said quickly. Of all their possible topics of conversation, that was the one she most wanted to avoid.

He cocked his head to one side, studying her face. "Actually we've got to talk about a few things," he said finally. "One of which is this marriage. People are asking more and more about it. We can't put them off forever with some vague engagement plans in the future."

Early-evening sunshine slanted through stained-glass windows, and the breeze through the church's open back door felt cool against Angelica's neck. "I know. It's Xavier, too. He wants to know when the wedding will be."

"Is there going to be a wedding?" He watched her, his face impassive.

Her heart skipped a beat. "Do you want to back out?"

"Noooooo," he said. "But I'm seeing some implications I wasn't thinking about before." Deliberately he reached out and took her hand.

It felt as if every nerve, every sensation in her body was concentrated in her hand. Concentrated to notice how his hand was bigger, more calloused than hers. To notice the warmth and protection of being completely wrapped in him. Waves of what felt like electricity crackled through her veins.

He was watching her. It seemed he was always watching her. "You feel it?"

Heat rose to her cheeks as she nodded.

"So...we're going to have to figure out what to do with that."

Somehow even admitting she felt something for him—something like physical attraction—made her feel panicky and ashamed. She looked away from him, focusing on the polished light wooden pews, on the simple altar at the front of the church. Her hand still burned, enclosed by his larger one, and she pulled it away, hiding it in the folds of her dress.

"It's not wrong, you know. It's a mutual thing, a gift from God, and He blesses it in the context of marriage." Troy's voice, though quiet, was sure.

Angelica wanted that quiet certainty so much. She wanted Troy's leadership in this area. Wanted to feel okay about her body and wanted to find the beauty in physical intimacy sanctioned by God. It had been so long since she felt anything but sadness and regret about the physical side of life. Here, in God's house, she wanted to hope. But did she dare? Was change possible after all these years? Could God bless her that much?

Xavier and Lou Ann came hurrying in through the side front door of the sanctuary. *Whew, relief.*

"Hey, you two." Lou Ann reached them right behind Xavier and leaned on the pew in front of them. "Some of the kids and parents are walking over to the Meadows for ice cream. Is it okay if I take Xavier along?"

"Please, Mom?" Xavier chimed in.

Angelica grabbed her purse. "I can take him," she said to Lou Ann.

"That's okay. I could use a rocky road ice-cream cone myself." Lou Ann reached over and put a hand on her shoulder, effectively holding her in the pew. She leaned down and whispered, "Besides, you need to talk to him."

"Do I have to?"

"Yes, you have to!" Lou Ann patted her arm. "I'll be praying for you."

"Thanks a lot!" She bit her lip and watched Lou Ann guide Xavier off, trying to remember what was most important: God was with her, always, and God forgave her, and God would help her get through this whole thing.

She drew in a breath, and the peace she'd been seeking during the service came rushing in. *Pneuma.* Holy Spirit. God.

She turned back to Troy and he took her hand again, and immediately that uncurling inside started. That opening; that vulnerability. She tried to pull away a little, but he held on. Not too tight, not forcing her, but letting her know he wanted to keep touching her.

Angelica let him do it, her eyes closed tight. She didn't want to like his touch. Didn't want to need him. It would be so much easier and safer not to open up.

He tightened his grip on her hand, ever so slightly. "I want you to tell me why you pull away all the time."

"I'm not sure—"

"Hey, hey, the engaged couple!" Pastor Ricky came over and clapped Troy on the shoulder, leaned down to hug Angelica, overwhelming her. She shrank back, right into Troy. *Aack.*

"Have you two set a date yet? Are you wanting to get married here? You'd better reserve it now if you're planning to do it any time soon. We're a busy place."

"We were just talking about that," Troy said.

"Make an appointment with me to start some pre-marital counseling, too." He made a few more minutes of small talk and then turned to another pair of parishioners and walked away with them.

"He's right," Troy said. "We've got to decide."

"I know." But inside, turmoil reigned.

Xavier needed a dad in the worst way, and Troy was the perfect man for the job. The three of them were already close.

Xavier needed it, needed Troy, but she herself was terrified.

Lord, help me. Her heart rate accelerated to the pace of a hummingbird. She could barely breathe. She looked up at Troy, panicky.

"You can talk to me." He slid an arm along the back of the pew behind her, letting it rest ever so lightly around her shoulders. "What is it you need to tell me?"

She took deep, slow, breaths. The fact that she was shaking had to be obvious to Troy.

What part could she tell him? What part did she need to keep private? What part would come back to bite her?

Tell him the worst right away.

Like yanking off a Band-Aid. She moved to the edge of the pew, away from his arm, and pulled her hand from his. Clenching her fists, she turned her head toward him, looking right at his handsome face. "I was…I was raped."

"Raped? What? When?"

It was the first time she'd ever said that word, even to herself. Her vision seemed to blur around the edges, bringing her focus to just his mouth, his eyes. She had to grip the edge of the pew, waiting for the expression of disgust and horror to cross his face.

His mouth twisted.

There it was, the anger she'd expected. She looked away from his face and down at his hands. His enormous hands. They clenched into fists.

She shrank away. Was he going to hit her right here and now? Frantically she looked around for help.

"Tell me." He sounded as though he was gritting his teeth. But his voice was quiet, and when she looked at his hands, they'd relaxed a little. He wasn't moving any closer, either.

"Troy, I'm sorry… I was drinking. I should have been more careful."

"Man, I'd like to kill the jerk who did that to you. When did it happen?" His voice was still angry, and she couldn't blame him. At least it was a controlled anger, so she wasn't at immediate risk.

Even though it would destroy their relationship, she'd started down this path and she had to keep going. *God, help me.* "It was…after my twenty-first birthday celebration. Remember I went out to that bar?" She heard the urgent sound in her voice. Couldn't seem to calm down.

His expression changed. "I remember that night. I had to work and couldn't go." He pounded a fist lightly against the pew. "I should have been there to take care of you."

"I was drinking."

He took her hand in his. "It's not your fault. Man, I

wish I'd been there." He shook his head slowly back and forth, his eyes far away, as if he were reliving that time.

Not her fault? She looked away, bit her lip. That was what her therapist and her aunt had said, but she'd never really believed it. Could Troy?

"Look," he said, "as far as any physical connection between us is concerned, you can have all the time you need. I'll be patient. I understand."

Tears filled her eyes. Was it possible that, even knowing this, Troy could still want her?

"So…wait. That's when Xavier was conceived?"

She nodded, staring down at her lap, kneading her skirt between her hands. He was being kinder than she had any right to expect. She blinked and drew in shuddery breaths as tension released from her body.

Telling him the truth was something she'd barely considered at the time because she was terrified of what his reaction would be. She'd had some vague image of yelling and rage and judgment, and the notion of Troy, her beloved fiancé, doing that had pushed her right out of town. Better to leave than to face that pain.

He didn't seem to be blaming her. She could hardly believe in it, couldn't imagine that his kindness would stay, but even the edge of it warmed her heart.

"Who did it, Angelica?" Troy's voice grew low, urgent. "Was it someone you knew? Someone we knew?"

And there it was, the part she didn't dare tell him.

"Did we know him?" Troy repeated.

Still looking down at her lap, she shook her head.

Did it count as a lie if she didn't say it out loud?

Troy looked at Angelica with his heart aching for all the pain she'd been through and his fists clenching with anger at the jerk who'd done this to her. He tried to ignore the tiny suspicion that she wasn't telling the whole truth.

His mother had constantly lied to his father. He didn't want to believe it of Angelica, but her body language, her voice, her facial expressions—all of it suggested she was keeping something from him. "We were engaged. You should have told me."

"I blamed myself," she said in a quiet voice. "And I knew how much my chastity meant to you."

Her words hit him like a physical blow. "You think that would be more important than taking care of you? I would've helped you."

"Out of obligation," she said, glancing up at him and then away. "But you wouldn't have liked it."

"Was I that kind of a jerk?" He didn't think so, but look how he was feeling right now. Compassion, sure, but with the slightest shred of doubt in his heart.

He grabbed the Bible from the rack in front of them and held it. For something to do with his hands, but also to remind himself to take the high road and think the best. "I can't believe this happened to you," he said, turning the Good Book over and over in his hands, thinking out loud. "It was a crime committed against you. It's not your fault, and you shouldn't blame yourself." He put the Bible down beside him. "And if you didn't report the crime then…" He searched her face, saw her shake her head, looking at her lap again. "If you didn't say anything already, you should now. The man should be brought to justice. I'll talk to Dion. He knows everything about the law."

"No!" She scooted away from him, an expression

of horror on her face. "I don't want to dig into it again. And anyway, it's not…it's not necessary."

"We gotta get the guy! Don't you want justice?"

She shook her head. "No. I don't want anything to do with the police."

"Are you protecting someone?"

"I just don't want to get the police involved. For all kinds of reasons."

Why wouldn't she tell him who did it? Was she telling the truth, that she didn't know the person?

And if she was lying, then how much did she really care for him?

He looked at her face and was shocked by the disappointment he saw there. Immediately he felt awful. She needed support, she needed help. She needed a dad for Xavier, and speaking of that sweet kid…wow, he was the product of an assault. And she'd mothered him despite that, wonderfully.

Whatever mistakes she'd made in the past, he was going to provide what he could for her. He reached out to put his arm around her. Felt her stiffen, but remain still, letting him do it.

There was none of the tender promise of before, though. There was more of a cringe. He reached out involuntarily to stroke her shiny hair.

She pulled away and stood. "I'm going to leave you to think about this. It's a lot to take in, I know."

"Angelica—"

"We'll talk later, okay?" Her lips twisted and she hurried off toward the back of the sanctuary.

Leaving him to his dark thoughts and guilt and anger, a mixture that didn't seem to belong in this holy place.

Twelve

"I'm terrified," Angelica admitted to Lou Ann as they dug carrots from the garden. "They hated me before and they'll hate me even more now."

The older woman shifted her gardening stool to the next row. "Troy's family isn't that bad."

Hot sun warmed Angelica's head and bare arms, and the garden smells of dirt and tomato vines and marigolds tickled her nose. Around them, rows of green were starting to reveal the fruit of the season: red tomatoes, yellow squash, purple eggplant.

Later today, she and Troy and Xavier were going to join his family at the small country club's Labor Day picnic. Just the words *country club* made Angelica shudder.

Not only that, but her relationship with Troy had felt strained ever since last Saturday, when she'd revealed the truth about how Xavier was conceived. Although he'd responded better than she'd expected, she still felt questions in his eyes every time he looked at her. It made her want to avoid him, but they'd had the plan to go to the Labor Day picnic for weeks.

And she had to see whether she could stand it and whether his family could accept Xavier. Had to see whether to go forward with the marriage or run as fast as she could in the opposite direction.

The older woman sat back on her gardening stool. "You put way too much stock in what those people think."

"What they think about me isn't that important," Angelica said, "but I don't want them to reject Xavier."

Lou Ann used the back of her hand to push gray curls out of her eyes. "I've yet to meet a person who could dislike that child. What God didn't give him in health, He gave him double in charm."

"Which he knows how to use," Angelica said wryly. "But what he doesn't know is which fork to pick up at what time. I don't, either. We've neither of us ever been to a country club."

"He never took you when you were engaged?" Lou Ann asked, and when Angelica shook her head, the other woman waved a dismissive hand. "Honey, this isn't some ritzy East Coast place. This is a picnic in small-town Ohio. I've been to the country club dozens of times. It's just a golf course with a pool and some tennis courts. Ordinary people go there."

"People like me? I don't think so." She remembered the girls from high school who spent their summers at the club. They wore their perfect tans and tennis whites around town as status symbols. Angelica could only pretend not to see their sneers as she scooped their ice cream or rang up their snack purchases, working summers at the local Shop Star Market.

"You've got the wrong idea," Lou Ann said. "Rescue River's country club has always been a welcoming place. Never had a color barrier, never dug into your marital status, never turned away families based on their religion. They're open to anybody who can pay the fee, which isn't all that much these days. I've thought about joining just to have a nice place to swim."

Angelica tugged at a stubborn weed. "You may be right, but Troy's family can't stand me. Not only did I dump their son, but my grandfather threw a wrench in their plans to dominate the county with their giant farm. We've been feuding from way back."

"Isn't it time that ended?" Lou Ann pulled radishes while she spoke. "The Lord wants us to be forces of reconciliation. I know Troy believes in that. You should, too."

Angelica sat back in the grass, listening to crickets chirping as a breeze rustled the leaves of an oak tree nearby. God's peace. She smiled at Lou Ann. "You're my hero, you know that? I want to be you when I grow up."

"Oh, go on." Lou Ann's flush of pleasure belied her dismissive words.

"But I'm still scared."

"You know what Pastor Ricky would say. God doesn't give us a spirit of fear, but of power and love and self-control."

"Yeah." Angelica tried to feel it. Sometimes, more and more often these days, she felt God's strength and peace inside her.

But this Labor Day picnic had put her into a tailspin. Steaks and burgers weren't the only thing likely to be grilled; she would be, too.

"Here's a little tip," Lou Ann said. "Pretend like they're people from another country, another culture.

You're a representative of your culture, bringing your own special gifts. You're not expecting to be the same as them, just to visit. Like you're an ambassador to a foreign land."

Angelica cocked her head to one side, her fingers stilling in the warm, loose dirt. Slowly a smile came to her face. "That's a nice idea. If I'm an ambassador, I'm not under pressure to be just like them."

"Right. You just have to think, that's interesting, that's not how we do it in my culture, but that's okay."

"Yes! And in my culture, we'd bring a gift." Angelica reached for a sugar snap pea and popped it into her mouth, savoring the vegetable's sweet crunch.

Lou Ann smiled. "Atta girl. What would you bring?"

"Food, probably. But that's the last thing they need, especially at a country club bash."

Lou Ann tugged at a recalcitrant carrot and then held it up triumphantly. "Anyone would welcome fresh vegetables from a garden."

Angelica flashed forward to imagine herself and Xavier walking onto the country club grounds. The image improved when she threw in a basket of zucchini, tomatoes and carrots. She threw her arms around the older woman. "You're a genius!"

Troy pulled up to the bunkhouse and, on an impulse, tooted the horn in the same pattern he used when he'd dated Angelica years ago. It was a joke, because he'd always insisted on coming to the door even though she urged him not to. It used to be something of a race, with him hustling to get out of his car and up to the door before she could grab her things and burst outside.

He couldn't beat her now, though. By the time he'd

grabbed his stupid cane and edged gingerly out of the truck—man, his leg ached today—Angelica had emerged from the bunkhouse. Her rolled-up jeans fit her like a dream, and her tanned, toned arms rocked the basket she was carrying, and Troy wanted to wrap his arms around her, she looked so cute.

"What do you have there?" Troy asked. He was proud of her, proud of bringing her to meet his family. Remeet them, actually; they'd all known each other forever. But Angelica was a different person now, and they all had a different relationship.

"Just a little something for your dad."

"For Dad, huh?" Troy tried to smile, but he wondered how that would be received. His father was notoriously difficult, and Troy had already warned Angelica that his dad's moodiness had gotten worse. None of them could go a whole evening without causing him to yell or cuss or storm out of the house.

Lou Ann came out bringing Xavier, fresh-scrubbed and grinning.

Troy gave him a high five. "You ready for some fun, buddy? They have a blow-up bounce house and a ball pit and face painting."

"Face painting is for girls," Xavier said scornfully.

"I just now saw your outfit," Lou Ann said to Angelica, then turned to Troy. "Have they changed their rules about denim?"

Angelica's face fell. "Aren't you supposed to wear jeans?"

"It's no problem," Troy said. "They did away with that rule a couple of years ago."

"I didn't even think of it," Angelica said uneasily.

He put a protective arm around her shoulder. "You'll

be fine. You look great!" But the truth was, he was on edge himself. It wasn't just his dad's bad moods; his older brother wasn't much better. Dad and Samuel, the two wealthiest men in the community, could be an intimidating pair.

"It'll be fine," he repeated. And hoped it was true.

When they got to the club, they were greeted with the smell of steaks and burgers grilling and the sound of a brass quartet playing patriotic songs. The whole place was set up like a carnival, with music and clowns and inflatables, and kids ran in small packs from one attraction to the next.

"This is so cool, Mom!" Xavier's eyes were wide, as if he'd never seen anything like this before. And knowing how poor they'd been, maybe he hadn't.

"It really is." She was a little wide-eyed herself.

He took Xavier by one hand and Angelica by the other and urged them forward. "We'll find you someone fun to play with," he told Xavier. "Samuel's girl, Mindy."

"A girl?"

"Girls can be fun!" He squeezed Angelica's hand, trying to help her relax, and looked around for his brother's daughter. Truthfully he worried about the girl. With an overprotective, suspicious father who tended to stay isolated, she often seemed lonely. "Hey, Sam!" He waved to his brother, gestured him over.

Sam walked toward them, frowning, holding Mindy's hand.

"Hey," Troy greeted his brother, glaring to remind him to be polite. "You remember Angelica, right?"

Sam gave him a quick nod and turned to Angelica. "Angelica. It's been a long time."

"And this is Xavier, Angelica's son."

"Say hello," she prompted gently.

But Xavier was staring at Mindy. "What happened to your other hand?"

"Xavier!" Angelica sounded mortified.

"I was born without it," Mindy said matter-of-factly. "What happened to your hair?"

"Leukemia, but it's gonna be gone soon and then I'll have hair."

Mindy nodded. "Want to go see the ball pit? It's cool."

"Sure!" And they were off.

"I'm so sorry he said that," Angelica said to his brother. "He should know better."

"No problem," Sam said, but to Troy's experienced ear, the irritation in his brother's voice was evident. He hated for anyone to comment on his daughter's disability. Plus, the man was frazzled; since his wife's death, he'd had his hands full trying to run his business empire and care for his daughter.

"Kids will be kids," Troy said as a general reminder to everybody, especially his brother.

"That's true," Sam said. "I'm sorry Mindy commented on your son's hair. Are things going okay with his treatment?"

"I'm hopeful," Angelica said quietly. "Lots of people are praying for him."

They strolled behind the two running children. Troy kept putting his arm around Angelica while trying not to actually touch her. He was being an idiot, but there'd been awkwardness between them ever since their botched conversation the other night, when she told him about her attack. He wished he hadn't pushed her to reveal her assailant, but he wanted to know because the guy deserved punishment. He also needed to be off the street.

Xavier and Mindy were chattering away as they zigzagged from craft table to ball toss. The adults, on the other hand, were too quiet. "Angelica brought some vegetables for Dad," Troy told Sam, trying to keep this reunion from being a total fail.

His brother nodded. "Too bad Dad hates vegetables."

"Oh." Angelica's face fell. "They're fresh from the garden back at Troy's house. I've been helping Lou Ann take care of it. Does he even hate fresh tomatoes?"

"Pretty much. But," Sam added grudgingly, "his doctor told him he needs to eat better, so maybe this will help."

"We made some zucchini bread, too. Maybe he'll like that, at least."

"I'm sure he will," Troy said firmly.

Sam didn't answer, and after a raised-eyebrow glance at him, Angelica shrugged and got very busy with examining the Popsicle-stick crafts at the kids' stand and checking out the tissue-paper flowers some of the older girls were making. The brass quintet started playing old-fashioned songs, of the "Camptown Races" sort, and the smell of grilled sausage and onions grew stronger, making Troy's mouth water.

"Where's Dad?" he asked to kill the awkward silence.

"I'll get him," Sam said. "Watch Mindy, would you?"

"Sure."

As Sam left, Angelica looked up at Troy. "He hates me. I can tell."

"Well, he doesn't *hate* you. He doesn't hate anyone.

He's a good guy underneath. But he's had people take advantage of him a lot, and his wife's death was really traumatic. So bear with him. He's protective of his family, and he thinks you hurt me."

"I did hurt you," she said softly. After a minute's hesitation, she reached out and lightly grasped his forearm, and the touch seemed to travel straight to his heart. "I never apologized about that. I shouldn't have left like I did, Troy. I should have trusted you more, and it was wrong of me to leave without any explanation. You can maybe understand how desperate I was, but still, I realize now that it was a mistake."

"Thanks for saying that." Seven years later, he found that the apology still mattered. His throat tightened. "I appreciate hearing those words from you. But I'm sorry, too."

"For what?" She looked up at him through her long lashes, and she was so pretty he just wanted to grab her into his arms. But you didn't do that with Angelica.

"For being the type of person who'd judge a woman for something that wasn't her fault." He saw Mindy stumble, watched Xavier reach out a hand to steady her. "Life's taught me not to be so rigid about everything."

"Isn't that the truth?" She laughed a little, looking off toward the cornfields in the distance. "We all learn as we get older."

"Well, most of us." He nudged her and nodded toward his father, who was being urged out of his seat by Sam and Daisy. "Some are a little more thickheaded and it takes longer."

"Here we go," she said, obviously trying to be funny, but he could hear the dread in her voice.

"Just don't let anything he says get to you. I've got your back."

"Thanks." She tightened her grip on his arm and then let go. Today was the first time Angelica had initiated touching him since they met again, and he had to hope that it meant there was some promise for them together.

Xavier and Mindy shouted for them, and they turned to watch the two kids skim down the inflatable slide together. Around them, people were starting to gather at tables covered by checkered tablecloths. Parents were trying to get their kids to come to supper, helped along by the smell of hot dogs and cotton candy.

The warm sun and music and patriotic decorations brought back memories of his parents in happier days, of playing baseball and Frisbee with his brother and sister here at the club, of eating and laughing together before everything had started to go wrong in his family.

Behind them, he heard his father's grousing voice. "I don't want to walk all the way over there. I just got comfortable sitting down and—"

"Come on, Dad." It was Daisy, and when he turned to look he saw that she was urging their father along by herself; Sam had apparently bailed on supervising this meeting. "Troy's fiancée is here," Daisy continued determinedly, "and you need to welcome her. Hi, Angelica!"

Angelica offered a big smile. "It's good to see you, Daisy. Hi, Mr. Hinton."

"Hello." His father didn't say anything rude, thankfully; that probably meant he hadn't had much to drink yet. But he looked Angelica up and down with a frown.

"Dad, Angelica brought you some vegetables from the garden."

She rolled her eyes at him, subtly, and he realized he was trying too hard.

"Humph." His father looked at the basket dismissively. "Green stuff."

Troy opened his mouth to smooth things over, but Angelica took a step in front of him, effectively nudging him out of her way. "Sam said you don't like vegetables, but there's some zucchini bread I made from Lou Ann Miller's recipe. I hope you like it." She held out the basket.

"Thank you." His father took it begrudgingly. "That woman always won the prize at picnics when we were teenagers. Even back then, she was a good cook."

Angelica smiled. "She still is. Maybe you could come visit sometime."

Troy gritted his teeth. He avoided inviting his dad over because the man was so difficult. He didn't like what Troy was doing with his life—being a vet, especially doing rescue. The Hinton sons should be making money hand over fist in the world of agricultural high finance, according to his dad.

"So you've taken to being a hostess at Troy's house, have you?" his father asked.

"Dad!" Daisy scolded before Troy could intervene. "Angelica has every right. She's marrying Troy."

As Angelica followed the group toward the long dining tables, Daisy's words rang in her ears like chimes foretelling her fate. *"She's marrying Troy."*

"Hi, Angelica!" A blonde in spike-heeled sandals approached, with mirror-image blond girls holding each hand. Ugh. She'd wanted a distraction, but not necessarily in the form of Nora Templeton—one of the country-club girls who'd been meanest when they were in high school together. Was her voice really prissy? Or was Angelica just defensive?

"Hi, Nora," she said, holding out a hand.

"Let Mommy shake hands, Stella," Nora said, pulling loose from one of her daughters to hold out a perfectly manicured hand.

Which made Angelica wonder if she'd gotten all the dirt out from under her own nails since her marathon gardening session that morning.

"Run along and play a minute." Nora shooed her daughters away. "How are you? I heard you were back in town."

"Yes." As Nora's daughters high-fived each other and ran off toward the dessert table, Angelica debated how much to tell. "My son and I wanted to spend more time with my grandpa."

"That's sweet. I see your grandpa sometimes at the Towers when I visit my aunt." She leaned closer. "Your son looks a lot like his daddy."

Angelica's world blurred as she stared at the other woman. Did Nora know Jeremy, her assailant, then? Who else did?

"He's got that same dark hair and sweet smile."

Around them, people stood in clusters or found seats at family-sized tables. Troy's friend Dion was sitting down with an older couple, and he saw her and gave a friendly wave.

Angelica fought to stay in the present and analyze Nora's words. Did she mean Jeremy? Had Jeremy talked about what had happened, then, after threatening her with a worse assault if she ever said a word?

Nora's eyes grew round. "Did I say something wrong? I just assumed Troy's your son's father."

Angelica's breath whooshed out. Troy. Nora thought Troy was Xavier's dad.

"If it's supposed to be a secret, I won't say anything to anyone. But I think it's just so sweet that you two are finally getting married."

Angelica stared at the other woman blankly while her mind raced. Should she just let this happen, let the misperception remain? Was that fair to Troy? To Xavier?

"Mom! Stella rubbed cake in my face and we didn't even eat dinner yet!"

"Girls! Stop that!" Nora looked apologetically at Angelica. "They're not always such brats. See you around!" She rushed off, leaving Angelica in a haze of self-doubt.

Oh, she'd been stupid, thinking she could bring Xavier here to live without putting this small, close-knit community on alert. Everyone had to be doing the math in their heads, figuring out that Xavier was of an age to have been conceived during her former engagement to Troy.

"Come on, Angelica." Daisy's voice brought her back from the brink. "They're about ready to serve dinner, and Dad likes to be first in line."

"Make me sound like a cad," her father grumbled.

The savory tang of barbecue sauce and the slightly burned scent of kettle corn filled the air as they straggled toward long tables heaped with potato salad, watermelon and enormous silver chafing dishes of baked beans.

Lou Ann had been right: the crowd included all skin colors, just like the town. There was even a man wearing a turban at one table and a group of women in brightly colored saris at another. Cooks and servers in pristine white aprons and chefs' hats shouted instructions to one another, punctuated by the laughter of family groups and the shouts of children.

Angelica ran a hand over Xavier's bald head and felt the tiniest hint of stubble. A bubble of joy rose in her chest, reminding her of what was really important.

As Angelica helped Xavier load his plate for dinner, Troy's father stood next to her in line. "I told my son not to get together with you," he said in what was apparently supposed to be a whisper, but was probably audible to everyone up and down the long serving buffet.

"Oh?" Ignoring the stares and nudges around them, she scooped some baked ziti onto Xavier's plate. "Why's that?"

"Because you dumped him before," Mr. Hinton said. "Fool me once, shame on you, fool me twice, shame on me."

Heat rose to her cheeks, but she just nodded. What could she say? She had left Troy, it was true.

"What's that man talking about, Mom?" Xavier asked in a stage whisper.

"Ancient history," she said.

"Actually history about the same age as you are."

The server behind the grill was openly staring. "Shrimp or steak, ma'am?"

"Xavier," she said, "take this plate over where Mindy's sitting. I'll be right there."

As soon as Xavier left, she turned to Mr. Hinton, hands on hips. "Any issues you have with me, you're welcome to tell me. But don't involve my son. None of this is his fault, and he has a lot to deal with right now."

Mr. Hinton narrowed his eyes at her. "Your son is part of the issue. Is he related to me?"

She cocked her head to one side.

"I mean, is my son his father?"

Light dawned. "No, of course not! Troy would never…" She trailed off. Mr. Hinton believed that, too? She'd known on some level that acquaintances like Nora might think Xavier was Troy's son. But she was shocked to realize that his own father suspected it.

Keeping Xavier's parentage a secret was hurting Troy. But revealing it would hurt Xavier.

Lou Ann's words came back to her. As a Christian, she was supposed to be all about reconciliation.

She turned to Mr. Hinton, gently took his plate and put it down on the buffet table and nudged him off to the side, ignoring the raised eyebrows of family members and bystanders around them. She pulled him by the hand to a bench out of earshot of the crowd and sat down, patting the seat beside her.

He gave her a grouchy look and then sat.

Aware that she didn't have long before he left in a hissy fit, she talked fast. "Look, I can understand why you're upset with me. And I can understand why you want to know whether Xavier is a blood relative. The answer is no. He's not."

Mr. Hinton crossed his arms and glared at her. "All the more reason for me to be angry, then. Isn't that right? Isn't my son opening himself up to a lying, cheating woman by getting back together with you?"

His voice had risen and people were staring; conversations in the area had died down. She'd *thought* this area was secluded enough to keep their conversation private, but apparently, with the volume of Mr. Hinton's hard-of-hearing voice, it wasn't.

It was her worst nightmare come true: she was a spectacle at the country club, looked down on by the other guests.

What's the right thing to do, Lord? The prayer shot straight up through the tears that she couldn't keep from forming in her eyes.

An arm came around her shoulder, and Troy sat beside her, pulling her to his side. His strength held her up where she felt like collapsing.

"Dad," Daisy said as she hurried over to clutch her father's shoulder, leaning over him from the other side. "Why are you making a scene? You know this isn't right."

"No." Angelica straightened her spine, pulled away from Troy, and stood. "He's not doing anything but protecting his son. That's totally understandable."

"Thank you!" Mr. Hinton's exasperated words almost made her smile.

"But, Mr. Hinton," she said, reaching out to clasp his arm. "That's what I need to do, too. Xavier's story is his own to tell, and he's too young to understand it and share it yet. So I'm just going to have to ask you to take it on faith that, when the time is right, you'll know the right amount about his parentage."

"That's about as convoluted as a story can get," Mr. Hinton complained, but his voice wasn't as loud and angry as it had been before.

"Dad. I know enough to understand what happened," Troy said. "None of it is Angelica's fault, and I'd just ask you to accept Xavier without any questions right now. That's what I'm planning to do."

"And that's what this family is about," Daisy said firmly. "We accept kids. All kids."

Angelica took deep breaths and shot up a prayer of thanks. Troy had supported her. And it looked as though Daisy was coming around to her side, too.

Mr. Hinton was a tougher case, but he was just trying to protect his child and his family. That was something she could understand.

"Come on," she said, and took the risk of clasping his hand. "Let's go get back in line before the food's all gone."

He cleared his throat. "Finally somebody said something that makes sense." As they walked together to the line, he leaned down to mutter in her ear, "You tell Lou Ann that nothing on the dessert table here holds a candle to her zucchini bread."

"Wait. You've been sampling dessert already?"

"Life's short. Eat dessert first. Right?"

"I think I'm going to follow that philosophy," Angelica said, grabbing a big piece of chocolate cake.

"You're not my favorite person in the world," Mr. Hinton said to her. "But I reckon I can back off of hassling you. Xavier's not accountable for your problems. And come to think of it, you're not accountable for your grandfather's."

Angelica gave the old man a sidearm hug and then sidled away before he could either embrace her or reject her.

"Humph." He glared at her and bustled off.

It wasn't a warm welcome, but Angelica felt that progress had been made. And she shot up a prayer of thanks and wonder to God, who was clearly the author of the peace and reconciliation she'd just felt.

Thirteen

After dinner, they all moved over to sit near the band. Xavier was fighting tiredness, but losing the battle, so Angelica talked him into lying down for a little rest on the blanket beside her. He resisted, but in minutes, he was asleep.

The gentle music prompted a few older couples onto the makeshift dance floor, where moonlight illuminated them in a soft glow. Most of the younger kids were quieting down or already asleep, while the teenagers paired off at the edges of the crowd. Nearby, most of the Hintons were spreading blankets and settling in to listen to the music.

She wanted this for Xavier. She wanted the community and the family and the security represented by life here.

She'd never thought she could have it. When she left seven years ago, running scared, she'd thought her connection with this community was severed. Now she had a chance to regain it, stronger than when she was young, to regain it as part of a connected, loving family.

She wanted it so badly, but was she just setting herself up for disappointment?

"Aw, he's so sweet," Daisy said, coming over to settle in the grass beside her. "He got along really well with everyone, didn't he?"

"I was pleased. But he's a great kid that way. He's always had an ease and charm with people that I can only envy."

Daisy cocked her head to one side, studying Xavier. "I wonder where he gets that."

The comment echoed in Angelica's head. Where did Xavier get his charm and people skills?

The thought pushed her toward his genetics, toward Jeremy and his superficial charm, but she shoved that idea away. "My aunt helped out with him so much when he was small. She was an amazing woman, and I'm sure he picked up some of her better traits."

"I'm sure he's picked up some of your great traits," Daisy said, patting her knee. "I really admire what you've done, raising him even though..." She stopped.

"Even thought what?"

"Look," Daisy said, "I'm guessing Xavier is the product of some kind of an assault. Remember, I'm a social worker. I see stuff like this all the time. I can tell you're wary of men in a way that suggests you've been treated badly, and I know you didn't use to be like that, so..." She spread her hands expressively.

Angelica stared at the woman, feeling defeated. Daisy had guessed most of the story of her past. As much as Angelica wanted to hide it, it was written and apparent in the existence of Xavier.

"I'm sorry." Daisy patted Angelica's arm. "There

I go blurting stuff out again. I should learn to put a sock in it."

Angelica let out a rueful sigh. "For sure, I don't want to talk about my past troubles. But am I going to be able to escape it? Is it wrong for me to want to keep it all private?"

"From me, it's okay," Daisy said. "I have no right to your private information. But I would think that Troy would want to know whatever information is available about Xavier's father."

"That's what I'm afraid of." Troy was the last person she wanted to tell. The trust developing between them was a beautiful thing, but fragile. Revealing the name of her attacker might downright destroy it. After all, Troy had looked up to Jeremy. Would he believe that a guy he admired, a guy who'd mentored him, who'd been a town athletic star, had done something so awful to Angelica?

Or would he turn on her instead?

"But maybe not," Daisy went on, lying back to stare up at the emerging stars. "Maybe he won't need to know. Troy is a rescuer at heart. He's taken in animals since he was a little kid, and in those cases you don't know what happened. But you deal with the results."

"Gee, thanks, Daisy." She whacked the woman on the calf, welcoming the distraction from her own uneasy thoughts. "Did you just compare me to a rescue dog?"

Daisy grinned. "If the shoe fits…"

"If the dog coat fits…" Angelica played along. She was glad that she and Daisy could joke. But what the woman had said bothered her. Why did Troy want to be with her, anyway? Why was he willing to put up with not knowing Xavier's background?

Was it because he saw her, not as an equal human being, but as a creature to be rescued?

"Today's the day, buddy!" Troy turned in the passenger seat to give Xavier a high five. "I get my cast off, and you get to start playing soccer on the team."

"Just to try it," Angelica warned as she swung the truck around the corner. "Remember, when we go to your checkup on Thursday, Dr. Ravi is going to let us know if soccer is the right thing for you to do."

Xavier's jaw jutted out, and Troy could almost see his decision to ignore his mom. He looked down, grabbed the soccer ball from the seat beside him and clutched it to his chest. "Hey, Mr. Troy, do you think you could be one of the coaches?"

"I don't know much about soccer, buddy." But the idea tickled his fancy. What a great way that would be to connect with Xavier. And to help kids. Coaches had been a huge part of his own childhood, giving him the encouragement his dad hadn't.

Xavier was bouncing up and down in the car seat. "You played football before. You could learn about soccer. Please?"

"We'll see, buddy. I have to get the okay from my doctor. Just like you."

"Really?" Xavier's eyes went round as quarters. "I didn't think grown-ups had any rules."

Troy and Angelica exchanged amused glances, and Troy reached back to pat Xavier's shoulder. "We have more rules than you know. And if we're smart, we follow the rules. We listen to doctors."

Xavier frowned and nodded, obviously thinking over this new concept.

Angelica flashed Troy a grateful smile as she pulled up to the door of the hospital. *Thanks*, she mouthed.

Looking at her made his heart catch fire. She was everything to him, and once he got this wretched cast off, he'd feel whole again and as if he could take control. She wouldn't have to drive him and he would be able to be a full partner to her and Xavier. They'd be able to set a wedding date and move forward with their lives, with a real marriage.

"Let me know if you need a ride when you're done."

"This should be pretty quick. Afterward, I'll just stroll over to the park and you guys should still be doing practice."

He gave in to a sudden urge, leaned over and dropped a kiss on her cheek. Her hair's fruity scent and the sound of her breathy little sigh made him want to linger, and only his awareness of Xavier in the backseat held him to propriety.

Especially when she didn't pull back.

He felt ten feet tall. They were making real progress as a couple. What a great day.

"What was that for?" she asked while Xavier giggled from the backseat.

"Just feeling good about everything."

He walked into the hospital easily, barely using his cane. After checking in and waiting impatiently in a roomful of people, the nurse put him in a room to wait for X-rays.

The technician came in and told Troy to hop up on the exam table. "First I'll cut the cast off and then we'll x-ray everything." He was bent over an electronic tablet, recording and filling things in. Finally he looked up. "Hey, I know you."

Troy studied the bearded man, who looked a little younger than Troy. "You do look a little familiar." Then it clicked into place: this was the man they'd seen outside the Senior Towers, that day they'd done the weeding. The one Angelica hadn't liked. His friend's younger brother.

"I'm Logan Filmore." He held out his name tag as if to prove it. "I was a couple years behind you in school, but I watched you play football with my brother."

"Right, right!" Troy reached out, shook the man's hand. "I'm sorry for your loss." Logan's brother had died in a car accident about five years ago. "The whole town came out for Jeremy's funeral. What a loss."

"Yeah." Logan frowned as he positioned Troy on the x-ray table. "I keep hearing that from everyone now that I've moved back permanently."

They made small talk as Logan took pictures of Troy's leg in every position. When the ordeal seemed to be almost over, Logan looked at Troy with a serious expression. "I hate to bring this up, but I heard that you're pretty intense with Angelica Camden. Is that true?"

"Yeah." Troy smiled to remember their exchange in the car. "In fact, we're getting married pretty soon."

"That's great." Logan moved the X-ray machine to another position. "Now, lie still for this one. It's a full 360 and takes a few minutes to get warmed up." He made a tiny adjustment to Troy's leg. "So, you feel okay about everything that happened before?"

Something in the man's tone made Troy's stomach clench. "What do you mean?"

"I mean, about her leaving town pregnant, staying away. You…" He shook his head. "I don't know if I could do that, raise another man's child."

Heat rose inside Troy but he tamped it down. "That's between me and Angelica. And anyway, a kid's a kid."

Logan took a step back, palms out like stop signs. "For sure. Didn't mean anything by it."

"No problem." He'd have to learn to deal with nosy people. It came with the territory of marrying a woman with a kid and a bit of mystery in her past.

"Anyway, I'm glad to see my nephew get a good home. After Jeremy passed, I always thought I should do something, but since Jeremy said she didn't want it…"

His *nephew*? Icy shock froze Troy's body. "Want what?"

"Well, any help with the baby. I guess she felt like, since it was just a one-night stand, he didn't owe her anything."

"Just a one-night stand." Troy repeated the words parrotlike, feeling about as dumb as an animal. "What do you mean? Are you saying Xavier is Jeremy's son?"

"Yeah. Oh man, didn't you know?" Logan's eyebrows shot up. "I thought sure she would've told you. Or you would've asked." He slapped the heel of his hand to his forehead. "Man, I feel like a fool. I'm sorry. What a way to find out."

Troy just lay there on his back under a giant machine, his heart pounding like sledgehammer blows, sweat dripping from his face into his ears. *He* was the one who felt like a fool.

"Okay, ready? Lie still now."

Troy forced himself to obey while the machine moved its slow path up and down his leg. Inside, anger licked slow flames through his body. It took massive self-control not to jump up and slug Logan, though none of this was his fault.

It wasn't Troy's fault, either, nor Xavier's.

It was Angelica's fault. Angelica, and the guy Troy had always looked up to, the guy who'd stayed after practice to help him when he was a scrawny freshman, the guy who'd argued his case when the coach thought Troy was too focused on his studies to play first string.

Troy's mind reeled. Angelica had called it a rape, and he'd 99 percent believed her. So why did Logan think Jeremy was Xavier's dad?

And why did he have details about Angelica not wanting Jeremy's help? Wouldn't she have wanted it?

Well, but if it had been a one-night stand...

Because Jeremy wouldn't rape anyone. Would he?

He felt as if a million little dwarves were hammering at his brain. He wanted out of this conversation. This room. This whole wretched situation.

"Why do you think Xavier is Jeremy's child?" he ground out after the infernal machine had done its work and Logan was back in the room, a sheaf of X-rays in hand.

"Because he told me." Logan crossed his arms over his chest, looking off into space. "Man, that was one of the last times I saw my brother, right before I went overseas. We were out drinking one night and got to talking. He told me they'd hooked up." Logan's gaze flickered down, and he must have seen the turmoil on Troy's face. "Oh man, I'm sorry to break that news. Especially to a guy who's having this kind of trouble with his leg."

"What?" What did his leg have to do with anything? Who cared about his leg now?

"Here, sit up. Take a look." Logan pinned Troy's X-rays up on a light board and pointed. "That didn't heal worth nothing, man. It's all wrong. I don't know if they'll rebreak it or just leave it." He studied the light board, cocking his head to one side. "I don't think I ever saw a break heal that bad before, dude. My sympathy." He went to the door. "Sit tight. Doc will be in any minute. And hey, sorry to be the bearer of bad news."

Angelica sat on the grass watching Xavier joyously joining in the soccer practice. She still felt a little out of place with the other parents, all of whom seemed to have known each other for years. People were friendly, but Angelica knew she was still an outsider. Had always been an outsider, even when she was a kid.

"Good kick, Xavier!" one of the other children yelled.

Coach Linda, Becka's mom, waved to her. "Your son's a natural! Hope he can stay on the team!"

She watched as her son, completely new to soccer, raced to the ball and took it down the field in short, perfect kicks. Or whatever you'd call it…dribbling, maybe? She was way short on soccer terminology.

She so wanted for Xavier to fit in, and truthfully she wanted to fit in with the community, too. During her early years with Xavier, scrambling with work and day care, sometimes struggling to find a place to live before she'd settled in with her aunt, she'd looked enviously at families watching their kids play sports, kids with not only parents but grandparents and aunts and uncles to cheer them on. Families that could afford the right uniforms, could get their kids private lessons or coaching. She'd never even had the chance to dream of such a thing for her and Xavier, but now, hesitantly, she was starting to hope it could happen. They could be a part of things. They could have love, and a community, and a future.

When Nora, the woman from the country club, came up to her with a clipboard, Angelica smiled at her, determined to keep her walls down, to make a fresh start. "Hi," she said, extending her hand. "Are your girls on the team? I'm hoping Xavier can join."

"I heard. He seems really good." The woman settled down on the bench beside Angelica. "I'm head of the parents' organization. We do fund-raising and plan the end-of-season banquet for the kids, so I wanted to get you involved."

Pleasure surged inside Angelica. "Great. I'm pretty new to all this, but I'm glad to help however I can."

"Let me get your contact information." Nora pulled out her iPhone.

As she punched in Angelica's address, she smiled. "So you're living with Troy already, are you?"

Angelica swallowed. *She doesn't mean anything by it. Don't take it personally.* "No, we're not living together exactly. Xavier and I live on the farm, in the guesthouse."

"Oh, I'm sorry! I just assumed, since you have the same address… Great job, Nora, foot in mouth as usual. Never mind."

"It's okay. I work at the kennels," Angelica said, hearing the stiffness in her own voice. "That's why we live there."

"Oh! I misunderstood." The woman leaned in confidingly. "You know, ever since I got divorced, people have been trying to match me up with Troy."

Angelica looked sideways at the woman's perfect haircut and designer shorts. She was tall with an hour-glass figure. What had Troy thought of her? Had they gone out?

Nora waved her hand airily. "It didn't work out. He's a great guy, though."

"Yes, he is," Angelica said guardedly. Why hadn't it ever occurred to her that Troy had other options he was closing off by being involved with her? That he could date, or even marry, someone like Nora, the gorgeous, well-off, country-club-bred head of the parents' group?

"So, I notice Xavier doesn't have a uniform yet," the woman continued. "They cost fifty dollars. And we ask that parents make a donation of fifty dollars to the group, for parties and snacks and special events."

Angelica swallowed. "Um, okay. I might need to do one thing per paycheck, if that's okay. Money's a little tight."

The woman laughed. "You're kidding, right? Troy has all the money in the world."

I want to fit in, God, but do I have to be nice to this busybody? "Like I said, we'll take it one thing at a time. I'd like to get him the uniform first, but if you need the parents' fee right away—"

"Oh no, it's fine." The woman shrugged, palms up. "You pay when you're ready. Or when you tie the knot! I know Troy's good for it."

That rankled, and then another truth dawned as Angelica realized how her engagement to Troy must look to much of the town. Here she was, in her ancient cut-offs, and Xavier in his mismatched holey T-shirt and thrift-store gym shorts, and apparently Troy was known as one of the richest men in town. Just like when they'd been engaged before. They were two people from opposite sides of the tracks. They didn't fit.

Did everyone think she was marrying Troy for his money?

Angelica's phone buzzed, and when she saw Dr. Ravi's office number on the caller ID, she wrinkled her nose apologetically at Nora. "Sorry, I have to take this." When the woman didn't get up to move, Angelica stood and walked out of earshot. "Hello?"

"Angelica, it's Dr. Ravi. I got your message about Xavier playing soccer, and I wanted to tell you I think it's wonderful."

"Really? He's cleared to play?"

"Not only that, but all the signs about the treatment are very, very positive. Of course, definitive cures aren't part of the language of cancer doctors, but we are looking at very, very good numbers."

"Oh, Dr. Ravi, thank you! That's wonderful!"

"I agree." In his voice, she could hear his sincere happiness. "One never likes to make promises, but if I were you, I would be planning a long, healthy future for that young man."

Angelica half walked, half skipped back to the bench and sat down, vaguely conscious that there were a couple of other moms there with Nora now. She couldn't even remember why she'd felt upset with Nora.

What an incredible gift from God. She looked up at the sky, grinning her gratitude. Wow, just wow. She felt like shouting.

"Could you give me your email and cell phone information for our parents' directory?" Nora was looking at her, eyebrows raised.

"Um, yes, I… You know what, can we do this later? I

just got some really, really good medical news. Xavier! Hey, Zavey!"

Xavier came trotting over. "Mom, did you see me score a goal?"

She reached out widespread arms and caught him in them, holding him so tight that he started to struggle. Reluctantly she let him go but held his shoulders to look into his eyes. "Guess what?"

"Mom, can I go back and play more?"

Her smile felt so broad that her cheeks hurt. "You sure can. In fact, Dr. Ravi says you're cleared to play, and that the treatment seems to be working."

His eyes and his mouth both went wide and round. "You mean I'm getting well?"

"Looks like it, kiddo."

"And I can be on the team? And have my own shirt?"

"Absolutely. Just as soon as I get my next paycheck, you'll have a uniform, buddy."

He took off his hat and threw it high in the air, and the other moms seemed to draw in a collective sigh at the sight of his cancer-bald head.

"You know," Nora said, "I'm sure that, between us, we can get him a uniform right away. Can't we, ladies?"

The others nodded, and one of them, an acquaintance from years ago, reached out to give Angelica an impulsive hug. "We're so glad you moved back. It'll be great to get to know you again."

"Yes, and with Xavier playing, maybe our team will win a game every once in a while," chimed in one of the other moms, and they all laughed.

"Hey, there's Dad!" Xavier pointed down the street. "Can I go tell him, Mom? Can I?"

She was so happy that it didn't even bother her that

Xavier had called Troy "Dad" in front of all these mothers, who, no matter how nice, were likely to gossip about it. She looked in the direction Xavier was pointing and saw Troy walking toward them, along the sidewalk. A part of her wanted to tell Troy the great news about Xavier herself, but she couldn't deny Xavier the delight of telling. After all, it was his news. "Go for it, honey. Just don't knock him down. He looks a little bit tired."

Angelica watched Xavier running toward Troy, soccer ball under one arm, and happiness flooded her heart. It almost seemed in slow motion, like a dream: she was surrounded by other moms who seemed, suddenly, like supportive friends. The warm, late-afternoon air kissed her cheeks, tinged with the scent of just-mown grass. Giant trees shaded them all, testimony to how long this park had been here, how deeply the community was grounded in history.

She wanted this, especially for Xavier, so much she could taste it. And here it was within their grasp.

Xavier got to Troy, shouting, "Mr. Troy! Dad! Guess what!"

Troy kept walking. Limping, actually, and he still had his cane.

Angelica's heart faltered.

"Mr. Troy, hey! Don't you hear me?" Xavier grabbed Troy's leg.

Troy stumbled a little.

Angelica sprang from the bench and strode toward them, ignoring the concerned exclamations of the other mothers.

"Hey, Mr. Troy, guess what!"

Finally Troy stopped and turned to Xavier. "What?" His voice was oddly flat.

"I can play soccer! And I'm gonna get all better!"

Knowing Troy so well, Angelica could see him pull his mind from whatever faraway place it had been. He turned and bent down awkwardly, slowly. "That's great news, buddy." He was clearly trying to show enthusiasm. Trying, and failing.

To which her excited son was oblivious. "So that means you can be my coach, right? Can you, Dad? Can you?"

"We could use a few extra coaches, Troy," Coach Linda called from among the group of mothers. "Hint, hint."

Troy looked toward them, forehead wrinkled, frowning. "No," he said. "No, I can't do that."

"Whaddya mean you can't, Dad? You gotta coach me! You said you would."

Angelica reached the pair then and, breathless, knelt down beside Xavier. "Give Mr. Troy a minute here, buddy." She studied Troy's face.

He was looking from her to Xavier with the strangest expression she'd ever seen. Eyes hooded, corners of his mouth turned down. She couldn't read it and for some reason, it scared her.

"What's wrong?" she asked, putting a protective arm around Xavier.

"Mr. Troy, watch what I learned already!" Xavier threw the soccer ball he'd been carrying up into the air and bounced it off his head. Then he dribbled it in a circle, then kicked it up into his hands again.

His ability to handle the ball took Angelica's breath away. He was well, or pretty close, and he was going to be able to develop this amazing talent. She clasped her hands to her chest, almost as if she could hold the joy inside.

"Don't you want to coach me now?"

Troy looked at the two of them for a minute more. Then, without another word, he turned and started limping toward the truck.

She felt Xavier's shoulders slump.

"Troy!" she said. "Come back here and tell us what's going on."

He didn't answer, didn't look at her, just kept walking. And now she could see that he had a pronounced limp from some new, big kind of bandage around his leg, beneath his long pants.

"Troy!" When he didn't answer, she put her hands on her son's shoulders. "Remember how tired and cranky you can get from going to the doctor?"

Xavier nodded. But his lower lip was wobbling. He was so vulnerable, and she could have kicked Troy right in his bad leg for hurting her son's feelings. "Well, I think that's how Mr. Troy is feeling now."

"Did he have a treatment?" Xavier asked. "Does he have cancer, like me?"

"He doesn't have cancer, but I think he must have had a treatment that hurt or something. So we'll talk to him later. Right now I think your team needs you." Gently, she turned him back toward the playing field. She waved to Coach Linda, ignoring the curious stares of the other mothers. "Hey, Coach, Xavier's coming back in to play some, okay?"

"We can use him," Linda called, and as Xavier ran toward her, she reached out an arm to put around his shoulders.

Angelica watched long enough to see the pair head

back toward the field. Both of them glanced back a
couple of times, Xavier still looking a little crestfallen.

She marched after Troy.

"Hey, what's going on?"

He didn't stop, but she caught up with him easily.

"Troy! What happened at the doctor's? Did you get
bad news?"

He got to the truck and looked at it. Shut his eyes
as though he was in physical pain. Then walked to the
passenger door and opened it.

"Troy! I thought you... What happened?"

He closed the door and sat in the truck, staring
straight ahead.

She reached out and pulled the door open before he
could lock her out. "Look, I get that you've had some
bad news, but let me in, okay? Tell me what's going on.
We're a team, remember? We're engaged! We're getting married!"

"No, we're not."

The three words, spoken in that same flat tone he'd
used with Xavier, pricked a hole in her anger. She felt
her energy start to flow out of her, like a tire with a slow
leak. "What do you mean? Talk to me."

He didn't.

"What happened? Why aren't we getting married
now? Troy, no matter what happened to you, which I'd
appreciate being told about, you can't just shut me out.
And I don't like your ignoring Xavier that way. You really hurt his feelings."

"And of course I wouldn't want to hurt the feelings
of Jeremy's son."

Jeremy's son.

A core of ice formed inside her. He knew. Troy knew the truth.

Jeremy's son.

She never thought of Xavier that way. Xavier was her son. God's son. Soon, she'd thought, he would be Troy's son.

Though Jeremy Filmore had had a role in his conception, a role she'd spent a lot of years blocking out, it had ended there.

Hearing Troy say that name made her feel like throwing up. She staggered and leaned against the side of the truck. It was hot, but somehow the sun's warmth didn't penetrate the icy cold she felt inside.

Her worst nightmare. Troy had found out her assailant, who wasn't some stranger he could hate from a distance, but his own good friend, someone they'd both known. "What did you hear?" she asked in a dull voice.

"Well, for one thing, I heard that my leg is permanently screwed up. That I'll have to wear this boot for six months and I won't be able to drive or exercise. After that, I have to have some surgery that might or might not allow me to walk without a cane."

She didn't answer, couldn't. She could barely focus on what he was saying, only realizing that it had something to do with his leg not healing.

That awful name kept echoing through her head. *Jeremy. Jeremy. Jeremy.*

It whirled her back to a night she'd spent years trying to forget. To a very handsome and charming older guy who'd flattered her at her birthday celebration, walked her partway home, then dragged her into his apartment and spent what seemed like hours hurting her in ways she'd had no idea a man could hurt a woman.

Her screams had been ineffectual; the other apartments had been empty. Her pleas had fallen on deaf ears, even made him laugh.

What he'd done to her physically was horrible enough. But his name-calling, his degradation of her as a woman, his comments about her past, her unworthiness, her asking for it… All of those words had stuck to her like poison glue, growing inside her right along with the baby growing in her womb. The ugly descriptions of herself had expanded until they were all she could see, all she could feel.

Only the tireless nurturing of her aunt, and intensive sessions with a skilled therapist, had been able to pull her out of the deep depression she'd sunk into.

"You cheated on me," Troy said now. "And you lied to me."

Cheater. Liar. Even though the words Jeremy had uttered had been much stronger and more degrading, the echo in the voice of her beloved Troy made her double over, the hurt was so sudden and so strong.

She knelt in the dirt beside the truck, holding her stomach.

"Don't even try to defend yourself. I won't believe a word you say."

His flat, angry, judgmental certainty slammed into her. It was just the way she'd figured he would react; it was the reason she'd thrown clothes into a bag and left town the day she learned she was pregnant.

Now, though, her automatic reaction was different. To her own surprise, she didn't feel like running. She felt her shoulders go back as she glared at him. "Did you just tell me not to say anything?"

"Yeah," he said, leaning out of the truck, breathing hard. "That's exactly what I told you."

Gravel dug into her knees. What was she doing on her knees? Holding on to the side of the truck for support, she climbed to her feet. "Don't you ever tell me I can't say what's on my mind. I spent a lot of years keeping silent, and I'm tired of it. I don't deserve what happened to me, and I don't deserve for you to blame me for what someone else did to me."

He looked at her with huge sags under his eyes, as if he'd aged ten years. "You wanted to be with him. Right?"

Whoa! Just like Jeremy! Her hands went to her hips as heat flushed through her body. "You can stop right now with telling me what I did and didn't want. No woman would want what happened to me, and any man who says otherwise is messed up." She walked closer to him, her heart pounding in her ears. "You hear me? Totally. Messed. Up." With each word, she jabbed a pointing finger at him. "If that's what you're thinking, you can get out of my life."

He swung his legs down with a painful wince. "I'm going, just as soon as I can get a ride. And you can get out of mine. I want your bags packed and you…" He trailed off, swallowed hard. "You and Xavier…off my property. By tomorrow."

Fourteen

Troy watched the woman he'd thought he loved draw in a rasping breath, then clench her jaw. "I'll drive you home," she said. "Let me get Xavier."

She turned before he could answer and marched down toward the playing field. Her back was straight, shoulders squared.

He stared after her, then squeezed his eyes shut and looked away. His heart rebelled against the sudden change he was asking of it: stop loving her, start hating her. Stop believing in her, realize that she'd been lying this whole time.

She *had* been lying, right? Because she'd said she hadn't known her assailant, but when he'd confronted her with Jeremy's name, she'd tacitly acknowledged him as Xavier's father.

But why would she have lied about it being Jeremy?

The answer had to be that she'd gone with him willingly. Just as Jeremy's brother had said.

Sliding out of the truck, he landed painfully on his bad leg, and the metal cane the doctor had lent him—

the old man's cane with four little feet on the end—
crashed to the ground.

A teenage girl on a skateboard swooped down,
picked it up, then skidded in a circle to hand it back
to him.

He wasn't even man enough to pick up his wretched
cane for himself.

Angelica came back, pulling an obviously reluctant
and angry Xavier by the hand. "Mom!" he was whin-
ing, almost crying. "I don't want to go."

"Get in the truck," she ordered.

"But—"

"Now." Her voice was harsh.

Tears spilled from Xavier's eyes, and his lower lip
pouted out, but he climbed into the truck.

"Mr. Troy!" Xavier said as soon as they were all
in. "Mama says we have to move away. But that's not
true, is it?"

Troy looked over at Angelica and saw a muscle
twitch in her cheek. Her jaw was set and obviously she
wasn't about to answer.

Troy was already regretting his hasty order that they
leave. He turned back to Xavier, looked at his hopeful face.

Looked into Jeremy's eyes. How had he not noticed
that before? "I'm sorry, but yes. You do have to leave."

"Why?" Xavier's face screwed up. "I love it here. I
hate moving."

Troy looked over at Angelica and saw a single tear
trickle down her cheek.

Well, sure, she was upset. Her game was up.

"Mom, you promised we wouldn't have to move
again!"

Angelica cleared her throat. "I'm sorry, honey. I made a promise I couldn't keep."

"Seems you make a habit of that," Troy muttered.

Angelica's body gave the slightest little jerk, as if she'd been hit.

The truth hurt. He tried to work up some more righteous anger about that, but he was finding it hard to do.

What she'd done was wrong, but it had happened a long time ago.

But she's been lying to you just in the past few weeks.

But she'd seemed to genuinely care about him. Hadn't she? "Look," he said, "maybe I've overreacted. I...I need to take a breath, think about this. I don't want to throw the two of you out on the street..."

"We've been there before." She spun the truck around a corner too fast, making the tires squeal. "We'll manage."

"I don't want you to just manage. I need to pray about this, get right with God, figure things out. I was blindsided, but we all make mistakes. I... Maybe I can work through it and learn to forgive you."

"Don't strain yourself." She pulled the truck into the long driveway and squealed to a jerky stop in front of his house. "Here you go."

There were a couple of unfamiliar cars parked in front of the house, and he couldn't deal with strangers. Didn't want to talk to anyone but Angelica. "I... Look. Let's talk before you go."

"I think you've said all you need to say. I know what you think about me. I know how much respect you have for me. All I want now is to pack my things and be gone."

"Mom! You should listen to Mr. Troy! Maybe we won't have to leave."

"Are you getting out?" she asked him through clenched teeth.

"No. Angelica—"

She pulled out fast enough to make the wheels spit gravel, drove past the kennels and down to the bunkhouse. She skidded to a halt and slammed the truck into park. "C'mom, Xavier. Out." As soon as the sobbing boy had obeyed, she faced Troy. "By tonight, we'll be gone." She slammed the truck's door and walked into the bunkhouse, back stiff, one arm around Xavier.

Troy sat in the truck, his legs and arms too heavy to move. He stared out at the cornfields and wondered what he could do now.

His life had been snatched out from under him. Instead of being active, doing everything himself, he'd need help. With the kennels. With his practice. Even with driving, for pity's sake. Instead of getting married to the woman he loved, instead of becoming dad to the child he'd come to care deeply for, he'd be alone.

Alone, with a big empty space in his heart.

He knew he shouldn't be sitting here feeling sorry for himself, but he couldn't seem to make himself move. He didn't know what to do next.

Well, he did know: he should pray, put it in God's hands.

He let his face fall forward into his hands. *God...* He didn't know how to ask or what to say. Even looking at the bunkhouse and knowing that Xavier and Angelica were inside packing made his throat tighten up and his heart ache.

Help, he prayed.

The word echoed in his mind, as if God was saying it back to him.

There was nothing to do but try to help them. He'd help them load their stuff into the truck, as much as a crippled guy could. Find someone to drive them to the station. He'd pay for tickets wherever they wanted to go.

Where would they go, though?

And what about follow-ups to Xavier's treatments? What would Angelica do for a job? She'd worried that this would happen, that the "us" wouldn't work out and that she'd be alone, unable to afford the rest of the cost of treatment. He'd waved her concern aside.

Had she suspected he'd find out the truth about her?

What *was* the truth about her? He pounded the seat beside him. Why had she cheated on him? Why had she given herself to Jeremy?

"Mr. Troy! Mr. Troy! Come in here!"

At first he thought he was imagining the sound, but no; it was Xavier pounding on the truck's door. He lowered the window and looked out. "You okay, kiddo?"

"I am, but Lily's not! She's having her puppies! And Mom says she's in trouble!"

Troy grabbed the bag he always kept in the backseat and swung out of the vehicle.

"Come on! Mom said you wouldn't still be here, but I knew you would!"

They hurried into the bunkhouse together and there in a dark corner of the living room was Angelica, leaning over Lily.

Her dark hair was pulled back with a rubber band and she was doing something with a towel.

"What's going on?"

"She's having trouble with this last one." The anger

was gone from her voice, replaced by worry. "She can't get it out. I've been trying to help her, but I'm afraid of hurting the puppy."

"Let me see." He squatted down and saw the puppy's hindquarters protruding from Lily, who was whimpering and bending, trying to lick at the new puppy while three other pups pushed at her teats.

"Get a couple towels," he told Xavier, and to Angelica, "Get the surgical scissors out of my bag while I try to ease the pup out."

It took several minutes, and when the puppy was finally born he saw why: it was half again as big as the other puppies. Lily sank back, too exhausted for the usual maternal duties, so Troy carefully removed the sac and cut the cord and rubbed the puppy vigorously in a clean towel until he was sure it was breathing on its own.

"Poor thing," Angelica cooed, stroking Lily's ears and head. "You did a good job."

The pup was breathing well, so Troy tucked it against Lily's tummy, where it rooted blindly until it found a teat to latch on to.

Lily lifted her head feebly and licked the new puppy a couple of times, then dropped her head back to the floor.

"You can rest now," Angelica said to the tired dog. "We'll help you."

A small hand tugged at his shoulder as Xavier peered past him to look at Lily. "Is she gonna die? Why's she bleeding?"

He'd half forgotten that Xavier was there. "She's doing great. There's always a little blood when a dog gives birth, but she should be just fine."

"The puppies look…yucky."

Troy glanced over at Angelica, not sure how much detail she wanted her son to know. She shrugged, so he gave Xavier a barebones account of placentas and amniotic fluid and umbilical cords.

Fortunately the boy took it in stride. "Is she gonna have more?"

"I feel one more little bump, so she'll probably have one more." He smiled at Xavier. "It'll be okay. Just takes a while."

"Can I watch?"

Troy looked over at Angelica, eyebrows raised.

"Sure, I guess." She stood up, stretched with her hands on her lower back, then walked over to the small bookcase. And started putting books in boxes.

Troy's heart dove down to his boots. For a minute there, he'd forgotten their conflict, forgotten that he'd kicked her out, forgotten they weren't a couple anymore. He opened his mouth to say something and then shut it again.

Should he take back his request that she leave? Beg her to stay? If she stayed, what would they do? Because the fact remained, she'd betrayed him.

Lily whimpered, and he looked down at her and petted and soothed her.

And then it hit him. Again. His revelation about how Angelica had cringed and held back from the physical.

If she'd consented to the relationship with Jeremy, then why did she act like an abused animal when a man tried to touch her?

Her phone buzzed just then, and he watched her as she answered it, wondering what to believe. Saw her frown and look despairingly at the half-filled box of books. "Are you sure you can't manage it? I'm kind of busy here."

She listened again.

"Okay. No, of course I can help." She clicked off the phone and sighed. "Lou Ann needs me to help her with something up at the house. Says she needs a woman, that you won't do. Can you…"

"I'll stay with Lily. And Xavier can stay with me." He felt so good being able to do something for her. Lord help him, he wanted to take care of her. Still.

"All right. I'll be as quick as possible. I still want to get going by nightfall."

"Angelica—"

"No time to talk." And she was out the door.

Angelica stalked into the house with her fists clenched and teeth gritted tight against the tears that wanted to pour out of her. "Lou Ann!" she called past the lump in her throat.

"Out here," came a voice from the backyard.

She walked through the kitchen, trying not to look at the table where she and Xavier had shared so many meals with Troy. The counter where they'd leaned together, talking. The window through which she'd watched him playing ball with her son.

The whole place was soaked in memories, and if she and Xavier weren't going to have Troy, if this wasn't going to work, then it was best for them to get out of here now.

She walked through the back door.

"Surprise!"

The sounds of female laughter, the pretty white tablecloth over a round table decorated with flowers, the banner congratulating her and Troy…all of it was totally overwhelming.

She looked around at Lou Ann; Daisy; Xavier's teacher, Susan Hayashi; Miss Minnie Falcon from the Senior Towers; and her two best friends from Boston, Imani and Ruth. She burst into tears.

Immediately the women surrounded her. "It's a surprise shower!"

"We're so happy for you!"

"Aw, she's so emotional!"

"Wait a minute." Lou Ann broke through the squealing circle of women to step right in front of Angelica and look at her face. "Honey, what's wrong?"

Something in her voice made the rest of the women quiet down. Angelica looked into Lou Ann's calm brown eyes and bit her lip. "It's not going to work. Xavier and I are leaving."

"What?" The older woman looked shocked, and around her, gasps and words of dismay echoed in Angelica's ears.

"Come on, sit down and tell us about it," her friend Imani said.

"I think I'll head over to see Troy." The deep voice belonged to Dion, and he waved a hand and headed for the front of the house.

"Go on, we'll catch up with you later," Lou Ann said. "He was helping us set up the canopy," she explained to Angelica.

"What did you mean, you're leaving?" Daisy asked.

So, haltingly, hesitatingly, Angelica explained what had driven her and Troy apart. What was the point in hiding it all now? And they'd be gone, so if any gossip came from this good group of women—which she doubted—it wouldn't hurt Xavier.

"But God's good," she finished, choking out the words. "It looks like Xavier's going to get well."

Hugs and tears and murmurs of support surrounded her.

"Men can be such idiots." Daisy pulled her chair closer to Angelica and squeezed her hand. "My brother most of all."

"That jerk Jeremy most of all," her friend Ruth said.

"So I don't *need* to marry Troy anymore, to help Xavier," Angelica explained, her voice still scratchy. "I mean, of course, he still wants a dad. But he's got time now, and he's got his health. And I can't be with someone who doesn't trust me."

"But what do you *want*?" Imani took her hand. "If Xavier weren't in the equation, would you love Troy? Do you want to be married to him?"

Angelica shut her eyes, and a slide show of memories played through her head.

The first time he'd asked her out, when she'd thought he must be joking, that no one as handsome and rich and popular as Troy could possibly want someone like her.

Riding horses together. Going to her first superfancy restaurant. Looking up to see his marriage proposal in skywriting, in front of the whole town.

Back then, she'd been in love in a naive way. Impressed with him, infatuated with him. And down on herself, seeing no alternatives.

Now things were different. She'd gotten through the past six years by relying on God's strength. With His help, she'd mothered Xavier through the worst moments a child could have and come out stronger. She'd built friendships like those with Ruth and Imani, who'd come all the way from Boston to celebrate a milestone. Now she could add Daisy and Lou Ann to that circle of life-time friends.

Now she didn't *need* Troy. But the thought of life without him was colorless, plain, lonely.

Now her images of him were different. She thought of him not only helping her get rid of a drunken Buck but also giving her cola and comfort and a shoulder to cry on afterward. She thought of him bent over Bull in the road, caring for the wounded animal and still remembering her son's feelings. Thought of him admitting he'd been wrong to accuse her of still dating Buck, apologizing, going on to find Dr. Ravi for Xavier.

"If he could accept my past without thinking less of me, then yeah." She looked around at the circle of concerned, supportive faces. "Yeah. I still love him."

"All right," Lou Ann said. "Then we've got to find a way to make this right."

A sharp rap on the door made Troy's heart thump in double time: *Angelica*. Maybe she'd decided not to go. Maybe she wanted to talk to him.

He didn't know why he was so eager for that when she'd betrayed him with Jeremy. *If* she'd betrayed him. Because now that his initial anger was fading, he was having a hard time believing that of her.

"I know you're in there, my man," came Dion's deep voice.

"Come on in." Although he was glad to see his friend, needed a friend, Troy couldn't hide his disappointment.

Dion walked in looking anything but friendly. "Angelica's a mess. What did you do to her?"

Troy gave a tiny headshake, nodding toward Xavier. "We're watching Lily. She just had her last pup, and we're making sure she's okay."

"I'm helping," Xavier chimed in, bumping his shoulder against Troy. "Right, Mr. Troy?"

"Yep." Troy could barely choke out the word. How was he going to let this kid go?

Dion narrowed his eyes at Troy and flipped on the television to an old Western, complete with flaming arrows, bareback-riding Navajos and gun-toting cowboys. "Take a look, Xavier. You ever seen a cowboy show before?"

"Angelica wouldn't let..." Troy broke off. A little old-fashioned violence wouldn't hurt the kid. Xavier was immediately engrossed, leaving Dion and Troy free to move to an out-of-earshot spot at the kitchen table.

"What happened?" Dion glared at him.

Troy sighed, laced his hands together. "I found out who Xavier's dad is."

Dion looked at him expectantly.

"Jeremy Filmore."

Dion reared back and stared. "No kidding?"

Troy nodded. "No wonder she didn't want me to know, right? She could hardly claim assault with Jeremy." As he spoke, his anger came bubbling back.

"What do you mean? Does she say he attacked her?"

Troy nodded impatiently. "That's what she says, but I knew Jeremy. He wouldn't have done that."

Dion drummed his fingers on the table, frowning. "You sure about that, man?"

"You're not?"

"He had a pretty bad drinking problem." Dion studied the ceiling. "And he wasn't above clashing with the law. I broke up a few bar fights he started."

"True." And Troy had heard a few rumors, come to think of it, about how awful Jeremy had been to his wife.

"Not only that," Dion said, "but I was on duty for the car crash he died in. He was dead drunk. We didn't publicize that, and it was never in the paper—what would have been the point, when he was the only one involved, except to make his kids feel bad? But I can tell you it's so. I have the police reports to prove it."

"Wow." Jeremy, who'd had such potential, been a powerhouse of a football player, had died drunk. "So, what are you saying?"

"I'm saying that if Jeremy was drinking, he turned into an idiot. One who didn't have the ability to control himself."

"Even to the point of forcing himself on a woman?" The thought of Jeremy doing that to Angelica tapped in to a primal kind of outrage, but Troy fought to stay calm, to think. "Would he go that far, just because he wanted her?"

Dion shook his head. "It's about rage, not desire. They drill that into us at the police academy."

"But why would he be mad at Angelica? It just doesn't compute." Slowly he shook his head. "But it doesn't compute that she's lying, either."

"He was mad at women, period. Remember the so-called jokes he used to tell?"

"Yeah." Troy turned his cane over and over in his hand. "I guess I didn't spend much time with him once we were done with school."

"There could be another reason he kept his distance." The sound of televised gunshots and war whoops punctuated Dion's words. "He could have felt guilty about what he'd done."

"Getting her pregnant?"

"By force."

Troy pounded his fist on his knee.

"You have some apologizing to do."

Troy heaved out a sigh. "I screwed everything up."

"You might have, but pray Father God forgive you, and He will. Might even help you to make things right."

Troy nodded, staring down at the floor.

"And pray fast," Dion said. "Because there's a lot of estrogen coming our way."

Troy looked out the window Dion was looking out of. Marching in a line toward them, arms linked, were seven or eight women, his sister, Daisy, included. Angelica was at the center, and she looked shell-shocked. The rest of the ladies just looked angry and determined.

Man, was he in for it! But at least Angelica was still here.

Just before the women got within earshot, Angelica pulled away. The other women gathered around her and seemed to be urging her forward, but she shook her head vehemently. Then she broke away from the women and climbed into his truck.

Daisy marched over and yanked open the truck door. She and Angelica exchanged words, and then Angelica slid over to the passenger seat.

Daisy climbed into the driver's seat and they drove away, leaving clouds of dust behind them.

It was a mark of how upset Troy was that he didn't even care that his reckless sister was driving his vehicle.

He just wanted to be in there with Angelica.

The women watched her go and then headed toward the bunkhouse, looking more serious and less angry now.

"You better go out there and face them," Dion advised.

Xavier pushed in between them to look out the window. "Those ladies look mad."

"I know. But they're not mad at you, buddy." He spoke the reassuring words automatically, but his mind wasn't on Xavier. Mostly he wanted to know where Angelica had gone.

As the women reached the bunkhouse, he went out the front door and stood on the porch, arms crossed.

"You stay in here with me, Little Bit," he heard Dion say behind him.

The women stood in a line in front of Troy. "Come down here," said a dark-haired woman he'd never seen before.

Troy used his cane to make his way halfway down the front steps.

"You've hurt that girl something terrible," Lou Ann said.

The dark-haired woman added, "You accused her of stuff she didn't do."

"She'd never have cheated on you."

"I… Yeah." Troy sat down on the edge of the porch and let his head sink into his hands. He was only now realizing the enormity of what he'd done. He'd made a terrible mistake, maybe lost the best part of his life— Xavier and Angelica. He looked up. "Where'd Angelica go?"

The women consulted and murmured among themselves for a couple of minutes. "We think she went out Highway 93," Lou Ann said finally.

Dion came out behind him, clapped a hand on his shoulder. "If you want to follow her, I can drive you. But not if you're going to make a fool of yourself again."

"No promises. I've already been an idiot. But I want to tell her how sorry I am."

That seemed to make the women happy; there were a couple of approving nods. "Take him out there, Dion," Lou Ann said, "but keep an eye on him."

Angelica knelt at the white roadside cross. *Jeremy Filmore* was painted on the horizontal board; *In loving memory* on the vertical one.

It wasn't his grave, but this was where he'd had his fatal accident. Somehow it had seemed to make more sense to come here, to this place she'd driven by dozens of times, getting mad and hating him with each pass. Never before had she stopped, gotten out of the car and studied it.

Now she saw the plastic flowers, the kids' football, the baby shoe and picture that decorated the cross, all looking surprisingly new, given that he'd died almost five years ago.

It reminded her that Jeremy had had a life, kids, people who loved him enough to keep up a memorial.

How could he be loved when he'd done something so awful?

Her legs went weak and she sank to her knees as regret overcame her. If only she hadn't been drunk that night. If only he hadn't. If only a friend had walked home with them. If only Troy had come out with her.

She'd never understand the why of it, no way. Why had God let it happen, something so awful?

She sat back and hugged her knees to her chest, aching as she remembered the years of hating herself, all the loose, ugly clothes she'd taken to wearing, scared of provoking unwanted male attention. Afraid of being the tramp Jeremy had accused her of being.

"I wasted the best years of my life hating you!" she cried out, pounding the ground, as if Jeremy lay beneath the memorial, as if he could still feel pain. She wanted to hurt him as he'd hurt her. Wanted to make him feel ashamed and awful. Wanted him to lose the love of his life, the way she'd lost Troy, twice now.

"Hey," Daisy said, getting out of the truck. "You okay?"

Angelica kept her eyes closed, her whole body tense as a coiled spring. "I hate him," she said. "I can't make myself stop hating him. I can't forgive him. I thought I could, but I can't."

Daisy knelt and put an arm around her. "He was awful. A complete jerk. No one deserves to be treated the way you were treated."

"I hate him, hate him, hate him! I want him to suffer like I did. I want him to lose everything."

"Can't blame you there. Stinks that he lived in the community like a good person, and meanwhile, you felt like you had to leave."

"Yeah."

A breeze kicked up, and a few leaves fell around them. Fall was coming. Maybe it was already here.

Something was tugging at her. She thought about the years since the assault. "I hurt a lot in the past seven years."

"I know you must have."

"But I also had Xavier and got closer to God and… and grew up. Where Jeremy…he must have always had this in the back of his mind, what he did."

"Nah." Daisy let out a snort. "Guys like that are jerks. He didn't suffer."

"I think he did suffer. I think that's one reason he drank so much."

"Don't try to humanize him. It's okay to hate the guy who assaulted you!"

Angelica hugged Daisy; half laughing through her tears. "You're wonderful. But I don't actually think that it *is* okay to hate."

Daisy rolled her eyes. "Don't go all holy on me."

"I'm not very holy at all." Angelica shifted from her knees to a more comfortable sitting position. "I've always felt guilty myself, because I…" Tears rose to her eyes again. "Because I dressed up pretty and flirted with all the guys at the bar. Including Jeremy." She could barely squeeze the words out past the lump in her throat.

"Oh, give me a break. Men flirt every day and no woman commits assault on them. It wasn't fair, what happened to you." Daisy squeezed her shoulder. "And you totally didn't deserve it."

"You don't think so?"

"No! You'd probably make different decisions today, and you'd probably see more red flags with Jeremy." Daisy's voice went into social-worker mode. "Our brains keep developing and learn from experience. But no way—no *way*—did you deserve to be raped. Whether you flirt or dress up or get drunk, no means no." She squeezed Angelica's shoulder. "And you have to forgive yourself for being a silly twenty-one-year-old."

Daisy's words washed over her like a balm.

If she could forgive herself—the way God forgave her—then maybe she could forgive Jeremy. And get on with her life.

But it wasn't easy. "I'm still mad at myself. And even though I'm figuring it out, I still feel pretty hostile toward Jeremy."

Daisy was weaving a handful of clovers into a long chain. "I have a terrible temper," she said. "Pastor Ricky always tells me that forgiveness is a decision, not a feeling."

Forgiveness is a decision, not a feeling. The words echoed in her mind with the ring of truth.

Behind them, a truck lumbered by, adding a whiff of diesel to the air.

Forgiveness is a decision, not a feeling.

Angelica reached out a finger to the baby shoe that hung on the crossbar. "I know, I've known all along, that God worked it for good by giving me Xavier." She drew in a breath. "Okay. I forgive you, Jeremy."

"And yourself?" Daisy prompted.

"I forgive…I forgive myself, too."

No fireworks exploded, and no church bells rang. But a tiny flower of peace took seed in Angelica's heart. For now, it was enough.

"Now, don't go ballistic," Dion warned Troy. "I think I see Angelica and Daisy up there."

"Why are they out of the car on the highway?"

"They're by a roadside memorial." Dion paused, then added, "For Jeremy Filmore."

Troy's hands balled into fists as Dion slowed the truck to a crawl and drove slowly past Daisy and Angelica. "If this doesn't show she's got feelings for him—"

"I'm sure she does have feelings." Dion pulled the truck off the road and turned off the ignition. "Wouldn't you hate the guy that did what he did?"

"That's not what I—" And Troy stopped. He was doing it again, being a jerk. He had to stop jumping to conclusions about Angelica, about how she felt and what she was doing. It wasn't fair to her or to him or to Xavier.

He sat there and watched while Daisy and Angelica held hands and prayed together. Man, his sister was a good person.

And so was Angelica. Talking with Dion had confirmed what his heart had already suspected: No way would she cheat on him.

He was a fool.

Troy dropped his head into his hands. If Angelica was praying, he should do that, too. She was amazing, always plunging forward and trying to do the right thing, to make a change, to live the way she was supposed to despite the horrible circumstances life always seemed to be throwing at her.

And he, what did he do?

He got his feelings hurt and suffered a minor disability and he fell apart.

He'd tried to fix her life and Xavier's on his own, giving her a job, letting them live on his place, getting medical help, even the marriage proposal. Looking back, it seemed as if he'd been waving his arms around uselessly, acting like some comic-book hero, trying to fix problems way too big for him.

For the first time in his life, he saw—just dimly—
that there might be another way. The way that gave Dion
his uncanny peacefulness. The way that made Angelica
able to kneel by that jerk Jeremy's memorial and pray,
after all she'd suffered.

He wanted, needed, that ability to let God in, to trust
Him. Most of all, to ask Him for help. To recognize that
he himself wasn't God and that God could do better than
he could on his own poor human strength.

I'm sorry, God. Help me do better.

It was a simple prayer, but when he lifted his head,
he felt some kind of peace. And when he looked over
at Dion, he saw his friend smile. "What do you say I
take Daisy home so you and Angelica can have some
time?" he asked.

"That's a good idea."

Troy got out of the truck then and limped over to the
two women. When he got there, Daisy stood and studied his face. Then, nodding as if satisfied, she walked
back toward Dion's truck.

Leaving Troy to kneel beside Angelica.

She finished her prayer, turned and looked at him.
Eyes full of wisdom but guarded against the pain he
might inflict.

He reached out hesitantly and touched her dark hair.

She didn't flinch away. Just studied his face.

A car whizzed by behind them. Another. The sound
faded away into the horizon, and quiet fell.

He looked down at the cross for Jeremy. A man
who'd done something so horrendous to the woman he
loved. Reflexively his fist clenched. "I could kill him."

Angelica reached out and put her hand over his. "He's
gone. Leave it to God." Her voice shook a little, and

when he looked away from Jeremy's cross and into her eyes, he saw that they were shiny with tears.

One overflowed, rolled down her cheek. "You kicked us out. You didn't believe me."

"I'm so sorry." He relaxed his fist and reached out slowly to thumb the tears away. "I love you. I never stopped loving you. Can you forgive me?"

There was a moment's silence. Long enough for him to feel the cooling breeze against his back and smell the sweet, pungent zing of ozone. It was going to rain.

"I don't know." She knelt there, her face still wet with tears, and studied him seriously. As though she was trying to read him. "I love you, too, Troy. But I can't live with being distrusted, and I can't live with someone who thinks I'm a bad person inside."

"You're the best person I know!" The words burst out of him and he realized they were the exact truth. She'd gone through so much, and with such faith, and there was humility and wisdom and dignity in every move she made, every word she spoke. "Look, I screwed up, and I screwed up bad. I want to spend the rest of my life making it up to you. Even that won't be enough, but I want to try."

"Really?"

"Yeah, really." He touched her hand, tentatively, carefully. "I can't guarantee I'll never make another mistake, but I can guarantee it won't be about who you are inside."

She didn't look convinced.

He blundered on. "Like, I tend to be jealous."

She lifted an eyebrow. "No kidding. Right?"

"It's just, I know how incredible you are, and I see other men seeing it, and it makes me crazy."

Her lips tightened. "I'm not flattered by that, Troy. It's not a good thing."

"I know. I'm willing to do whatever I need to do to fix this. Read self-help books. Get counseling. Join Dion's men's group at church."

"That," she said instantly. "That's what you need. Other men to rein you in when you go all macho."

"I'll call him tomorrow." He took both of her hands in his. "Look, Angelica, I'm nowhere near as good of a person as you are. But I need you to know that I'll do everything in my power to protect you and Xavier. I'll take care of you and love you for the rest of my days. And I will never, ever tell you to leave again."

She looked steadily into his eyes as if she was reading him, judging him. And she had the right. She had to protect her son.

Finally her face broke into a smile. "I'm not a better person than you are. I've made plenty of mistakes and I'm sure I'll make more."

"Does this mean…" He trailed off, hardly daring to hope.

To his shock, she laughed, a pure, joyous sound. "You caught me on the right day," she said. "I'm on a forgiveness roll."

He took her face in his hands and was blown away by the sheer goodness of who she was. "I don't deserve you. You're…you're amazing, inside and out. I…" He ran out of words. *Way to go, Hinton. Smooth with the ladies, as always.*

She lifted her eyebrows, a tiny smile quirking the corner of her mouth. "Does this mean… What does this mean?"

She looked at peace about whether he wanted to

marry her or not, whether they had a future or not. She had that glow of faith. She'd always had it, but it glowed brighter now.

He had so much to learn from her. And what could he, with his gimpy leg and his ignorant rages and his general guy immaturity, offer her?

Little enough, but if he could ease her parenting burdens and listen to her problems and protect her from anyone—anyone!—who so much as looked sideways at her, he wanted to do it. Would devote his life to doing it.

"It means," he said, "that I want you to marry me. For real. Forever. I want to help you and support you and be Xavier's dad. And I want it for the rest of our lives, through thickheadedness and illness and whatever else life throws at us. If you'll have me."

She looked at him with love glowing in her eyes. "Of course I will."

And as they embraced, the sky opened up and a warm, gentle rain started to fall, offering God's blessing on their new beginning.

Fifteen

"That was awesome, Mom!"

Angelica turned toward her son's excited voice, only slightly slowed down by her wedding dress. Pure white. Traditional. What she'd always wanted.

"What was awesome, honey? The wedding?"

"No, the ride in a Hummer!"

Of course, her healthy, normal son had loved their unorthodox ride back from the church more than fidgeting through the wedding ceremony and receiving line.

Now they were back at the farm for the reception, which Lou Ann had insisted on orchestrating. There were two canopies set up, in case the warm October sunshine turned to rain, and Angelica could smell the good hearty dinner that was on buffet tables for the guests.

A small wedding, but meaningful. Just what she'd hoped for…and for many years hadn't dreamed possible for herself.

Since forgiving Jeremy that day by the side of the road, since feeling the sincerity of Troy's love and belief in her, she'd felt light enough to fly.

Gramps hustled over to give her a hug. "Did I tell you how beautiful you look?"

"About a dozen times, but it's okay." She kissed his grizzled cheek. "Thank you for walking me down the aisle. You've been wonderful today. I'm so grateful."

"Not sure about the rest of those Hintons, but Troy is all right." Troy had tried to talk Gramps into moving out of the Senior Towers and into the bunkhouse. When Gramps had refused, insisting on staying with his friends, Troy had helped him move into a bigger apartment at the Towers, paying the difference in rent secretly to save the old man's pride.

That was part of what she loved about Troy: he was willing to change, to break from the long-held Hinton animosity toward Gramps, to embrace her family with all its flaws.

Lou Ann had ridden from the church with Troy's father. As she emerged, radiant in a maroon dress and hat, from Mr. Hinton's vintage Cadillac, Gramps sniffed. "I'm gonna go over there and make sure he's not bothering Lou Ann. He always did have a crush on her."

People were all arriving now, and Angelica watched Lou Ann rush away from both men with an eye roll, hurrying on to direct the caterers and welcome guests. Angelica hadn't wanted a big fancy reception, but thanks to Lou Ann, everything was simple and perfect, from the centerpieces—a pretty mix of sunflowers, orange dahlias and autumn leaves—to the bluegrass band strumming lively music.

"Hey, Mom, look!" Xavier came out of the kennels, his suit knees dusty. "I have a 'prise for you!"

"You'll want to watch this," Troy said, coming up behind her. He wrapped his arms around her middle and she swayed back against him. He made her dizzy…in a good way. A very good way.

"Mom, pay attention!" Xavier stood frowning, hands on hips.

Troy chuckled into her ear, and Angelica laughed with self-conscious delight. It amazed her that she could feel so attracted to Troy, that it was easy and good to be close to him. No more cringing, no more fear. She trusted him completely.

She was getting back the girl she'd been, with God's help. He truly did make all things new.

She eased herself over to Troy's side, where she could breathe a little more easily. "What's the surprise, sweetie?" she called to her son.

"Lily's dressed up for the wedding!" Xavier yelled, so loud that everyone turned to see.

The rescued pit bull, her collar decorated with yellow roses, emerged from the barn with a line of puppies behind her. Amid the happy murmur of the guests, Xavier's voice rang out again. "Look what else!"

He whistled, and Bull came running full tilt from the barn.

Angelica did a double take. How was Bull moving so fast?

And then she realized that his back legs were supported by a doggie wheelchair, also decorated with yellow and white flowers. As he zigzagged after Xavier, Angelica pressed her hands to her mouth, amazed.

"We've been practicing with him for a couple of weeks," Troy said. "Xavier was determined that Bull could come to the wedding and play."

And trust Troy to make it happen, to take the time to work with Xavier and the dog and to keep the surprise for her.

"Come and get it, everyone!" Lou Ann called, and people flowed toward the tables to eat, stopping to greet them on the way. And there were hugs. So many hugs.

As she and Troy stood there arm in arm, welcoming their guests, Angelica lifted her face to the afternoon sunshine and thanked God for all He'd done for them.

Xavier barreled up toward them, and at the same time, both Troy and Angelica reached out to hold him. "Our whole family," Angelica said, rubbing her son's head, roughened by newly sprouted hair. Joy bubbled up inside her, rich and full and satisfying.

"Well..." Troy said, sounding guilty.

"Mom? There's one other thing. Dad and I have been talking about it."

"What?" She stepped out of Troy's embrace to frown in mock exasperation at her two men. "Are you guys conspiring against me?"

"What's 'spiring?"

"Hatching a secret plan, buddy. And...kinda. Tell her, Zavey."

Her son reached out and took one of her hands and one of Troy's. "I want a little sister."

"Oh, Zavey Davey..." She looked up at Troy as her mind flashed back to a family she'd seen in the park. Mom, Dad and two children, one an adorable little girl. She hadn't thought it was possible God could be so good to her, but now she knew He could.

The last of her old doubts about the future faded away at the sight of Troy's smile. "What do you think?"

"I think it's a distinct possibility." He gave her a quick wink and reached out to pull her back into his arms.

* * * * *

We hope you enjoyed reading
LAUGHTER IN THE RAIN
by #1 *New York Times* bestselling author
DEBBIE MACOMBER
and
**ENGAGED TO THE
SINGLE MOM**
by LEE TOBIN McCLAIN

Both were originally Harlequin® series stories!

From passionate, suspenseful and dramatic
love stories to inspirational or historical,
Harlequin offers different lines to
satisfy every romance reader.

New books in each line
are available every month.

SPECIAL EXCERPT FROM

H
HQN™

Surprise fatherhood, Southern charm and a heartwarming family Christmas—read on for a sneak peek at Low Country Christmas, *the conclusion to Lee Tobin McClain's Safe Haven series!*

Cash remembered coming out to Ma Dixie's place at Christmas time growing up. The contrast with his own foster family's home had been extreme. There, six themed Christmas trees were spread throughout the house, decorated perfectly by the commercial operation that brought them out each year and took them away after the holidays. That same company had wrapped garlands around the staircase and strung lights outside the house.

It had all been grand. He remembered being shocked and impressed his first year with the family, because it had been so different from the humble holidays back in Alabama. But he hadn't been allowed to invite his brothers over; too much noise and mess, his foster mother had always said. If he wanted to see them, he had to find a ride out to Ma Dixie's, which he had done frequently.

Here, Christmas really felt like Christmas.

He opened another box of ornaments, pulled out an angel made of hard plastic and handed it to Holly to place on the tree.

"Is this your tree topper, Ma?" Holly asked, holding it up.

"Yes, it is. I usually have Pudge put it up, but...could you do it, Cash, honey?"

He did, easily reaching the top of the small tree. "Is Pudge okay?" he asked Ma. "Is that why the place isn't decorated yet? He's too sick to help?"

Ma arranged the last figures in the Nativity scene and sank down onto the couch. "That's part of it. Mostly, it's me feeling blue. I'm not used to Christmas with no kids around."

Holly tilted her head to one side. "Did you have a lot of kids?"

"Dozens," Ma said with a wide smile. "That's the beauty of being a foster parent."

"Oh," Holly said as she sank down onto an ottoman beside Ma. "Do you…not foster anymore?"

Ma sighed. "I really can't with Pudge having all these doctor appointments. I guess maybe we're getting too old for it." She looked wistfully at the tree. "I just, you know, always enjoyed having the little ones around."

Holly looked thoughtful. "Is that why you wanted to take care of Penny? Not to help me out, but to have a little one around?"

"That's part of it," Ma said, "but don't you worry about it. I understand being picky where your child is concerned."

"It's not pickiness," Holly said. "If I were being picky, who better than an experienced foster parent like you?" She reached out and rubbed Ma's arm back and forth, two or three times, an affectionate gesture that made Ma smile.

Cash came over and sat at Holly's side, leaning against the ottoman. His heart, like that of the Grinch in the movie playing muted on the television, seemed to be expanding.

He'd taken plenty of women to high-end Christmas parties and fancy restaurants. But sitting here in Ma Dixie's house, talking with her about holidays and kids and family problems, decorating the tree with her, felt different. Like coming home.

Like coming home, with Holly beside him.

He put that feeling together with the questions his brother and Pudge had been asking. He was getting the horrifying notion that he might be falling in love with Holly. But he wasn't the falling-in-love type, or the settling-down type. And Holly wasn't the type for a short, superficial fling.

So what exactly was he going to do with all these feelings?

Don't miss Lee Tobin McClain's
Low Country Christmas,
available October 2019 from HQN Books!

Save **$1.00**
on the purchase of ANY
Harlequin Love Inspired or
Love Inspired Suspense® book.

Available wherever books are sold,
including most bookstores, supermarkets,
drugstores and discount stores.

Save $1.00

on the purchase of any Harlequin Love Inspired or Love Inspired Suspense book.

Coupon valid until December 31, 2019.
Redeemable at participating outlets in the U.S. and Canada only.
Not redeemable at Barnes & Noble stores. Limit one coupon per customer.

52616479

Canadian Retailers: Harlequin Enterprises Limited will pay the face value of this coupon plus 10.25¢ if submitted by customer for this product only. Any other use constitutes fraud. Coupon is nonassignable. Void if taxed, prohibited or restricted by law. Consumer must pay any government taxes. Void if copied. Inmar Promotional Services ("IPS") customers submit coupons and proof of sales to Harlequin Enterprises Limited, P.O. Box 31000, Scarborough, ON M1R 0E7, Canada. Non-IPS retailer—for reimbursement submit coupons and proof of sales directly to Harlequin Enterprises Limited, Retail Marketing Department, Bay Adelaide Centre, East Tower, 22 Adelaide Street West, 40th Floor, Toronto, Ontario M5H 4E3, Canada.

5 65373 00076 2 (8100)0 12430

U.S. Retailers: Harlequin Enterprises Limited will pay the face value of this coupon plus 8¢ if submitted by customer for this product only. Any other use constitutes fraud. Coupon is nonassignable. Void if taxed, prohibited or restricted by law. Consumer must pay any government taxes. Void if copied. For reimbursement submit coupons and proof of sales directly to Harlequin Enterprises, Ltd 482, NCH Marketing Services, P.O. Box 880001, El Paso, TX 88588-0001, U.S.A. Cash value 1/100 cents.

® and ™ are trademarks owned and used by the trademark owner and/or its licensee.

© 2019 Harlequin Enterprises Limited

BACCOUP08108